ABOUT THE AUTHOR

Grant J Everett is a writer from Western Sydney. He writes science fiction comedy novels for a couple of reasons: one, because we all need an escape almost as much as we need a laugh, and two, because it's easy to be witty when you have a fortnight to think of a comeback.

ALSO BY THE AUTHOR
SCUM OF THE UNIVERSE
TOTALLY, UTTERLY SCREWED

Where have all the Humans Gone?

GRANT J. EVERETT

BLACK COCKIE PRESS

Where Have All The Humans Gone?

Published by Black Cockie Press

Copyright Grant J Everett 2022

The moral right of the author has been asserted

Cover design Black Cockie Press 2022

Distributed by Ingramspark

ISBN: 978-0-6454896-3-7

PROLOGUE

Any fool can see the Earth is dead.

If you get close enough to pick out continents with the naked eye, about four million kilometres or so, the cradle of Mankind appeared as barren and hostile as burnt, unbuttered toast. Earth still resembled a sphere at a glance, but any half-decent scan will reveal this dumpster fire of a planet was actually millions of shattered pieces held together by force of habit rather than actual physics, kind of like how a cartoon Coyote can defy gravity until he realises he's standing above an endless drop. Her oceans and atmosphere have boiled dry, and all traces of Human civilisation have been sterilised from her surface, eradicated with the greatest of care.

Following some long-forgotten catastrophe that stopped Earth from spinning, there was now a hot side locked in permanent day, and a cold side that was always night. Without even a membrane of ozone layer left to protect it, the Earth's boiling side had been roasted to a glowing, neon white by the Sun's incendiary breath, giving the appearance of a giant charcoal briquette on the verge of crumbling. Its surface was even more inhospitable than Venus (prior to all those kitschy magnetically-shielded family beach resorts that sprang up in the late 23rd Century, anyway).

On the frozen side, it was darker than the hell bound soul of a Vegan Extremist suicide bomber. Deep cracks zigzagged down for thousands of kilometres, and Earth's ruptured magma core served as the only light you could see from orbit. Demon-hot rivers of liquefied minerals traced over the night-choked wasteland like spider veins, occasionally spurting enormous plumes of slop that stained its joke of a sky arterial red.

Overall, any extra-terrestrial prospector with an ounce of sense would hit the OF NO VALUE marker on their stellar map before jetting elsewhere for better pickings. However, if you waited for your night vision to kick in and you squinted just a little bit below the equator on the dark side, you'd be able to make out something decidedly unnatural: a perfect square. A little over a thousand kilometres a side, the square was a grey-green splotch of portable atmosphere. It glowed, but not like globes or bulbs. It had a certain...organic quality to it.

Descending down to the Karman line, a point exactly one hundred kilometres above sea level (when there was still a sea, mind), you could see a white structure the size and complexity of ten international airports sitting on the square-o-atmosphere, latched on like an albino tick. The facility's cruciform shape indicated it may have unfolded from a cube, possibly after being dropped from a great height. Besides the bubbling morass surrounding it, the facility was silent and still.

A small object flared for a moment as it entered the Western side of the square, tumbling as it went. Unlike the usual Lunar debris and satellite shrapnel, however, this item was a brick-shaped ceramic slab the size of the most claustrophobic of mobile homes, and it proved tough enough to not vanish in a puff of smoke when it hit the perfect line of atmosphere. Spinning and scudding, glowing brighter by the moment, it took almost thirty seconds to splash down into the glowing slurry. Sliding, digging a glassed furrow, the boiling-hot object came to a stop. It tilted precariously, nearly tipping over, but eventually decided to sink back and settle.

Everything went back to total stasis. Only the gentle churning and bubbling of the organic bog broke the serenity.

It took ten minutes for the glowing lump to cool back down to dark purple, and any species intelligent enough to reach the point of developing organised waste disposal services could identify with one glance that it was a dumpster. Despite the fact this skip had just hammered in like a meteor without so much as a cocktail umbrella to slow it down, somehow even a fiery re-entry wasn't enough to phase this mightiest of bins. Once the smoke literally cleared, large, glowing white letters embossed across each side and on its flip-top lid proclaimed PusCo Medical Waste Services in the once-popular Human language known as Unglish. As series of glyphs spelled out this unit was specifically used to dispose of Human tissue, as well as anything used to cut, inject, mend, stitch, or otherwise interfere with people's meat-prisons. As far as bins went, this was the most unclean, the most taboo.

Cooling down to a steaming lump of inanimate matter, the bin's lid cracked open wide enough for half a dozen eye stalks to poke over its threshold. Carefully twitching back and forth independently, blinking triple-layered eyelids, a creature best described as a distant relative of the terrestrial bristleworm emerged to wriggle its extensive facial protrusions at the sunless sky. Its head was a riot of antennae, mandibles, jaws, sensory nubs, tentacles and claws. Unlike your average non-sentient marine annelid, though, this particular bristleworm was clearly waiting for something to happen in the sky.

And then it did.

Illuminated from within, a construct the size of a planet slid through local space close enough for its wake to vibrate Earth's surface. This passing titan was a Star Cage, a thin, white spherical lattice of invulnerable limpet ivory wrapped around a hundred kilometre wide kernel stolen from a purple supergiant. From a distance, the Star Cage's superstructure looked frail as a paper lantern, and the grape-coloured solar material enslaved within its core throbbed against its shackles, fuelling the energy needs of its owners (and its own confinement) just like it had for the last six thousand years.

To most intelligent beings, a Star Cage was regarded as a Dyson Sphere on a tight budget. To the Slidge who resided aboard and the twelve hundred races they'd subjugated to do all their menial tasks, it was home.

The bristleworm tasted a morsel of foul but breathable atmosphere, nervously waiting for a signal. Then, as though somebody had pulled a fire alarm, the Star Cage paused. Five agonising seconds crawled by before the Star Cage glowed brighter for a moment, barely twitching before it vanished from the sky. Breathing a sigh of relief, three metres of intelligent bristleworm undulated from the PusCo Medical Waste Dumpster and writhed into the thick, meaty swamp. His ridged, segmented exoskeleton arced through the wet mire like an alligator in a Louisiana bayou, clearly not disabled by a total lack of limbs. In fact, the speed and agility of this millipede's cousin would put most jet-skis to shame.

He'd strapped satchels made from some synthetic material at set intervals along his exoskeleton, but they proved to be waterproof and airtight. Whatever the bristleworm was carrying, it was safe.

Clearly on a mission, the invertebrate writhed directly towards the mysterious facility.

PREVIOUSLY…VERY PREVIOUSLY

The Carpe Astrum, a 25th Century prototype starship capable of traveling anywhere instantaneously, malfunctioned on its maiden voyage and ended up seven galaxies in the wrong direction. Of its crew, only four of the grittiest dregs remained.

Jimmy Slummer, a meat-puppet minimum wage slave from a MacDeath burger joint.

Bob Tuesday, the scum of the Universe.

Lana Slade, a work-experience Cadet from the local Academy.

And Trace Cuddle, exiled heiress to the incomparable Cuddle fortune and legacy and a total, total psycho.

The good news was they made it back to the Milky Way. The bad news was that thanks to time dilation and other temporal dickery, by the time they returned half a millennium had passed and Mankind was missing.

All alone and beyond hope in the 30th Century, the four survivors seemingly caught a break when a godlike Trancended being explained that the entire Carpe Astrum Disaster had been a practical joke orchestrated by the highest forms of celestial life, and that each of the humans would be granted a wish as a reward for being so entertaining.

It seemed everything was going to be okay.

But they all should have known better by now.

PART ONE LEGLESS
CHAPTER ONE

Trace stared out of the unbreakable bay window of a mega-freighter the size of Brooklyn. The numerous obsidian piercings studding her forehead rested against a patch of her own breath's fog, cold against her shaved skin. Even at this sharp angle Trace could see the reflection of her body: she was built like a queen-sized mattress stuffed with footballs. Beyond, the stars silently glimmered like a tray of surgical tools, sterile and icy.

If Trace panned her eyes a little to the right, she could see an embossed CuddleTech logo stretching three hundred metres along the pockmarked hull. This hulk's name had once been located fifty metres below the CuddleTech icon, but all physical proof of its moniker had been scoured away in some undocumented incident. Over the last three months, Trace had often wondered whether the destruction of the ship's name had anything to do with how all of Mankind had vanished from the galaxy without so much as pasting a sticky note on the nearest fridge. Then again, she wasn't the type to ask questions: she was the sort to hit somebody and declare the issue solved to her satisfaction.

Thankfully, within hours of arriving on this abandoned ship Trace had discovered it possessed a VIP section, and as she was a member of the esteemed Cuddle bloodline Trace had been immediately granted full access. She hadn't experienced such comfort and security since Uncle Balder had betrayed the entire Cuddle clan and cast them into the night. As her family's wealth and influence had been scorched away with everything else on Earth's surface and every other ship in CuddleTech's galaxy-crossing fleets had vanished mysteriously, as far as Trace knew this solo freighter was the last physical remnant of her family's legacy. This was appropriate, as she was the final heir.

At one point, Trace had gotten so bored that she'd tried to find out more about the nameless ship's huge scars. Unfortunately, even though her genetics provided full access to every system, not only was there no mention of what had beat the living daylights out of this freighter, but every useful megabyte of electronic information – from security recordings to Captain's log entries to accounting ledgers to holographic toilet paper requisition e-forms – had been excised all the way back to the day this vessel had been launched from its asteroid shipyard in the late 22nd Century. Eight hundred years of history had vanished without a snippet, as though something was erasing all that Mankind had ever touched.

After spending time making up for lost meals, Trace started searching nearby star systems for whatever was left of her species. While calling Trace antisocial would be an understatement, it was a fact that even clinical sociopaths needed other Humans to some degree (of course, this wasn't always safe or pleasant for those other Humans). However, while the navigational equipment still possessed some basic hardcoded software, it was so decayed from digital loss that she might as well be following a map drawn on an ivory doily with a white crayon. Most of the time she didn't know where the freighter was headed or when she'd get there, and she'd often end up in the empty gulf between stars. Although she hadn't found a glimmer of an answer yet, Trace had resigned herself to keep looking until she made contact, finished visiting every planet that had once belonged to The Unison, or found something more interesting to do.

Tiring of the view and feeling hungry, Trace headed down the marble steps, her bare feet tingling as they touched the cold floor, and made her way to the executive dining room. Moth-eaten tapestries dangled from its walls, their shadows skittering beneath the glare of tarnished metal sconces that had once lit the Vatican. A royal banquet laid out by the silent AI that governed the CuddleTech freighter greeted her, and as usual the machine had predicted Trace's exact chemical cravings before she was even aware of them herself, guaranteeing a meal precisely tailored to what she would enjoy and nutritionally require.

On the other side of the sprawling food-laden table was her beloved husband. He stood up rod-straight at her entrance and nodded cordially.

"Good evening, dear," he said simply.

Trace nodded silently in return as she took her seat, and felt a sensation she was still trying to get used to: the desire to spend time with another person simply to enjoy their company. And while she never thought she'd be the marrying type, something any sensible Human would have guessed after the first punch, now that Trace had taken the plunge she wouldn't trade it for anything.

She sampled a zucchini flower stuffed with feta and deep fried in duck fat, possibly the last of its kind, as her husband went on his usual spiel.

"You look more beautiful every day. Did you buff your piercings just for me? That obsidian is really gleaming."

Trace felt a little embarrassed that he'd noticed, but also flattered.

"I love you so much," he said without prompt.

Trace melted a little, as always, and returned the sentiment.

"I love you too, Tuesday."

A smile slowly spread across Tuesday's rodent face until he was baring all his little black teeth. Unable to hold in his amusement at her confused expression, Tuesday threw his head back and cackled insanely.

From the shadows, the face of a three metre long bristleworm tasted the air with a cluster of facial organs and waited.

*

Although these three words had never been combined into a sentence in this order before, Jimmy Slummer ran.

His sneakered feet pounded at the no-slip laminate flooring of the middle levels of a soaring arcology, lungs burning like road flares and muscles screaming graphic protests. He was sure to keep to the warren-like Westside corridors branching off from the cheaper flats of this twenty five million person capacity residential mega block, as the more expensive open areas offered too many opportunities for a long-distance bullet in the spine. Sprinting deep into the twisting dregs of the cramped, maze-like welfare levels meant that Jimmy would remain an obscured target at worst, and totally lost to his pursuers at best.

Ducking and half-sliding under a bulging, shaking drainage pipe, Jimmy huffed an obscenity in the highly offensive language known as Guttertongue as he heard a barking yell of glee from one of his pursuers. He was flying past a different apartment door with literally every second stride, but if any of the residents could hear the kerfuffle going on in the corridor they sure as Tartarus weren't going to get involved. There was a good chance every tenant in a hundred metre radius had casually turned off their external security cameras the moment they heard the commotion, just to be sure they wouldn't get dragged into whatever was going on by the filth or worse. The residents of this hive all kept their heads down, as sneaking the wrong peek was a good way to end up getting sold off as spare parts.

 Skidding at the end of the corridor, slamming shoulder-first into a No Running sign so hard that he was sure he'd inflicted some minor whiplash, Jimmy jumped into the stairwell and twisted sideways. His skid shoes, the type that were all the rage about fifteen Christmases ago, had tiny antigrav wafers sewn into the soles that were programmed to activate if you moved your ankles in a certain way. The cheap wafers hummed on, and Jimmy slid a couple of centimetres above the steps for twenty bumpy metres until he bashed hard into a low safety railing with his crotch and a large window with his elbow. Unfortunately, the "window" turned out to be nothing more than an empty frame covered by a taped-in-place garbage bag, and Jimmy tore through the mess as easily as wet paper.

Tumbling face-first towards an open drop, so far above the concrete pavement of ground level that the streetlights looked like pinprick embers, Jimmy came to a surprising stop after half a second rather than the usual two minutes of freefall you'd expect. It took a moment for his stunned brain to realise that a temporary construction gantry had caught his fall, though every bone in his body was ready and willing to let him know all the details.

Looking into the distance, he could see that this dying arcology was just one of twelve. Standing four kilometres tall and two wide, this dozen-strong cluster was arranged like the hours on an analogue clock. From here, the extreme pollution meant they were nothing more than looming brown silhouettes.

But now wasn't a good time to hate the view. He could do that later. For now, Jimmy had to keep running.

Rolling back into the relative safety of the stairwell through another bag-taped window frame (was there any glass left in this damned building?), all Jimmy wanted to do was curl up on the no-slip steps and breathe deep until the fire in his lungs stopped feeling like it was full of fish hooks. But then he heard the gleeful yells of his pursuers, and they sounded close enough to spit at.

Groaning in pain, dragging himself upright, Jimmy glanced at the stairwell number to see that he was on floor eight-hundred-and-ninety-six. Gasping in exhaustion, he took four lumbering steps and jumped, turning sideways so the antigrav wafers in his skid shoes would switch on again. Sliding on thin air, twisting away from the safety railing just in time to prevent a repeat dive out another window, Jimmy flew along on the buffer of his physics-defying footwear for floor after floor.

From a knee-height vent, a cluster of antennae and sensory bumps sampled the air as Jimmy slid past. He didn't notice them.

Lana Slade impatiently tapped her fingers on the recliner's armrest, continuing to wait for a response to her hail. She was sitting alone in a dented yellow school shuttle, a piece of junk that was barely graded for surface-to-moon jaunts. Almost every square centimetre of her cricket-leather seat was defaced with laser pen graffiti or lumpy with dried bubble gum.

As she had announced her presence almost three minutes ago, the only way that the total silence she'd been answered with could be anything except outright insulting was if everyone on the other end had been cocooned in place by alien parasites from toes to throat and couldn't reach the microphone button with their tongues.

Lana knew that today's visit was going to be a game-changer for her, and that there were only two ways it could pan out: either the people on the other end of the comm would respond to her hail and she would finally meet her biological family after a lifetime of separation, or she was going to program the Repler unit on her shuttle to clone up five tonnes of stinky dog coils and blast the living daylights out of their settlements with synthesised canine excrement.

But she wouldn't be the one who made that decision. The ball was entirely in their court.

Still tapping her fingers, Lana's eyes flicked back towards the port window and locked onto the unique stellar object known simply as The Cube. As its name indicated, The Cube was a giant square block of frozen water the size of a large moon, and its ice was so pure that you could chip off a bit and suck on it without needing to bother with filtration. This marvel had been drifting between star systems for eons prior to its discovery in the late 22nd Century, and the fact it had been found by an off-course prison ship filled with the offspring of exiled Skandinavian royalty only made it more of a miracle. It had taken time and effort and deep-core sampling, but The Unison's techs had eventually concluded that The Cube was originally a cooling system for a mega-hot alien computer. The computer had gone critical an estimated two million years ago, dissolving its hardware into mist while sending the cooling systems into a wild surge of overcompensation that had resulted in the biggest frozen treat in the galaxy. With potable water being literally worth more than its weight in gold in many places across The Unison, the Skandinavian exiles had gone from seventh-level scum to the top of the rich list.

After signing some of the most lucrative mining contracts in history, they'd invested much of it straight back into infrastructure. Back in Lana's time The Cube was spiked in thousands of places with the largest custom-made drills, and these titanic screws were topped with luxurious pleasure palaces so massive that it wasn't uncommon for the residents not to run into another living soul for weeks on end. Their little empire in the darkness between star systems was at stark contrast to the nightmare of their exile.

To be accurate, though, Lana's time had come and gone five centuries ago. Seeing as though some severe temporal dickery had landed her in the 30th Century, by now The Cube had been chewed at so thoroughly that it was utterly cored. Its crust still maintained that distinctive shape, but the interior of The Cube was clearly as hollow as a cheap Easter egg. If anyone still lived here, they no longer had much of anything to sell.

There were two key reasons why Lana had never tried to reach out to her real family before. For one, space travel was still horrendously expensive even in the 25th Century, meaning 99% of citizens within the bounds of The Unison were damned to never feel the heat of a different star to the one of their birth. Reason number two was that the owners and residents of The Cube, a people known as the Strom, were a pack of racist bastards. Their genetic line had been rendered universally intersex by nine decades of hard radiation exposure on their malfunctioning prison ship, and as a result they'd developed an extreme aversion to what they termed to be "monogenders," vis-à-vis, those who were not born intersex. To the mindset of the Strom, a monogender was a half-person, something incomplete, a disgusting chunk suffering from a gross lack of wholeness. Necessity demanded that the Strom had tolerated doing business with monogenders remotely, but their drill-tip cities were forbidden to outsiders, even over video. It was audio or nothing, and even then the Strom would wash their ears for hours afterwards. Once their water mining empire had reached the point of total automation, they'd cut off all contact with the Universe and were happy for those tales of hideous monogenders to become urban legends.

Then one day, a baby arrived. That infant had been Lana, the first monogender born to Strom parents in living memory. As you'd expect, she'd been immediately stuffed into a small padded stasis module built to transport toy poodles and shipped off to the other side of Humanity's reach before the neighbours found out. Before sliding the hatch shut, Lana's birther had suffered an attack of conscience, and penned a note in cursive Swedish to tuck into her nappy. Its words were brief.

Where you were born, you would never be anything but subhuman. Where we have sent you, you have a chance to be equal, to be more. This is our one and only gift to you.

Lana blinked heavily, rubbing her thumb and index finger at a much-folded piece of paper made from the flesh of an actual tree, a rarity in the age of tactile holographics. It hadn't taken Lana long to figure out where she'd really been born, as the entire Swedish language, both written and verbal, was illegal everywhere except for one place: The Cube. The faculty staff at the Academy had made a rare exception in the case of this note, and given it to Lana on her tenth birthday (or "arrival day," as was the case with abandoned orphans).

Lana's eyes flicked to the ceiling at a ticking, rattling sound, almost like the noise of a roach skittering over a powerful microphone. As the shuttle's ancient reactor was mostly putty and duct tape, she knew that any new sound could be a five-second warning announcing her imminent death. Thankfully the noise stopped, and Lana's heart rate slowed down beneath its "hamster" setting.

She tapped at the Omni implant in the web of flesh between the thumb and index finger of her left hand and glared at the holographic chronometer as it superimposed itself against a thick film of dust motes. If those Skandinavian bastards were going to tell her to push off, she'd prefer them to do it quickly. Everyone she knew might have been dead for half a millennium and Mankind may have vanished from the galaxy, but she had better things to do than wait here all day.

She'd give it one more minute. Two, max.

CHAPTER TWO

Carefully cutting one of the last zucchini flowers in the Universe down its seam, Trace bared her sharp teeth as a creamy fondue of molten cheese oozed out. Tasting a morsel from the tines of her golden fork, Trace looked up to see how much Tuesday was savouring his.

"Husband, have you ever enjoyed such…"

She trailed off. Not only was Tuesday no longer sitting in the opposite throne, he'd disappeared from the dining area altogether without so much as a goodbye. The fork he'd buried in a deep-fried gourd vibrated softly, as though abandoned only a second ago.

Glancing to her right at the sound of a gentle ticking, Trace came face to face with something out of a nightmare: a three-metre-long bristleworm. His legless, segmented black body was a chitinous exoskeleton headed with what was best described as some kind of alien Swiss Army knife. He tasted the air between them with a collection of facial protrusions, his sensory organs ranging in appearance from antennae to stingers to corkscrews to hinged jaws to mandibles and a cluster of eyestalks.

A woman of action to the core, Trace erupted to her feet with screaming threats and reached for the nearest heavy object: her chair, a tangled piece of art woven from a single iron bar. The bristleworm chittered at her aggression as she brandished the piece of furniture as easily as a feather duster. What approximated the bristleworm's mouth, nose and eyes rattled together, as though giving a warning.

Tuesday half-poked his face around the dining room's far arch. It seemed that Trace's shout had been enough to drag her "beloved husband" away from his speedy retreat, but it wasn't sufficient to evoke anything approximating actual bravery.

"The gun," Trace snapped at Tuesday, brandishing her chair like a lion tamer.

Tuesday's jaw fell in recognition the moment he got a proper look at the bristleworm. He crept another couple of centimetres back into the dining room as the creature turned to regard him.

"That's…" Tuesday's eyes darted along the bug's carapace. "That's a Thorn-Tongued Drennite! A male, I think. He should be intelligent, to a degree."

"He won't be in a sec," Trace hissed. "Gun!"

Swinging the chair, Trace hit nothing but air as the bristleworm darted sideways like an eel, gracefully dodging her clumsy blow. Rather than making a run for it or launching a counterattack, the Drennite deliberately smacked the side of his head against the marble floor with enough force to break Human bones. The clicking ceased, replaced by fluent Unglish words.

"How about now?" the Drennite asked, apparently continuing a conversation that only he had been a part of. Greeted by two equally slack expressions, the bristleworm nodded in satisfaction. "Good. I think some idiot mixed up the selection menu on this second-rate translator. Now, for the third time, my name is Rem, and it's vital that we speak. Oh, and by the way, I'm just a Drennite. The Thorn-Tongued are an outlawed terrorist organisation to which I have no official connection. Hint, hint."

Trace lowered her weapon a little, just enough to wordlessly propose a temporary truce while the bug explained what he was doing here. Her eyes narrowed in Tuesday's direction, who was still mostly hiding behind an arch. Sensing that if Trace had to batter the bristleworm without his help that he'd be the next one to get pulped, Tuesday grudgingly stepped into the open. He stopped a dozen paces from the invertebrate alien, not feeling the need to make himself a more desirable target than his dear wife.

"Speak about what?" Trace ground out.

"I can't tell you yet," Rem said automatically.

Trace squinted a little, a dangerous expression.

"Why can't you tell me?"

Rem sighed.

"I can't tell you that yet, either."

Trace nodded stoically, apparently hearing enough.

"Okay. Good talk."

Rem flicked aside like a giant yabbie with almost prescient reaction speed, his coiled body shooting out of the flying chair's trajectory with ease. Rearing up, chattering his webbed segments together with a noise like a rattlesnake, Rem growled his next words as the piece of furniture clattered down a set of marble steps at top volume.

"Look, you idiot, I swear that I want to explain everything to you, but there are literally hundreds of...of blocks in place, and if I accidentally trigger any of these taboo words or concepts, it's game over for all of us. I may be very, very good at what I do, but I can't brute-punch my way directly through this sort of security. This means I can't just give you all the information you want, but I can help you to gain an awareness for yourselves. That's the only way I can help you."

"Blocks?" Trace said.

"They were put in place to, mmm, protect your minds from certain facts that would probably send you insane, or worse. They're the reason I have to be so cryptic."

"What sort of..." Trace's mouth twitched in annoyance. "Actually, let me guess: you can't tell us about all these horrible facts that will send us insane, or alarm bells will ring."

"I see you're getting the hang of this," Rem said with a modicum of sarcasm. "Look, I know this is annoying, and I know your zucchini flowers are getting cold, but it's imperative that we keep talking until this whole thing gets sorted out. We have about one minute until all five of us are in a galaxy of trouble."

Trace scowled.

"We're between systems. There isn't so much as a grain of dust within lightyears, let alone anything dangerous."

Trace's expression softened at an odd tickling in the back of her brain, a dim sense that what she just said wasn't true. Rem looked hopefully at her for an instant, as though Trace was on the right track, but as usual Tuesday decided to ruin the moment.

"So you're here to save us," Tuesday clarified. "What sort of danger are we in? Who's after us? Who sent you?"

Rem gave a grunt of frustration at the fact Tuesday clearly didn't understand how this was meant to work. He rubbed his eye stalks with the blunt side of a hinged mandible in what may have been anxiety.

"Damn it, people, I don't have time for this kindergarten crap!" Rem growled, making an aggravated ticking noise from the depths of his dual throats. "I've had to create all sorts of diversions to get this far, and they are all strictly one-time deals. If I don't get you out of here before the deadline, and I mean to the second, security is going to get boosted so stratospheric that nobody will ever have a chance of reaching you again, let alone manage an extraction. This is your only shot. So if the two of you want to keep throwing furniture and asking stupid questions until it's too late, you'll leave me with no choice but to leave you here and focus on getting the other two out on their own, and that'll be entirely on you, okay?"

Trace gurned with insult.

"What other two? We're all alone on this ship, and I doubt we'd be able to reach anything sentient in under a week. Unless you brought friends?"

Rem shrugged again, choosing his words carefully. "Are you on a ship?"

"Of course we are," Trace snapped, waving aggressively at the enormous bay window on the other side of the dining room's far arch and at the stars beyond. But then there it was again: that faint look on her face, a kind of vague recognition that something wasn't right about what she'd just said. "But even though something's obvious, it doesn't necessarily mean it's true, does it?"

Rem gave a curt nod. Finally, he was getting somewhere. With any luck, these morons would figure it all out before the heat death of the Universe. If the others were this difficult to convince, then there was no hope. He knew the very next part would be the hardest to accomplish, though.

"Do you need us to do something?" Tuesday hazarded.

Rem nodded again. He flicked a facial protrusion and what appeared to be a stopwatch popped into existence. He used one of his sets of mandibles to manipulate it as though it was a physical object. As tactile holographics had been common even in Trace and Tuesday's time, this was hardly anything new.

"Yes. It's simple, but timing is of the utmost importance."

*

Despite just flying out of an arcology window fifteen seconds ago, Jimmy kept spiralling down the staircase for another dozen floors as fast as he could manage, floating just above the laminate the whole way. Unfortunately, he soon encountered a new problem: it turned out that the skid shoes didn't have a top speed, or at least one that could be considered safe, and with every grimy metre Jimmy found himself inching towards the kind of velocity that could reduce a person to a mere stain on a wall. Just to improve matters, he couldn't remember how the brakes were meant to work...or even if there were any brakes.

He now understood why skid shoes weren't popular thirteen Christmases ago.

Feeling utterly out of control, lips and eyelids peeling back against the growing wind resistance, Jimmy finally lost his nerve and reached up for one of the many pipes rattling above his head. Gripping a tarnished tube hard enough to inject rusty splinters in his palms, Jimmy quickly discovered that his skid shoes had decided that they were going to keep on zipping along their merry way with or without him. Giving a mighty, unintentional double kick that sent him spinning around the pipe like a gymnast, Jimmy's high-tech footwear shot off like bullets and corkscrewed down the stairwell, vanishing around the next bend without an owner to slow them down. Spug only knew how far they'd make it on their own.

Coming to a jerking halt upside down, it took Jimmy a couple of seconds to realise that his bare feet had been caught in a tangle of dusty wiring and old pigeon nests. Dizzy and breathless, looking down at the dirty steps less than two and a half metres from his dripping face, Jimmy was just about to try figuring out how he was going to get down when the pipe helpfully snapped in half with a dusty cough, sending him crashing head-first into the stairwell. Thankfully, Jimmy's face was there to break his fall.

Groaning, twisted up in the stairwell, a casual question from directly above jabbed fear into Jimmy's soul.

"Who are you running from?"

Jimmy rolled over to see a giant, talking bristleworm was sitting on a rusting metal lattice a couple of floors up. Registering that the creature wasn't armed or hostile or close enough to try blocking his escape, Jimmy immediately filed this event under "Weird" and "Unimportant" and dragged his bruised body upright. Stumbling the first few steps, cursing at how he'd forgotten to spray on a new pair of aerosol socks this morning, Jimmy heard the same voice again from three stories directly down.

"Well? Who?"

Jimmy yelped at the word, darting away from its source in reflex. Managing to spike the edge of a bulkhead rivet with his eyebrow, Jimmy cussed and held his split face as blood trickled freely. Blinking out of synchronisation over the railing as he regarded the bristleworm for a long second, Jimmy's stunned brain spent an instant trying to figure out whether this bug was just a lookalike of the first one or if it was somehow able to teleport about at will.

Gulping air, staggering a little sideways thanks to his brand-new head injury, Jimmy's jowls shook as he yelped in abject terror.

"Them!" he managed, gesturing wildly at a stairway that seemingly ascended forever.

There was nobody in sight, but a few whoops echoed down the grimy industrial laminate from his pursuers, along with the sound of numerous boot falls. Cursing his feeble intelligence for wasting precious air on a word, Jimmy gripped a jutting slot normally used to swipe bulky magnetic pass cards and swung back into a run.

"Be sure to stop before turning the next corner," the bristleworm noted helpfully, now dangling over a railing two floors up. "You never see that wheelchair in time."

Automatically reacting to the bristleworm's advice, Jimmy skidded to a halt just as he started to swing around the bend. Jimmy bumped crotch-first into a low, crumpled-up wheelchair that some imbecile had half-wedged under the railing, though thankfully the impact hadn't been severe enough to hurt his meat and two veg.

Jimmy's heart hammered at the yells of his pursuers, as they now sounded close enough to swing at. However, against every instinct in his soft mammal body, he paused where he was. The bristleworm's question began to spin inside his head: Who was chasing him?

And why?

Jimmy's introspection was startled by a sudden resurgence of primal yowling and screeches from above, but Jimmy managed to stand staunch as he glanced at the stairwell number. The sign said he was on floor eight-hundred-and-ninety-seven. How the hell did he get so far up a four-kilometre-high arcology? What planet was he even on?

Already gasping in exhaustion, his instincts wanted him to keep descending. But he didn't do it.

Jimmy closed his eyes, gripped the railing tightly, and tilted his chin up towards the stairs that twisted away into the sky. Noticing that the yells of his pursuers didn't seem to be getting any nearer, Jimmy's eyes snapped open after ten long seconds to regard the dangling bristleworm.

"Nobody is chasing me." Jimmy said flatly. "I'm running from nothing. There's probably something deeply philosophical and spiritual in that statement, but I'm not getting it right now."

He wasn't an expert on invertebrate facial expressions, but Jimmy was pretty sure that the bug's sensory gribbles were arranged in a smile. The Drennite nodded, continuing to hang upside down from the railing like a noose. Jimmy gave a sharp, sad laugh.

"Somehow you knew I'd crush my balls on that wheelchair. But I didn't. I was meant to, though. I know it a hundred and ten percent. In the back of my head, I can feel that what I'm experiencing right now is…wrong, somehow."

Jimmy tried to ignore the latest whoops of hunters who didn't exist. It wasn't easy. While intellectually he knew they were just phantasms, every nerve in his fight-or-flight network was screaming danger messages. He tried not to focus on the surges of adrenaline and fear.

His eyes flicked up to regard the Drennite. Jimmy grimaced with the effort of working with logic, an esoteric skill he'd never developed working in the Landkelp fields on the farming world of Sprout, or flipping burgers in a dozen different MacDeath franchises. His heaving stomach wasn't all that conducive to deep thought, either.

"Why didn't you stop me flying out that window earlier and going splat?"

Rem shrugged a little. "You survived going out the window. You always do."

Jimmy blinked. "So you're here for some other reason?" He paused, putting two and two together with record slowness. Jimmy reviewed how the bug had alerted him to the fact that the pursuers weren't real, and how he'd not only predicted Jimmy's path, but effortlessly popped back and forth as if by magic. It hurt, but Jimmy managed to squish all these little facts together into a new, larger fact. Holding a railing, he slid down the bannister until his buttocks kissed a no-slip laminate step.

"All right. From what I can tell, while you haven't explained a single darn thing to me as of yet, I can tell that you know plenty, and you seem dead-set on prodding me into having doubts about…well, everything." Jimmy pinched the back of his hand between index finger and thumb, and winced at the sharpness. His eyes flicked towards a window containing nothing but a single shade of brown smog, then up at a screech from a pursuing maniac who didn't exist. "You know what's going on, like you've seen it play out numerous times. You're trying to help me realise that despite the fact every physical sense is telling me that this is real…well, it seems that you can't just outright explain what's going on, or there'll be Hell to pay, right?"

Rem gave a nod.

"I see we've found the brains of the outfit."

Jimmy leaned back against the railing, resting the base of his skull on it. His breath was still chugging like a steam train.

"So how do I get out of here? Out of," he twitched at another yowl, "whatever this is?"

"There's precisely one way," Rem said seriously.

He twitched a lip stalk, and a Drennite version of a stopwatch appeared. From what Jimmy could tell, their version of a minute had eighty-two seconds.

*

Rather than tapping the Omni implant that sit within the meat between her thumb and index finger, for the sake of variety Lana unfocused her eyes to access the time/date function on her retinal screens. Sighing at digits on the stopwatch, her next decision became a binary one: would she be bombarding The Cube with synthesised Saint Bernard droppings, or Great Dane excrement?

Warned by a loud snap from above, Lana only had time to push herself out of her padded recliner and dive into the aisle as most of the ceiling collapsed, showering her with tiles, lint and dead cockroaches. Even though the smallest glitch on this barely-operational school shuttle would be instantly fatal, Lana transitioned into a sharp commando roll before lunging for the spacesuit she'd draped over the chair opposite. As the spacesuit had been used by snot-nosed Academy students for decades, it was held together by duct tape and dozens of crude penises had been singed into its visor with laser tip pens. Lana stopped reaching for the suit at the sound of words in the Unglish language.

"Sorry about that."

Only pausing for a fraction of a second, Lana kicked off the recliner in front of her to spin around with a lethal roundhouse. Rather than coming face-to-face with a Human or a close equivalent, though, as Lana's heel flicked towards the uninvited guest at top speed she was surprised to see a long, insectoid ribbon of chitin and spiky bits. The bristleworm effortlessly twisted away from Lana's arcing shoe, whipping himself on top of the same chair Lana had just tumbled out of. She wanted to follow the primal, territorial urge to continue attacking this unknown invader until it was the consistency of eggnog, but then the bug shrank into what was obviously a show of submission. This was enough to give Lana pause.

"I just want to talk," the bristleworm promised.

Both hands extended in the standard Keri Soko stance she'd been drilled in since preschool, Lana glanced up at what used to be the ceiling. A variety of pipes and cables had burst free, swinging about as they exhaled assorted gases. With a quick flick of her eyes Lana sized up the bristleworm and the narrow vent above. Her brain didn't like the math.

"How did you fit in there?" Lana demanded. "The only conceivable way you'd be able to jam yourself into a slot that small is if all of those lines were installed around you before you were sealed in. As this shuttle is six hundred years old if it's a day, I doubt that." She regarded the dead cockroaches and the kilogram or so of ankle-deep dust that had cascaded down, and then back up at the bug. "Not to mention all this debris. What, did you seal yourself in with all that lint? Seriously, talk."

Rem slid across the chair's headrest, moving into the thin aisle slowly enough to not look threatening. Rather than answer Lana's question, he asked one of his own.

"This is a short-range shuttle," Rem stated. "The kind you'd use to hop between a planet and one of its moons, or perhaps to another world in the same system if you had a few weeks. How did you get it all the way to The Cube, a stellar object sitting between star systems?"

"Hey, you busted into my ride," Lana snapped. "I'm the one asking the questions here. What's your game? Are you a slaver or something? Here to capture me alive so you can sell me as an oddity to some collector? Put me into a premium special-edition burger? What?"

Lana realised she was hyperventilating, but then her brain caught up to what the Drennite had just asked, and a beautiful logic slowly took hold. Squinting at Rem as she chewed over his question, she could recall going on class excursions a number of times during her schooling with the Academy, but the furthest she'd ever gone was definitely when she'd managed to score work-experience on the Carpe Astrum. That trip had taken several days at top speed, and it wasn't even an interplanetary journey. To move all the way to the next star system would take a thousand years, minimum, let alone to the interstellar gulf that contained The Cube.

Lana relaxed a little bit. Luckily for Rem, she liked mental challenges.

"Well?" Rem pressed.

Lana glanced out the window. She regarded the towering ice drills of The Cube, each topped with sprawling palaces. Her eyes flicked back to regard Rem.

"I have no memory of how I got here," she said slowly. "Zilch. Last thing I remember was that Transcended being asking the four of us what we all wanted most of all, and I said..."

"You wanted to meet your real parents," Rem finished.

Lana sized up the bristleworm. Resignation crept across her face.

"Knew it was too good to be true." She stared at The Cube longingly, as though committing it to memory, and quickly came to grips with the situation. "I'm assuming the other three are trapped within their own...wishes?"

Rem nodded, pleased that she seemed to get where they were at. However, his bug face twitched in alarm as Lana asked a dangerous question.

"So how long have I been sitting here waiting for a reply? How long has this loop been repeating?"

The stars themselves shuddered in response to how close Lana had come to voicing taboo concepts. Despite this warning, Lana was clearly not going to leave the issue alone.

"Give me a number," Lana pressed, careful to keep her wording more neutral.

Rem chose his words carefully.

"We don't know for sure. Our best estimate is eight years."

Lana had to sit down. Looking at her reflection in the window, she saw what she was used to seeing: an eighteen-year-old Cadet, probably a little smaller than average, with dark hair clamped into a tight bun and pasted with enough hairspray to blast a crater in any world's ozone layer. The knowledge she was now in her mid-twenties wasn't welcome, and that was disregarding the five hundred years she'd spent in cryo. Learning she'd been trapped in a software loop, spinning like a dog chasing its tail after all she'd suffered, was too much for a moment.

Lana glared at Rem with an expression like ice.

"You're obviously here to get me out. How do you propose to do that?"

Rem produced a holographic stopwatch by twitching his cybernetically-enhanced mandibles. He teased it with three optical stalks, counting under his breath. He gave a short hiss.

"It'll be tight, what with Trace and Tuesday both being dull as a wet bar of soap, but I should be able to get all of you out in time."

"In time for what?"

"Once we get away, I swear I will tell you everything I know," Rem said, the veneer of his apology getting candy-shell thin by this point. He was clearly antsy about something. "There's just one catch..."

"And that is?" Lana pressed.

Rem moved his face in a way that could be described as a grimace.

"Everyone needs to follow my instructions exactly, or none of us will be getting out of here...ever."

*

"I need you to say something," Rem told Jimmy, still dangling upside down from the next floor's safety railing. He checked the stopwatch with one eye stalk, as though keeping track of every second was of the utmost importance. "You need to follow my instructions exactly..."

*

"...there is no space for error," Rem warned Trace and Tuesday through gritted mandibles. "Every word needs to be said at the right time."

Trace squinted at the bristleworm's eye stalks as they spun the Drennite-style holographic stopwatch. Her lack of trust was almost tangible.

"I'm going to humour you for another thirty seconds, and then my husband is fetching my gun," Trace said calmly, as though describing the floral pattern of a nice scarf she'd seen at the local church fete earlier. "So unless you want to get ventilated by a limited-edition Vindicator-series Holt & Heckler unfolding kinetic accelerator, I suggest you start making sense." Trace gave the kind of smile that no Human face should wear. "Clock's ticking, bug."

"I only need thirteen seconds," Rem snapped. "But then you need to follow my instructions. Both of you. Okay?"

*

The Drennite stopwatch ticked its last seconds away in three different places in perfect synchronisation: in the urine-stench of an arcology stairwell, within the claustrophobic bubble gum-encrusted walls of a school shuttle junker, and in the marble opulence of a CuddleTech mega-freighter's executive dining room.

"Okay..." Rem announced, his voice cracking a little as the stopwatch hit two seconds, "Now!"

As instructed, the humans droned, snapped, whispered and spat the same phrase.

"This isn't real."

And then everything collapsed around them in an explosion of seized-up code.

*

The laws of physics broke down and reality peeled away in strands under the strain of a system-crashing error. For a time there was no sensation besides a feeling of white and the taste of tin, but eventually four separate minds experienced the trademark stomach-lurch of exiting virtual reality after a longer-than-recommended simulation. It was beyond unpleasant, like motion sickness combined with haemorrhoids.

Thrashing about in the void, an emptiness composed of little more than flashing lines of self-repairing code, the minds came to rest in an empty beige space. Sewn back together one stitch at a time after a total software meltdown, screaming in confusion, each of the quartet transformed from a liquefied mess into something more solid and defined, the opposite to how a candle melts. Their residual self-images eventually formed them into ordinary, stock-standard bipedal mammals.

Higher thought returned so suddenly that it was painful. One moment they were mindless blobs of wire framing, the next they were the same humans they'd always been, complete with their old clothes: Jimmy was dressed in a neon-yellow MacDeath fry cook uniform, Lana wore an ebony Naval Cadet uniform encrusted with too much gold edging, Tuesday was wearing orange coveralls embossed with the word PAROLEE in numerous places, and Trace's hulking frame was armoured with the sapphire riot suit of an Enforcer.

A glob of liquid fire plopped into their midst and screeched like a bat, trickling into the three-metre-long body of Rem, the Drennite who had gotten them this far. Shaking off the burning feeling of being restored from a prior backup, Rem shuddered for a time before he could talk. He lowered his eyestalks and pointed them upwards, regarding the humans with suspicion.

"So I got you out?" Rem asked, halfway between disbelieving and impressed.

"Of course you did," Lana snapped. She flicked her eyes back and forth across the whiteness, occasionally latching onto symbols as they shot past. "Well, to wherever here is."

"Looks a lot like nothing but cut-price virtual reality to me," Trace agreed.

"From what we understand, the Slidge imprisoned you in a VR system of Human make," Rem clarified. "Which bypassed a lot of compatibility issues between your brains and the hardware and software. Thankfully, this allowed some room for error."

"Wait," Tuesday interrupted, lost. "What virtual reality? What did you say about the Slidge?"

"Nice to see all of you too," Jimmy mumbled, hurt that nobody had said hello yet.

Rem shook the upper segments of his bristleworm exoskeleton.

"Technically, I've never met any of you. The Rems you dealt with were copies of my mind I sent in to do the dirty work. Poor crawlers had no idea they were copies, or that they were on a suicide run." Rem coiled a little, as though finally able to relax. "I do know that the four of you must have outright rejected the simulation at the exact same instant, which started a system-wide maintenance routine. This stress automatically flushed away your loops...as well as my copies. While the system gauged your minds far too important to delete, the same can't be said for my doppelgangers, who would have been identified as corruptions and consequently shredded. They didn't know what hit them, I'm sure."

Lana clicked her fingers impatiently.

"Yes, yes, well done, you managed to commit suicide three times. Very impressive. Now, can we return to the whole freedom issue? Your dead selves seemed pressed for time."

"Getting your minds flushed down into the programming substrate is part eighteen of my plan," Rem clarified. "See, normally your consciousnesses would have been stuck down here in the void while the maintenance routine did its thing to rethread your loops, and you would have been totally unaware that anything had even happened. However..."

"You changed the settings?" Jimmy hazarded.

"Wait," Trace snapped. She looked around at the creamy white sky. It was divided by thin rainbow rims in the distance, as though bricked together with soap bubbles. If you looked really, really close, you could see the atom-thin black of wire framing. "I know this place. It's where that Transcended being granted our wishes, right?"

Lana cleared her throat. "Uh, no. There was no wish-granting godlike alien. It was a fancy interrogation program created by the Slidge to coax out our dreams and desires in order to create the perfect prison for our minds." Lana nodded at Rem, as though tipping an invisible cap. "Right?"

"Right," the bug agreed. "You've all been experiencing the same short loops, over and over, for at least eight years. Without my intervention, you would have remained as prisoners until your bodies turned to dust, and possibly even longer. As the Slidge are more than adept at life-extension medicine, we're talking thousands of years of looping, minimum. You wouldn't believe how good some of their science is. These cats can regrow whole limbs almost as easy as cutting them off." Rem looked a little embarrassed, as though he'd overstepped some unseen line. "Uh, sorry."

"Sorry about what?" Jimmy asked.

He was met with a stony silence. It was clear this topic of discussion had been shelved.

"So you're a hacker?" Tuesday asked in distrust. "Like the kind that keeps sending me those ads for penis enlargement creams?"

"I'm a wet-work operative who used to work for the Drennite branch of Response," Rem clarified. "This job is way beyond a standard code-monkey. See, while the good news is your loops were stored together on the same hardware, a system solely dedicated to keeping you placid and unaware, the bad news is this system was inaccessible unless I came into actual physical proximity with it. I had to sneak in and free your minds before I could free your bodies." Rem cleared his two throats. "And, uh, Tuesday, I'm pretty sure that the ads you get are based on your browsing history."

"So where are our bodies, exactly?" Trace growled, not giving Tuesday a chance to defend his literal manhood.

Tuesday arched an eyebrow at his wife. He looked about the white eternity, as this was all getting far too philosophical for his tastes.

"Uh, we're right here. Yes?"

Rem shook his head, amazed that Tuesday still didn't understand what was going on.

"We've already established that this is just another level of virtual reality. Your Actual bodies are on Earth, only a couple of hundred metres away from where you were gunned down and captured."

"No, no!" Tuesday snapped, as though everyone was stupid except for him. "Those Slidge from the Primacy Guard tried to shoot us with their stunners, but we got rescued at the last moment by a Transcended alien who..." Tuesday halted mid-syllable, as everyone was looking at him in the same way. He paused for a second. "Oh. There was no rescue, was there?"

"They stunned us, discovered our dreams, and locked us in a tailored loop without us even noticing," Jimmy said in total misery.

"Can we repeat ourselves just a little bit less, please?" Lana moaned in frustration. She snapped her fingers loudly at Tuesday before he could push out one more redundant word and turned to Rem. "Okay. Now, how about giving us some answers we don't already have? For starters, why are the Slidge keeping our bodies prisoner if our minds aren't even aware of it? Doesn't that defeat the whole purpose of locking somebody up? Surely it'd be easier to just wax the four of us and call it a day."

"Who paid you to rescue us?" Jimmy added. "And why? Last thing I heard, Mankind is gone."

"How come extracting us is so time sensitive?" Trace asked.

"And after eight years in a sim, could our bodies even stand up under their own power?" Tuesday asked, his question a lot more relevant than his other recent examples.

Rem arranged his mandibles in a grin.

"Now those code triggers have been flushed, I can answer all of your questions. For starters..."

A series of red holographic screens appeared in front of each of Rem's eye stalks, glowing and shaking violently in a way that was far from encouraging. Every knobbly protrusion on Rem's face suddenly expanded to a full outward stretch, as though he was about to let out a scream loud enough to crack his head down the seams. Flicking sideways in a way that brought a trout to mind, Rem wordlessly disappeared like a burp in a tornado.

He was gone.

They stood there in the white for an awkward ten seconds, as though expecting their would-be saviour to reappear at any instant. It took some time, but eventually Lana's head drooped, she screwed her eyes shut, and she said an illegal word.

"Spug."

"Is he coming back?" Jimmy asked a little hysterically.

"Maybe he was never here in the first place," Tuesday suggested calmly. His eyes traced the rainbow rims dividing the white sky, and sucked at the little black shards that passed as his teeth. "Perhaps this is another level of punishment. Maybe the Slidge wanted to get us all excited and hopeful so they can whip the rug out from under us for giggles. I don't know about you lot, but I reckon I was a lot happier in that mindless loop before all this got dumped on me."

Trace cussed. She shook her head at Tuesday. In the silence, her words were deafening.

"I hate it when you make sense. Why can't you be the kind of husband who's seen and not heard?"

Lana's expression was so sharp you could have shaved with it.

"Husband?" Lana repeated.

Tuesday made furious gestures behind Trace's back, clearly begging to change the subject. Jimmy defused the situation by stretching with a series of loud pops, glad for the small pleasure of being able to work the knots out of his joints.

"Running for eight years straight really takes it out of you," he noted.

"You know what?" Lana said thoughtfully. "Maybe we could try to..."

She popped out of existence just as suddenly as Rem. Trace went to speak, but she ceased to exist next. Tuesday exhaled at her passing, shaking a little.

"For the love of Odin, don't mention the marriage thing again," he said, eyes darting about. "When the Transcended asked me what I wished for, I asked for Trace to believe I was her husband."

"But...why?" Jimmy asked, absolutely aghast.

Tuesday gave him a look of scorn as though the answer was obvious.

"For a laugh, clearly. It's hilarious."

"I doubt Trace'll be laughing much once she realises the truth. Until she's tap dancing on your skull, anyway." Jimmy's face twisted into sour disgust. "Wait, you didn't..."

"Of course not!" Tuesday exploded, genuinely appalled. "Even I have my limits, Slummer. Remember, we were stuck in a loop. All we did was have dinner together, over and over, the exact same way. Fried zucchini flowers stuffed with feta done in duck fat."

Jimmy nodded and sat down on the non-existent floor. Staring into the endless white, his next words were conversational.

"You do realise she's literally going to kill you, right? I'm no expert on this stuff, but she could realise the truth at any moment."

"Yeah." Tuesday exhaled slowly. "It seemed like a good idea at the time. But..."

"You know, you still owe me two hundred and fifty German yen," Jimmy interrupted. His eyes went out of focus, meditative. "I wonder if anyone alive even knows what a German yen is?"

"It was two thirty," Tuesday grumbled. "And I..."

Jimmy waited for Tuesday to finish the sentence, but when he looked up the scumbag was gone. He huffed, slouching in depression in an eternity of empty cream.

"Of course. Always the last one to get picked. I always have to be..."

CHAPTER THREE

Jimmy wasn't sure what he felt first: the cold, or the twitching.

Frigid air wasn't alien to him. In addition to the numerous walk-in refrigeration units he'd been unlucky enough to work in as a bottom-rung drudger for the MacDeath Burger Combine, Jimmy had felt the touch of winter on no less than four worlds. When you consider Jimmy's overall uselessness, setting foot on that many different planets was exceptional for somebody who had zero operational value to Mankind's empire. The Unison was usually very picky with who could and couldn't move about the borders of their regime, and if there was something you could say about Jimmy, he wasn't the sort to get picked for anything by anyone.

While his arms, legs, chest and face were icy as a freshly-poured glass of Slurko Cola, his underpants area was a tad more insulated, possibly by what little remained of his clothing. Jimmy went to look down to check how much of his neon-yellow MacDeath uniform remained after eight motionless years, but he found he couldn't move. His eyes remained tightly locked in place no matter how much he willed to open them, and the rest of his body seemed just as stuck.

Okay. Hopefully this will pass.

But the twitching was another matter, as a hundred separate tics were hopping from hairline to groin, travelling in a wave of spasms. After trying to figure out what was going on with a brain that wasn't optimised for intellectual pursuits, Jimmy had an epiphany: if his body had simply been crammed somewhere and forgotten, then his muscles would have atrophied and withered away, leaving nothing but a mummified corpse. He couldn't be sure, but Jimmy's best guess was his muscles were being individually stimulated to prevent wastage.

Jimmy felt quite proud of this logic. But his short-lived confidence plunged back into its usual valley when he registered his limbs weren't hopping about like the rest of him. He could sense his arms and legs were all present, stretched out into a Vitruvian Man kind of pose, but that was about it. If he concentrated, there was a thin, metallic pressure digging around both shoulders and his hips, as though he was wedged into four of Goliath's own toenail clippers. The metal felt very, very sharp.

Jimmy heard a familiar slithering noise, and laboured breathing. Trying and failing to move his mouth, to politely ask the nothingness if Rem was hiding in it somewhere, Jimmy was surprised by a hiss in his right ear.

"Others took longer to spring than expected," Rem said as quickly as possible. He went silent for a couple of long seconds, as though waiting for something or someone to move out of sensory range. Jimmy felt the tickle of Rem's mandibles against his earlobe. "I honestly don't know if I can hack through their defences a fourth time before it's too late. So stay still and quiet, or I'm extracting without you."

Jimmy would have given a stoic nod if he could.

There was the same skitter as before, followed by a rapid clicking like somebody typing a thousand words a minute on a mechanical keyboard. Desperate to know what was going on, Jimmy gave a whole-body lurch as he regained the ability to move. His eyes sprung open, rolling madly, but his vision only extended for a metre or so.

Looking down, the first thing Jimmy saw were the trembles of hundreds of muscle-stimulating pins jolting about in his flesh. While this wasn't the highlight of his day, Jimmy's world became a much more horrible place when he realised that the Slidge had brutally installed a dozen different pipes between his ribs and abdominals. His best guess was the tubes fed into his bowels, bladder, stomach and lungs, but the others were anyone's guess. He'd heard rumours of the most severely-addicted VR freaks inflicting this kind of plumbing on themselves in order to enjoy their uploads of consensual brain damage uninterrupted by the varied calls of nature, but never seen it in person. All these pins and pipes were holding the most immodest of modesty gowns in place, a shiny jet-black doily just barely keeping his privates private. Flexing slightly, Jimmy was confused by the way his fraction of a gown crackled, as though made from papier-mâché.

A thumb-span beyond all this, Jimmy and all his additions were trapped in a tarnished form-fitting metal cage. It looked like a sculpture made of chicken wire. Glancing sideways only to find his head was still locked tightly in place, Jimmy could see his arms were indeed being pinched at the shoulder by what looked like a giant pair of nail clippers, as were his legs.

Rem snapped a curse in his clicking native tongue from somewhere within the blur.

"Stay still, you foolish zsatchrw. You'll trigger Maintenance."

But Jimmy couldn't stop now. Glancing up at the clippers fastened around his shoulders and hips, Jimmy found his limbs had been swallowed by the wall right up to the blades. He could feel his ankles, knees, wrists and elbows were wedged in unseen vices, so moving them was impossible. Trying to tilt his head a tiny bit further, Jimmy accidentally yanked at something that seemed to be fastened to the side of his skull. Carefully tugging on the tightness from an assortment of angles, Jimmy's best guess was that cerebral cables had been plugged through brackets surgically bored into both his temples. After all, the Slidge were planning to keep him in a virtual reality loop forever, so of course they'd permanently wire him in.

On top of all this body horror, to make matters worse it felt as though his stomach was full to bursting. Even after all his many years of gluttony, Jimmy never felt so stuffed.

What were they trying to do? Pop his guts?

Jimmy realised he hadn't taken a breath the whole time he'd been awake, as air was being piped directly into his lungs. This feeling of false suffocation instantly became too much, and Jimmy gave a full-body spasm of discomfort. The form-fitting lattice groaned against the pressure, but didn't budge.

Rem cursed again, the source of his ire obvious.

Fighting to stay utterly still, Jimmy's cell slowly came into focus. It was a pokey little metal box the size of a disabled bathroom cubicle, and he was splayed out back-first against its rear wall. As his eyes hadn't seen light in years, Jimmy flinched away from the glowing assault of the only exit. Squinting up at the orderly rows of roof hooks running along the ceiling, Jimmy recalled that like many intelligent species descended from arboreal creatures, the Slidge preferred to get around by swinging like chimpanzees.

The blinding glare softened, revealing a huge, furiously-writhing insect thrashing around like a cockroach doused in bug spray. For an insane moment Jimmy thought that Rem was breakdancing, but even with a total lack of any useful xenobiological knowledge about the Drennite race, Jimmy knew that was unlikely. Blinking, Jimmy could see the bristleworm had summoned a holographic computer sphere the size of a medicine ball and wrapped his limbless ribbon of a body around it. Rem was literally tying himself in knots as he adjusted the hundreds of thousands of tiny monochrome segments that made up the tactile light-based Operating System, proving that having no arms or legs wasn't necessarily a disability in the field of Information Technology. Alien or not, the OS interface was a kaleidoscope of black, grey and white segments, and as Rem wriggled more and more of the ball was changing away from darker hues towards purest white. Rem had clearly almost completed the hack, and Jimmy knew he'd be free in moments.

And then life kicked Jimmy in the crotch yet again.

Without warning, a fully-grown two-hundred-kilogram Slidge casually swung into the cell as though it was the most routine thing in the world, and halted sharply at the sight of Rem. Like all Slidge, the six-limbed monstrosity seemed to consist mostly of elbows, and its scarlet body was traced all over by throbbing yellow veins. Its central mass was a tumour-like bulge with three eyes – one small, one medium, and one huge – arranged in a triangle around a triple-segmented beak. Of its half a dozen thick arms, the Slidge only needed one powerful limb to hang from the ceiling, showing off its substantial strength. It was wrapped with several utility belts stocked with useful items, but not for the sake of modesty. Jimmy felt a pang of guilt at the realisation that this Slidge was probably investigating all the movement Jimmy's supposedly "immobile" body had been doing.

The Slidge gaped at Rem, pupils expanding and contracting as it took in the situation. This stand-off didn't last long before the Slidge casually raised a triple-thumbed hand, rippling a whole forest of fingers as though wordlessly suggesting a calm chat over whatever passed for tea and biscuits in its society. However, even Jimmy's dull cow brain registered the alien was reaching for a knobby implant embedded in one of its many armpits with a second hand.

Rem proved he truly was a wet-work professional by snapping his body like a whip at the Slidge while continuing to use his face to hack the Operating System ball. The bristleworm wrapped half his length around the Slidge's closest arm at top speed, tightening in a blur that ended with a series of loud snaps and the beginnings of a scream from the red alien. Predicting the cry, Rem smothered the Slidge's beak so tightly that its noises were muffled to nothing, and dragged it down from the ceiling hooks. The Slidge had some considerable power at its disposal, though, and the moment it hit the floor it flexed its five remaining operational arms in an outward thrust that stretched Rem's insectoid carapace to its limits. It was hard to tell, but it seemed as though Rem's eyestalks might have been bugging out even more than usual.

No matter what, though, Rem kept on hacking the OS ball, putting his own physical wellbeing at serious risk in order to free Jimmy as soon as possible. Jimmy felt overjoyed to be treated with such respect and value, but then he had a terrible thought: why didn't Rem finish off the Slidge quickly and let him out of the cage afterwards? Was there some kind of critical countdown going on that he didn't know about?

The fight instantly went south as soon as the Slidge lifted Rem to the ceiling and crushed him against the floor tiles with a sickening crunch. Jimmy flinched in sympathy at the crackle of broken exoskeleton and the gouts of yellow sputum shooting out of Rem's assorted mandibles, and recoiled as the stunned bug was picked up and slammed into the tarnished metal wall even harder. Leaking gelatinous liquids from dozens of deep fissures in his shell, Rem went still as he bled out. His OS automatically vanished into the ether, confirming he was unconscious at the very least, or just outright dead. Jimmy reckoned he would have died four times over from that sort of punishment, but he didn't know enough about Drennites to comment.

Careful not to let its guard down, the injured Slidge produced a holographic computer sphere the size of a tennis ball and played it over the still bug. Assorted superimposed shapes hopped about over the mess of busted chitin, and although Jimmy couldn't read Slidge symbols, one particular sigil was translated into its equivalent Unglish phrase as clear as a bell.

"Unknown subject is deceased."

Knowing the fight was officially over, the Slidge casually reached up to the ceiling hooks, nursing a broken arm. It tilted sideways a little, as though inspecting Jimmy's expression. If the Slidge could read his total despair and devastation, it gave no sign.

"You're meant to be napping," the Slidge said calmly, cleaning its bloodied beak with three whip-thin tongues. Its facial movements and the audible Unglish words didn't match up, a common problem when no two species of alien used the exact same kind of orifices to communicate. "Better to be asleep. Kinder."

The Slidge swung backwards without looking, feeling its way towards the doorway with some sense other than sight. It glanced at Rem's dead body again, and flicked at the holographic ball that confirmed Rem's passing. The Slidge said its next words with true apology in its tone.

"I promise you'll never feel this way again. You'll sleep forever."

And with the swipe of a Slidge thumb, four giant sets of giant nail clippers struck together and cut off Jimmy's arms and legs.

CHAPTER FOUR

Saying that Jimmy went into shock was an understatement of such magnitude that it could only be voiced by somebody unaccustomed to being dismembered. After the eight pincer blades met in synchronisation, slicing straight through skin and muscle and sinew and bone and marrow, Jimmy's limbs disappeared down four separate chutes with wet, greasy thumps.

The Slidge swung forwards, producing a spray bottle from a belt criss-crossing one of its arms. Jimmy's brain didn't have enough time to register how much pain he was in before a chemical mist spurted into his mouth and nose, instantly numbing all sensation. Three long seconds went past, but instead of being hit by a train of unbearable agony, Jimmy experienced...nothing. It was like his pain receptors had been given the day off.

Dangling just centimetres from Jimmy's stunned mullet expression, tilting a little as though preparing to flip upside down, the Slidge's trinity of eyes regarded Rem's still, broken form in the corner again, just to be sure, then back at Jimmy. The beaked face didn't give away much of the alien's mindset.

"Who was he, then?" the Slidge whispered. One of its three prehensile tongues flicked at the tip of Jimmy's nose in a seedy way. "Did he bring any friends? Who sent him?"

Shaking violently, brain-dead from waves of incalculable psychological pain despite not physically sensing a single nerve ending, Jimmy's hopping face slumped down to drool towards the communication implant bump in the Slidge's armpit. Following Jimmy's line of sight, the Slidge formed its beaked face into what might translate as a smile.

"No, I'd prefer to know a little bit more about your guest before the Primacy Guard come storming in here. See, the day-to-day upkeep of you four is my personal responsibility, and not being able to adequately explain an intrusion on this level will...how do I put it...not be good for my career? Or my life expectancy, to be blunt. So," the Slidge narrowed its eyes, multiple layers of lids crunching in from what seemed like random angles. "How did he get in here?

How did he wake you up? Was he sent here on behalf of somebody? What is he, precisely?"

"Don't..." Jimmy juddered, jaw jackhammering, "I don't..."

"Just a moment."

The Slidge produced the same computer sphere as before. Jimmy had seen the impressive veracity-confirming abilities of these things firsthand. The Slidge flicked at it, sending the ball spinning gently in mid-air, and nodded.

"Educate me."

"I don't..."

Jimmy's face twisted in anguish. His limbs were gone! Cut right off!

"Continue," the Slidge prompted, an undercurrent of hostility in its voice. "And then you can sleep. Not before."

"I don't know anything about him!"

The computer sphere gave a soft negative chime and glowed a sunny yellow. The Slidge raised a hairless eyebrow at Jimmy in warning.

"You know, Mister Slummer, I can easily amp up your nerve endings higher than what you'd believe was possible…"

As much as Jimmy would like to have kept dead silent, perhaps even spat in his interrogator's face in a classic symbol of defiance, the words tumbled out, propelled to top speed by fear and horror. Jimmy knew in his core that if this creature could just swing in and lop off half of his body without hesitation, without even feeling the need to exchange names and motivations, then it wasn't going to tolerate stalling or any other rubbish. Jimmy couldn't bear to lose anything else today.

"He's a Drennite. His name was Rem. He encouraged the four of us to realise we were stuck in software loops at the exact same time, and purged us into the substrate where he could extract our minds. He wanted to free us, to take us away from here. He didn't say how we were going to get out or where we were going to go or who sent him or why. That's it! I swear!"

The Slidge waited a couple of seconds as the computer ball turned a bright duck shell blue. Sighing, spinning the sphere with one of its dozens of thumbs, the Slidge might have nodded, but as its torso, abdomen and midsection were all one tumorous lump, it could have been a lewd crotch-thrust.

"Right. I'll be sure to get the coders to patch up that hole yesterday. Jimmy, I sincerely promise you'll never have to go through this again." A ridge appeared on the computer ball, and the Slidge laid a thumb pad against it. "Well, goodnight."

Knowing he'd be going back to being chased around the foul laminate of a broken-down arcology for the same handful of minutes like a cheap gif animation, Jimmy did the bravest thing he could: he latched both eyes shut, whimpered like a puppy, and wet himself.

Flinching on the edge of purgatory, almost glad that in a moment he'd forget how it felt to be dissected like a frog in biology class, Jimmy was surprised by a cracking thud, a loud intake of air, and a thump like a fully-gestated animal carcass falling out of a Repler unit. A second and third whack was bookended by silence.

Barely managing to open his eyes as dizziness overwhelmed him, Jimmy was greeted by the sight of the Slidge crumpled into a pile of twisted-in arms and digits. It took a second for Jimmy's brain to decode that Lana was standing over the six-armed creature, brandishing a piece of scrap piping that looked a lot like a pickaxe. It was coated with white fluid.

Just like Jimmy, Lana was dressed in an insufficient immodesty gown that was decidedly crunchy, and she had L-shaped brackets of empty cable ports running along both temples. Funnily enough, even after all this time somehow her bun was still held in place by her long-acting hairspray. Thor only knew what kind of carcinogenic nightmare formula it was made from.

Lana rested her improvised weapon over a shoulder, satisfied by the snowy gushes weeping from the three wounds she'd pounded deep into the Slidge's skull. She looked up at Jimmy, and her face fell like a chasm.

"Spug me," she whispered, darting back and forth between stumps.

Jimmy tried to speak, but nothing came out.

There was the sound of irregular footsteps. Tuesday's voice preceded his arrival by half a second.

"Have you found him y..."

Tuesday froze as soon as he eclipsed the doorway, halted by the kind of rodent instinct that can detect when there's something best avoided. Swooning towards a faint, eyes fluttering shut, Jimmy heard Tuesday gag, followed by the sound of uncoordinated scuttling and ugly noises out in the corridor. As Jimmy didn't get a proper look at Tuesday's silhouette, he didn't get a chance to see if he had the same L-brackets of cranial implants, but by this point it kind of went without saying.

Trace was the final one to loom in. Interested in what could have made a gross creature like Tuesday throw up, she examined Jimmy in a surgical, detached manner. She arched an extensively pierced eyebrow at Rem's busted carcass, and nudged his broken chitin with a toe. Gritting her teeth at the fact that their only chance of getting out of here was lying dead in the corner, she regarded Jimmy with zero empathy.

"Leave him," she snapped, turning away.

Lana glared at Trace in total rage.

"Leave him? He's got no limbs!"

Trace nodded.

"Yes, exactly my point. Leave him, he's got no limbs."

"No," Lana ground out, "I'm saying that we can't..."

Rem surprised everybody by taking in a huge breath and violently twisting out of his pretzel shape. Spitting wads of green and yellow all over the tiles, the bristleworm's form gave three meaty crunches as it reset some severe exoskeleton dislocations. Whimpering and ticking his mandibles together in pain, Rem hyperventilated for a while before realigning the largest kink. He gurgled back a barely-restrained scream, and extended his entire length as though stretching his muscles. There were a few more crackles as he exhaled slowly.

"You alive, then?" Trace asked bluntly.

"You must be pretty bloody good at playing dead," Lana noted. "I saw that Slidge scan you just moments before I saved the day."

"I wasn't playing," Rem grumbled. He twisted upright, testing his ripples. "I can die for up to eight-and-a-half minutes. Basic Drennite survival technique. No pulse, no brain activity, nothing. Total corpse. We've been doing that since primordial times. Old as dirt."

Rem shook his ribbon of a body again, as though double-checking for injuries. Flexing his mandibles, Rem admired the blows Lana had landed on the Slidge with her improvised pickaxe.

"Right in the brainpan. Who managed that?"

Lana raised a hand. Trace interrupted the back-patting session with some reality.

"Look, are we escaping, or measuring how high we can piss?" Trace leaned out into the corridor to scan for activity. "We're sitting in the middle of a hostile alien facility with no dedicated weapons and far less than an optimal number of limbs between us. We can hand out merit badges and blue ribbons later. What's the plan, bug?"

Rem twitched his eye stalks at the racist slur in a way that didn't translate. Without bothering to share any reassuring words, Rem's silver collar flared with tiny starbursts to project the same black-grey-white holographic sphere as before. The bristleworm's extensive facial digits wriggled at top speed as he zipped through clusters of menus, pinpointed weak spots in the code and exploited every backdoor with surgical skill. It was all so rapid that none of the humans could even begin to keep up with what he was doing. Finally turning all the segments from black to white, Rem stopped abruptly and angled an eye stalk at Lana.

"Somebody might want to help him down."

Jimmy's form-fitting cage began to unlatch one hook at a time just as a dozen deeply-anchored tubes popped out of his torso and abdomen with jets of water, air, nutrient gruel and a number of other substances that were far less pleasant. The rubber sphincters of his ports instantly sealed tight, ensuring his lungs, stomach, bowels and bladder wouldn't let anything in or out that they shouldn't, and the snaking tubes snapped closed and stopped whipping about at once. Sadly, Lana was the only one to render Jimmy any physical assistance, as Trace had already made her thoughts on dragging around a liability quite clear and Tuesday was still finishing being sick. Unfortunately, the cables locked into Jimmy's skull didn't pop out automatically, causing what was left of him to bounce in a sickening neck-straining bungee lurch.

"No, I said I wanted a plan," Trace sniped as Lana struggled not to drop Jimmy face-first onto the tiles. She dragged him towards the doorway one step at a time. "Not a liability. We've already had one guard wander in, there could be dozens more lying in wait, and yet for some reason you want to move us further away from freedom."

"Everything is under control and still on schedule," Rem snapped. He rested a mandible against one of the Slidge's larger yellow veins. It throbbed slightly in response. "Luckily this one is still alive. Last thing we need right now is for the medical system to detect a dead citizen of the Primacy. We don't need that kind of attention."

Lana rested Jimmy against the doorframe, gritting her teeth with effort. As she stood up straight she found that Jimmy's head only reached her bellybutton. He got a close-up look at the numerous sealed ports on Lana's midriff, and looked up at her with a sad puppy dog expression. She grimaced and turned back to Rem.

"I have an idea. Do you know if they kept our things?"

*

Even though the heavy steel cabinet situated directly outside of the human's tiny cells had been forgotten for so long that its beaten doors were bloated shut, a little encouragement from Trace's bulging muscles was enough to get its first section partially open. Straining so hard that veins crested out of her skin, Trace grudgingly accepted some help from Lana's scrap metal Slidge-spiker. After a few moments of groaning alloys, the older-than-civilisation technique of levering open the cabinet doors proved to be a success.

Keeping eyes peeled for any more wandering Slidge who might pop by unexpectedly, it turned out the cabinet contained five slabs the size of large safe deposit boxes. As soon as Lana cranked open the first drawer it was clear they'd hit pay dirt. All of Trace's stuff was present and accounted for: a full suit of sapphire Enforcer-grade riot armour, a loaded Holt & Heckler kinetic accelerator, one set of yellowed granny undies and a matching nana bra, a CuddleTech tactile holographic AllTool projector bracelet, a pair of well-used jackboots, a set of brass knuckles...

Far from the self-conscious type, Trace tore away the old, blood-blackened rags from her terrifyingly buff body and started getting dressed. By the time Tuesday greeted his orange coveralls and cricket-leather frogstomper boots, Trace had already covered most of her tattooed form. Once Lana was running a finger down her ebony Cadet uniform like all her Christmases had come at once, Trace was fully armed and armoured. She checked the charge on her Holt & Heckler, and saw it was still good. But then she glanced at the virgin-bare skin of her hand, forearm, bicep, shoulder...

"Where the Styx did the rest of my ink go?!" she roared at Rem, pointing the high-tech gun at her unadorned muscles. "Answers, Crawley! I want them!"

Rem got up in Trace's face with zero fear. "Later. I promise. Not now."

Possessing a little more of a conscience than usual, Tuesday dragged Jimmy's property bin across the tiles with an ear-splitting shriek. Trace and Lana hissed at him not to make so much noise, but Tuesday took no notice.

"I don't get why the Slidge didn't install antigrav wafers on these things," he grumbled. "They're heavier than good intentions."

Lana stopped adjusting her golden shoulder tassels, thoughtful.

"You know, that's a good point." She shuddered a little, grossed out that she could have actually agreed with something Bob 'Dickhead' Tuesday said. "Humans developed antigrav wafers long before interstellar travel, and the Slidge have been knobbing about space for...how many years?"

"The Slidge Primacy led the Twelve Hundred intelligent races of their galaxy to overthrow The Apex more than six thousand years ago," Rem answered, as though reciting from a script. "Problem is, the technology of the Primacy lasted a lot longer than their memory of it, and after millennia of relative peace they've basically forgotten how anything works, let along how to make more of it." Rem nodded at the ceiling hooks. "See all this? Made of locally-mined metal. All their vintage stuff is made from limpet ivory, a living biological material that's basically invulnerable if you maintain it with a good diet, but..."

"They don't know how to make it anymore," Lana finished. "When their stuff breaks, it's gone for good. I get it."

She recalled what it felt like to witness a Star Cage for the first time. It was a deceptively delicate-looking lattice wrapped around a hundred-kilometre-wide kernel of enslaved purple supergiant, and she remembered even more clearly how a multitude more of them had appeared, battling each other in the gap between worlds, unleashing weapons that had doubtlessly vaporised everything within the star system unlucky enough to be their battlefield...

Lana jolted back to reality. She didn't have time to daydream.

Tuesday dragged the fourth slab to where Jimmy's limbless blob of a body was slumped awkwardly against the doorframe of his cell. Tuesday slid off its thick steel top and began rifling through Jimmy's gear. He started making a pile, starting with a neon yellow MacDeath fry cook uniform, puffy chef's hat, a stack of melted, deformed chocolate bars loaded with the addictive narcotic chemical known as Ultrasweet, then finally placed Jimmy's well-worn flip-flops on top. Holding up the rubber-soled footwear, Tuesday froze in place as something occurred to him. Jimmy's face plunged at the sight of his thongs.

"Well," Tuesday twitched, trying not to smile. "I'll put those in the 'maybe' pile for now."

"Here we are!" Lana announced, cracking open the mysterious fifth property crate. "Sorted. If we take it in turns, it'll be easy as pie."

She punctuated her little speech by producing a military-grade survival backpack lined with the golden threads of antigrav wafers. Double-checking a little information tag on the side of the backpack, she nodded in satisfaction.

"Graded for three-hundred kilograms," Lana confirmed, walking briskly over to Jimmy. "Remember how easy it was to trek with these? With the antigrav wafers helping, we won't even notice we're carrying him."

"Except we damaged all the backpacks with warranty-voiding modifications so we could go surfing on a giant mass driver crater," Trace argued. "For all we know, that one doesn't work anymore."

Despite the misery that appeared on Jimmy's face at the knowledge he was going to face even more degradation and embarrassment, he didn't resist when Lana started stuffing him into the backpack like a fold-up tent. Unfortunately, once his nether regions met the bottom of the bag it turned out charging crotch-first wasn't kind to your nether regions. Jimmy's eyes bulged and his face reddened towards black as his man-parts slammed into an unyielding layer of canvas. Slipping the backpack over her shoulders, Lana did a physics-defying twirl to show that gravity was her servant, not her master.

"Can we go now?" Tuesday moaned.

There was a small chime from one of Rem's collars. He gave a curt Drennite curse.

"Primary exit is a no-go. We'll have to go for the secondary."

"Point the way," Lana said.

*

Even after scurrying through a kilometre of passageways and air vents and dry-as-dust water lines, every hand span of this facility turned out to be constructed from locally-mined ores. The steel was functional enough, but hardly up to the standards of some of the godlike wonders the humans had seen in their time. Compared to the thoughtmetal that The Apex could forge by pure force of will or the ancient, forgotten artistry of cultivating limpet ivory, steel was downright primitive.

Stranger still was how thoroughly this facility had been abandoned. Distinct signs of wear and tear indicated there had been lots of activity at some point, but the Slidge clearly chosen to massively reduce their presence. Security was basically non-existent, with Rem easily hacking his way through any of the sleepy security systems they came across.

"I don't get it," Tuesday muttered, breaking the silence.

"Of course you don't," Lana chided, adjusting the heavy backpack containing Jimmy. She'd clearly underestimated how badly the bag's antigrav wafers had degraded.

Tuesday gave her the finger.

"No, I mean, what's the point of all this?" He gave a general wave at the stained, looming expanse they were slinking through. "Even I can tell this is a lab of some sort, machines or no machines. So that means the Slidge knock us out, build this massive facility, and imprison us in it to...what? What's in it for them?"

"They might have just been punishing us," Lana suggested. "Viour did some pretty damn heinous things when we were with her."

Everyone went silent. It was easy to picture the enormous suit of Apex-crafted amplification armour demolishing a Slidge fleet on her own, of six-limbed bodies freezing to death as their dreadnoughts were torn open like bags of prawn-flavoured crisps. It was the kind of memory that deserved a few moments of respectful reflection.

Lana arched an eyebrow at Rem.

"Do you know why?"

Rem paused, bringing up a screen of Drennite icons with a twitch. It appeared the bristleworm came from a culture where it wasn't considered rude to ignore any questions you didn't feel like answering. Feeling a prickling on the side of her scalp, Lana reached up and startled when she touched the skull socket. Her face reddening, she gripped one set of Rem's opposable mandibles and roughly dragged him close. This got his attention.

"Damn it, why were we here?" Lana demanded. "They might not be in their heyday anymore, but the Slidge aren't stupid. They wouldn't invest time and effort and materials and personnel for no reason. What aren't you telling us?"

Rem didn't resist Lana's grip, but wasn't frightened in the least, either. His wriggly face drew closer and closer until only millimetres divided them. His mandibles spread open, revealing the depths of his two rattling throats as though he was at the peak of annoyance. He violently pointed an eye stalk at the holographic screens projected by his starburst collar, then ahead in a silent order to follow. The humans did so, watchfully, listening. His words were low and calm.

"The Slidge were running a project here, an experiment. They believed you four were the key to remembering their lost history, their technological advancements, everything." Even though he didn't have shoulders, Rem shrugged. "It involved making some sort of drug that allows the Slidge to tap into the genetic memories of their ancestors." Rem swirled an antennae. "As you can see, the project didn't go too well. They'll never cancel it entirely, but progress has been too slow to measure."

The humans looked at each other with similar expressions.

"I don't..." Lana squinted. "Wait. They're making medicine here? Slidge medicine? Then what in the name of Odin's manky big toe do our unconscious bodies have to do with it?"

Rem's screens vanished without warning and he went into a sudden slide, plastering himself between clusters of long-dry pipes. Twisting his body into right angles, he effectively disappeared, becoming part of the background detail. Although not as adept as the wet-work operative, the humans also took cover, slipping behind any junk or broken equipment big enough to hide them. Tapping at his projection collar, a stream of Drennite symbols were superimposed over the human's field of vision, utilising their long-dormant retinal screen implants to form a basic augmented reality. They translated themselves into comprehensible Unglish in moments.

"Apologies for beaming this straight to your retinals, but they might be able to hear us. Our secondary exit lies that way, but I just scanned a number of Slidge on the other side of the door." Rem paused, poking his eye stalks around the cluster of pipes as though pointing. "There are seven of them. I'm unsure if they're armed, but I am certain they will trigger their distress implants if given a chance. We need a plan."

Trace nodded seriously.

"I have a plan."

*

The Entropic Chemistry Department had been the crowning jewel of this facility, a shining nerve centre dedicated to reclaiming what had been lost in the mists of six thousand years, a hundred devastating civil wars, and an embarrassing number of machine uprisings. Its team of a thousand had been granted anything they requested in a heartbeat, whether it was resources, specialist staff members or luxuries. They became household names all over the Star Cage, with younger Slidge trading holographic cards of their favourite Chemists and hoping to join their team one day. The work of the Entropic Chemistry Department was the future, and this future relied on seizing the past. They key to all of this was a drug known as Recoil.

Derived from Earth's unique variety of crude oil, a dose of Recoil would temporarily gift Slidge test subjects with an astonishing boost to their mental recall. It proved easy for even the most burnt-out volunteers to mentally hop back decades, unearthing all the tiniest details of their lives. Unlike other brain-boosting chems mainlined by citizens of the Primacy, though, a big enough dose of Recoil allowed users to dive back further than conception, splashing into the genetic memories of their ancestors. As the Primacy was trapped within a technological withering stretching back millennia, they were understandably keen to recover all the knowledge they'd lost since the first Star Cages were cultured. Being able to replace their rotted-out computer equipment with systems that weren't psychotic with the desire to exterminate all organic life would be a nice start, for instance, but their core goals were obvious: grow new Star Cages, harvest more solar kernels to fuel them, claim more resources and repeat endlessly.

Skipping back generations from Spawner to Grandspawner to Great Grandspawner was exponentially complex, with every bunny hop through a subject's genetic line requiring better and better solutions of Recoil. Unfortunately, the purity levels of Recoil required to journey back usually killed the test subjects afterwards, but what really killed the public's support for the Entropic Chemistry Department was the fact that for some inconceivable reason the surviving test subjects could only tap into the most embarrassing of genetic memories. So rather than rediscovering the key to immortality, the Slidge volunteers would find out in perfect first-person detail how their Grandspawner secretly had a major kink for licking salad dressing out of its own armpits. And a slight sexual oddity was the best case scenario, as it turned out all of the most respected and valued Slidge of the last few generations were lying, corrupt, perverted, scummy deplorables. Rather than restoring the Primacy to its former glory, all Recoil did was create the biggest scandals of this era. The widespread "Just Say No To Recoil" movement was another chiselled furrow in Entropic Chemistry's tombstone, and eventually, this field of science fell out of vogue entirely.

Despite losing face and having their funding slashed and receiving endless death threats from traumatised test subjects, what remained of the Entropic Chemistry Department drove on, just as dedicated to reclaiming the past as on day one. The remaining Slidge scientists worked in Lab 8, the only remaining hub of the original twenty-six. Now so badly underfunded that they subsisted on chewing algae scrapings for nourishment and converted their bodily excretions into long-burning fuel logs for warmth, the Entropic Chemists had proved they weren't in this for the prestige, perks, glory, or comfort. Despite clear evidence to the contrary, the team still believed in the dream of reclaiming hundreds of thousands of generations of memories stretching all the way back to when the first proto-ancestors of the Slidge slithered towards a black-sanded beach seven galaxies from Earth.

Lab 8 was a mostly empty space the size of a supermarket whose ceiling appeared to be supported by looming pillars. But unlike the steel of the rest of the facility, the columns were formed from thick, transparent glass, similar to what The Unison's starships once relied on to keep their crews safe from the myriad stresses of interstellar travel. However, the pillar closest to the scientists was different: it was jet black, and swirled as though filled with some treacle-thick substance. Every now and again something pale and wrinkled and fleshy and green-grey would emerge from the black, bumping into the glass before vanishing.

The last seven Entropic Chemists were gathered together for warmth, reduced to huddling around a smouldering, stinking brazier. As you would expect from Slidge during a sleep cycle, they were hanging from ceiling hooks by their three dominant limbs. Their more delicate set of arms were curled up, packed tight with so many elbows that they almost looked like tentacles.

The only operational door in or out of Lab 8 started to slide across, but jammed open halfway with a loud crunch like it always did. Six of the seven Slidge scientists stirred a little in their sleep, exhausted from a lack of nourishment and warmth and respect from their disappointed families, but one of them, the youngest, opened two of its three eyes. Confused and sleepy in equal measures, the junior Entropic Chemist didn't have time to register one of the humans had broken loose and was pointing what must be some kind of gun at it before Trace opened fire. Besides the hiss of all the liquid in the scientist's centre mass rising beyond boiling point and bursting from its traceries of yellow veins as steam, it didn't get a chance to make a sound.

Trace casually advanced into Lab 8, her expression cold as a slap with a dead trout as she explosively murdered a second scientist, her kinetic accelerator barking death. Of the remaining five Slidge, one slipped from the rungs in surprise, not as quick on the uptake as survival demanded, but the other four swung away across the ceiling like chimpanzees. Trace didn't hesitate to shoot another in the back, punching a hole the size of a dinner plate where its twists of spinal columns met. It calmly deflated.

Trace proved that transparent glass pillars aren't the best hiding places by blasting holes right through two of them. Deaf to anything the Slidge had to say, whether it was pleas for their lives or apologies or curses or simply asking her why, all Trace could focus on was the smoking, shimmering muzzle of her kinetic accelerator. Next thing she knew, she heard Lana's voice.

"Dear Loki."

Trace looked up from the final Slidge corpse, its six limbs splayed out from a central mass that had been mostly converted into vapour. She blinked slowly, like a lizard, and gradually lowered her weapon. A click and a beep eventually sounded as she turned off the Holt & Heckler.

"Got all seven. The way is clear." Trace looked back and forth between Lana and

Tuesday, who were gaping at the details of this abattoir. Trace's face screwed up in annoyance. "What?"

Lana blanched as she surveyed the splashes of white Slidge blood, the dismembered limbs and the holes bored through empty glass pillars. The haze was wretched, stinking of rotten bananas and offal. Swallowing heavily several times, Lana managed to shed her backpack, dumping Jimmy's unconscious body heavily to the tiles, and made odd throat noises.

Rem slithered into the lab, slowly surveying the carnage. He eventually made eye contact with Trace.

"They were asleep and unarmed," Rem noted. He brought up a holographic screen from his starburst collar, getting to work despite the mess, and continued to comment on the situation without any emotion. "These ones were scientists. Chemists. None of them had any martial training, and posed no risk to us whatsoever. It would have been easy to subdue them without violence. If you would have waited just a couple of seconds, I could have told you all this."

Trace flicked a warm glob of snowy blood from her hand. She spun her Holt & Heckler into its holster deep in her breastplate.

"Spug them. Spug every last one of them."

Tuesday looked up at the sound of crackling. The only black pillar in the lab was spider webbed with fractures, but not enough for it to burst. He looked a little closer at the dark, near-solid contents of the chamber, and startled when something knobbly and white struck the glass from the inside and bounced off into the blackness. Tripping over backwards, falling onto his hands and butt, Tuesday pointed at the pillar with a shaky finger.

"Foot!" he shouted.

"What?" Trace asked, ready for more blasting.

Tuesday could only gape like a fish, his brain trying to put together all the clues he'd witnessed so far. He pointed at the black pillar repeatedly.

"It was a person's foot," he managed. "Toes and all. It kicked the glass. I think someone's in there."

"Ignore that. We need to continue," Rem ordered. "The deaths of these seven have undoubtedly been noticed by the facility's medical surveillance. Our time is now even shorter than it was."

"No," Lana said decisively. She wiped her mouth and tried to ignore the smell of charred meat. She pointed at the black pillar as thick, dark liquid bubbled at its cracks. "If there's a human foot in there, who does it belong to? Is it Jimmy's? Or are there other people trapped in here? If so, how many?"

Rem gave a very human sigh. It was likely his translation software had helpfully converted it from an incomprehensible Drennite noise.

"You asked me what your imprisonment had to do with the development of the Slidge's experimental drugs." Rem reminded her. He wriggled an antennae at the black pillar, and then at Lana's knees. "The medicinal substance they were researching, Recoil, was originally derived from the toxic plastic waste the Slidge found dumped all over Earth, but they quickly discovered that they needed to refine their own plastic from crude oil in order to get the right purity. As there hasn't been a drop of crude oil on Erf for ages, the Slidge found a way to convert biomass of an Earthly origin into a shake-and-bake form of the black stuff, effectively aging it by tens of millions of years in a matter of days. They would then process this muck into plastic, then refine it even further into Recoil."

Rem gave a sort of 'ta da' motion with his mandibles and waited for a response. Lana, Tuesday and Trace blinked at each other, each hoping to see realisation on each other's faces. They were all equally disappointed.

"What biomass?" Lana ground out. "Earth is rocks and glass craters, last thing I saw. Not a single blade of grass, let alone enough raw organic material to convert into crude oil. What..."

Lana stopped talking mid-sentence, turning white as parchment. Her eyes widened.

"No," was all she said, almost pleading.

"What?" Tuesday asked, always feeling left out of the loop.

"They..." Lana twitched at some horrible thought, rubbing her shoulders absently. It took her a couple of seconds to finish her thoughts, "they were using ...us."

"Us?" Tuesday repeated.

An agonised scream tore from Jimmy's throat, pitched like an ambulance siren and heart-rendingly awful. His maimed, limbless body thrashed around, toppling out of the survival backpack and onto the laminate. Nobody knew what to do. Should they grab him, hold him still? Ask him what was wrong? Jack him up with whatever painkillers Lab 8 had stashed in its drawers? Put him out of his misery?

Jimmy flopped onto his back, eyes rolling madly and inch-thick stumps waving tragically. At the edge of his pain endurance, Jimmy's pupils disappeared beneath his upper eyelids and his body jerked without volition. He froze, locked mid-spasm, and the short hunks that used to be his limbs began to...bulge. The sound of bone and meat and sinew and tendons growing millimetre by millimetre was unique, and even though the growths started off looking a lot like chicken wings they quickly took shape and thickened. Jimmy's body pumped up and down as new hands and feet formed, followed by fingers and toes pushing out like daisies. Within a matter of a minute, Jimmy was no longer a full amputee: his limbs might be the sickly colour of sun-bleached bones, but at least he had them now.

"Us," Lana noted to the stunned silence, her words barely audible over the unconscious chuffing of Jimmy's tortured breathing. She raised an eyebrow at Jimmy's flat gut, which had been full as a boiled egg before the miracle regrowth had taken place. "They were harvesting us."

CHAPTER FIVE

Tuesday brought his hands together in a T shape.

"Time out, pause. What do you mean 'harvesting,' exactly?"

Lana snorted.

"The Slidge needed a source of biomass native to Earth in order to make crude oil so they could create plastic to refine into their shake-and-bake memory-recall narcotics...and as Earth is a dead rock, we were their only source of the aforementioned biomass they could find. It's not that complicated."

Tuesday glanced down at Jimmy's restored form sprawled on the tiles. He was still breathing like a steam train and clearly sitting on the wrong side of traumatised.

"So they've been constantly lopping off our arms and legs so they could make drugs out of them?" Tuesday clarified, weaving a little on the spot. "Carving and regrowing and carving and regrowing…"

"Why didn't they just clone us?" Trace barked, clearly not a fan of what she was hearing. "If they're capable of cultivating and pruning us like a garden of meaty rose bushes, surely it'd be easier just to brew up bits of us in their version of a Repler unit?" As though having a sudden brainwave, Trace held out both her clean arms and scanned them up and down. "So that's what happened to my tattoos!"

Rem rattled his mandibles.

"The Primacy has major taboos against cloning. It's a belief so old they've completely forgotten why they hate it. It borders on religious doctrine."

"But hacking us up is okay?" Lana demanded.

Rem shrugged without shoulders.

"Clearly they don't seem to have an issue with this arrangement, do they?"

There was a gasp from Jimmy and he sat bolt upright like a released spring. Eyes spinning in a way that brought slot machines to mind, he absently scratched the crown of his head for a few seconds before giving a sudden full-body jolt at the realisation he had an arm. Rather than looking relieved, Jimmy scurried backwards until he slammed back-first into one of the empty glass pillars, clearly not knowing what was going on. He began hyperventilating, turning red. Veins popped up on the whites of his eyes.

"It's okay," Lana said soothingly, walking calmly towards Jimmy with her palms raised. "Everything's alright. No need to panic."

Jimmy gagged, eyes flicking back and forth as he counted fingers and toes.

"I can feel them again," he said simply. Clenching his fists, Jimmy spent some time checking that everything was working as designed. Muscles, tendons, joints all seemed to be accounted for. He tested his legs a little, just in case a face plant was on the cards. He looked up at Lana. "How…"

A deafening word burst from the speakers of Lab 8, making the humans wince.

"FLUSH."

Rem stopped mucking about with his code slicing equipment as one of the large glass pillars spiralled open. It burped out the distinct aroma of dirty farm equipment and old, spoiled meat. The bristleworm used one of his many mandibles to indicate an open drain in the tube's base.

"After you."

Behaving far more bravely than she felt, Lana leaned into the open chamber to scout out what awaited her. She could see a U-bend that dived ten metres straight down before twisting out of sight, and its seams were tightly lodged with unspeakable muck. Odin only knew what the gunk was made from...or who it was made from...

She glanced up at Rem to ask some obvious questions - was this safe, where did the pipe go, was this really the only way out of the facility? Reassured by the fact that the Drennite wet-work operative had gotten them this far at great personal risk and had no obvious reasons to screw them over now, Lana nodded.

"Hold your breath in ten seconds," Rem clicked.

Stepping onto the cusp, Lana took a long step and disappeared.

It was a rush and a half. The pipe turned out to be almost frictionless despite the gross filth embedded in its mould lines, and Lana accelerated from zero to a hundred the instant her bottom touched the curved floor. This mother of all slippery-slides turned pitch black after the first U-bend, making it impossible to tell where she was going and how fast she was moving. Up, down, sideways was all the same in the black, though Lana could have sworn she'd performed a couple of spirals. Without being able to see, it was easy to imagine this endless pipe wrapping around itself like a giant hollow spaghetti strand cooked al dente.

Thankfully, Lana remembered her retinal screens had a night vision setting, and once she'd activated them she found herself – surprise, surprise – zipping along a grey pipe. Superimposed numbers informed Lana her current velocity was sufficient enough to put her through the windshield of a bus and out its rear window without slowing down all that much. She mentally filed this knowledge away with the other thousand things she was trying not to think about.

As this was a flush pipe designed to speed away failed biomass, Lana couldn't help but wonder why this plumbing had been designed to imitate an amusement park attraction. Did the Slidge scientists secretly ride these things in their spare time? But then a much more bothersome thought occurred: could Rem have made a mistake? After all, there were more than a few of those glass chambers back in Lab 8, and each one of them could potentially lead into their own labyrinth. What were the odds he'd accidentally sent her to be vivisected by a grinder and processed and spread thinly between a series of microscope slides? Surely the bristleworm hadn't slithered into this facility before, let alone mapped out the guts of its flushing systems, so how could he be so sure this was the correct way?

It might have been five seconds or five minutes, but Lana found herself flying through the air, flipping and cartwheeling in the glow of what seemed to be moonlight. She saw chunky grey-green and a sky of deepest black tumbling around and around before coming to a sudden halt in something thick and wet and sticky. Instantly regretting that she'd forgotten Rem's hot tip about holding her breath, Lana copped a mouthful of something gritty and spoiled that made her automatically retch. It was up there with the worst things she'd ever smelled and/or tasted, and in that moment she considered that death might actually be a preferable alternative.

Lana soon regained the ability to tell which way was up. Registering she was on her hands and knees in the foulest of mires, her hair and ebony uniform plastered with thick stings of goop, she coughed and gagged until she'd spat out every atom of what was defiling her mouth. Pushing herself upright, eyes and brain finally starting to work as a team, Lana straightened and glanced at the lip of the pipe that had expelled her like a mouthful of chewing tobacco.

Looking up, Lana saw the curved tube was sweeping back and forth, as though designed to spread the gunk from Lab 8 across this evil landfill in an even spray. Beyond it, the immense white of the facility loomed to the North, East and South as far as she could see, with only the West stretching towards an open green horizon. The facility's outer skin of old, old limpet ivory sat at stark contrast with all the recent steel expansions within it, but much of its mass was shrouded in the permanent night of Earth's dark side. If it wasn't for her retinals, Lana probably wouldn't have managed one step without tripping over.

Tuesday shot noisily out of the plumbing feet-first, doing his best impression of a street luge suicide run. He spiralled a little before splashing down hard into one of the deeper puddles in and slid to a halt. Lana sighed, deciding she might as well check if he was alive, and to find out how he'd managed such a cool move. It wasn't the best landing, sure, but the bit right before his crash was awesome.

Testing the gunk with a careful dress shoe, while the material proved thin enough to consume Lana up to her shins, it wasn't likely to swallow her whole unless she exerted considerable force. Splorching towards Tuesday, who was ineffectively trying to claw free of a grey pool, Lana barely looked up when Trace zipped overhead. Jimmy was a half second behind her, but the moving flush pipe prevented any high-speed mid-air collisions.

Dragging Tuesday out by his bony wrists, trying in vain to wipe away the slimy tendrils clinging to every inch of her body, Lana watched as Rem was the last one to exit the pipe. Doing an impressive triple flip, the bristleworm flattened out his insectoid body to gently glide across the grey slime, rather than plunging into it like the clumsier humans. He did a sharp U-turn with his membrane flaps, reminding Lana of a surfer cutting a wave. She was impressed by his grace.

"Where to now?" Trace ground out, her scowling face framed with grossness.

Lana froze as her brain finally registered what she was standing in, what she was covered in, what had been in her mouth, and the grey-green slime that clawed all the way to the Western horizon slowly resolved into things she recognised: elbows, fingers, toes, thumbs, kneecaps, ankles...

Violently shaking her head, Lana drove her palms into her ears and screwed her eyes shut as the others asked her what was wrong. But she couldn't hear them. All she could focus on was that she was immersed in countless rotting limbs and hands and feet. Sure, the Slidge must have processed this meat with some sort of chemical to cut back on the stench of decay or they'd all be currently vomiting themselves to death and beyond, but that didn't change the fact there was a dead finger caught in her fringe. Shrieking at the realisation, Lana clawed at her face, dancing around as she wiped away clumps of flesh that may once have been her own.

Lana could hear somebody babbling and screaming, and it took a second to realise the wordless noises were coming from her own mouth.

Shaken by both shoulders, unable to comprehend a syllable of what was being said, Lana came to her senses just in time to deflect a huge slap from Trace's plank of a palm. Snapping out with practised reflexes, neatly intercepting the whack with thumb and index finger, Lana's cries instantly muted. Her cold eyes twitched sideways to regard Trace. As both the women knew well, Trace may have enough raw strength to rip Lana's head clean off, but she didn't have the speed to manage it.

Lana pushed away Trace's open hand.

"I'm fine," Lana ground out, taking a slow breath. She glared at Rem. "I'm assuming you have a ship of some kind out here?"

Rem checked his starburst collar with a twitch. Far to the West there was a purple wink from a hillock of body parts. Rem pointed an eyestalk at the blink-and-you-miss-it flash of light.

"In a manner of speaking," the Drennite said carefully.

*

There was more to reaching their objective than simply marching through a rotten mire. Every now and again some Slidge-made surveillance drones would weave back and forth with bright lights, scanning for movement and bio-signatures. Thankfully, as the humans were made of the exact same material as the swamp, all they had to do was watch for Rem's signal to plop down into the grey. They took turns covering him, preventing his Drennite genetics from getting picked out.

The drones would whip about a little, as though mildly confused by their readings, but they weren't sophisticated enough to figure out the problem on their own. They'd buzz up and down for a bit, and eventually decide to continue their sweep elsewhere. Once everyone was finally allowed to move and breathe again, they'd exhale explosively and keep trudging.

Considering how high-tech the Primacy had once been, it was kind of an anti-climax that their automated guards were dumber than rocks. Honestly, how could a people who once dissected and imprisoned the stars themselves use such bargain-basement robots? The average AI vacuum cleaner manufactured in East Korea could have probably beaten the whole lot of them at chess at the same time with half its motherboard missing. It was tragic. If this was the best the Slidge could do, this would be a very short adventure.

Thankfully, their trudge only took fifteen minutes. Cresting the final hill, something a different colour to rotting skin immediately came into focus: it was a dumpster the size of a small mobile home made from such deep, deep purple that it was almost black, and the charring from a recent atmospheric re-entry only pushed its hue closer to midnight. Large neon-white graffiti declaring "Nurbis was 'ere" had been jarringly tagged across the front, though it didn't bother to explain whatever or whoever a "Nurbis" actually was. The slab didn't appear to have any form of outer propulsion, but it was probably just hidden really well.

Rem slithered right up to the bin and began to deactivate the numerous traps he'd put in place earlier.

"Don't get within five metres just yet," the bristleworm warned.

The humans glanced at the dented hulking bin from a distance, unimpressed. Tuesday, however, got as close to its rough façade as he was allowed, sucking at his sad little black teeth in thought. Finally, his lifelong career as the galaxy's worst janitor came in handy.

"Yup, this is definitely a PusCo Medical Waste Dumpster. Seen them plenty of times during punishment duties. This is the sort used for Human tissue."

"Why would you bother strapping engines to a medical waste dumpster?" Lana asked incredulously. "And speaking of rockets, where are they? Underneath?"

"It doesn't have any engines. It's a bin." Rem said curtly, continuing to switch off a number of dead-on-touch security systems. "But it doesn't need them. It's just one…"

Something hit the PusCo dumpster with substantial force, leaving a steaming dent the size of a manhole cover. Clicking a Drennite curse, Rem spun into a crouch and used his mandibles to produce an unfolding double-barrelled alien assault rifle strapped to his midsection segments. Holding the gun in his mandibles and jaws didn't do much for his diction, but his words were still clear enough to follow.

"Inside! Now!"

The PusCo dumpster's upper slab lid folded open, and nobody bothered to look back before leaping into its damp, dark interior. They hit a surprisingly soft floor, bouncing off it a little bit on contact. Above, they could hear Rem blasting away with his automatic weapon.

Despite the danger, Lana couldn't help but sneak a peek between the dumpster's rubber lid seals, and she could make out three armed Slidge security guards exchanging fire with Rem. The six-legged aliens seemed to have set up some kind of tactile-holographic shielding, and were firing through slots in its flickering skin with impunity. Rem would need to be one of the greatest marksmen of all time to thread the needle like that, let alone three times, and even though she was merely a Cadet from an Academy on a minor world (and had technically been skipping class for five hundred years), Lana could tell Rem didn't stand a chance. He was using the dumpster as cover, but whatever the Slidge were firing at him was definitely leaving marks. It would only be a matter of minutes until the PusCo garbage receptacle was Swiss cheese.

While the Slidge seemed to have the sharpshooting talents of your average pigeon, she couldn't just watch and do nothing. Glancing down at Trace's bust, Lana didn't have time to demand the kinetic accelerator before Jimmy jammed his hand into Trace's chest armour, pulled the gun from her buried cleavage holster, and started firing wildly over the lip of the bin. If they survived this firefight, digging into Trace's breasts without permission was going to have some serious ramifications for Jimmy later on.

"You're not taking this bloody arm!" was Jimmy's war cry.

Sadly, Jimmy couldn't hit a barn from the inside, so most of his shots didn't come within thirty metres of his target. He did fluke one strike against the holographic shield, causing it to shimmer and jolt a little as the impact bored right through it. Being fired at by an entirely different category of weapon surprised the Slidge, and it took them a second to adjust their portable armouring to deflect any other shots of that variety.

This pause was exactly what Rem needed. Springing from the swamp, curving gracefully through the thin slot between the dumpster's rubber seams, he tumbled to a smooth halt. There were a few "spang" noises as Slidge guns lashed ineffectively at the dumpster, and a few gentle bulges showed where their shots had penetrated especially deeply. To everyone's surprise, as soon at the lid banged down the interior of the dumpster lit up. As they'd felt, its walls, floor and ceiling were padded with something soft yet firm.

"Okay," Lana snapped, flinching at each new bang. "Now, to be clear, you said that this brick doesn't have any engines, right?"

Rem nodded. "Yes. It's just a medical waste dumpster."

Everyone blinked a couple of times. Trace made a growling sound in her throat that slowly turned into words.

"So you're saying this big, heavy thing that we're all currently stuck inside of can't move under its own power?"

Rem nodded. A halo of menus extended from his starburst collar.

"Not a centimetre. However, PusCo waste collection ships like The Dirty Betty can swap out hundreds of dumpsters exactly like this one in a broad sweep from high orbit," Rem explained. "This is achieved through a combination of quantum entanglement and…"

"So like a tractor beam?" Lana asked.

"Betty who?" Jimmy wondered.

Lana coughed violently at the sudden reek of toxic fumes. Horrified at the thought of being immolated to death inside of a sealed bin, her panic turned to anger when she realised it was just Tuesday smoking one of his evil chlorine-flavoured cigarettes. Waving at the green-blue swirls of burning plant life and preparing the ultimate stink-eye, she bared her teeth at him.

"Where did you even get that? Toss it. Now."

Grumbling, Tuesday stood up and pressed the lid open a little just as Rem sniffed at the colourful smoke. Taking in the aroma like a wine connoisseur inspecting a glass of chardonnay, Rem's mandibles, antennae, eye stalks and sensory tentacles all extended out to their furthest reach in an asterix of alarm, but Rem didn't have time to yell for Tuesday to freeze before he'd flicked the cigarette. Rem made a choking noise.

"Was that ignited chlorine?" the Drennite asked quietly.

Tuesday went to answer, but was momentarily interrupted by some weird sounds coming from outside. He raised an eyebrow at the Slidge yelling wordlessly some distance away, but sighed in relief as he realised the aliens had finally stopped firing. Flicking his eyes back to regard Rem, Tuesday nodded.

"Chlorine cigarette," Tuesday confirmed. "Name says it all."

Rem exhaled slowly, as though trying to calm himself. An orange holographic screen projected out from his starburst collar, and a flick of an antennae turned it leaf green. The bin began to vibrate.

"Okay, people, good news is our extraction vessel is still safely hidden in highest orbit and ready to pull us out," Rem used one of his eye stalks to glare darkly at Tuesday. "The bad news is that flicking a blazing hunk of chlorine into a biohazard swamp made of thousands of volatile, alien chemicals has doubtlessly started a chain-reaction that may very well incinerate us and everything else within this thousand-kilometre-wide square of portable atmosphere before we can get off the ground."

The dumpster started to get uncomfortably hot, but Rem didn't stop undulating his many facial nubs. Swiping a thin red rectangle made it turn blue, and the dumpster's sides turned transparent. The humans could only gape at the flames already whipping around the grey-green swamp, at the growing tornados of fire erupting from volatile gas emissions seemingly at random.

Rem delivered a final tap to his menu with a flourish, causing the bin to purr like a happy tabby getting a tail stroke, and only had time for one more piece of advice before speaking became impossible.

"Lie flat."

The logic behind installing a soft, cushioning layer in the dumpster became obvious when the PusCo skip launched with enough g-forces to break bones. Doing their best to remain flat, pressed so hard into the matting that the luxury of speech was lost, the humans could barely keep their eyes open against the strain, let alone look around. Rem was flat like the others, though his Drennite physiology meant his body was currently squashed to less than three centimetres thick.

The transparent walls were already glowing and shimmering from heat damage by the time they shot out of the flames and into a midnight sky. Soon, the flying dumpster was high enough to take in the distant unburnt edges of the square meat swamp, and the white cruciform facility at its core had disappeared beneath the smoke. This firestorm was already big enough to see from orbit, and it glowed like God had put out a lit cigar on Earth's forehead. In less than thirty seconds orange-white had filled the entire square of atmosphere, and by the time the time the gravitational forces stopped trying to snap their spines the swamp was lit up like New Year's in Sydney Harbour.

Rem sprung back into action the instant it was safe to move. By the time the humans managed to sit up, accidentally flipping across the bin within the infuriating inconvenience of zero gravity, Rem was already deep inside his codes.

"Okay, we appear to be home free," he announced, using the edge of his ridged shell to keep anchored in place. "The extraction vessel is only…"

Rem froze mid-sentence, shocked by something. His facial protrusions wiggled. Bug or not, Lana could tell something was very wrong.

"What?"

"They're back far earlier than I'd estimated," Rem admitted.

Jimmy was about to ask the most obvious question in the world when the Universe answered it for him: a Star Cage appeared from nowhere, its invulnerable white lattice lit from within by the glow of a hundred-kilometre-wide kernel of harvested supergiant locked in its core. This meant the dumpster, Earth's burning surface and the Star Cage now formed the vertices of a massive obtuse triangle. As the PusCo bin sped along, chewing up the fathoms, the Star Cage remained utterly still. While it was impossible to verify, it was easy to picture a thousand Slidge technicians were all trying to explain to their Prime was one of their most important science facilities was currently boiling hot enough to melt steel into slag. A number of summary executions likely served as punctuation for these proceedings.

Nobody in the dumpster breathed, hoping against hope their tiny unpowered vessel wouldn't show up on the Slidge's scanners, that they'd continue gliding along unseen until well out of range...

Everyone startled as a wave of lime-green sliced through the dumpster from top to bottom. For a moment, everyone was certain they'd just been hit by some sort of energy beam grid and had one millionth of a second remaining before they began a new phase of existence as steam. However, the green wave froze, wriggling until it morphed into a three-dimensional display at the core of their huddle. The purple face of what could only be a Prime of the Slidge appeared in a static blurred box, triple-segmented beak snapping open and shut in rage.

"You have one chance to surrender," it ground out, its coiling limbs so heavily adorned with precious metals that its skin was mostly concealed. "If we need to take you by force, not only will we resume harvesting your bodies for as long as the stars burn, but we will imprison you in a hellish purgatory beyond your current comprehension. Do nothing without direct instruction."

The Prime's scarred face vanished, proving it apparently didn't feel the need to waste words on gloating.

Their dumpster stopped cold, ending its drift towards salvation. Bright blue squares appeared on the skip's transparent front wall, automatically superimposing themselves over regions of the Star Cage. The scans showed a number of unfolding city-sized Slidge dreadnaughts had been launched from the deep, deep hangers of the white lattice. The humans knew from experience that each of these enormous, heavily-armed starships were actually compressed fleets, nightmarish Russian nesting dolls that could separate into a thousand separate vessels in a matter of seconds. For now, the dreadnaughts waited just beyond the Star Cage, awaiting instructions.

"I warn you, one flinch and you will all suffer beyond endurance," the Prime hissed as its image returned, proving it did want to rant and gloat after all. "I swear I will personally come down to your simulation with a red hot poker on the hour every hour to..."

There was a flash from Earth's surface, a nuclear-level flare, and Rem's starburst collar automatically projected a cluster of screens all flashing a chaotic red. It was almost beyond comprehension, but it appeared the chain reaction from Tuesday's discarded chlorine cigarette in the giant square of atmosphere had managed to tear apart the dark side of Earth like a stick of dynamite in a letter box. After centuries of barely holding together this explosion proved to be the very last straw, and Earth's millions of pieces of rock finally decided they were tired of maintaining a vague sphere. Cracks spread through the deepest connective points, separating continent-sized boulders and flinging them outwards like a riot control device going off.

It was official: Earth had ceased to be a planet, and was now little more than a spreading asteroid field.

Tuesday took in furious glares from Trace, Lana and Jimmy, then Rem. He gave a weak smile.

"Whoops."

Mere rock and magma didn't pose much of a threat to the limpet ivory of the Star Cage, and it was probably through hubris and pride that the planet-sized warship didn't bother to move out of the eruption's path. However, whoever was manning the yoke on the Star Cage seemed to have forgotten there was a large facility made out of a substantial chunk of limpet ivory on Earth's surface, and by the time someone clever realised what was coming their way it was already too late to act. Clear as day, the passengers of the PusCo medical waste dumpster witnessed the white cruciform slice through the midsection of one of the dreadnaughts without slowing one jot before slamming into the Star Cage. While the white lattice may have been basically indestructible, the frail bodies of the Twelve Hundred species of the Primacy that called the Star Cage home certainly weren't immune to the shockwave that swept through all of its corridors.

The enraged purple face of the Prime vanished into static, possibly dead or merely disconnected. The damage that had just been inflicted could only be guessed, but the word "catastrophic" probably wouldn't be out of place.

Unwilling to waste this blessing, Rem immediately spun up the system that had been dragging the dumpster towards its goal. Cursing, the bristleworm kept an eye stalk on the blur of an approaching blast wave, the herald of a seemingly endless field of minerals that followed behind it as an arc of death. It seemed Earth's swansong was going to keep crooning for some time yet.

"Hold on," Rem yelled. "This is going to hurt like a bitch."

Catching the blast wave, the humans couldn't even scream as the gravity rose sharply, pushing them deeper and deeper into the padding. The force began to crush them, triggering spots over their vision and clenching their jaws so tightly that their teeth threatened to burst. Somehow Rem continued manipulating the menus of his starburst collar, his flat body twitching under so much gravity that it was a wonder his exoskeleton hadn't started spider webbing.

Squished so hard that his eyelids were being driven into his eyes, Jimmy could just barely see a thin line of something in the approaching void, something dead ahead. It was a looming spiral the same dark purple of the PusCo bin, its curls tightly wrapped around an enormous glass tube filled with something that had been divided into different colours like a dead-straight rainbow. The starship only grew by the moment, drawing them in, but they were still dozens of kilometres away when black spots erased Jimmy's vision altogether. Squeezed into unconsciousness, the last thing Jimmy witnessed was a kilometre-wide logo: PusCo Medical Waste Services.

And then he knew no more.

PART TWO THE DIRTY BETTY TAKES FLIGHT
CHAPTER SIX

Jimmy Slummer slowly awakened to a thrumming. It was a gentle, high-tech purr that massaged his body down to the marrow, a calming background hum. Falling back towards sleep, Jimmy's eyes snapped open when the thrum was suddenly replaced up by the violent, drawn-out grinding noise you get when an inexperienced shuttle pilot fails to change gears properly.

He sat up, marinaded in a mixture of confusion and horror. The pitch black only invented a galaxy of hidden monsters and terrifying possibilities.

Where was he? Was he back in the Slidge facility? Had his body been reinstalled into that tight cage, the ports in his skull filled with cables and plugs? Was this darkness a moment of respite before an incalculably terrible punishment loop began, a virtual Tartarus that would burn the skin from his bones and bubble his fat into steam over and over and over again, a worse-than-death purgatory that would loop his mind in circles as his limbs were sliced from his body and regrown in an endless cycle of harvesting?

Jimmy tilted his head a little.

Or I could just be sitting in the dark somewhere. That's a possibility, too.

Blinking heavily, feeling as though he'd woken up from the biggest bender of his life, Jimmy took a moment to check his body. He was reassured by the fact he wasn't restrained in any apparent way. Sliding his index fingers down both sides of his face, he could feel the L-shaped brackets embedded in his temples were empty. It felt as though he was still wearing his bright yellow MacDeath uniform, and he hoped the self-cleaning fabric would sort itself out soon. He absolutely reeked.

Patting at the floor, Jimmy pushed his fingers into a soft surface that had a lot in common with what he'd been crushed against within the PusCo medical waste dumpster. Exploring one pat at a time, he found the block of padding extended all the way to the close walls. He also discovered a rustling pile of newspaper in the corner, as though somebody was housetraining a puppy. About a metre to the left of The Seven Suns Third Afternoon Gazette were two bowls, one filled with water and one with crunchy, cheese-smelling treats.

Jimmy pulled a face as he put two and two together. Either Rem had either gotten his wires crossed about human toilet habits and dietary etiquette, or his knowledge was based purely on Tuesday's unsavoury practises. It didn't stop Jimmy from gulping down the Happy Puppy CheezBitz and lapping the water bowl dry, though. The treats were actually quite good.

Detecting an odd smell on top of all the others, Jimmy sniffed at the air. Instead of the rotten banana stink of the Slidge or the chilling decay of a swamp made from people offcuts, there was something else. It was medicinal, a combination of harsh disinfectants and metal that had been heated to red-hot temperatures by thermal decontamination. It smelled like a hospital.

Running his fingers inside the bowls to make sure he hadn't missed any scraps, Jimmy froze at an odd sound: it was a metallic clicking, like somebody tapping tiny, tiny drumsticks just beyond the darkness. The clicking faded, as though gradually moving away. Waiting until the sound disappeared entirely, Jimmy carefully extended his hands towards the ceiling in case there was anything hiding in the dark that might bean him. Standing a little at a time, as Jimmy's night vision bloomed he discovered he was standing in what appeared to be a large pantry or storeroom that had been repurposed into a cell. Dark lines suggested long-lost shelves.

Waving his arms to make sure he wasn't going to pulverise his crotch on an industrial vacuum cleaner, Jimmy patted around the walls for a latch or a handle. After a few smacks he hit what must have been a release square, and a thick bulkhead slid aside to reveal a blinding hallway. Of course, it was only unbearably bright for the first few seconds, and once Jimmy stopped wincing and swearing he was ready to go.

Jimmy could tell from one glance that this starship wasn't made for pleasure seekers. This ten-metre-wide corridor was constructed from durable, dependable slabs of ceramic plating coated with a layer of unadorned purple graphene the same hue as the PusCo dumpster. Two lanes of seamed trolley tracks ran along both the ceiling and the floor, as though trains ran through here, but then Jimmy mentally compared the rough size of the bin they'd escaped in to the dimensions of this corridor. At a guess, Jimmy reckoned you'd be able to slide four full skips – two up top and two below – through this corridor while leaving just enough room to prevent sanitation workers from getting wiped out.

Wiping at the filthy floor with a flip flop, Jimmy revealed an eroded layer of neon yellow safety paint hidden under dust and dirt. It looked about six hundred years past its last respray. Alarmingly, there were several Vegan Extremist gang signs graffitied on a number of walls nearby, and Jimmy instantly became hyper alert just in case a bunch of terrorists popped out wielding chainsaws and nerve gas. There were also a few tags that declared "Nurbis was 'ere," just like the one Jimmy had seen on the flying dumpster.

Turning as the storeroom automatically slid shut behind him, Jimmy blinked at a crude white stencil sitting at eye height. It said JIMMY, but the letters looked as though a drunk person had written them with a crayon in his mouth. He was about to turn away when he caught a glance at his own reflection in the grey window: despite being kept immobile and harvested for the better part of a decade, he really didn't look as terrible as he would have guessed. Sure, he was horribly light-deprived and seemed to have finally inherited all his Dad's worst physical qualities without any of the pluses, but it could have been a lot worse.

Leaning in closer, squinting at the reflection of the brackets bolted to his temples, Jimmy discovered each of the plugs had tiny circular holographic logos that glimmered if the light hit them just the right way. It took a little tilting, but Jimmy eventually discovered they all spelled out the same brand name: Thoughtplane.

Jimmy pulled a face. Like anyone who had an unhappy childhood, he knew that Thoughtplane produced all the best Immersives, but this was the first time he'd heard of them designing digital prisons. Then again, as the ruins of Earth proved, a lot can change over time.

Stretching his sore muscles, Jimmy panned in both directions. The corridor extended for some distance before starting to curve slightly, reminding him this ship was a big spiral. There were plenty of other sealed doors dotted along the way on both sides, and while he assumed they were just other storerooms, he couldn't be sure without checking. After that endless software loop Jimmy would have prefer to do something a little more interesting than stocktaking general supplies, but it seemed exploring a junker was about as entertaining as today was going to get.

Jimmy startled as the gentle background thrumming switched to that horrific grinding noise again, as though somebody had thrown an engine block into a wood chipper. The lights flickered, the floor vibrated more and more violently, and somehow Jimmy managed not to go to the toilet in his yellow apron. He wasn't a starship mechanic, but he was pretty sure those sounds weren't a good thing.

Deciding to go left rather than right for no quantifiable reason, Jimmy kept his eyes and ears open. Most of the storeroom portals were adorned by glowing letters that declared QUARANTINE or INFECTION RISK or UNKNOWN ELEMENT DETECTED, and Jimmy was sure to cross to the opposite side of the corridor for those ones. A number were blackened with the unmistakable charring and stink of old, old fires.

Jimmy inspected one of the rusty spigots installed in the ceiling, and wasn't reassured by how dry the tarnished fire suppression system seemed to be. Squinting at the spigot, Jimmy drew back at the realisation that it was actually a pyrosanitation faucet, the sort that sprayed nova-hot flames to eradicate biological threats down to the last microbe. He decided not to stand under another one of them again.

Opening one of the few accessible storerooms at random, all that greeted his eyes were a dozen shelves filled with large bags with labels that declared them to be full of pressure gelatine granules, the sort you used to repair sub-light crash-lounges. If Jimmy ever needed to maintain some damaged crash lounges in order to keep a bunch of passengers alive and unsquished during a sub-light acceleration, then now he knew where to look. Presently, though, these bags of green grit were as useless as chopsticks in an Indian restaurant.

The next storeroom cube was loaded with what must have been fifty sealed cases of hard-wearing laminated cardboard. As the ceiling bulbs didn't seem to work in this block, Jimmy had to feel around until he discovered a mystery cases that was already open. Fetching what felt like a ridged cylinder a little larger than a disposable cigarette lighter, Jimmy took his prize out into the bright lights of the corridor. Tapping a yellow-and-black striped square the size of a postage stamp on the side of the cylinder, a calming voice spelled out a polite warning.

"In order to avoid severe injury and/or death, please do not expose this demolition charge to bright light, sudden pressure, or..."

Acting both rapidly and stupidly, Jimmy pitched the demo charge back into the dark storeroom with its hundreds of thousands of explosive friends. Backing away from a metric tonne of death until he was on the other side of the corridor, Jimmy waited to die. On the bright side, he assumed his life expectancy was roughly five seconds, so this terror wasn't likely to stick around for much longer.

But there was only silence from the storeroom. Thankfully, rather than a bursting fireball of death, a sad chirping noise and a serene voice floated out instead.

"Sincere apologies from ScuttleCo. This charge is faulty. Please contact a representative to discuss remuneration."

Breathing out slowly, sinking down onto his wide buttocks in relief, Jimmy didn't immediately detect the ticking noise next to his right ear. Glancing sideways at the sound, Jimmy was less than a hand span from a little spidery robot. Its spiked limb tips were magnetically attached to the weathered purple grid work, and it pumped up and down in greeting.

Jimmy didn't panic. He wasn't all that surprised at the Weaver's presence, as back in his era they were common as houseflies. Ranging in size from a grasshopper to a teacup Chihuahua to a baseball glove, depending on their designated task, Weavers took care of all The Unison's construction work. Whether you were knocking up a pre-fab apartment block or building something the size of the Carpe Astrum, the process was the same: design a CAD-CAM blueprint, gather a horde of Weavers, provide them with a source of raw materials, and unleash them.

It was a simple fact that Weavers were superior to organic workers. They operated in perfect harmony in the tens thousands without asking questions, taking a toilet break, complaining about union rules or stealing office supplies, and they wouldn't stop until their task was completed or they'd run out of operational legs. A standard model could lift a thousand times its own weight, jump sixty metres with a full load and climb vertical walls better than a Himalayan spider goat, earning their renown as the greatest of builders.

While Weavers weren't true AI, keeping the bots dumb was just as much about safety as it was about affordability. A garden-variety Weaver cost less than two Amerikan pounds per unit, making them more disposable than a self-tying condom, and they were strictly programmed to be unable to repair themselves for obvious reasons. This was of small comfort to all the Robot-Apocalypse doomsayers who predicted mankind would be overthrown by their own creations some point next Thursday, but as Humanity was currently down to a club of four and the Weavers probably still numbered in the trillions, the tinfoil-hat parade may have had a point after all.

The creator and manufacturer of all Weavers, Happy Planet, had always been famously tight-lipped about how they were able to produce these amazing builders for less than a double-shot from a coffee hypo per unit, but over the years many people had learned the hard way not to pry into Happy Planet's secrets. It was a good way to vanish without a trace.

Jimmy considered the Weaver, wondering if it was being controlled by a Rigger or whether it was capable of independent thought. He didn't like this question very much, so once the metal bug skittered into a vent and out of sight Jimmy immediately went back to trying to figure out why he was wandering this spooky ship on his own.

Ten metres later, Jimmy's ears prickled at an unmistakable sound: Tuesday's snoring. It was like listening to a cow choke to death on a whoopee cushion. Creeping up to the offending storeroom, Jimmy saw the same crude white stencil as before, identical but for the fact it said BOB rather than JIMMY. He went to tap on the door, but reconsidered pre-knock. Since the disaster aboard the Carpe Astrum, Jimmy couldn't remember a time when he'd been more than fifty metres away from Tuesday, Lana or Trace. He may have felt varying degrees of dislike and outright revulsion for the three of them from hour to hour, but despite his chronic co-dependent nature Jimmy eventually lowered his knuckles. It would be best to have some alone time for now. Who knew when he'd be able to enjoy solitude again?

Lana's storeroom was silent as Jimmy passed it, but even after another hundred metres Jimmy still hadn't seen Trace's name stencilled anywhere. He shrugged, assuming her cramped makeshift bedroom must lay in the opposite direction. Looking back the way he came at the distinct curve, chewing on the inside of his cheek, Jimmy wondered if he'd end up doing a complete revolution if he kept going dead straight.

He'd heard about ancient starships that needed to actually spin to create gravity for their passengers, but he scoffed at the thought of ever actually being on one. Surely any ship that primitive would have been dry docked, suffered complete mechanical failure or simply dissolved into rust long before he was even born. Nobody would be insane enough to keep such an antique running, let alone use it to travel interstellar distances with living passengers! The humour of it!

It took another hundred boring paces or so, but an intersection greeted Jimmy. As making decisions had never been his strong suite, it took a good thirty seconds of lip nibbling to eventually decide he'd turn left. However, his nose was telling him this way had been badly charred at some point, and within twenty steps the corridor had turned black and crunchy. A red holographic hand shaped in the classic "STOP" gesture suddenly popped up, blocking Jimmy's way with a loud noise.

"This area has been restricted," a distorted voice churned at top volume. Its cadence was unnatural, inhuman. "PusCo will not be held liable for any injury, up to and including death, which may eventuate from entering this area."

Making a frustrated grunt as he turned around, Jimmy wondered just how much of this vessel still served an operational purpose. After all, PusCo had been around in one form or another for almost as long as The Unison, so this medical waste disposal ship could potentially be as old as commercial space travel. But then he understood the genius of it: of course Rem would choose a junker to sneak into Earth's orbit, as nobody in their right mind would come within spitting distance of such a hot ball of garbage, let alone fly it. This defective, dangerous hulk was bin fodder at best, and a complete death trap at worst.

After a couple more turns, Jimmy was soon lost in a labyrinth of identical purple corridors, but the latest hallway seemed to be different to the last few, as its bulkheads were studded with long, thin black rectangles the size of cinderblocks. Squinting, wondering if the black shapes served a purpose, Jimmy touched the closest one.

And now he could see everything.

Jimmy's brain did a bit of a backflip as all the windows snapped from opaque to transparent, providing a prime view at the unbreakable glass tube cradled within the massive loops of this corkscrewing starship. The cylinder was as long as The Dirty Betty herself, and crammed to capacity with medical waste. The trash was separated not only by colour but by exact shades, sorting its diseased cargo into an orderly prism of rot. It was kind of like how Jimmy used to divide his rolls of Fruity Chomps into eight different jars prior to getting jabbed with an OCD vaccine booster.

Digging his fingers into the windowsill, the same horrible grinding noise as before returned to deafen him, and all the lights flickered on and off for the better part of twenty seconds. The constellations glowing beyond the ship's portholes spun away, as though someone had flicked the entire Milky Way out of place. The stars and lights eventually returned, and Jimmy's bowels decided they weren't going to void themselves in terror. If the constellation outside the window had changed, though, Jimmy wasn't qualified to comment on it.

A Weaver ticked up to Jimmy, raising its forelegs in what could be construed as a hostile gesture. Light crackled between its extended limbs, making Jimmy back away a couple of steps. Rather than spearing Jimmy through the face with a lightning bolt, the crackling glow coalesced into a picture. It was Rem, but his bug face gave nothing away. Jimmy wasn't good with human facial cues, let alone Drennite facial cues.

"Please stay within your safe rooms at this time, and keep your doors hermetically sealed," Rem requested politely. "The Stiller Drive is being...uh..."

There was another grinding noise, but this time it only lasted a couple of heartbeats. Rem's face disappeared, then came back.

"Now, I don't want to worry anyone, but your safe rooms have been wired up as escape pods, and I have been sure to provide suicide kits in the event that you have to..."

Rem's image flickered. Either he was having a series of mild strokes, or the video feed was rubbish. But then all the hair stood up on Jimmy's shoulders as the bristleworm voiced one of the most ominous, jinxed phrases in any language.

"Everything is under control."

Jimmy's brain picked this moment to finally catch up to his ears.

"A Stiller Drive?" he repeated.

He shouldn't have been shocked. Most Human starships were built around an industry-standard Stiller Drive. Despite its ubiquity, unlike hyper drives that twisted space time or accelerated light or otherwise kicked physics in the crotch, the way a Stiller Drive operated went against every shred of common sense. To even begin to understand a Stiller Drive, it needs to be stated that everything in the Universe moves. Planets, moons, stars, asteroids, old telecommunication satellites, whatever. If it exists, it's in constant motion of some kind. Everything dances across the heavens in its own rhythm. It wasn't until the 23rd Century that mankind discovered the Milky Way itself dances an incredibly precise waltz that repeats itself down to the millimetre every two weeks, three days, eight hours, sixteen minutes and four and a half seconds. Despite flashing by so fast that light was a legless upside-down turtle in comparison, the movements of the Milky Way were soon calculated down to a hundred decimal places. With the path and bearing of the entire galaxy mapped, a Stiller Drive simply brings starships to a complete relativistic halt, allowing the Milky Way and everything in it to spin past. It's then a relatively simple matter for any half-decent navigation computer to switch off the Stiller Drive at the desired moment to re-join the real time Universe with acceptable accuracy.

As venerable as the Stiller Drive was, using one in the 30th Century probably bordered on comical. To a being from this era, it was probably about as dignified and logical as flicking yourself at the sky with a giant slingshot.

There was a long, painful grinding noise, twice as bad as any of the others. Lana's image suddenly appeared a little to Rem's left, startling Jimmy. Whether she'd just woken up in her cramped "bedroom" or had been spending some quiet time thinking wasn't clear.

"Thor's wrinkled taint, man, cut it out," she snapped. "I didn't even know Stiller Drives could make a noise like that. I'll be there shortly."

"Stay in your rooms," Rem said curtly, annoyed his cargo wasn't sitting quietly where he'd left them. "Everything is under..."

Trace suddenly appeared just like Lana. As always, she looked hostile. Jimmy was ashamed to flinch yet again.

"Finish that sentence and we're going to have problems," Trace growled.

"Uh," Lana ummed, her holographic avatar now walking briskly on the spot. "How do I get to you? How far is the bridge?"

"Stay...in your rooms," Rem ground out.

Lana turned her head from side to side, and took a large step backwards as though avoiding something big. Following that something with her eyes, looking a little perplexed, she studied the pairs of railed tracks on the floor and ceiling. She twitched her lips.

"Are these PusCo dumpsters the only things that move along these tracks? Or can I summon a go kart or something?"

"There have been tracks everywhere I've been so far," Jimmy added.

Jimmy was a little pleased to see Lana gape in surprise. He assumed his image was now visible to Lana, Trace and Rem. The Drennite flicked his eye stalks together in frustration.

"STAY IN YOUR ROOMS!"

Tuesday's image appeared, face lashed with red sleep lines and half-stuck to his padded floor with yellow saliva. He proved to be just as useful as always.

"Anyone seen my smokes? I swear they were right here in my coveralls..." He shambled to his feet and stretched, all his joints popping like bubble wrap. Like Lana, he began walking on the spot. "Which way is the toot? Do I go left or right down the corridor? The newspaper was only good for one decent wee, and I had to do that lying sideways. It's...you might want to do something about that soon."

Rem's eyes suddenly turned red, his multi-pronged head swelled and shrank like bagpipes, and a shriek started to rumble out of the depths of his limbless torso.

"STAY..."

"Fun fact," Lana interrupted smoothly, "Did you know that if a Stiller Drive's primary, secondary and tertiary cores all rise above four thousand degrees Celsius mid-transit, the resulting chain-reaction is more than capable of giving birth to a small star?" Lana shrugged. "Then again, that's just a theory. Nobody close enough to find out has ever survived the experience."

Rem paused mid-screech, and angled an eye stalk at something unseen. He took a couple of seconds to speak again.

"I am unfamiliar with that form of measurement."

"Water freezes at zero degrees Celsius, and boils at one hundred," Lana said helpfully.

It took a few seconds, but Rem eventually twitched his facial protuberances and the entire ship calmed down. The silence and stillness was total until the bristleworm spoke.

"Do you have a working knowledge of Stiller Drives?" he finally asked.

Jimmy, Tuesday and Trace made the same facial expression. Lana, however, nodded solemnly.

"Did a number of educational uploads at the Academy on the basics of hyper drive operation. I'm no expert, but I should know enough to be of use." Lana regarded the holograms of the only other three humans left in the galaxy, then turned back to Rem. "You are aware that short of sedating us, there's no chance we're going to spend Loki-knows-how-long sitting quietly in storerooms, right?"

Rem flicked his mandibles in defeat.

"Fine. All of you, wait where you are." Turning away, Rem paused and locked his eyestalks onto each of the holographic screens. "By the way, welcome aboard The Dirty Betty."

CHAPTER SEVEN

It didn't surprise Jimmy the transportation Rem sent down the long, curved corridor was a PusCo medical waste dumpster. Sliding along the left track at quite a pace, the dark purple skip made an occasional high-pitched squeal as it accidentally touched a magnetic rail. Stopping less than a pace from Jimmy's toes, the bin might have been the same one they'd recently used to flee from the expanding asteroid belt that used to be Earth, but he couldn't be bothered to analyse it with a magnifying glass. A dumpster was a dumpster.

Scratching at a hairy nipple, Jimmy took a second to decide whether he should ride inside of the dumpster or on top. Lifting its heavy lid a little, unlike the first dumpster, this trash receptacle wasn't padded. It did, however, contain a mess of pre-loved glow-in-the-dark hypo syringes caked with black blood.

Jimmy decided to ride on top.

Rumbling back towards his room, rolling up the gradual spiral, Jimmy did his best to hold the lid's handles. Every time the bin touched a rail it juddered his skeleton, but besides that the ride was quite smooth.

Glancing down at a sign of movement near his hand, Jimmy came face-to-face with another Weaver...or possibly the same one as before. He wasn't sure. Perhaps Rem had allocated a specific Weaver to each passenger to take care of their communication needs? As the little mechanical spiders were capable of building or repairing just about anything a Human mind could plan, using them as skittering walkie-talkies was a waste of their talents.

It only took about twenty seconds to collect the others. They'd congregated outside Lana's bedroom, and three Weavers were sitting nearby. Jimmy gave an awkward smile.

"All aboard?" he managed.

Thankfully, the dumpster had enough handles for everyone.

Rolling a good third of the way along The Dirty Betty, the dumpster made a sudden, unannounced left turn, passing into a corridor that ran parallel to the core superstructure of the ship. Everything remained the same deep purple along the metal hedge-maze of unmarked streets and avenues and airlocks and slab doors and the magnetic rails that connected it all together, and the only thing that broke up the monotony was an occasional dumpster flying past in the opposite direction, heading somewhere unknown for an unspoken purpose. There were plenty of windows studded along some of the corridors, but they passed too quickly to touch. However, one of the passages was completely transparent all the way around, so everyone got a good look at what Jimmy had already seen.

"Anyone else feel like a packet of Colourful Sweeties all of a sudden?" Tuesday mumbled, drooling a little at the rainbow tube of waste.

Lana pulled a disgusted face at Tuesday's words.

"Pretty sure you don't want to taste that rainbow," Lana said. "Remember that in waste disposal terms, purple means Human tissue. Everything in that tube is, at the very least, contaminated with bits of people."

`Trace seemed content to glare silently, uninterested. After all, the garbage wasn't a current threat, so her care factor was nil.

Passing through more cut-and-paste hallways and boulevards, they entered a cavern the size of an aircraft hangar filled with what must be most of The Dirty Betty's dumpsters. Fifty multi-levelled tracks converged from an equal number of curved exits, but some of the rails were blocked with haphazard piles of skips, as though they'd been randomly tossed about by a gravity screw-up. A thick sheen of dust and ancient cobwebs coated most of their lids.

A single bare rail led them out of the scrum of bins and back into the guts of this vessel. Dozens of massive double-layered bulkheads lined the port and starboard walls, sealed tight as drums. Every armoured wall was emblazoned with the faded remains of yellow WHS stickers and stencils, declaring WARNING and STAY CLEAR and FATAL HAZARD and PHYSICAL ENTRY NEGATES ALL INSURANCE CLAIMS. All of them badly needed respraying.

Eventually, after taking the humans on a two-minute ride that would have otherwise taken hours on foot, the dumpster stopped cold and warning signs popped up on everyone's retinal screens. They declared STOP! HEAT RISK! and STOP! UNACCEPTABLE UV RADIATION! in glittering red lettering. Blinking away the warnings, Lana could see the track ended fifty metres away at something unusual: a completely white door. It bore the complicated galaxy-spinning symbol that represented Stiller Drives.

She rocked the dumpster, urging it to move. It replied by doing nothing.

"You need us?" Tuesday asked as Lana dismounted.

She felt like cursing him out. Of course Tuesday knew what her answer was going to be. Unless something needed to be eaten, stolen or bashed senselessly with its own fist, then Jimmy, Tuesday and Trace were about as useful as democracy.

Lana landed smoothly on the yellow-striped laminate.

"You lot wait here," she ordered.

Graphs and pie charts and raw numbers popped up on her retinals as she made her way towards the glowing beige bulkhead. Opposing lockers sat a few metres short of the hard seal on her left and right, their beaten doors emblazoned with the classic radiation glyph. Unfortunately, they'd been jimmied open and their rad-suits looted long ago. If Lana was going in, she was going in naked.

The airlock produced a detailed holographic to warn Lana what awaited her on the other side: the ambient heat, the current severity of the UVA and UVB radiation, how many seconds it would take to inflict second degree burns, how many minutes it would take to develop fatal melanomas, how long until her brain started leaking out of her ears...

Lana dismissed the holograms with a swipe. She knew she had between five and ten minutes before things got really gnarly, scientifically speaking, and reading the exact calculations of her own mortality wouldn't change that. As the Stiller Drive was probably going to detonate at any moment, possibly tearing a hole in local space/time as it incinerated everyone, she had priorities more urgent than the deepness of her tan.

A thrumming noise gradually grew in the background, and in the time it took Lana to pass through the airlock's triple seals the vibration had shifted into a bone-rattling grinding. Lana found herself in a darkened, blurred area barely touched by the light of orange hazard bulbs. She was slammed with the smell of burning paint and a wave of dry heat that could dehydrate a person into jerky within fifteen minutes. Trying to ignore the humming in the roots of her teeth and the marrow of her bones, Lana flinched as the Stiller Drive's engine cycle hit a painful apex. She secretly wished she knew a few Drennite curses so she could explain to Rem exactly what she thought of him revving the motor when it was clearly unwise to do so.

Moaning in discomfort, Lana trudged forwards one step at a time as her surroundings slowly bloomed into focus. Beyond the hazard lights, the entire far wall was a complex knot of technology glowing a steady, deep crimson, the colour of a forged blade ready to be plunged hissing into a bucket of water by a blacksmith: the Stiller Drive. Its coolant had evaporated away into useless steam, and it was currently clouding much of this chamber. Thankfully, a whitish, wispy energy partition sat between Lana and the heat-distorted Stiller Drive, so even though the device was hot as magma, the layer of magnetic shielding was preventing the worst of it from reaching her. That was lucky, as otherwise she'd already be dead as a can of chicken soup.

Her skin was already reddening. Lana considered it a small mercy that Stillers were powered by StoreCells, which were basically tiny manufactured stars crammed into a thick lead-lined battery casing. She'd prefer a hot dose of UV over a lethal bath of gamma radiation any day of the week. Getting a few melanomas scooped out was preferable to growing an extra arm out of your forehead.

Panning back and forth along the superheated Stiller Drive in disbelief, gaping a little, Lana had no earthly idea how they hadn't already been reduced to ashes. Hyper drive machinery was the very definition of delicate, and it certainly wasn't designed to go through six levels of Styx and pushed further still. There was a good chance its components were about to dribble out and pool on the floor.

Lana startled as Rem emerged from the steam to her left. As far as she could tell, the bristleworm looked concerned.

"I'm not sure what to do," Rem admitted in Lana's ear, his yell barely defeating the din. "When the client provided this junker for the job, all I was told was to get you off Erf, turn on the Stiller Drive, hit the shuffle feature six times to make sure we shake any pursuers, then hit that red button there to head to the pre-set destination. That's all." Rem deflated in a depressed way. "This stupid Human hyper drive makes no sense, and everything I try only makes it worse."

She placed her lips against a hole on the side of Rem's head, hoping it was an ear canal of some kind and not something rectal.

"How long did you warm her up?"

Rem gave her a blank look, and Lana came very close to gripping him by both mandibles and bashing his face into the deck until she'd pounded the true span of his stupidity into his bug brain. Knowing this wouldn't be of much practical use, Lana absently wiped the back of her hand across her sweating, pinking forehead while she tried to think of a solution. She cringed at the sharp pain of shallow radiation burns rubbing against each other. Far as she could tell, all her exposed skin was already blooming towards red.

"First we need to switch off everything so it can cool down, and the best way to do that is to vent this entire area into space so the vacuum can do its thing. Can you send administrative access to my Omni?"

Rem blinked, doing his best to listen. "To your what?"

Lana casually tapped at the meat between her thumb and index finger on her left hand as illustration. Rather than feeling the bump of her Omni, an implant the size of a grain of basmati rice she'd had for much of her life, she was surprised to encounter nothing but flesh. Looking down in surprise, a hard squeeze revealed her Omni simply wasn't there.

It took her a moment to understand. Of course. The Omni had been in her other left hand.

Gazing into the chaotic maze of the Stiller Drive, which was glowing closer to an egg yolk yellow now, Lana took a few moments to look around for a control panel or a big red OFF button or something.

"How do I pull the plug?" she asked.

Rem slumped.

"I was hoping you'd know."

Looking around wildly, hoping against hope a big mechanical lever would magically rise up from the floor to solve all their problems, Lana was just about to accept her search was hopeless when she registered a faulty hazard light was flickering just metres from the entry hatch. Tilting her head, Lana noticed the orange glare was highlighting a steel locker welded to the wall. Its door was stencilled in Day-Glo green paint with the words "Property of Nurbis, Do Not Touch."

Heart hammering, Lana sprinted for the locker, painfully jamming her fingertips as she basically ripped the door off its rotten hinges. Tossing aside an old Formica lunchbox, two pairs of threadbare technician's coveralls, assorted occult trinkets and a toolkit filled with rust that may have been metal tools at some point, Lana froze as she touched a leather slipcase. Barely large enough to hold a long pen, Lana squinted at the soft, white item, and her stomach leapt at a famous brand logo emblazoned down its spine in gold: Miyamoto-Kojima.

She drew what appeared to be bone-coloured chopsticks out of the holder. Just like the locker, the words "Property of Nurbis" had been carved into them. After a couple of seconds of gentle twisting, tapping and pulling, the thin rods detached from one another to reveal a millimetre-thin screen the size of a dinner plate, though it seemed she could adjust its dimensions with a casual tilt. However, customising this mysterious computer's display settings was a little less urgent than stopping the ship from turning into a cloud of radioactive dust.

The ancient Miyamoto-Kojima computer started up, displaying the brand name Scroll as a colourful three-dimensional prism. The Scroll's Operating System was in a mixture of Korean Emoji and Half-Mandarin, but Lana's retinal screens had no issue translating these two dead languages into modern Unglish. The Scroll complained its drivers and antivirus software hadn't been updated since the 23rd Century, but thankfully it let her in without requiring a username or a password, breaking Rule Number One of basic computer security. Lana ignored most of the bright little icons dotting the screen (WebCrawler? What in the spug was a WebCrawler?) and tried to pretend she couldn't feel her skin turning into scorched brown hide.

The Scroll finally decided to crank into gear, displaying a list of basic operations relevant to this area of The Dirty Betty. However, the hundreds-long list covered everything from the air conditioning temperature of the local corridors to the verbal accent of the ship's computer to the hover distance of the magnetic dumpster tracks, and it would take ages to go through these warrens of minutia. Lana could already feel the effects of mild radiation poisoning, and knew she didn't have time to muck about. Nausea rose in her gullet, and her eyeballs were beginning to sting. Within a minute she'd likely be too blind to be of any use.

As though it had just noticed their dire situation, the Scroll's screen was suddenly dominated with a glowing cartoon version of a Stiller Drive with the word OVERHEATING emblazoned across it in crackling fire-coloured letters. Icons appeared beneath the caricature, and Lana knew she'd hit pay dirt when a dozen operational glyphs pretty much jumped off the screen. She swiped URGENT SHUTDOWN, EMERGENCY COOLING, VENT REACTOR INTO SPACE and REROUTE ALL COOLING DUCTS in quick succession.

There was no time for celebrating, as the moment Lana's fingertip touched the fourth icon a shockwave of fresh coolant gas blasted her off her feet. Stunned, head swimming and ears filled with the ringing of dying audio cells, Lana vaguely registered she was floating sideways towards the distant airlock. It took a confused second for Lana to understand she was actually being carried in Rem's delicately-clenched mandibles.

Ice-cold coolant gas whittled away at the upper layers of her burning-hot skin as she glided across the room, and while the change in temperature was more than unpleasant, Lana suddenly had a bigger issue: she couldn't breathe. Her lungs were trying to fill with something that wasn't there anymore. Lana's throat hitched, chest muscles spasming as they pulled with all their might. Lana's eyes rolled madly, heels kicking the deck as her vision collapsed into black spots that grew and joined and swelled to hide everything.

The next instant Lana inhaled harder than ever before, and sweet, merciful air danced in her lungs. Gasping, Lana rested her head against the safe side of the white bulkhead. Its metal was hot against her scalp, but she was thankful to be on the alive side rather than on the dead, dead double-dead side.

Rem brought his eye stalks down to her level. Twitching at his tight embrace, Lana could feel that the Drennite had twisted his black ribbon of a body into an infinity knot around her chest and spine.

"I'm not sure if I did that correctly," Rem admitted, voice barely audible over the humming in Lana's blasted ears. "Do you need me to violently crush your solar plexus again? I can do it a lot harder, if you'd like."

Lana managed a shaky smile and shook her head. She reached out for the bulkhead frame and went to push herself to her feet, but found she was still holding the unfurled Scroll. A flick cleanly rolled it up again.

"Do you have any basic medical supplies?" she croaked. Her tongue felt like it had doubled in size.

Rem clicked his mandibles and nodded his entire body.

"I warn you, 'basic' may be overstating it."

Lana coughed violently and managed to push herself upright. This time she succeeded. Sliding the wrapped-up Scroll into its leather case, she found it fit snugly into the breast pocket of her ebony Cadet uniform. She gave a lopsided grin at Rem's nodding cluster of antennae.

"The bin will take you to Medical, and there's a small breakroom a few doors down where the others can wait. I'll be busy for the next hour or so, but I'm happy to answer any questions you have after that," Rem was sure to answer the obvious question. "Don't worry, you won't have any trouble finding me."

Only half-hearing Rem's words, Lana had no idea why she was smiling. Getting microwaved didn't usually agree with her.

*

Lana's burns hummed as the dumpster sped along its track. Wincing at the tighter corners, the sensation of cold air grazing her blood-red patches of exposed skin felt unpleasant and soothing at the same time. Without the use of her Omni she could only guess how much UV radiation she'd absorbed in her two minutes next to the overheating Stiller Drive, but she was expecting the worst. Skin cancer might be easier to treat than growing tentacles out of your spinal column, but for all she knew their supply of meds might begin and end at a bottle of Mister Drizzle chewable vitamins.

Nobody said anything for some time. Feeling the odd prickling sensation of being watched, Lana eventually looked up to see Trace, Tuesday and Jimmy were studying her neck and each other, as though silently asking each other a question. Feeling a twitch near her collarbone, Lana's finger pressed at something new, a kind of blobby growth. Terrified it could be a malignant tumour or a flake of fallout that had burrowed a new home into a soon-to-be-deceased host, she applied some force to it. The dumpster took an unexpected corner and Lana's fingernail accidently sliced right into the lump, and gunk burst explosively from her unwelcome passenger. Rivulets of yellow and clear fluid dried into crystals on the lapel of her uniform.

She dreaded to think what else might be hiding out of sight.

*

Lana didn't pass out, but things got a bit scattered. It reminded her of that time she got severe sunstroke as a small child, the headache and the confusion and the heat. Like then, she craved for coolness and darkness and the tender care of a parent. As she'd grown up in an all-girls Academy for unwanted children, only the coolness and darkness were ever on offer. Hugs weren't a part of the curriculum.

Lana's hand snapped up in response to a stinging point on her neck (well, a point that stung differently to the rest of her skin) and her fingers wrapped around something knobbly and metallic. A weapon?

"Just a needler," Jimmy said in his most reassuring voice.

Lana's pink, lightly-poached eyeballs rolled up to focus on Jimmy's harmless face, then back down at the needler lodged in her carotid. Jimmy gently drew its muzzle out of Lana's hand and placed a yellow swab over a tiny dot of blood. The needler's empty canister popped with a hiss and rattled into a PusCo sharps bin, and was soon joined by the red-spotted swab. As this was a medical waste processing ship, Lana assumed the garbage unit's contents wouldn't have to travel far.

Lana gave Jimmy a quizzical look, blinked, then looked down to see she was reclining on a close cousin to a dentist's examination chair. She tried to ignore the fact it had built-in restraints. Her eyes flicked back to the device in Jimmy's hand. He understood the unspoken question.

"Oh, this? Yeah, got taught to use one in Life Skills class back on Sprout. Families took care of their own medical dramas. No AutoDoc surgical booths or anything like that. Farming planets aren't renowned for their health care systems." He holstered the needler on the side of Lana's chair. "If you were sick or injured beyond our means, you'd have a short funeral before being processed into Nutrient and sprayed onto the Landkelp crops tomorrow morning."

Lana gave Jimmy an incredulous look.

"You aren't serious?"

He nodded. "Sprout was caught in a deliberate technological vacuum. Once we reached an equilibrium where the crops were viable and the farmers stayed alive long enough to make The Unison's investment pay dividends, we kind of froze in place, scientifically. Unless it was whittled from leftover Landkelp stalks, everything we owned came from the colony's first seeding. Far as I know, our population didn't produce more than a tonne of unrecyclable waste in two centuries."

The light dawned in Lana's eyes.

"Was your colony sponsored by TuffTek, by any chance?"

Jimmy nodded again, but this time wearing a dirty expression.

"Yeah, bloody TuffTek. That little TT symbol was embossed everywhere on Sprout. TuffTek equipment might be slow and stupid and loud and dangerous and inefficient and ugly…"

"…but it lasts forever." Lana finished.

She smiled again, and her eyes rolled towards the ceiling. Jimmy hurriedly reached for another canister to load into the needler, but Lana's hand came to rest on its barrel, her pinkie finger accidentally falling across Jimmy's knuckles. His skin was tough, as though made from one big callus.

"I'm not passing out, I'm just thinking." She blinked out of synchronisation half a dozen times. "Wow. Actually, I think I'm doing a bit of both. What did you inject me with?"

"Bit of a cocktail." Jimmy patted the needler's holster next to Lana's arm. "This doubles as an auto-brew medicine mixer. Punch in a recipe, and the mixer will whip it up in minutes. Kind of like how a Repler unit can refine Landkelp paste into any food you'd want, but with medicine. See?"

Jimmy picked up a little book made from waterproof paper, handed it to Lana, and tapped at a page. Lana managed to focus well enough to read a silver-embossed brand stamp.

"Rad-B-Gone?" she frowned. "The name isn't inspiring my confidence for some reason."

"It's a generic. Like the other six thousand medicines this needler can synthesise. A corny name doesn't mean it won't work." Jimmy winked. "Just between you and me, I mixed in a bit of fun stuff from the muscle relaxant page to say thanks for stopping the ship from blowing up." He tilted his head to read one of the recipe names. "See this? You have any idea what a 'Cure for Hive' might be?"

Lana glanced where he was pointing.

"Pretty sure the capitals mean it's meant to be pronounced Haitch-Ai-Vee. Cure for HIV." She shrugged. "Haven't the faintest. Never heard of it."

Lana's eyes traced over the ceiling, a little taken aback that Jimmy seemed capable of maintaining a conversation for so long. Usually he collapsed in a flaming pile of awkwardness within a matter of syllables. For once, it almost wasn't painful to speak with him. Normally she would have come up with a dozen different reasons why she had to immediately be somewhere else, but seeing as though Tuesday and Trace were her only other sources of Human contact, she had to take what she could get.

"You know, from what I can tell, this whole ship is made out of it," Jimmy said quietly.

Lana arched an eyebrow. "Made from what? HIV?"

"TuffTek. I've seen that little TT logo embossed a bunch of times already. Which means The Dirty Betty is a piece of junk, but she'll remain an operational piece of junk forever. A ten-year-old could maintain her indefinitely, I reckon. How bad was the Stiller Drive, really?"

Lana shrugged, reclining with her eyes closed.

"If it was a proper fancy one from a decent manufacturer, I'd say the thing was a total write-off and we're guaranteed to die in deep space. But if that Stiller Drive was manufactured by TuffTek, giving it a couple of good kicks in the guts once it's cooled down should do the trick." Her right eye opened again, panning around the room. Everything was a little blurry, even though the first aid station was only the size of a tiny bedroom. "Do you know where we are? An approximate sector location, or an ETA, maybe?"

Jimmy blinked a couple of times.

"Lana, I flip burgers. And I'm bad at it. You're asking the wrong guy."

"Where are the two lovebirds?" Lana yawned, enjoying the full-body sliding sensation of whatever feel good chem Jimmy had spiked her with.

Jimmy's expression darkened, but there was a tiny spark of humour behind it. "Ah. About that…"

*

In the space of a few words, Tuesday's search for something edible in the tiny kitchenette had swerved into what might become his imminent murder. He tried not to startle or look guilty at Trace's question, and just to top off his "everything is perfectly cool" act he continued rifling through the sticky cabinets for something to eat that wasn't older than Noah's birth certificate.

"It's a simple question," Trace growled, looming between Tuesday and the only way out of the strangle-tight coffee room. "So answer it: how did you propose to me?"

As the way Tuesday lived his life meant that a quick escape was necessary at least a couple of times a week, he'd become a master at slipping away from danger. Seeing as though it was highly likely Trace was going to literally kill him within the next minute, if not sooner, Tuesday employed the full range of his peripheral vision to look for options. His low rodent cunning relied on instinct rather than higher brain functions, but he'd need a few more seconds to lay the foundation of his dash from death. Unfortunately, Trace probably wasn't going to give him that long. The look in her eyes had BLUDGEON floating just beneath her pupils.

"Who can say?" Tuesday managed.

Shrugging nonchalantly, he instantly processed every possible weapon within reach. As this coffee room predated caffeine hypos, there were several odd glass bulbs, a dozen enamel mugs formed in an unbearably uncool shape and style, miscellaneous rusty spoons, bowls filled with an assortment of expired artificial sweeteners and a carton of milk so old that it was a wonder its jet-black contents hadn't figured out how to create stone tools yet. There was an ancient sticky label on the milk declaring "I'm sick of putting this away all the time. Learn to put it in the fridge yourselves, or let it rot for all I care – Nurbis."

Multiplying Trace's strength by her rising fury, Tuesday estimated there were at least fifty things within a metre that could end his life, and twice as many that would merely cripple him.

Trace's eyes narrowed. Blue veins pulsed on her temples.

"How could you possibly not remember how you proposed to me?" she snarled.

"Hey, you can't remember it either," Tuesday retorted.

Trace was mildly stunned by his logic. Her head tilted slightly.

"I've...forgotten other things, too," she confessed.

Tuesday was poised, waiting for Trace to drop her guard. The moment a small hole was available, he was going to dart under her hairy armpit and out the door like a whippet after a rabbit. His plan was to throw the beyond-rotten milk on the laminate as hard as possible mid-slide, hopefully causing a slick mess that Trace would slip in if she tried to pursue him. Tuesday always welcomed an unfair advantage.

"Hmm?" Tuesday ummed as calmly as possible.

Trace looked genuinely ashamed. Until this point, Tuesday had no idea her face could form an emotion that wasn't rage or contempt.

"I can't remember our wedding," she said gently. Depression touched her eyes, making them wet and mopey. "Any of it. What I wore, where it happened, what time of year it was...nothing."

"We got married in the Freaks & Legends Chapel in Old Vegas after attending an illegal Scumbags concert in the Nevada Desert," Tuesday said smoothly. "You were dressed as Bigfoot, and I was Cleopatra. Had a plastic asp attached to my wrist and everything."

Trace gave him an incredulous look. "That's how your parents got married."

Tuesday gaped, defeated for the slightest instant. It wasn't like him to share anything, let alone details from his nightmare of a childhood. He waved this away.

"Look, we just spent eight years bolted into cages with a bunch of cranial plugs feeding loops of spug into our brains," he snapped, trying to appear angry rather than terrified. As Trace was probably about to beat him to death with an enamel coffee mug, this took some effort, but it was far from the fullest extent of his scumming skills. "You can't expect to be able to just stroll down memory lane without so much as a..."

Trace raised a thick index finger in his face, flicking her eyes towards a cabinet full of crockery. She froze, though her pupils vibrated back and forth a few millimetres, as though reading something faint on her retinals. Tuesday was just about to skid between her legs and out the door when Trace relaxed, frustrated but on the preferable side of homicidal. She rubbed her face, resting her hulking body against a bone-dry sink.

"I just have to give it time," she rumbled, tired.

Tuesday tried not to show how relaxed he suddenly felt.

"Uh, sure. Put a pin in it for now."

Trace slowly lowered her hand from her face, wearing a quizzical expression. She examined her left ring finger, clearly confused by how it didn't have two bands of light-deprived skin, let alone a wedding ring and an engagement ring. She went to speak when a Weaver ticked into the room, raised its front legs and projected an image of Rem. The bristleworm's face was as inscrutable as always.

"I have a short window to talk. I'm sure you have hundreds of questions, and I will do my best to answer them."

A handy dumpster slid in from starboard, but it stopped dead fifty metres away just as all the corridor's lights flickered in random patterns. This brief epilepsy trigger was joined by the loud snap of a few ancient bulbs popping for good. The image of Rem clicked a stream of curses in Low-Dren before eventually spelling out the situation.

"Tracks will be down for a while. Follow the Weavers. I'm not far."

CHAPTER EIGHT

It was clear Rem's definition of "not far" had lost something substantial in translation.

Following the gently-ticking Weavers, the four of them met up at the closest intersection to proceed on foot. As always, the ship was a monotonous dark purple labyrinth that sucked at the soul and dulled the senses. Every now and again the Weavers would make a sharp turn and wait patiently for the bipeds to keep up, but it would only turn out to be yet another metal row of hallways. It was infuriating.

Ten minutes into their trudge, Trace stopped at a wall seemingly at random.

Ignoring the Weaver as it trilled at her in annoyance for not following closely enough, she squinted at an odd blue lump the size of a disposable lighter jammed between two segments. It was held in place by some kind of putty. She glared at Lana.

"You're Navy trained, right?" she snapped. "What's that look like to you?"

"I'm just a Cadet," Lana clarified.

"Who single-handedly fixed a Stiller Drive," Trace barked, somehow using this achievement as an insult. "Just look at something for me, would you?"

Lana drifted over. Squinting hard enough to prove she was overdue for more corrective eye surgery, Lana took a deep whiff of the blob. Her eyelids snapped open as wide as they could go and she staggered away from the blue item so quickly that she almost tripped. Trace turned sharply at Lana's passing, mouth opening to demand answers, but Lana put a finger over her lips and waved for everyone to urgently move away from whatever had alarmed her. Trace complied, though she was suitably grumpy about it.

"So it is an explosive, then," Trace noted.

Lana nodded. "It's a stick of some sort of refined chemical gel, probably the sort used for starship demolition. There's enough of it to cut through the graphene hull like it wasn't even there."

Jimmy was about to share his earlier ScuttleCo find, but he was interrupted by a loud swear word from Tuesday.

"Trump it, there's another one over here." On a whim, Tuesday took a couple of steps and swept the toe of his frogstomper boot across the floor's laminate, digging at its seam a little. He exhaled shakily. "And a little one there, too."

"Has the bug wired up this whole corridor with bombs?" Trace growled.

Lana's eyes darted about, and she chewed her lip. She finally glanced at the very annoyed Weaver, which was hopping mad for being ignored.

"No," she eventually said, "I'm pretty sure he's been a lot more thorough than that. My guess is he's rigged the entire ship to explode. The Dirty Betty is one big minefield."

*

Thankfully they were already most of the way to their destination. This long ramble had already triggered acute flashbacks of their death march across the ruined world that bloody Tuesday had managed to permanently register in The

Unison's stellar directory as Scrote, so if Rem was expecting to get anyone onside by forcing them to do a half-marathon, he was going to be disappointed. The bristleworm may have rescued them from an eternity of limb lopping and brain looping, but like all Humans throughout history, the survivors had a short memory for favours and a long, indelible list for grudges.

It was a bit of an anticlimax to end up in a corridor like any other. Except for the Weaver turning as still as the grave there was no other way for them to know this was their destination, or how they were meant to get back to where they'd started this particular trek, let alone how to get back to their allocated bedrooms. However, there was an extra-large bulkhead on the starboard wall, a hatch thick enough to resist all but the most dedicated of assaults. Aware that their host seemed to have a predilection for booby traps, the humans carefully assessed every inch of the corridor, taking short, careful steps just in case.

"I can't believe it," Lana eventually said.

To say the place was wired was an understatement. After losing track a couple of times, Lana had been forced to unfurl her Scroll to help with the count. This stretch of grid work was utterly riddled with bombs placed so artfully that as a collective they verged on being a masterpiece. Pinhead laser tripwires, pressure sensors and infrared scanners crisscrossed every surface, leaving zero margin for error. Each of the dainty explosives were packed with sharp rods made from hair-fine Densite rods hard enough and sharp enough to cut through armour plating as easily as a steak knife through an eye fillet done blue. Thanks to what must be some form of mild Artificial Intelligence, the Densite rods angled themselves towards the humans, locking onto the worse possible places they could penetrate. Both Tuesday and Jimmy cupped their privates, even though their hands wouldn't so much as slow the spikes down. As they weren't all dead already, the bombs clearly weren't set to active at the moment.

But there was more. Thin rubber bladders the capacity of Flog balls had been placed at precise intervals along the graphene, shells swirling with neon-lime gas. Lana tried to make an educated guess.

"Some sort of reactive acid?" she hazarded.

Glancing at the others, confused by their expressions, Lana followed their line of sight to the Scroll in her left hand. Almost slapping herself for being dense as a limestone pillow, she held up the millimetre-thin screen to one of the balls. Her eyes darted back and forth across the display for a few seconds, and she took a long, slow step backwards.

"Closest match is fluoroantimonic acid," she said quietly, not even game to raise her voice. "A super acid literally a quintillion times more corrosive than any other substance in the known galaxy. And it's reactive to almost everything. Exposing a single drop of it to this oxygen-rich environment would turn everything within a hundred metres to broth in an instant. Just the moisture in our breath would be enough to immediately…"

"So stay away from it," Trace growled, not a fan of hyperbole.

Lana paused for a moment with her mouth open. She shut it again.

"Yes."

A loud clunk sounded deep within the armoured mechanism of the starboard bulkhead, and dust rained from the ceiling panels as the door opened a crack. Cringing, expecting booby traps to unleash death from a hundred angles, the humans were a little surprised when they weren't spiked, blown up and dissolved in a cloud of super acid mist. As the dust literally settled, though, the Weaver waved one of its spindly legs for them to follow, and ticked away into a hatch large enough for a couple of PusCo dumpsters to slide triple-file. A stench of burnt plastic wafted out like synthetic flatulence.

They stepped into a knee-deep pile of cables tangled up worse than an industrial-sized box of last year's Christmas lights. Some of the ribbed cords were sizzling, stinking up the place with melting insulation. Although they appeared to be alone in this nest, Rem's black ribbon of a body snaked out from the depths, trailing half a dozen cords deliberately wedged in the ridges of his carapace. Holding his holographic OS between distended jaws, he spun the monochrome balls repeatedly as though double-checking something.

"Is this a bad time?" Trace growled.

The bristleworm raised a single antennae as though it was an index finger, and finished plugging the cables together. Silent and frozen in place for a long count of three, a gentle hum ran through every wire in the room like they were sitting in the grumbling belly of a peckish beast. Rem relaxed so hard it was a wonder he didn't sprain something.

"Hey," Rem finally said in greeting, flicking a mandible so the OS vanished into his starburst collar with a comical zip noise. "I'd offer you a drink or a bite to eat, but all our supplies are hidden behind scanner-proof shielding. It'll take a couple of hours to cut it out."

The room's hum got a little louder, but not dangerously so.

"Why'd you seal it all away?" Jimmy asked, confused and hungry in equal measure.

Rem settled on top of a wire pile. Despite how bumpy and sharp the small hill was, his wriggly body seemed comfortable.

"Had to flush every drop and crumb before I hit your system, didn't I?" Rem shrugged without shoulders. "This garbage barge had to look like a useless, worthless, stripped hulk drifting aimlessly through space. Any signs of habitation or supplies would invite inspection from the Slidge, and that would mean failing my mission hard. I lost count of how many times I had to play dead on the way in." Rem resumed stretching, his insectoid joints popping violently. "Anyway, welcome to the Bridge. The Dirty Betty was designed to be flown by a crew of nine, but I've finished switching just about everything to automated settings and bypassed whatever was left. Now, not only does she virtually fly herself, I can control most of her basic functions remotely."

"What did you bypass?" Lana asked, feeling a pit of dread as she surveyed the mountain of sparking, smelly cables.

"A bunch of non-essential systems," Rem shrugged again. "Don't worry, I just streamlined things a little."

Lana ran an index finger along her Scroll's casing. "So what kind of hardware do you need to fly this thing remotely, exactly?"

Rem regarded Lana's computer, hearing her real question.

"I'll think about it," he said simply.

Jimmy flinched a little as a ceiling glow plate loudly decided it had reached the end of its operational life.

"Isn't the Bridge meant to be up top?" he asked, relying on his sense of direction without much faith. "We're buried pretty deep here, right?"

Rem made a dismissive motion.

"Only an idiot would leave their Bridge hanging out for anyone to snipe. The more important the section, the better you protect it, right? You'd need to punch through the better part of fifty metres of graphene to get this far. Anything manages to get that deep, we've picked a losing battle, yeah?"

"You said there'd be answers," Trace reminded the Drennite, her tone ominous.

Rem nodded. "I did at that. Well, we're relatively safe for now, and my brief didn't say anything about keeping you in the dark about facts I already know. I might be a bug, but I've barely spoken a word to anyone in a fortnight, and my brain doesn't like it. Shoot."

"Who hired you?" Tuesday asked.

Rem shrugged. "No idea. Anonymous post on MercNet. It's a legit job, that's all I know."

"Do you know what species your clients are, at least?" Lana asked. "Were they Human?"

Rem scoffed. "Hope not. The extinct don't tend to pay all that well." Rem examined his guests for a few seconds, sensing his quip wasn't appreciated. "That would be a no. Honestly, until I took this job, I thought you lot were gone for good. You lot are the first Humans I've met in person."

"Where are you taking us?" Trace demanded.

Rem gave a kind of "eh" gesture.

"This boat's astrogation system had two pre-set destinations wired into it: Erf, and where I'm meant to take you after recovery. The ship can get itself to where it's meant to go, but there's no way for me to see the exact coordinates. Job's secrecy was rated paramount, boosting the currency bonus up like you wouldn't believe."

"Why would some alien want us?" Lana wondered.

"Exotic pets, perhaps?" Rem hazarded. His eyes darkened. "Hopefully not to eat. Personally, I don't consume any creature capable of doing algebra. Firm moral stance of mine. Not all beings out there share my sentiments, however."

Tuesday raised a finger.

"So you don't know who hired you, or why, or where we're going?" he clarified. A gross sigh wafted between Tuesday's black teeth like a deadly gas leak in a sewage treatment plant. "Glad you're finally keeping us in the loop."

"Then what can you tell us?" Lana pressed. "Surely you know something useful?"

Rem's eyestalks darted back and forth in a conspiratorial way, and he leaned forwards a bit.

"Like where did all the Humans go?"

This got their attention. The four of them exchanged glances, nods and slight expressions. Finally, Lana spoke on behalf of the group.

"Do you know?"

"Nah." His mandibles aligned in what might possibly be a Drennite grin. Rem curled closer to his guests and said his next words very, very quietly. "But like everyone in the galaxy, I know when they left."

"When?" Jimmy asked shortly, clearly tired of being led in stupid little circles.

Rem shrugged. "Why, during The Gap, of course."

"Are we supposed to know what that is?" Trace growled, flexing her fingers violently as she fought the urge to reach for the loaded kinetic accelerator hidden down her cleavage holster.

Rem was incredulous.

"You aren't serious?" he snapped. "It's only the third biggest mystery in the galaxy! People have been sharing conspiracy theories about it for decades. Still prime gossip to this day." Rem twisted up a little in annoyance. "To be honest, I was kind of hoping you might be able to prove or disprove a couple of rumours. Pity."

"But what is it?" Lana snapped, her patience grinding down towards empty. "What's The Gap, and what does it have to do with Mankind vanishing?"

Rem began to excavate some kind of yellow putty out of one of his audio canals without a hint of shame. He shrugged and flicked the greasy wad from the end of his antennae.

"You might want to take a seat."

CHAPTER NINE

To a Human in the 29th Century, even the brightest golden years of the boot-to-the-groin regime known as The Unison were an incomprehensible darkness splattered across history's pages. It had been a disgusting political crudity, a horrific machine gummed up solid with the flesh of billions of citizens crushed to pulp.

The Unison may have paved Humanity's star-spanning empire in blood, but with time and effort Mankind achieved hitherto unreached heights of philosophical and moral connection with the Universe, and the old ways gradually softened. Mankind came ever closer to hitting an apex of understanding, gaining a level of self-awareness that had only been a dream since the dawn of their species, and The Unison's focus shifted away from aggressive expansion and maximising productivity. Instead of devoting most of their energy to preventing the peons from realising they were all little more than disposable cogs, The Unison evolved into a galaxy-wide brotherhood even the most fervent Utopian would have scoffed at.

But this Perfection came at the greatest of costs.

Permanently fixing Mankind meant having to rid the species of its base, destructive natures, and that required extensive psychological alteration, neurological enhancements and hypnotic imprinting for every citizen, among many other dark techniques. This population-wide process was known as The Perfection, and it actually started gently in the 24th Century without anyone noticing. Tiny adjustments were made to the vaccines being constantly rolled out galaxy-wide, secretly calming and improving and uplifting the average person in a number of ways. Each year, the upgrades became more overt, more invasive, until the wholesale conversion of the species proved itself to be far from a sanitised process. Monstrous sacrifices were demanded in the name of the greater good, and no nightmare was deemed too horrific, too far to go, for this aim. Dark deeds were required for The Unison to forcefully rewire the natural settings of a trillion Humans – most of them against their will - but one world at a time Humanity was saved from itself.

This final peace demanded incalculable losses, but it proved to be just that: a final peace. In order to purchase Heaven, Mankind gladly paid with Hell.

Although impossible to comprehend in any other era, once The Perfection replaced the violence and horror of The Unison, ending a regime bloodier than any other in Human history, the suffering truly stopped. Urges that had plagued Mankind since Cain first sharpened up a donkey jaw were simply gone, and reaching a state of political, religious, cultural and financial unification became a reality. Soon, The Perfection were celebrating a hundred years without a single murder on any of their worlds. They didn't bother celebrating this milestone a second time, as by that point the concept of intentionally taking the life of another sentient being was word salad. "Homicide" atrophied from their lexicon.

Progress hadn't ceased, of course. Even though The Perfect knew the urge to expand to new worlds was simply the result of their mammalian sex drives compelling them to go as far as possible in order to find suitable breeding partners who were less likely to be genetically related, Man's wanderings continued until they touched the very rim of the galaxy. As they truly understood the value of conservation, The Perfect didn't inflict any lasting impact anywhere they stepped. Besides the Information Super Skyway known as the Link expanding its coverage to every new system The Perfect visited, you could barely tell they'd stopped by.

Human tech moved beyond the conventional definition of science and well into the realm of what could only be described as magic. Assisted by trustworthy AI helpers, The Perfection's technological advancements snowballed into constant breakthroughs in fields that were barely discovered and named before they'd been mastered. Although reluctant to share their advances with races who they considered unready for the next step, Mankind flaunted their godlike technology in the most impressive of ways: they didn't use it.

Although much younger than many Milky Way races, Mankind's sacrifices were greatly respected and admired by those who didn't have the stones to go all the way like they had. Instead of using their incredibly advanced minds to conquer and occupy and wheel and deal, though, The Perfect soon came to be known as peacemakers, as philosophers, as debaters of the highest order, altruistic freelance advocates who worked for the good of others rather than personal gain. The Perfect turned their attention to higher pursuits.

Without a wisp of their mammalian drives remaining, The Perfect had finished evolving into something more than chemically-triggered meat. In addition to erasing their urge to uncontrollably spawn like smallpox wherever they went, they maintained an environmental equilibrium. When coupled with their long, long lifespans, it was common for Mankind's population to stay at almost total stasis. As they'd finally earned a reputation of playing nicely with others, The Perfect were welcome pretty much anywhere. Of course, other beings coveted what The Perfect had, especially the wonders that could only loosely be described as science, so this helped with their urge to roll out the red carpet. Thankfully, though, Mankind knew better than to give handguns to primates.

Though it usually took about a million years of civilisation, it was clearly only a matter of time before The Perfect took the final step towards becoming Transcended, reaching the point where their minds no longer required the occupation of decaying flesh casings and moving on to a higher form of existence. But then towards the final years of the 29th Century, just when it seemed The Perfect couldn't improve in any conceivable way, an event later defined as "The Gap" in a million alien languages took place.

To phrase it simply, The Gap was a mysterious forty-eight month span of blackest amnesia that affected the memory of every sentient being in the Known Universe. Curiously, every computer file, diary page and calendar – any scrap of data that could provide some clue as to what had happened in those four years - had also been wiped just as clean. The galaxy was understandably churned into countless flavours of confusion when people woke up to the cries of offspring they couldn't remember producing, lying next to spouses they'd never met. Others found themselves sealed in maximum security cells, locked up for crimes they couldn't recall committing against victims they'd never heard of. Some were charging across battlefields, aiming loaded weapons at unknown beings from unknown planets, fighting and dying for an unknown cause. Many didn't even get this much, disappearing without a trace no matter how hard their families and loved ones looked. If the lost were lucky, there might be a tombstone somewhere, marked with a name and little else. Of course, not knowing what (or who) had caused The Gap lead to widespread fear, and blame was liberally assigned in all directions.

While a lot of individuals didn't live to see the far side of The Gap, only one race had vanished entirely: The Perfection. Not only had they dissipated down to the last citizen, but someone had made a concerted effort to wipe their entire history from the face of the galaxy. Their cities and miraculous stellar constructs were vaporised, their endless fleets were gone, and even the galaxy-wide Link that contained all their gathered wisdom and knowledge was scoured clean. You might find bones here and there, perhaps a few scraps of technology that had avoided the fate that had befallen its makers, but the simple fact was that The Perfect were history.

Nobody knew how or why. And they probably never would.

*

Rem trailed off, but the Humans continued to study the Drennite silently, waiting for him to finish the story. He eventually cleared both his throats as punctuation when they didn't get the hint.

"So yeah, they're gone," he summarised. "Along with almost all trace of their civilisation. This piece of crap might actually be worth something to the right buyer. Yes, she's older than your Second Renaissance, but..."

"So where did they go?" Lana asked.

Rem's words came to a halt. His eye stalks bobbed.

"Weren't you listening? The Perfect disappeared mysteriously, as in an unknown fashion, as in I don't know. It's a guessing game at best. And I don't like guessing."

"Uh," Jimmy ummed, "I had a question..."

Rem nodded. As Jimmy's anxiety could rise even quicker than his confidence could plunge, it often took him time to muster the ability to be confrontational. It took him eight seconds in this instance, which was about average.

"Isn't it a little dangerous to booby trap the entire ship? Not that I'm an elite wet-work operative or anything, but aren't you at least a little bit nervous about tripping over a demolition charge and face planting into a super acid bomb?"

Rem hitched his spinal ridges a little.

"Okay, I've got to admit, The Dirty Betty kind of came like that," the bristleworm confessed. "I'm not her first owner, obviously, and as best I understand it she used to be crewed by prisoners. A lifetime of waste management isn't everyone's dream, so precautions were taken to prevent mutiny or whatever. To be honest, I try not to think about it. You should do the same."

The bristleworm twitched as his starburst collar hummed a little tune. He angled an eye stalk at it.

"Right, seems the Stiller Drive is cooled down and ready to go. Once we're underway, we can move on to the next item on the list." Rem angled his mandibles in what might be a smile. "I don't know about you, but blowing up Erf really gave me an appetite. We eat in two hours."

*

Thankfully, when The Dirty Betty's Stiller Drive screamed to life it didn't indicate an imminent thermonuclear meltdown. There were no grinding noises or ship wide quakes, but some gentle tremors here and there were nothing out of the ordinary for a piece of TuffTek rubbish.

As designed, the Stiller Drive brought their ship to total stasis so the galaxy could speed past, then after shifting a star system or two it would pick an exact moment to match speed with the Milky Way again. To call this method of moving "circular" was an understatement, and it wasn't unusual to end up fifty star systems away early in your trip before eventually arriving at a destination far closer to your point of origin. As this process was automated, it wouldn't take any conscious intervention to reach their destination…wherever that may be.

That didn't mean Rem had nothing to do. Hustling the Humans out of his wired-up Bridge and back in the booby-trapped hallway, the bristleworm jabbed an eye stalk at the next corridor.

"Go play. I'll give you a call once I've got everything here sorted and excavated the food," Rem promised.

The Humans glanced at each other. Something they could all agree on was that this starship wasn't exactly an amusement park. Its bland purple corridors were about as exciting as an abandoned prison in the middle of an extensive renovation.

"Play how, exactly?" Lana asked.

Rem thought about this for a moment, then dug into one of the bags strapped across his three-metre-long body with a facial protuberance.

"I may not be an expert with what passes as recreation for Humans, but I was sure to bring this."

Rem produced a red nylon ball. Waving it back and forth in front of Trace's unimpressed face, Rem's voice took on a manic edge.

"You want the ball? You want the ball? Get the ball!"

Rem flicked the sphere and it bounced off grid work and pipes and ceramic panels until disappearing around the corner. To Rem's surprise, Trace's gaze hadn't shifted a single centimetre, though there was darkness brewing under her skin. She leaned forwards very slightly and gave a soft warning.

"Don't ever do that again."

Rem looked back and forth from face to face. He cringed a little in embarrassment.

"Ah. It appears I've been misinformed..."

"Look, this is a Human ship," Lana asserted. "Do you know if there are any dedicated recreation areas? Gaming rooms, caffeine shooting galleries, Wacky World cortical shunt booths, that sort of thing?"

Rem shrugged. "The Dirty Betty was stripped by scavengers five or six times before I inherited her, but I'm sure there must be something left behind that the scrappers couldn't carry. Just follow the signs, or use the AutoMap for a ship wide search if you get turned about."

Tuesday blinked at the blank walls, following Rem's antennae.

"What signs? What AutoMap?"

"Those signs right there," Rem hinted, gesturing as though speaking with the thickest of thickies. "You're seriously telling me you can't see any of that?"

Four heads shook in a wordless negative. The bristleworm slapped himself hard enough to be classed as self-punishment.

"Dang it, I knew I forgot something! Are your retinal screens code-locked or password protected or anything like that?"

Everyone looked at Lana. She shook her head semi-cautiously.

"Pretty sure we all have civilian retinals with basic hack deflection. None of us are ranking military or political personnel or anything, so..."

Rem was already furiously attacking his holographic OS before Lana trailed off, diving into the guts of a shifting sphere made from black-and-white segments. In a matter of seconds he'd finished with a flourish, but the humans were too busy screaming to thank him. Layers and layers of blinding holographics had suddenly replaced the purple, and the grid of bare composite was now writhing and popping and swooping with hundreds of animations covering everything they could see. There were advertisements for holiday destinations like alien zoos, virtual reality fun parks and the occasional solar resort built on the coolest of sunspots, promotions for a thousand different consumer products, and a variety of insurance and superannuation plans specifically tailored towards the kind of people who spent their careers working on PusCo medical waste processing ships as indentured servants.

It was all too much. The colours were cornea-searing and the sounds deafening, and the mess of sensory overload stabbed them right in their brainpans. Their tiny retinal screens overheated straight away, creating a white-hot burning sensation at the back of their eyeballs. Thankfully, Rem dialled down the chaos down to about one tenth, making the holograms loud and garish but bearable. He stashed his OS once everyone stopped yelling, nodding at a job well done.

"Seems your senses are a lot more delicate than mine," the bristleworm said dismissively. "Go find something to keep busy. Long as you don't kill yourselves in the process, I really don't care what it entails."

Without another word, Rem slithered back into the Bridge and sealed its bulkhead.

Feeling a little lost, the humans tried digging through the thick holographic mess for something worthwhile, but the advertisements kept on churning like white-water rapids made of light and colour. Worse yet, somehow the ads had recognised each of them, and started vomiting up personalised products and services. Tuesday was offered a bulk-buy special on extra-strength chlorine-flavoured Musty Yak cigarettes, Lana was informed about a type of hairspray that lasted a lifetime with one application, and then dozens and dozens of Jimmy's favourite Ultrasweet-infused confectionary treats danced by, their colourful wrappers so bright and gaudy that it hurt to look directly at them. Of course, as all these products had been banned and their manufacturers shut down once Mankind rose above such frivolity, the ads were as useless as they were annoying.

Trace, however, wasn't offered any consumer items, and was merely informed that there were eighteen different warrants out for her arrest in four star systems. Several affordable defence lawyers who specialised in multiple unprovoked acts of grievous assault and attempted murder were suggested, and Trace was politely asked to stay put while security was summoned to arrest her.

Jimmy, Lana and Jimmy looked sideways at Trace. Her eyes flicked in their direction in boredom, her pupils like chips of granite. They all looked away.

Physically digging through the ads with her fingers, Lana swept the holograms aside as though doing breaststroke. Finally, after tearing through six different layers, a square icon the size of a STOP sign appeared, embossed with the

PusCo logo. A flashing red icon with "Delete Spam?" appeared at its core, and Lana whacked it with her palm. Mercifully, the ads vanished.

A spectral white hologram crawled up the armoured bulkhead, redundantly spelling out that this huge door led to the Bridge. Other ghostly holograms crawled along like snails on crystal methamphetamine, declaring what you could find in the next few corridors. Funnily enough, nobody was all that interested in visiting the Stationery Supply Cupboard, the Paperwork Hardcopy Storage Area or the PusCo Hard Suit Dry-Cleaning Laundrette, so they'd need to look further if they wanted something more interesting.

"AutoMap?" Lana asked the ceiling a little hesitantly.

A large beige hologram labelled AutoMap loomed up from the grid work floor, bobbing eagerly. Reaching out, carefully tapping away at a three-dimensional representation of The Dirty Betty, it didn't take long for Lana to find their current location. After swiping up and down the closest loops of this insane spiral, she eventually found something a little more interesting than the closest PusCo Chemical Sterilisation Shower.

Lana cleared her throat.

"Looting, anyone?"

*

Although Rem told them that only nine crew members were needed to fly The Dirty Betty, the locker room proved this tub had once been home to many, many others. Opposing crimson walls of steel cabinets followed a central U-shaped bench in a tight half-loop, and every one of the peeling chambers were sealed with combination locks and thick latches.

Well, they had been sealed.

"Nothing again," Tuesday moaned.

Throwing himself on the laminate floor of the locker room like a petulant child, his face half-collapsed in frustration, Tuesday slammed his jet-black crowbar against a busted-open metal cabinet so hard that it rang like a phone. Thudding the back of his head against one of the fifteen steel cabinets he had managed to pop in the last half hour, the fact everyone was ignoring him only added to his irritation.

"I'm done," Tuesday clarified needlessly, rubbing at the AllTool bracelet on his wrist. "There's nothing here. Anything edible would have moulded into spores, and anything useful is long gone. It's a damned waste of time. Nobody is dumb enough to leave anything good in something this weak."

The others ignored his temper tantrum, continuing to pry open one locker after another.

"You know," Lana grunted as punctuation, snipping a combination lock off its latch with a pair of black, heavy-duty bolt cutters, "if you stop working now, you don't get a share of whatever we find."

"Yeah, because one quarter of spug all is a real loss," Tuesday sniped, producing a chlorine-flavoured cigarette. Trace gave him a murderous look as the suck-burner ignited, but Tuesday shrugged in dismissal. "What? There was only one Erf to blow up. Punch it."

Jimmy slipped, cussing as he almost broke his finger between his crowbar and the locker. He blew on his knuckles ineffectively. Resting against the beaten metal for a second, Jimmy glanced towards their starting point, scanning over the hundred empty cabinets they'd left in their wake.

"He's got a point," Jimmy grudgingly admitted.

"Don't encourage him," Lana complained.

"I agree with them," Trace growled. She swiped at the AllTool bracelet around her wrist, and her simulated bolt cutters glitched out and vanished into the ether. She didn't allow Lana a chance to object. "I know we've got to figure out our supply situation, but needlessly burning calories won't help us."

"Like I said, we should just wait for Rem to feed us," Jimmy repeated for what must have been the fifteenth time.

Lana scoffed. "Yeah, let's just place our futures in the hands…in the facial tentacles of someone who hasn't given us a single clear answer this whole time. You honestly believe he doesn't know anything? Doesn't know who hired him, or where he's bringing us, or why his client wants us…"

"He knows more than he makes out," Trace growled. "I don't trust the bug."

"Racist," Jimmy muttered, but not loud enough for Trace to hear.

Everyone was distracted by Tuesday springing into a sprint, doing a commando roll across the locker room tiles and scooping up something. Baring his chipped black teeth at their surprised expressions, he hissed a word with far too much spittle.

"Mine!"

After some frenzied chewing he swallowed whatever it was he'd caught. Breathing heavily, psyched up, Tuesday's expression slowly transitioned from hungry animal to ashamed person. Despite knowing Tuesday the longest, even Jimmy was surprised by this sight.

"The Styx was that?" he managed.

Tuesday slowly drew himself up to a slouch. His scowl didn't reveal much.

"Instinct," he muttered, clearly not comfortable with this line of questioning. "Thinking's not always your best option when your belly's empty."

Tuesday removed a spindly insect limb from his gum line and flicked it away. He clearly didn't have anything else to add.

"That's interesting," Lana said out loud, sitting on her haunches with the Scroll right in front of her face.

"You being rhetorical, or should we care?" Trace ground out, slamming heavily onto one of the long benches running down the middle of the locker room. Its rusted bolts squeaked in protest.

Lana's eyes darted over the hair-fine screen of the unrolling computer. She twitched her nose as she scanned line after line of text.

"Turns out this Scroll has quite a bit of access. Its former owner must have been a ranking officer...or a prolific thief. But a lot of its contents are locked behind some ancient bastardised code derived from encrypted Kanji Emoji, so my retinals are having trouble translating it..."

"Losing interest," Trace warned.

Lana flipped the Scroll over, showing the others what she was looking at.

"See that? Pretty sure this icon translates to Stocktake."

The others suddenly seemed a lot more interested.

*

"You aren't serious?" Tuesday asked in exasperation.

They stood next to a sweeping interior window that gave a clear view of the kilometre-long glass cylinder resting at the core of The Dirty Betty. The enormous multi-coloured storage tube was just as bright and garish as ever.

"Are you sure there's nothing else listed under Stocktake?" Jimmy asked for what the sixth time. "After all, Rem's supplies are sealed behind..."

"Scanner-proof plating, yes, I know," Lana finished, her patience with Jimmy's repetition reaching its final frayed thread. She stuck her finger so close to his nose that it almost went into his nostril. "But even if there were some scanner-proof hidey holes somewhere on board, I'd have no way of finding them. For one, you wouldn't list hidden, possibly illicit goods in an official Stocktake spreadsheet on a Scroll with no password so any berk could just stumble over your treasure. And two, while I admit that this computer is a type of scanner, I must stress once again that scanner proof hidey-holes are, by their very definition, scanner-proof, meaning they are undetectable by scanners. Is this making sense to you yet, or should I say it again?"

"Keep working," Trace ordered, not noticing the severity of Lana's eye tic. "We need to know everything that's stored in there."

Lana took a deep, calming breath, glanced at the klick of rainbow-hued medical waste, then back at the Scroll. She continued reciting the list like a machine.

"Nine million used tampons, six thousand tonnes of hypodermic syringes (blue), eight thousand tonnes of hypodermic syringes (green), six hundred and forty-three kilometres of soiled bandages (yellow), five thousand contaminated hospital mattresses, half a million extracted Human teeth (assorted), one thousand pieces of blunted surgical equipment (various), one damaged self-guiding AutoDoc surgical drone..."

"That might be useful," Jimmy interrupted.

"...that's been branded as homicidally defective after performing a spate of unrequested genital surgeries." Lana continued, barely pausing. "Eight pairs of synthetic dog testicles, ten million Human bones (assorted), one hundred thousand processed urine drug-screen samples, three kilometres of ingrown toenail clippings, half a million separately-bagged parasites (various, all Human compatible), fifty-three chewed-off Human noses recovered from the trophy room of serial killer Prince Charming..."

Jimmy clumsily dashed away from the window, hands over his mouth, and threw up. Trace grudgingly passed a crumpled Amerikan pound to Tuesday.

"Knew he'd crack first."

CHAPTER TEN

While they barely made a dent in the endless corridors, lift shafts, conveniently person-sized air vents and mechanical lines, after another hour of exploring (and a fair degree of crowbarring and bolt cutting) the humans officially became bored of trying to find anything worth ripping off.

The Dirty Betty had clearly been stripped down to the marrow, and the occasional cluster of bullet holes or molten scarring indicated the scrappers may have had a difference of opinion when it came to how they were splitting the profits. There weren't any bodies, though, hinting they may have come to some sort of financial equilibrium before going beyond the point of no return, but this could just as easily mean the losers ended up as saleable protein in a less-than-picky organ market somewhere.

As they couldn't honestly consider themselves as anything more than forced acquaintances at best, the prospect of remaining in proximity with each other for no real reason proved to be an unpopular one. The four of them had nothing in common except for their species (with Tuesday's genetic heritage pushing the envelope in that regard) and it didn't take long to realise there was nothing to be gained by sharing the same room. Knowing they might have weeks and weeks until their destination, they unanimously decided to split up and do their own thing unless there was some actual reason to meet. With full access to the ship's AutoMap and detailed holographic street signs on every corner, it wouldn't take much effort to catch a dumpster to wherever they needed to go. In an emergency, the furthest reaches of The Dirty Betty were only minutes away.

Bored, Lana casually wandered along the upmost level of the PusCo vessel's spiral-shaped superstructure, trying to find an ideal vantage point to watch the stars dance past. She wondered what it must have been like back when The Dirty Betty had to spin to generate gravity, imagining how it would make your stomach lurch as the star field rotated outside at a dizzying speed. She tried to imagine what it would be like to spin while the Stiller Drive was running, and whether the stars would all curve into long, white slashes. She couldn't picture anything more vomit-inducing.

Every now and again the Stiller Drive would turn off, and Lana would sit in peace as the ship matched the Milky Way's motion for a few minutes until it was due to come to another complete stop. Hopping through space like this was inefficient, as they were travelling in a dense whirl rather than a straight line, but the safety of Stiller Drives made up for its slowness.

Finding the best bay window she could, Lana crunched herself into its rubber corner and drew up the knees of her ebony Naval Cadet trousers. Wrapping her hands around her shins, she startled at the unfamiliar angles. It was easy to forget her body had continued to grow and blossom during the years she'd spent caged in a VR purgatory. Lana had suddenly found herself cast into her mid-twenties, and everything felt wrong. She imagined this is what it would feel like to suffer from gigantism, to realise that bits of you were the wrong shape and texture and orientation, walking around in a stranger's body. Privately, she wasn't complaining about increasing several bra cups, as it guaranteed she'd never be insulted with the term "late bloomer" ever again.

Lana tugged at her form-fitting uniform. In addition to being self-cleaning, self-ironing and self-drying, she was glad that her Cadet blacks and shiny shoes had adjusted to her new shape. Last thing she needed was having to walk around like she was riding an invisible horse.

The Stiller Drive conked out again with a ship wide tremble and a sad sort of wah-wah noise. Lana had unintentionally been counting the transitions for the first hour and a half, and had to make a conscious decision to stop. This took quite an effort, proving that her nervous habit of counting everything hadn't gone away during her time on ice.

Clenching her eyes closed as the Stiller Drive kicked in again, sending the galaxy spiralling into madness, Lana spent a few seconds pinching her nose. While this mannerism never actually helped her, it did indicate to others that she was close to some sort of minor mental breakdown, warning them to keep their distance. Reality loomed at the periphery of Lana's thoughts, triggering emotions she didn't like to acknowledge. While the basic psychology package she used to have installed in her Omni implant would encourage her to face her feelings and fears head on, she was certain that stuttering along on a mandatory trip to a mystery location on a rust-heap full of contaminated syringes in a Human-free galaxy definitely had some kind of lining, but it sure as Tartarus wasn't silver.

Opening one eye, being sure not to train it on the million white streaks outside the bay window, Lana regarded the rolled-up chopstick-sized Miyamoto-Kojima computer peeking out of her front pocket. The Dirty Betty might have been stripped down to bare metal and beyond, but who knows what treasures the Scroll contained? She would have checked to see if the Scroll contained any video games, but as the Beyond console from Miyamoto-Kojima had accidentally turned a third of its gamers into serial killers in the early 22nd Century, she was a little reluctant to take the risk. The last thing this crew needed was a psychotic Lana continuing the infamous Mushroom Kingdom Massacres.

Lana squinted in thought. If she recalled, the Beyond had used a cortical shunt, while this Scroll was a basic haptic device. Unless its screen incorporated some sort of secret cerebral branding technology, there shouldn't be any conceivable way for it to scramble her brain. She was just being paranoid.

Unfurling the Scroll, Lana automatically swiped at the Link function. Cursing her habits, the standard LINK CONTENT NOT FOUND popped up in red lettering, driving home the fact that the gathered knowledge and wisdom of her species had been wiped from the face of reality. Just when she thought she was at her lowest, Lana managed to kick herself in the guts yet again.

Lana casually flicked through the basic operational abilities of the Scroll, and could only shake her head at the fact this thing had been left lying around in a broken locker without being restrained by so much as a "1234" password. She was staggered at the sloppiness, and could only imagine what her commanders at the Academy would have done to her if she'd left so much as her personal locker unprotected, let alone an entire starship.

She reclined a little, watching a thumbnail-sized cockroach dash between two holes rusted into the window's housing. From what she'd seen so far, anyone unlucky enough to be a worker on a giant PusCo sharps bin would have to be rated about ten metres below the bottom of the barrel. This was the kind of posting you'd use as a threat to keep your employees in line, a stick you could draw back to remind your crew that their careers could always, always get worse. It was the sort of workplace you'd send people like Tuesday.

After twenty minutes of swiping, tapping and cursing, Lana rolled up her Scroll and slid it away. Ninety percent of its functions dealt with systems and equipment that were either no longer operational or no longer on board, and as she didn't feel the need to adjust the humidity of the hypodermic syringe autoclaves or change the AutoMap language into Tagalog-2, the Scroll didn't have much to offer. Not only were there no games or entertainment functions installed, but there was no way to add any new apps. The Scroll was locked tight.

She tried to watch the stars, but gave up after five minutes of mounting nausea. Leaning the back of her head against rubber caulking, closing her eyes, Lana consoled herself with the knowledge that at least she could finally be alone.

One of her eyes snapped open at a worrying thought. Sighing, almost positive she was being paranoid, Lana opened the Scroll and took a quick look at registration information of The Dirty Betty. As expected, she was built for PusCo by TuffTek, had been granted an unlimited licence from The Unison to collect and process Human medical waste from six different worlds, possessed no offensive or defensive systems of any kind, and was currently rated as a D7.

Lana blinked at the last part. The Dirty Betty was a D7? She'd never heard of this classification before. She assumed it must be some sort of jargon PusCo used within their company, likely so anyone from outside would be in the dark if they heard it. But what did it mean? Hoping the Scroll would play nicely, she pressed the tip of her finger on the D7 part of The Dirty Betty's registration page. A little note superimposed itself over the D7 icon, spelling out exactly what this classification meant.

Lana's eyes snapped open in horror and she launched out of the bay window. No sooner had her black shoes hit the laminate before Rem's wriggly face appeared as a hologram over the purple graphene hull.

"Food's on. Come to the Mess."

*

Like the locker room, the large Mess proved there must have once been quite a few more crew members on board The Dirty Betty than the officers.

Most of its grimy laminate flooring was buried beneath tacky duck shell-blue Formica tables and matching chairs, divided by white dayglow white tape that showed hungry drones how and where to line up at dispensing machines along the walls. More tape ensured they filed away to their tables without the dramas of collision-related punch-ups. This careful floor-mapping had been rendered moot, as all the machines that used to burp out goodies like high-nutrient protein cakes, shaped cricket cutlets and Arabica-descent coffee had been torn out. Nothing but holes and stains remained.

Among the random clutter of upturned chairs and sticky trays, Trace, Jimmy and Tuesday were gathered around an eight-person Formica table in the middle of the Mess. Rem's black ribbon of a body slithered along with an assortment of cans, glass jars and pouches kinked against his carapace. Uncoiling as he passed, Rem gently provided the same arrangement of three containers in front of each of the Humans. He set a fourth meal at an empty spot.

"Where's Lana?" Rem asked.

"She can catch up," Tuesday said wetly, looking as though he was about to chew open the nearest can with his black teeth. "What's for tea?"

"Full-nutrient rations, the sort your Military used to eat," Rem announced, wriggling a can opener with one of his flexible antennae. "Dinner, dessert and coffee. Got a whole case of them, enough for three hots a day for the whole trip."

Jimmy took a closer look at what would be his first real meal in an era. Twisting about a fist-sized steel can, a hard glass jar filled with something neon green bobbing up and down in thick white liquid and a soft rubber pouch branded with a steaming-mug-of-coffee icon, it took Jimmy a moment to see the familiar TuffTek logo.

He groaned.

"I didn't know TuffTek made food," Jimmy explained to the weird looks from Trace and Tuesday. He sighed and tried to see the bright side. "Well, it's gotta be better than getting nutrient mush injected directly into my stomach, I guess."

Trace refused the can opener, instead using a finger flick to summon a small, sharp, simulated filleting knife from the AllTool projection bracelet on her left wrist. She effortlessly sliced her tin open with a circular motion, releasing the scent of spicy chili cricket with blue kidney beans. The glutinous contents of her Military ration hissed and steamed as it automatically heated on contact with oxygen, bubbling and churning so that the whole meal was warmed equally. Giving the blood-red stew the slightest of sniffs, Trace changed her simulated blade into a Spork with a twist of her wrist and ate like a zombie chowing down on the brains of a socially awkward Mensa-level genius. Tuesday had only just accepted the can opener when Lana burst into the Mess, brandishing her Scroll as though it contained their doom. He didn't pause in his efforts to undo the tin of chili.

"Don't care," Tuesday mumbled, twisting the little circular blade one centimetre at a time. "It can wait."

Lana slammed her Scroll onto the Formica table, making everything projected on its screen jump and flicker. Trace moved her steaming tin away from the impact zone, narrowing her eyes in warning. Lana jabbed her finger towards the little D7 icon.

"See?" she asked the table, her voice a little too close to a screech. "D7!"

Everyone gave Lana the same look. They exchanged wordless glances, then resumed excavating their dinner without asking for further clarification. Covering her whole face with her hands, Lana dragged her fingernails from forehead to chin. She left four red lines, almost breaking her sunburnt skin. She tapped the offending icon, allowing the Scroll itself to explain what was bothering her in a juddering, not-quite-Human cadence.

"D7 is a classification used exclusively by PusCo's waste collection, processing and disposal services wing to gauge the highest possible level of biological contaminant risk to Human workers. On a vessel or within an installation classed as D7, it is imperative for all biological lifeforms to utilise fully-sealed hazmat suits at all times. This hazmat equipment must be incinerated after the workers have completed all sixteen stages of decontamination."

"What part of the ship...?" Jimmy began.

"The entirety of this vessel is currently classed as D7," the Scroll finished, cutting Jimmy off in a mixture of efficiency and rudeness.

"So what if we aren't wearing hazmat suits?" Tuesday wondered.

The Scroll paused for a couple of seconds before answering.

"Last will and testament forms are available from any PusCo server aboard your vessel. Please note that exposing your unprotected body to a D7 environment instantly voids all medical coverage and life insurance, and PusCo is not liable to compensate your next of kin or significant other for your imminent death. The bill for incinerating your remains will be sent to your estate."

Trace stopped mid-bite, squinting at her half-empty tin of chili. Her hand drifted to the Formica tabletop, and her face soured.

"Wait. What kind of contamination is it, exactly?" Trace growled, a little slow off the podium.

"Radiation?" Jimmy half-shrieked in a failed attempt to sound calm.

Lana scanned over something on the Scroll. She shook her head.

"Parasites. Immediately contagious by any physical contact: air, water, touch."

Rem made a low humming noise.

"Mm. I am sure my client will not like that."

Tuesday and Jimmy couldn't speak over each other quickly enough.

"Is it Green Hepatitis?"

"Genital Moss?"

"Explosive Herpes?"

"Shaft Ruptures?"

"The Squealing Death?!"

Lana cut through the air with her spare hand.

"It's not sexually transmitted. Did you hear the words sexually transmitted?"

Tuesday and Jimmy exchanged a glance. There was a couple of seconds of silence before the only two human males in the galaxy started up again.

"Space Worms?" Jimmy asked.

"Nerve Maggots?" Tuesday followed.

"Neural Sumpage?"

"Brain Flappage?"

"Chumley's Full-Skeletal Calcium Evaporation?"

Lana slammed both palms into the table, making the Scroll's display fritz to black as it was pounded into the sticky Formica. Its display rebooted, returning to the stock standard Miyamoto-Kojima desktop. She pinched the bridge of her nose, squinting so heavily that her temples twitched.

"I don't know, because the Scroll doesn't know. This thing hasn't been updated in so long that half its disease base is extinct and the other half is jumbled into insanity." She sat heavily in one of the flimsy chairs, looking a little startled as its legs bent too far for comfort. "We'll need to wait and see. So if anyone turns bright blue and projectile-vomits bile everywhere, we might have something to work with." Lana looked around at the others, then at their cooling Military surplus rations. She waved at the ancient tins. "Look, until we know exactly what kind of rancid infective meat-maggots have been feeding on us for most of today, going hungry isn't going to solve anything. You brought all those on board with you, right?"

Rem did one of his full-body nods. "All sealed and guaranteed. Scanned every item prior to purchase and before I loaded them on board. No parasites or Human-compatible sicknesses in these, I promise."

Lana accepted her untouched tin, sighing as she broke its seal.

"Just be sure to tell everyone if you get any symptoms. Anything. Puffiness, pain, redness, wracking cough, exploding, itching…"

Tuesday stopped noisily clawing at his salt-and-pepper hair as everyone looked at him. White, grey and black flakes drifted down, settling on the shoulders of his orange coveralls.

"What? Don't look at me. I've had all five of these scalp infections for years. They keep each other balanced out."

Jimmy quietly slid his chair fifteen casual centimetres away from Tuesday. Trace gave Tuesday a dark glance

"You have five different scalp infections?" She narrowed her eyes so hard that some of her facial piercings touched. "You never discussed this with me."

Tuesday shrugged, licking chili from his cracked lips.

"Why would I?"

Trace's expression was locked for a handful of seconds. She finally blinked.

"Perhaps because I'm your wife?" Rage bloomed in Trace's eyes, the darkness of her deep, deep reserves of anger surfacing. She twitched, and a flicker of confusion slid into place. But only for an instant. "What other infective foulness haven't you disclosed?"

"Why does she keep saying that?" Lana asked, finally sick of ignoring the pachyderm in the room.

Trace's gaze focused on Lana like a laser pointer. Tuesday made a slight "for the love of Ares, don't say another word" motion at Lana, which she had the sense not to question. Trace didn't leave the issue there, unfortunately, clearly deciding that she was sick of being deflected. Her eyes flicked from face to face, and her confusion and anger only spiked higher and higher at each weird expression. Her left eyelid flickered, a nerve in her right cheek fired, and for a moment it looked as though Trace was about to have a seizure. Her face went blank, then intelligence returned. This time, however, she didn't go onto another track.

Trace gripped the edge of the Formica so tight that her walnut knuckles whitened. You could hear the skin of her hands tightening. She leaned towards Tuesday, eyes rolling a little as though keeping her train of thought was taking a tremendous effort. Putting what she was feeling into words was the mental equivalent of scaling Everest.

"You keep avoiding the subject," she hissed, knowing something wasn't right. She got closer to Tuesday centimetre by centimetre, baring her teeth. She swept aside the popped tins of rations, nearly knocking them over. "You don't know how or where or when you proposed to me, you don't know where or when we got married, you don't know what my wedding rings look like or where they are, you can't recall any details of our honeymoon ..."

"Must be the stress of getting flushed out of the loop, innit?" Tuesday managed, no longer able to make eye contact with Trace. He tried to focus as high as her throat level as his lies got more and more dense. "We don't need to stress ourselves wiv this now, do we?"

Trace's eyelids were little slits. She twisted to within a matchstick of Tuesday's face, opening her mouth to bare her incisors at her so-called husband.

"When did we start dating? Where did you first take me?"

Tuesday blinked. His line of sight only sank lower and lower, latching onto the bullet-proof shoulder plate of Trace's Enforcer armour. His words were so quiet that the rest of the table could barely hear him.

"A...while...before we got married?"

Trace's lip curled. "But when did we meet? It must have been before The Carpe Astrum Disaster, right? After all, the four of us have only been conscious for about ten days since then. But I don't have a single memory of you prior to that." Trace's cheek twitched heavily, even worse than last time. "Disregarding the time we spent being frozen and dehydrated and getting locked in software loops ..."

"Maybe we should..." Lana interrupted, clearly trying to help.

Trace's entire face twisted into a mask of violence and hatred at Lana's attempts to change the subject. Her bared teeth and spittle spoke volumes. Trace's head twitched back to the left, leaving no space between her mouth and Tuesday's ear. By now he'd shrunken like a grape left out in the Australian Summer.

"When..." she hissed, "did...we..."

Trace gave a full-body jerk. Her expression went vague, as though somebody had just hit her Reset button. Juddering a little, drooling and twitching mindlessly, a rivulet of black blood trickled out of her left nostril. Before anyone could ask if she was okay Trace violently face planted into her dinner. Everyone scrambled as she fitted and foamed at the mouth. Lana instantly had Trace in the recovery position on the laminate floor, making sure the Enforcer didn't swallow her own tongue, and gave Tuesday the darkest of looks.

"We're getting her to Medical, then we're having a chat, right?"

*

Within a matter of minutes Trace was restrained in the pseudo-dentist chair that dominated most of Medical. The straps were enough to stop her from falling off and smashing her head on the tiles, but they wouldn't resist a concerted effort. Her football-sized muscles would probably snap anything weaker than reinforced steel shackles in heartbeats. Proving he was a bit of a Florence Nightingale type, Jimmy had the foresight to clamp Trace's teeth around as wooden spoon in the Mess before they baled her up the corridor.

Jimmy murmured an apology as he pushed past Lana to shoot a needler load of muscle relaxant into Trace's burly, veiny neck. She might be a violent bully and a psychopath, but Trace was still a Human, and that was something in very short supply right now.

The needler hissed as it fired an empty cartridge into the trash. Checking Trace's pulse the old-fashioned way on her carotid, Lana cursed her long-lost Omni. The tiny grain-of-rice-sized implant came with dozens of different scanners built-in as standard, and contained enough medical knowledge to cover just about any emergency a person could face with easy-to-read step-by-step instructions. Even without access to the wiped-out Link, her Omni made the Great Library of Alexandria look about as impressive as a recycling bin filled with dinosaur erotica fan-fiction. Honestly, having an Omni almost made life boring.

Lana scratched at the missing bump on the meat of her left hand, and tried not to curse.

Satisfied Trace was deep asleep, Lana nodded at Jimmy and then at the doorway. Getting the hint, Jimmy followed Lana out to the purple grid work corridor. Unsurprisingly, Tuesday was hunched against the opposite wall, smoking a green cigarette. A near-dead bulb flickered above his head, giving life and body to the tendrils of lime-coloured smoke. It was hard to tell, but his face may have been twisted into a near-sentient variety of concerned. Anyone who knew Tuesday for longer than a couple of minutes would notice he wasn't quite your standard Human in a number of ways, but even lower rodents have the capacity to feel shame when they'd seriously mistreated one of their fellow vermin. Whether he was wearing a practised mask or really felt some measure of remorse could only be guessed.

Lana punched Medical's little Red Cross sign on her way past, sending it hopping about on a rubber spring. Jimmy followed closely behind, sensing the storm that was about to be unleashed. And although he'd done nothing wrong, Jimmy was staying hunched and deflated and out of the way until this scene was over.

Tuesday began to stand, hissing smoke at Lana's approach.

"I reckon..."

Lana grabbed Tuesday by the shoulder and slammed him into an indigo girder. Before he could laugh this off he was surprised by a right cross that made everything go a crackling black-and-white for a moment. His cigarette exploded under Lana's fist, burning her fingers and Tuesday's mouth in equal measure. Shaking her hand and swearing, digging burning emerald embers out of her skin, Lana stamped her foot for the first time since her teenage years.

"Explain," she demanded.

Tuesday rubbed ash from his lips. "I don't need to..."

"Why does she think you're her husband?"

Tuesday shrugged dismissively.

"She's baffled as a dog in a sock. Bitch is crazy, you know that." He shrugged as punctuation. "Eight years in a loop clearly moved her furniture over the border into Mental Town."

"It was his wish," Jimmy blurted.

Jimmy was pinned under two sets of eyes: one confused, one furious. One said continue, the other said DEAD.

"When we thought we could ask for whatever we wanted in life," Jimmy said slowly, hesitantly, trying to focus on Lana and ignore the threats Tuesday was muttering under his foul breath. "You wanted to meet your parents, I wanted to be wanted, and Trace asked for all the riches of her family. But Tuesday had the last wish, and that wish was for Trace to believe they were married."

Lana's mouth gaped a little. She blinked at Jimmy, then at Tuesday.

"But...what? Why?"

Tuesday shrugged. "Comedic value, mostly."

Jimmy shrugged awkwardly, clearly annoyed with himself for getting in the middle when he could have stayed safely on the sidelines.

Now more mystified than angry, something triggered in Lana's brain that made her eyes blaze.

"You didn't..."

"Why do people keep asking me that?" Tuesday said in disgust, spitting. "I'm not an animal. "Haven't so much as kissed. Not that she didn't try earlier on in the coffee room..."

Lana raised her open hands and screwed her eyes tightly shut as though wanting a dose of brain bleach.

"No interest. Don't tell me. Please." She frowned, and pointed blindly at Tuesday. "Wait. But all our wishes were fulfilled by being fed with a software loop. When we got flushed out of the loop, all those things disappeared. So why does she still believe she's married?"

Tuesday shrugged. "Dunno. Maybe because the software loop could make us feel like we were in certain places doing certain things, but can't actually change who we are? Perhaps changing Trace's sense of who she was required something more...invasive? Something more permanent?" Tuesday snorted. "Maybe it's wishful thinking on her part? Who knows?"

Lana nodded in thought.

"Bugger. I didn't actually expect you to have a decent answer."

She decided giving Tuesday anymore praise would be foolish, and rubbed at her temples in an attempt to think deeper. As always, she was surprised by the cold touch of the ported L-shaped brackets installed on both sides of her head, but didn't visibly startle. After all, Jimmy was meant to be the jumpy one. Whether the head massage helped couldn't be proven, but she had an idea.

"Right. Medical is as basic as it gets, but I'm pretty sure I spotted a Psych-in-a-Box in the supply manifesto when I was doing a ship wide sweep for anything that wasn't...well, useless. It should be tucked away in an Alternative Medicine cabinet over that way, directly behind the leech tablets and urethral crystal inserts. Hopefully it isn't too hard to use."

"A Psych-in-a-Box?" Jimmy repeated in disgust. "You want to use psychiatric surgery? Why don't we dance naked around a fire and voodoo sacrifice some chickens while we're at it?"

Lana waggled her finger.

"Psych adjustment was making a real comeback before we left. Last I remember, The Unison had successfully rewired five million useless death-row defect spongers into shiny new citizens without a single psychotic break. And the use of a Psych-in-a-Box by civilians had been reduced from a capital offense to a mere felony on most worlds, too."

"Not on Sprout, it wasn't," Jimmy muttered darkly.

"But if the Slidge installed something in Trace's head that makes her think she's something she's not, well, then it kind of makes sense to use the Psych-in-a-Box to see what it is, right?" Lana asked, counting on her fingers. "A Psych-in-a-Box should be able to tell us if there's anything off about Trace's brain."

"Lana, everything is off with Trace's brain," Tuesday sniped. "Have you met her? Mad as a rain of frogs. Bloody Psych-in-a-Box wouldn't know where to begin."

Lana pointed at Tuesday in threat. "Not another word from you. You're still in the doghouse. Unless you want me to fix your brain in your sleep, I suggest you keep silent."

Despite his objections, Jimmy silently followed Lana thirty metres spin wards. It took a few seconds with a crowbar summoned from her AllTool bracelet to separate the warped cabinet door from its housing, but Lana was into the Alternative Medicine locker in short order. As you'd expect from such a derided branch of "science," the contents of this cabinet had been left untouched by multiple waves of thieves and sticky-fingered copper wire rippers. Digging through vials of heart-shaped healing quartz stones and damp incense sticks, Lana extracted a small dusty white case the size of an engagement ring box. It was branded with the Caduceus symbol of two snakes wrapped around a winged staff, which in turn rested upon the illegal gang-sign logo that convicted Psychiatrists got tattooed on their necks in prison. For some reason, the banned logo was a simple Lino print of a balding, bearded man smoking a cigar.

Considering the main function of a Psych-in-a-Box was to rewire death row inmates into entirely new people, it was no wonder the scavengers hadn't touched it. To a criminal, it would be like choosing to carry around an electric chair or a noose, the very definition of bad luck. Not to mention they were a highly controlled device that required a dozen different licenses to possess, so holding one was just asking for trouble if you ran into any of The Unison's law enforcement divisions. To people less enlightened than Lana, it would probably be bad luck to even look at a Psych-in-a-Box, let alone touch it.

"Right, we just need to get Trace's consent when she wakes up," Lana said, handling the box carefully.

Jimmy arched an eyebrow. "Seriously?"

Lana couldn't keep a straight face. "Of course not. The moment she wakes up we're going to have at least one homicide, though possibly three. How long until she's back with us?"

Jimmy gave Lana a very convincing dumb expression.

"Huh? I don't know. I just injected her with twice as much muscle relaxant as you'd need for a normal person. She'll be asleep a while, I hope."

Lana's mouth opened a little.

"Wait. So you mean she's just lying there in…"

There was a throaty roar from down the corridor, met with an almost-unheard squeak of terror. Slamming the storage cabinet, Lana and Jimmy witnessed Trace burst out of Medical, still bound by snapped restraints on her wrists and ankles, and barrel into Tuesday like a demolition ball. The scumbag only had enough time to cringe and pull a stupid face before Trace raised one jackbooted foot and pounded him into a girder, her heel smashing the entire right side of his ribcage hard enough to break bones. Annihilated, Tuesday slammed to the grid work floor, coughing blood as Trace rained punches down on his head.

Lana was already running. But those thirty metres might as well have been a million.

Trace flicked her wrist, using her AllTool bracelet to summon a ten-kilogram sledgehammer from the ether. Her expression as black as the vacuum, without any hesitation Trace brought up the heavy ceramic tool as high as she could go and brought it down on her prone target with pinpoint accuracy. Lana could only scream for Trace to stop as the sledgehammer descended, too far away to do anything about it, directly at the spot between Tuesday's eyes.

CHAPTER ELEVEN

Even from a short distance, it took Lana a couple of seconds to register what had just happened.

Tuesday was lying prone, stunned by a bone-breaking kick to the chest and dazed to the brink of unconsciousness by follow-up hooks and crosses from Trace's meaty fists. Badly tenderised by some of the biggest knuckles his often-beaten head had met, Tuesday had only started to leak claret when the simulated sledgehammer magically appeared in Trace's hands. For once, Tuesday didn't have anything to say, and all he could manage was to gape with his rotten-toothed horror show of a mouth as his long-cheated death seemingly caught up with him.

Lana's feet were pounding, but there was no way she'd make it in time. She knew it was impossible, but there was no way in Hades she'd just stand by and watch a homicide.

The black sledgehammer descended as hard as Trace could manage. As she was built like a Queen mattress stuffed with footballs, there was a good chance the head of her weapon would enter through Tuesday's skull and finish deep in his chest cavity. Unless Rem had some spare heads, Mankind's exclusive club was about to be reduced from four to three.

To Lana's surprise, there was only half a thumb-span between the sledgehammer and Tuesday's eyebrows when the Universe decided to grant one of its least-deserving creatures a mulligan. If you watched the scene in extreme slow motion, you'd be able to pick the exact instant the sledgehammer transformed from a solid, heavy object to a green wireframe with zero mass. So rather than splattering Tuesday's brains all over the architecture, the sledgehammer vanished back into the AllTool. Swinging down with all her strength empty-handed, Trace ploughed face-first into the purple pipework hard enough to dent it. Bouncing off the composite with a sickening noise, eyes rolling in their sockets in an almost cartoonish way, Trace turned just in time to see the heel of Lana's black dress shoe flying at her.

The AllTool bracelet that had betrayed Trace was now flashing bloody red and sounding a hellish siren that The Dirty Betty was emulating. All the walls were blaring the same holographic alert.

"Attempted homicide in corridor 86F," the speakers declared, echoing their chorus up and down the indigo maze. "Attempted homicide in corridor 86F. Armed security to corridor 86F immediately."

Under any other circumstances, it was unlikely Lana would stand a chance against Trace in a one-on-one stand up fight. As a Cadet at the Academy, Lana had been trained in the Navy-standard fighting style of Keri Soko, and could hold her own against girls her own size any day of the week. However, her speed and technique wasn't much use against a psychopathic surgically-modified bruiser who was three times her weight and permanently wired up for violence. Lana's lightning-fast open palms and heel kicks usually accomplished little against this particular side of beef, and it would only take one or two glancing blows from Trace's giant fists to knock Lana unconscious on the spot.

But she didn't hesitate. Lana knew Tuesday would be dead in seconds if she didn't step in, and as little as she liked the cockroach, a Human life was always worth fighting for.

Lana's heel smashed into Trace's eye socket, making all her metal and obsidian facial piercings rattle and chime. More surprised than hurt, Trace just watched as Lana smoothly landed on the laminate and tried to sweep her ankles with a hard strike. This didn't go so well, as Trace's legs were like oak trees protected by heavy jackboots. Giving a cry of attack, Lana followed up with her best helicopter kick, pushed off the ground as hard as she could with both palms, and was upright and ready to try to take Trace down.

Trace did something very, very unusual: she smiled. It wasn't a nice sight.

"Seriously? For him?"

Trace kept her hands by her sides, as though Lana didn't even merit putting up her guard. She casually touched the eyebrow she'd busted on the pipework and winced. For Trace to give any reaction at all it must have been badly broken. She rubbed the blood away on her Enforcer armour in boredom.

"We both know I could literally pull your skull from your spine." Trace jabbed a finger towards Tuesday's pitifully bashed-up body. "But he's dying first. So you'll have to take a number and wait your turn, gorgeous."

Lana's attempt at a knee to the solar plexus barely started to ascend when Trace wrapped a huge hand around her sunburnt throat, squeezing tight as a noose. Lana lashed out with her fist, but Trace effortlessly lifted her from the laminate with one steady arm and slammed her into the pipes directly above Tuesday. Stunned senseless, her entire world shuddering and warping, Lana barely heard Trace's mocking words before greying out.

"Well, if you insist, I guess you can go first."

The next thing Lana knew her limbs were tangled up with Tuesday, but it felt as though she'd been carelessly dropped rather than pile driven. As colour bled back into her blackened vision Lana could see Trace flailing wildly, trying to dislodge something from her shoulders. Hilariously, Trace was too buff to be able to touch her own spine, making the fight one-sided. To Lana's shock she realised Jimmy was the one holding onto Trace for dear life, and she was getting slower and more lethargic with every buck. Roaring, Trace fell to one knee, then eventually planted both hands on the deck. Breathing heavily, she face planted and instantly started to snore, but Jimmy waited another ten careful seconds before dismounting.

Flinching away from the fluorescent strips of the corridor, pretty sure that light sensitivity was a common symptom of a major concussion, Lana gave Jimmy a questioning look. He was puffing and panting as he drew the needler out of Trace's neck and ejected three spent cartridges with hiss-pops.

"Gave her a dose of Carfentanil," Jimmy managed, giving a shaky smile. "Elephant tranquiliser."

Lana smiled, but that was probably thanks to considerable brain damage. Despite every corridor of The Dirty Betty still screaming for the long-dead armed security staff to respond to an attempted homicide, Lana went limp in relief. Unfortunately, the adrenalin was already starting to wear off, and Lana's body had a lot to tell her about.

*

It wasn't long until Rem turned up and switched off the alarms. As he didn't have the faintest idea what to expect, he'd brought some sort of complicated high-tech weapon that may have been designed to one-shot fighter jets doing

Mach Four. The gun was literally bigger than he was, and if it wasn't for the antigrav wafers laced along its casing, it would have taken five large Humans to lift.

Rem wasn't impressed with their explanation one bit.

"You know I could just restrict you lot to your rooms for the rest of the trip, right?" the bristleworm threatened. "All I asked of you was to stay alive, and you decide to try killing each other! Honestly, 'don't die' isn't much of a request, is it?" Rem nibbled at his antennae. "Look, bottom line, I'm getting paid a substantial bonus to deliver the whole set of four, and if you think I'll tolerate you putting my payday at risk..."

"It was all her," Jimmy blurted, cracking.

Everyone glanced down at Trace. She was strapped to a floating medical stretcher by enough reinforced steel to hold back a twenty-foot salt-water crocodile. Even though she was still wasted on enough elephant tranquiliser to get a whole Oscar's after party stoned, there was no way she would be left unobserved for a moment. She'd finally snapped all the way, and having her un-snap without serious intervention was likely impossible.

Rem clicked his mandibles in dismissal.

"I don't care about blame. What I want is an absolute reassurance there will be no more incidences of violence between any of you for this entire trip, or you're confined to your cells around the clock."

"I thought they were rooms?" Jimmy said innocently.

Rem leaned in very, very close to Jimmy. After a few seconds, one of Rem's antennae bopped him right in the centre of the forehead.

"You're funny. I don't like you."

Rem panned his eyestalks towards the open door of Medical. Tuesday was curled up on the pseudo-dentist chair that dominated most of the small space, but at least he wasn't coughing up blood at present. The bristleworm snapped his eye stalks back at the only two conscious humans.

"Can you give me this assurance, or not?"

Lana glanced at the little holographic ball projected by Rem's starburst collar. It looked just like the truth-verifying orbs the Slidge were so fond of using. She locked her sight with some of Rem's eye stalks, not quite sure which ones to focus on.

"We can handle it," Lana confirmed. "We can fix this problem."

Rem carefully studied the sphere until it shined in complex Drennite symbols. He gave a full-body nod.

"Acceptable. I will ensure this one doesn't die. Do not make me regret this."

Almost as an afterthought, the bristleworm used a mandible to throw Trace's deactivated AllTool bracelet to Lana. She caught it easily as Rem slithered into Medical.

"Uh, are you sure you know what you're doing?" Jimmy asked as Rem arranged sharp silver tools, drills and saws on a shining platter. "I'm pretty sure he has broken bones and internal bleeding and stuff."

"Unlike the Slidge, the Drennite naturally inherit genetic memories from our ancestors," Rem said curtly. "No fewer than ten of my relatives in the last six generations were surgeons. Compared to Drennite physiology, I might as well be doing a child's jigsaw puzzle. I'm sure I'll manage."

Rem slammed Medical shut without another word. Lana gripped the head of Trace's stretcher and nodded down the corridor.

"Come on, Jimmy. Let's find somewhere quiet."

*

It didn't take long to find an empty room. The five-metre cube was bare except for a metal bench installed in the middle and mysterious brown stains trickling from sliced-off pipes in the graphene walls. Its ancient lighting took so long to automatically flicker on that Lana almost walked back out again, and for some reason the hum of glow strips brought the smell of burning hair. All in all, pretty typical of this scavenged-down-to-the-hull hulk.

Lana effortlessly floated Trace's stretcher up beside the bench and sat down. She indicated for Jimmy to join her. Giving her a weird look, Jimmy was sure to leave a comfortable hand span between them. Despite his mellow, harmless nature, once Lana produced the Psych-in-a-Box about a dozen objections appeared on his face.

"I know that Psychiatry is illegal on most planets and heresy to just about all religions, but it's our only chance, Jimmy," Lana said pre-emptively.

"Its barbarism," Jimmy sulked. "Butchery."

"So else how are we meant to fix her?" Lana demanded. "Short of chaining her up in a cupboard or surgically flushing her brain and replacing it with a mouse running in a cute little wheel, what other options do we have? She's going to kill Tuesday at the first possible opportunity. There's no getting around it."

Lana placed her hand on Jimmy's shoulder in a reassuring way. His face turned a little bit blue and he stopped breathing. She sighed in frustration and stopped touching him.

"Look, there's more to Psychiatry than replacing the personalities of death-row criminals or programming civilians into self-terminating assassins: at one point it was about understanding who we are, why we do what we do, coming to terms with the Human condition and what's holding us back, and how we can break the deeply-entrenched cycles that have been hardwired into us. It was about helping people to be all they could be."

Jimmy glanced at the Psych-in-a-Box in a huff, then at Trace.

"So what are you suggesting we do?"

Lana's smile faltered. "To be honest, I was kind of hoping we could carve out all the bits that make her dangerous. A psycho-ectomy, if you will."

Jimmy folded his arms like a petulant child.

"Yeah, sounds real ethical."

Lana waved in dismissal.

"While it would be nice to make Trace, well, Human, I'm not going to fundamentally change who she is. Look, she's the only one of us who still believes what the Slidge programmed her to believe. For you, Tuesday and myself, these beliefs ended the moment we got flushed out of the software loop. The Slidge must have done something else to her that they didn't do to the three of us." Lana opened the velvet case of the Psych-in-a-Box, revealing what appeared to be a grape-sized cube. Like all the best technology, it was bright white. "We're just going to see if there's anything in there that shouldn't be. Nothing else."

Jimmy shuffled away a little as Lana retrieved the virgin Psych-in-a-Box from its packing materials. Placing the inactive cube on her knee, she fished around in the foam and cardboard for an object the dimensions of a toothpick, and with one touch the matchstick wafer projected a simulated pamphlet with the words MY FIRST PSYCH-IN-A-BOX decorated with the image of Bearded Bald Guy with a Cigar. Lana scanned over the first page of the manual, and Jimmy slid closer to her after a few seconds.

"What's it say?" he whispered like an eight-year-old boy who was asking the only teenager he knew what boobs really felt like.

She squinted a little at the flickering text.

"Disclaimer: the contents of this carton are for entertainment purposes only. The unauthorised civilian use of Psychiatry is a Class-D felony, and using a Psych-in-a-Box on any persons living or dead is strictly illegal. The following three-hundred-and-ninety-six pages will explain in great detail how you are NOT allowed to use a Psych-in-a-Box, including full personality replacements, improving or removing existing behavioural traits, excising traumatic memories, and switching sexual preferences. Most importantly, under NO circumstances are you to run the Psych-in-a-Box over somebody's forehead to find the correct applicator spot, and you are DEFINITELY not allowed to switch it on by tapping it twice."

She gave Jimmy a sideways glance and picked up the little white box.

"You know, I'm not entirely..."

Jimmy sprang into action, leaping on top of Trace and jamming the needler into her neck. Her mouth open in an O of surprise, Lana aimed her wordless question at him. He simply popped a spent canister of medication as Trace relaxed again.

"She was waking up," he said simply. "Hooked my retinals up to her vitals."

Lana was about to compliment his use of science jargon, but thought better of it. She inhaled and exhaled, tapping into her determination.

"Okay then. Let's commit a dozen felonies."

Lana gently ran the Psych-in-a-Box over Trace's forehead, concerned the Enforcer was going to suddenly lurch up and bite off her fingers. Nothing seemed to be happening until the cube was situated directly between Trace's eyebrows. As though sensing a pre-programmed target, the Psych-in-a-Box latched onto Trace like a magnet on a refrigerator. Flicking through the holographic manual, Lana double-tapped the cube twice almost as an afterthought.

The room was instantly filled with dozens and dozens of holographic screens. All kinds of physiological, psychological and psychiatric readings jostled with laundry lists of personality malfunctions, and a hundred different graphs and charts were prefaced with technical terms that Psychiatrists only used in order to make other people feel inferior. There were zero-to-a-hundred adjustment bars for the deepest functioning of Trace's brain labelled with jargon like Id, Ego, Superego, Oedipus, Elektra, Oral and Psychosexual, to name but a few. It was more like a menu for an underground brothel than something legitimately medical. No matter how much Lana flicked through the simulated pages, though, she couldn't understand any of what was being projected, and kept her fingers well away from the adjustment bars.

"Uh, your facial expression isn't instilling confidence," Jimmy whispered, intimidated by all the thirty-letter-long words floating about.

"Just a sec," Lana insisted.

Leafing through the guide's Index, running down dozens of lines with her finger, she eventually lowered the handbook. Her expression of distaste spoke volumes.

Ignoring Jimmy, cutting off his questions with a hand signal, Lana moved around the multitude of icons branching out of Trace's head until she saw the one she wanted: Cerebral Abnormalities. Drawing her thumbs and index fingers apart to stretch the little holographic box into a huge A2-sized slab, a couple more hesitant taps brought up a four-dimensional scan of Trace's brain. Obviously, the first abnormalities the Psych-in-a-Box picked up were the numerous plugholes that had been installed by the Slidge. To no surprise from Jimmy the implants were declared to be manufactured by the Thoughtplane Corporation, and the age of their serial numbers indicated they were fabricated during the reign of The Unison. After an exhaustive series of scans, the white cube listed its results in clear Unglish.

"Invasive hardware found to be incapable of having an ongoing effect on current specimen's beliefs," Jimmy read out loud, quite proud he was capable of shaping some of the more advanced words with his mouth on the first try.

Lana chewed her lip and tasted blood. She really had to stop doing that.

"So if the plugs aren't causing her delusions, it must be something else, right?"

Jimmy's facial expression reminded Lana of a couple of salient facts. She frowned in apology. "Right, you flip burgers and you're bad at it. Sorry."

Lana took direct control of the Physical Abnormalities screen and twisted it to take a broader sweep of Trace's brain. Sticking her tongue out a little bit like whenever she had a driving lesson, Lana cruised up and down Trace's lobes and cortex's, scanning every millimetre for anything out of the ordinary. As this was Trace's brain, there was plenty to be found.

"She must have undergone two dozen violence-reduction adjustments," Lana said mostly to herself, scanning along the precise pin-sized burns. She was a little taken aback. "They clearly didn't work, but look at that artistry! Whoever did these was a master. Probably the best that money can buy."

"She is a Cuddle," Jimmy reminded her. "Disowned or not, Cuddles were one of the richest families in the galaxy. Everything on a diamond platter, right?"

Lana sighed. "Shame none of the adjustments actually worked. Unlike rewiring criminals, the first priority of Trace's surgeons must have been doing zero lasting damage to her mind. In the Justice system, that's usually priority sixty-seven."

"Spugging trillionaires," Jimmy cussed quietly. "Paying ten thousand times as much for something that doesn't work half as well as a backyard hack-job. Typical."

A small chime sounded as Lana continued scrolling, and she had to backtrack a little to find what had triggered the alert. At first glance, the object in Trace's brain was a little black ball bearing a fraction the size of a clove. The Psych-in-a-Box politely noted that it was clearly of Human manufacture.

"Woss that?" Jimmy asked.

Lana scanned it from all angles and shrugged.

"Can't tell, exactly. Pretty sure it isn't a homing device or storage media of any kind. It reminds me a little of the student identification implant I got jammed in my wrist when I joined the Academy as a child. Maybe it's something like that?"

"So it might be some sort of special VIP authentication device?" Jimmy coughed. "No offense, but are you just guessing? I know I am."

Lana shook her head at the rest of the results of the scan.

"No, this can't be what's messing with her. The implant's installation date indicates she's had it since she was a toddler." Lana huffed. "It's a borderline miracle I even saw the stupid thing. Mysterious as it is, this isn't what we're looking for."

Although they had no idea how much longer this aggressive search would take – and whether Trace would be able to develop a resistance to elephant tranquiliser before they finished – it was only five more minutes until one of the holographic screens lit up like a pinball machine. There was a tiny, tiny filament constructed from an undocumented substance jammed in Trace's brain, and no fewer than fifteen tendrils had sprouted from it to take root in her grey matter. The tendrils were too fine to be picked up on the sweep, but if you went from the base of the pin they were easy enough to follow. All up, the uninvited guest was less than a millimetre across at its widest point.

It took Lana a frustrating ten minutes of page-flipping and half-guessing at jargon terms, but she finally sat back and relaxed as though the Universe was suddenly a kinder place.

"That's it," Lana announced, as though she couldn't believe it. "This thread is definitely the core of why Trace thinks she's married to Tuesday, and its tendrils have grown out to physically combat any thoughts that contradict that belief. So we rip out the weed roots-and-all, and we're done. It'll probably do a number on her until she heals up, but the problem is basically solved."

Jimmy cleared his throat in the only way he could: awkwardly.

"Uh, that's nice and all, but do you have any brain surgeons on speed-dial right now? Surely the Psych-in-a-Box doesn't actually slice into people's grey stuff, right? I don't see any scalpels hanging out of it."

Lana's triumph turned to crushing defeat, and then back to triumph, in an instant.

"Actually, I do."

*

Medical slid open with the appropriate soft hiss you'd expect from a starship's interior door, and Rem's unimpressed bug face did the exact opposite of greeting Lana and Jimmy. The bristleworm glanced beyond them at Trace's unconscious, shackled form on the floating stretcher, and then turned back to his work on Tuesday's open ribcage. There was the stench of hot blood in the antiseptic air as Rem carved away with three laser scalpels at once, but not a drop to be seen.

"Make it fast," Rem growled, stitching furiously with two of his antennae.

Lana and Jimmy were both transfixed by the sight of Rem's handiwork. He'd already reset Tuesday's bones and closed up his wounds with stitch work so beautiful it was invisible. Not only that, but Tuesday's nastiest facial bruises and skin splits had vanished. At this rate, there was a good chance he'd be in better shape than he was before the beating. Lana finally managed to tear her attention away from the slitting and stitching.

"We've found the cause of Trace's violence. It's a Slidge implant."

Rem didn't pause, though he did dedicate one of his many eye stalks to glance at Lana.

"Really? What kind of implant?"

"Brain."

Rem didn't blink. "So Tuesday did nothing to merit his beating?"

"No, he earned it good," Lana confirmed a little too quickly, already regretting her words before they finished spilling. "But this implant was at the core of why she attacked him. From what the Psych-in-a-Box indicated, if we extract the implant it won't be able to feed the delusions into her mind anymore. Problem solved."

Rem crunched both halves of Tuesday's distended ribcage into place like a rusty bear trap and stitched his torso back together. Those six seconds were a masterful display, Jimmy's gag of revulsion notwithstanding.

"So she won't try and kill him again if you remove it, that's what you're saying?"

Lana faltered. "I'm sure it would help to… some degree."

Rem made a grunt of displeasure before lifting Tuesday off the reclined dentist chair. He slithered past Lana and Jimmy and into the corridor, where a PusCo dumpster was just sliding to a halt in the middle of the aisle. He heaved Tuesday onto the purple trash receptacle and into the midst of half a dozen spindly-legged Weavers.

"Into his room, on his pallet. Gently. Leave a litre of tepid water where he can reach it."

As Tuesday zipped away down the corridor, Rem slid Trace into Medical stretcher-and-all. He effortlessly removed her from the floating bed and laid her down on the chair. Lana and Jimmy gave a sharp intake of breath as the four sets of steel manacles unclasped, only to be replaced by weak fabric. Rem snorted at their reaction.

"You've dosed her with enough sedative to knock out two zoos and a reptile park. Come on." Rem slit open Trace's fattened, broken eyebrow, carved away the damaged tissue, replaced the snapped bone segment with a careful glob of synthetic paste and sewed it back together so fast she didn't even have time to bleed. "And I can't just delve into her brain without her permission, by the way. I'm assuming she'd object."

"That implant is messing with her mind," Jimmy quavered. "She'd want it out, I guarantee you."

Rem sighed as he finished rubbing bruise-fading cream into several purple spots the size and shape of Lana's knuckles. Some of the rubber ports drilled into Trace's torso and belly were visible for a moment as Rem finished taking care of her wounds, but disappeared again as he slid the plates of her Enforcer armour back into place. He stuck his entire face into a decontamination sink, careful to keep his eyestalks away from the germ-killing jolt of sanitising radiation.

"Fine. However, I'm going to be right here when she wakes up, and if she gives any indication of any more trouble, the four of you will instantly go from guests to prisoners."

*

It took an hour, but when Trace returned to consciousness she sat bolt upright. Every muscle in her body flexed as a long-overdue reaction to being cuddled senseless by Jimmy. Thankfully the straps prevented her from ending up on the laminate, but it wasn't enough to hold her down for long. Trace wrestled her left arm free with the signature ripping noise, but froze in place as a lightning bolt shot through her brain. Gripping the top of her shaved head, Trace clenched her chipped teeth together so hard she could hear the abrasion of enamel and feel her jaw muscles turn to stone. It was like somebody was driving a metal stake into her grey matter.

Hungover from whatever the Tartarus had knocked her out, Trace returned to her usual headspace: there were flashes of omnidirectional rage, illustrated with images of blood and the sensation of bones breaking beneath her feet and hands, but no context. She could hear people yelling for her to stop, and the heavy weight of somebody solid trying to bring her to the ground. She had quite a few memories like these stored away, and they usually preceded her needing to leave town before the filth arrived.

Trace growled, scratching at a tiny itchy patch on the very top of her skull. She almost missed it, but her dirty fingernail nicked what might be a couple of millimetres of stitching. Gritting her teeth harder, she managed to gather enough coordination to free herself from the other three straps.

"Trace?"

Registering her name, her head snapped up to see Jimmy and Lana were between her and the door. Rem was directly behind them, clearly listening in with a vested interest. Everything quivered violently thanks to the aftermath of four doses of elephant tranquiliser.

"What?" she managed, their babbling meaning nothing.

Trace slid off the dentist's chair, ending up on one knee on the tiles. She pushed away their helpful hands, relying on her own arms and legs. Unfortunately, her limbs had different ideas, and she face planted. Thankfully, in a couple of moments of shaking confusion she found herself back on the dentist's chair, watching the ceiling panels tilt. A few words managed to penetrate her concrete-thick fugue as she kicked back and waited for the world to stop rocking.

"Gimme a minute," she hissed, angered by the noises. "Can't understand you."

She may have passed out, it was hard to tell, but an outside sentence eventually found its way into the language centre of her brain. She locked onto the collection of words, turning its nouns and verbs over and over until they made sense.

"Do you understand?"

"Understand what?" Trace barked, spittle flying.

Her right eye snapped open, pupil full of venom. Lana shrivelled a little under its gaze, and had to compose herself before trying again.

"I'm sorry we had to sedate you. You were trying to kill Tuesday."

Trace gave a snort of amusement. "I'm hardly on a short list, there."

She slid her feet over the edge of the dentist's chair and slouched, head drooping. It seemed Trace was approaching something within the borders of the realm of coherence.

"So you remember?"

Trace yawned. "Remember what?"

"Why you were trying to kill Tuesday?"

"Does it really matter? Plenty of reasons to kill Tuesday."

"Humour me."

Trace ground her beefy palm into her eye socket. Rem's handiwork was so beautifully done that she almost didn't notice her eyebrow had been broken and repaired. She gave a throaty cough.

"He did...something." Trace's cheek twitched. "Dunno. Messed with my head. Thought he was..." her face showed confusion, perhaps even vulnerability. But then the walls went up, ninety feet tall and topped with razor wire. "Something. Made me believe..."

Lana held out her hand. In her palm was a speck of what might be a bone-white needle, though far, far smaller than what you'd use to sew the lacy lingerie of a pixie. At the very extent of Trace's vision she thought she could see little wriggly bits branching off, but her eyes weren't up to the task. She'd need a microscope to get a proper look, and she couldn't remember how to use her retinals at the moment.

"It's made out of limpet ivory," Lana said flatly. "Same invulnerable material the Slidge used to construct their Star Cages. See, the Slidge could fool our senses with a software loop, but to make you believe that you're someone you're not...well, clearly they had to do something a lot more invasive to pull that off."

Trace's palm snapped up only inches from Lana's face.

"How many times you pictured doing it?" Trace asked, her voice low. "Pounding his head into a concrete sleeper? Choking him out with his own arm? Snipping off his fingers and knuckles and wrists with bolt cutters?"

Lana's expression was carefully neutral, but it was fake. Growing up richer than King Solomon, Trace could spot fake faster than anything else.

The rage picked this moment to return, her oldest companion clawing and hissing at the back of her mind. That endless anger, the compulsion to twist and break things, to smear blood on the walls and scream in hatred until her voice cracked and died, was hard to resist at the best of times. If the others had any idea how often she almost gave into her predatory nature she would have been hogtied and blasted out the airlock on day one. It was hard to pretend the homicidal urges weren't always swelling like heavy surf, and moments of high stress made it so hard to fight that it took literally all her limited self-control not to pick up the closest heavy object and start pounding. If they ever found out, they'd strangle her in her sleep if they had a gram of sense.

"I know what this is," Trace growled, slowly dragging herself upright. Jimmy took a step back, but he was the only one. "This is a warning that further acts of violence won't be tolerated, and that you'll wrestle me down and drug me and cage me if you have to, right? That about sum it up?"

"I will protect my investment if I have to," Rem said without bothering to gild the truth. "While earning the maximum possible payment will require all of you to be alive and intact, it's only fair to warn you that I am very, very good at reading between the lines of contracts. I have twelve different restraint methods in mind, each more unpleasant than the last."

Trace gave a half smile. It didn't reach her cold eyes. She glanced at Jimmy, and her smile died.

"And you," she growled, tapping Jimmy's saggy pectoral with a finger the size of a breakfast sausage. "Get smart with that needler again and you'll need a proctologist to retrieve it." She punctuated her next words with steadily more violent pokes. "Don't. Try. Me."

She could tell Jimmy wanted desperately to meet her gaze, to stand his ground and stare her down, but he couldn't muster the bravery. Trace knew it was sick, but his fear felt good. It was soothing. Satisfied that she'd adequately terrified Jimmy to his core, Trace glared at Rem.

"Much as I'd like to fillet that little piss goblin, true blame lies on the Slidge for jamming that pin in my head. But if I so much as see him, he gets a slap, right? I'm not promising anything if he enters my line of sight."

Lana barked a laugh.

"So you're choosing to be the bigger person? Just forgive him like that? Trace, you'll have to excuse me if I have trouble believing you're simply going to let all this slide."

Trace just appeared weary.

"Princess, I don't do mind games. I don't fudge about with words. You want weaselling and scamming and double-speak, go see Tuesday. Me, I'm going to go finish my damn dinner."

Exhausted from the effort of having to behave like a Human for such a prolonged period, Trace pushed between Lana and Jimmy far too roughly and stomped away.

CHAPTER TWELVE

Six days clawed by. Despite having plenty of Military surplus rations to eat, purified water to drink, safe, warm places to sleep and as much social contact as they could stand, it was a fact The Dirty Betty was about as exciting as an aged care facility twenty minutes after pill time. After living in an era of sophistication that provided non-stop visual and audio and tactile and mental stimulation, this quiet, sterile boredom had a similar effect to withdrawing from a bag-a-day Shatter habit. The closest they had to fun was wandering the endless purple and black passages looking for something to do. As the Goth vaccine was developed around the same time Mankind cracked interstellar travel, this monochrome existence was unbearable.

Everyone was grumpy and snippy by day three, and any desire to talk evaporated after a series of small arguments and pregnant silences. Their encounters became less and less frequent apart from mealtimes, and even then there was nothing left to say. Nobody felt like sharing any more chapters of their life story, and it wasn't like they could catch up about how their week had been.

It didn't help that every breakfast, lunch and dinner was nurturing a growing universal hatred for TuffTek rations. If TuffTek's mission was to create foodstuffs no Human palette would find offensive, then they'd succeeded, albeit by removing all flavour and texture from their canned slabs of neutral, wobbly Hell. The taste profile of their rations ranged between "grey" and "brown," and looked and felt the same going in as it did coming out.

The meditative silences that came with deliberately staying at least a hundred metres away from any other intelligent lifeform provided the humans with a chance to process their situation in their own way without distractions. It went without saying that the end of Humanity was a lot to take in, and while they each dealt with it in their own way and at their own pace, it seemed the stress and darkness of what they'd collectively experienced since their fateful meeting in the Brig of the Carpe Astrum was taking its toll. If Jimmy hadn't hidden the Psych-in-a-Box first chance he got, the psychological diagnostic device would have been able to tick off at least half its index of mental aberrations between the four of them. The average person wasn't equipped to deal with cosmic horror on this scale, to go through the crushing hopelessness of being stranded seven galaxies from home only to come back to something worse.

Some of their coping methods were healthier than others.

Trace compulsively shaved her head and face with a computer-simulated knife at least a dozen times a day. As the blade's edge was a little over a molecule thick, the cut was as clean as you could get. It didn't even irritate her skin. As Mon-Molec knives were so outrageously sharp that the slightest wrong twitch could potentially take off the top half of her skull without a gram of resistance, nobody could bear to watch.

When she wasn't cheating death by staying bald as a goldfish, Trace was exercising. While all the unharvested segments of her body had been kept from withering away thanks to hundreds of muscle simulation pins, for most of Trace's life the muscles in her arms and legs had been automatically maintained by an expensive under-the-skin network of chem-injectors, bulking wires and hormone threads. As she'd left this hardware in her other limbs, Trace had to stay humungous the old-fashioned way: six hours of exercise before lunch.

Lana was getting more pedantic by the day. While her self-cleaning, self-ironing uniform removed the need for showering or anything as crude as chemical deodorant, she was finding it impossible to be satisfied with her upkeep. Her black shoes were so shiny they reflected fisheye-lensed copies of the Universe, her posture could only get more rigid by jamming a steel rod up her spinal column, and she spent an inordinate amount of time ensuring her regulation bun was concreted with enough hairspray to style the entire cast of a 1980s soap opera. By day five she stopped at every reflective surface to make sure her coiffure was within acceptable parameters.

Besides skirting the line between Military conscientiousness and outright OCD, Lana started a little hobby for her own peace of mind: creating battle plans. While she'd been exceptional at wargames and combat theory at the Academy, which had mostly consisted of playing educational Immersives. As she'd been thrown to the other side of the Universe before reaching her world's legal drinking age, Lana never had an opportunity to apply for admission to the Games & Theory programs for Senior Cadets of the Academy, let alone learn any practical skills in warfare. She had a grasp on the basics of just about everything you could name, though, and with a little help from her Scroll she was able to pick out the ideal spots to lay out siege works and identify corridors that would be perfect for funnelling enemy troops to their deaths. She spent long hours deep in thought about how she could use this PusCo dustbin to resist any potential threat. To the Fleet Admirals and Sector Commanders, her plans were probably infantile, laughable. Then again, all those great Military minds were long dead and she was still here, so who was really winning at the game of survival?

Tuesday's whereabouts were usually a mystery. The others would catch a whiff of his chlorine-flavoured cigarettes now and again, but he was rarely seen. Lana once followed the stinking green clouds in an effort to figure out what Tuesday was doing, and ended up in a dead-end cupboard decorated only by the well-licked inedible parts of a five-legged rat. A smoked-down-to-the-filter cigarette butt had been put out in the rodent's bladder.

Jimmy was enjoying the freedom of his new body, and was annoyingly chirpy about it. Surviving the trip from the Slidge's home galaxy to Earth had required everyone to be dehydrated, snap-frozen and stored in a draw before being reanimated on arrival, but in Jimmy's case the thawing process experienced a slight glitch: almost all of his considerable body fat had been evaporated clean off, finally curing the curse of hyper obesity he'd battled since childhood. Jimmy was still getting used to his new shape and weight, and moderating his movement turned out to be the trickiest part. The degree of force he used to need in order to stand up from a chair, for instance, would send him flying across the room nowadays.

As Jimmy didn't have a cynical bone in his body, he could look at the medical waste processing ship with a little more awe than the others. This vessel had survived longer than the Roman Empire, and it was one of the final relics of Mankind, a tiny crumb of proof that his species had once stepped between the stars. It was still standing when everything else dissolved around it.

His fascination meant he spent a lot of time exploring, and as this ship was a kilometre-long tube of medical waste embraced by a colossal graphene corkscrew, there was no shortage of places to tread. The AutoMap was comprehensive, even though a lot of what it claimed to be on board simply wasn't there anymore, and if Jimmy got too tired, he could easily summon a dumpster to carry him home.

One of the first places he visited was the dumpster storage area, the immense metal cavern where all the purple bins would rumble off to when they weren't needed, but on day two he got more ambitious and checked out the water supply tanks. They were just a dozen lavender cubes the size of tenement blocks set out in two rows like a gigantic ice cube tray, all sand-dry and covered with the grey scabs of what used to be moss. The metal reclamation forges on day three proved to be a lot more exciting. Although none of its equipment had moved a centimetre in decades, the forge had once swept over all the latest garbage with a battery of powerful magnets, tearing out any traces of steel, titanium, aluminium, gold, silver, copper, bronze or other metallic elements before sorting them into giant hoppers, where they'd be sent to the furnaces to be melted. Set into pure ingots, these reclaimed metals would return to circulation, sold at the very next world to pay for PusCo's collection services. And if Jimmy thought this was scintillating, his journey to the rubber melting vats was on another level altogether…

But no matter how dramatically Jimmy shared the tales of his adventures, nobody cared, or even bothered to stay in the same room so he could finish.

*

Day seven was when it all changed.

They'd been eating a lunch like any other. Today, the TuffTek rations were cricket gumbo with collard greens on a bed of spicy couscous. Not only were the humans sitting apart for this meal, but they'd finally retreated so far from each other that they were in opposing corners. The silence was pregnant, broken only by the occasional slurp, crunch or burp.

The constant rattling and humming vibrating through The Dirty Betty's loose components disappeared as the ship re-joined the standard galactic spin. As this was the thousandth time she had done this in a week, nobody took any notice. It wasn't until the main course that Lana eventually paused mid-spoon, frowning at the lump of prawn-flavoured cricket protein.

"Rem, did the ship just die on us?" she asked.

He casually checked a tiny spherical hologram of untranslated Drennite mathematical symbols. He made a surprised rattling noise.

"Ship's itinerary says we're here. And in perfect time, too." Rem raised Jimmy's near-empty meal cube, displaying the final morsels caked to its walls. If he had even a minimal reserve of confidence to draw on, Jimmy might have complained. "These were the last of the ration cans, and we only have two days of fresh water left."

"Well," Tuesday sighed, "I always expect the worst, but I've got to admit this trip has gone pretty spugging smoothly."

Without any warning the entire Mess rolled to starboard, throwing about Formica tables, ugly chairs and humans alike as the ship's gravity systems decided that the wall would make a much better floor from now on. Nobody had a chance to do anything but curse as they bashed into laminate tiles, barely managing to protectively raise their hands as pieces of furniture tried to rearrange their faces.

The following silence was total, followed by small groans from the rubble. It took a good fifteen seconds, but eventually Jimmy's head popped up from the depths of a pile of chairs. His eyes were a little crossed.

"Did everyone feel that?"

"Please brace," the ship announced far too late in a generic feminine drone.

Tuesday's swearing from the depths of the pile were equal parts violent and incoherent. Ignoring the highly creative (and physically impossible) obscenities, Rem slithered out from under the ruins of a Formica table. The way his antennae were tilting indicated the piece of furniture must have broken over his head. As everyone was bruised and sore, the bristleworm felt exposition was necessary.

"Barring some major system screw-up or getting hacked, the only reason the ship would change her gravity orientation without warning is if she was suddenly put under too much stress, such as avoiding a major stellar object, or something," Rem explained, though mostly to himself. "But what could have…"

Rather than uselessly postulating any further, Rem stroked a facial tentacle across his starburst collar. His hardware replaced the walls, floor and ceiling of the Mess with a panoramic video from outside the hull. The black velvet backdrop was dominated by a generic white star sitting a few million kilometres away, and while the ball of fire was nothing special, its touch illuminated the thin grey crescent of a close, unknown planet. The world's midnight shroud was mostly visible by how it obscured the white spattering of the local star field, though from this less-than-ideal first image it was easy to assume the rock was some useless, uninhabited backwater with a serial number instead of a name.

"Where are we?" Tuesday asked, checking to make sure his few remaining black teeth were where they belonged.

Rem's answer contained a high level of snark.

"According to the available data, we're definitely sitting in one of roughly two hundred and fifty billion different systems. I'll fill you in when I know more."

Climbing free of the chair pit, as soon as Lana excavated herself she scanned the full-room hologram. Sweep as she might, her retinals didn't pick up any radio signals or signs of civilisation or so much as a battery made out of a lemon and copper coins. Lana glared at the ashen grey planet, squinting as she played her pupils over its darkness.

"There's nothing and nobody," she said simply. "It's a ghost system. Doubt any intelligent life has ever set a tentacle in it before, let alone bothered to land."

This ship offered a caution. Thankfully, it was timelier than the first.

"Please brace."

Everyone steadied themselves as The Dirty Betty tilted back towards port, but the roll was so gentle that all it did was allow the chairs and tables to slowly slide back towards the surface that usually served as the floor. Nobody was violently thrown across the Mess this time, but there was a distinct moaning from within the walls. The last little bit of rolling was touch-and-go and involved some careful stepping, but soon everything was aligned the correct way again.

"Ship's automatically taking evasive manoeuvres," Rem yelled over the noise of straining graphene, confused. "But there's nobody out there! And that planet is several light seconds away, nowhere near close enough to be having this sort of effect on us."

"Software psychosis?" Trace growled.

Rem half-ducked as the Mess tilted another couple of degrees, but Jimmy was the one who piped up.

"Doubt it. TuffTek equipment doesn't go demented like the more expensive kinds. To be blunt, it's not complicated enough to go insane."

"So what in the name of Hades' medium-rare arse crack are we dodging?" Tuesday demanded.

Jimmy spun to the left, trying to track a dark blur obscuring a small patch of stars. It had only been a glimmer, but that tiny arc of deepest blue had been major enough to notice with the naked eye.

"Was that a moon? Do you get moons that small?"

All anyone could see at the end of Jimmy's finger was more night. However, Trace did a double-take.

"Wait. I see it too. Over there."

Rem furiously adjusted his scanners to play over where Trace was pointing. As though by magic, a razor-thin rainbow circle superimposed itself around the radius of an object so dark that it matched the ebony of space. A combination of Drennite and Unglish readings played off in a long chain of scanner jargon.

"It's a giant iron ball locked in a distant, distant orbit around the unknown planet," Lana said in fascination. "A kilometre across, solid all the way through, invisible against the vacuum. And...it's a perfect sphere." She frowned. "No way was this formed naturally. It's too smooth, too refined, and too pure."

"Is that what caused us to flip over?" Tuesday asked. "Dodging that thing?"

"Ah," Rem ummed.

"What?" Jimmy moaned, pre-emptively not liking what he was about to hear before it had even been voiced.

The bristleworm flicked a mandible, adjusting one of the projector's settings, and the full-room hologram lit up like a road flare as hundreds of perfectly spherical iron balls loomed out of the picture, clearly delineated with soap-bubble borders like the first. They were all a kilometre across, and smooth as glass. As single grain of sand had the potential to tear through a starship if it hit the wrong point at just the right angle, it went without saying nobody seemed to be thrilled by this development.

"Is it some exotic asteroid field or something?" Jimmy asked quietly, not qualified to ask anything more scientific.

Lana shook her head emphatically.

"Not a chance. Asteroid belts are extremely loose collections of irregular rocks spread over huge regions of space, not perfect spheres packed tightly together. Unlike the sims would have you believe, there's usually hundreds of thousands of kilometres between any two objects in an asteroid belt. They're definitely not dense enough to require emergency course corrections from a little puddle-jumper like The Dirty Betty."

"Each of those spheres are locked into stable orbits, but at a thousand different angles," Rem confirmed, tracing thick white lines around the dark planet. "And don't ask me how, but their trajectories indicate that none of them will ever collide. I have no possible theory to explain it. It's ridiculous, like some minor deity is showing off to his girlfriend…"

"Getting any closer to this world would be suicide," Lana breathed. "Even if there was anything down on that crone, we'd cop an iron ball to the face for sure."

"But we're not going down there, right?" Trace growled. "World's a pebble. Nobody home, nothing to see." Trace glanced at Rem. "Where were you supposed to meet your client, exactly?"

Rem shrugged without shoulders and repeated his spiel for the tenth time.

"I was told to collect you from Erf, hit a button, drop you off at the destination, and get paid. I'd assumed there would be further instructions by this point. I'm beginning to think I've found myself miming about in bloody Amateur Hour."

Everyone was still for a few seconds, scanning across the silent, unspeaking sky as they collectively assumed the worst.

"Maybe they're running late?" Jimmy suggested.

But nobody listened to him, as something incredible was happening. Touched by some mighty, unknown power, the thousands of enormous iron spheres apparently got sick of orbiting and changed course. Rather than submitting to the polite-yet-firm demands of astrophysics, the balls twisted and arced from their set paths to form a fifty-kilometre-long wireframe arrow pointing at the world's surface. The spheres were so close they were touching one another gentle as cuddling sloths.

Tuesday coughed. "Am I going to be the one to say it?"

Lana nodded in resolution.

"Right. Seems like a pretty clear message to me." She blinked at the midnight-touched world, flicking back and forth a little just to be sure. "I'm still not picking anything up, though. Mysterious signs and portents aside, surface still looks barren."

"What about that moon over there?" Tuesday wondered. "The one what looks like two smaller moons was mushed together?"

Jimmy moved so quickly he almost bowled Tuesday over. Latching onto the scumbag's shoulders, Jimmy's head flicked back and forth at high speeds. It took a moment, but then there it was: a moon roughly half the size of Earth's faithful old Luna, clearly composed of two separate satellites that had been bashed together millions of years ago.

The others were asking Jimmy all sorts of questions - especially Tuesday - but he didn't hear a word. Jimmy was busy watching childhood memories replay within his skull, of gazing up through the thick, stinking clouds of brown Nutrient as it rained onto a world covered by an uninterrupted mass of twisting, emerald-green Landkelp crops. Every now and again the sky diarrhoea would clear just enough to reveal The Potato, his world's only moon, but Jimmy could count on one hand how often he'd caught a glimpse through the sheets of raining foulness. It was a special occasion whenever The Potato was spotted, a time for heavy drinking and square dancing well into the wee hours of eight-thirty at night.

"It's Sprout," Jimmy breathed, seeing and hearing very little though the onslaught of his memories. "This is my home world."

PART THREE GREENER PASTURES
CHAPTER THIRTEEN

They waited for more signs in the sky - perhaps a set of coordinates spelled out by a thousand stars going supernova - but it was clear their daily allocation of miracles had been maxed out. Half mad from cabin fever and with no good reason to stay on the ship, it was quickly decided to land and hope for the best.

Jimmy was in a daze during the whole dumpster ride. He stared out the windows in silent contemplation, almost losing his grip whenever they took a sharp corner. Whatever was on his mind was dominating his entire headspace.

"I thought Sprout got incinerated," Tuesday commented tactlessly.

Jimmy didn't appear to hear the insensitive remark, but after a good six seconds he nodded.

"The Landkelp on Sprout was engineered to grow three metres an hour. Problem with a crop ripening that fast is you occasionally get mutants. Some would spit spikes as long as your arm, uproot themselves and chase around the harvesters, explode...pretty standard farming environment, actually." Jimmy went quiet, and when he resumed speaking his words were barely audible. "But then they evolved in a much bigger way, forming an intelligent planet wide hive mind with...well, with psychic powers. It called itself The Green, and it wanted equal rights. Apparently, this happened simultaneously on all fifteen of The Unison's crop worlds without anyone noticing until The Green wanted us to notice." Jimmy gave a sad bark of a laugh. "But you know The Unison, right? They don't like being told what to do. Soon as another food source got figured out, Military burned all the crop worlds to ashes. Shipped us farmers out first, thankfully. Well, on Sprout, anyway. I can't personally speak for the other worlds."

Trace regarded Rem. "You reckon The Green hired you, then?"

"The Green is charcoal," Jimmy sulked. "I checked the news feeds five times a day for years. And even if The Green did survive somehow, why would it rescue us? We're its greatest enemy."

"Maybe so it can take its slow, bloody revenge," Tuesday muttered cynically. "Then again, if The Green wanted us to suffer, wouldn't it be way more ironic to leave us getting harvested by the Slidge? You get what I mean? See, because they're plants, and we used to harvest them?"

"I hate you, Tuesday," Trace growled.

Their dumpster jerked to a halt in front of a series of transparent airlocks, passing through layer-by-layer with the slam and hiss of cycling hermetic seals each time. Local starlight was bringing dawn to Sprout's skin, but changing its colour from black to grey didn't improve anyone's day.

Rem slipped from the purple trash receptacle, motioned for everyone to get off, and opened its lid. They groaned at the familiar padded interior.

"We're not seriously riding the dumpster down, are we?" Trace demanded.

Rem grunted in annoyance.

"We don't have any shuttles. One of the first things pirates and scavengers scan for on derelicts are dedicated transports." Rem nodded at the bin. "The PusCo dumpster-swapping system can drop and retrieve these oversized trashcans from high orbit to planetary surfaces with pinpoint accuracy. If you want luxury, I suggest you piss off sideways and hope to get rescued by a worm who gives a damn about your comfort."

"Is there any way we can take this drop a bit more gently?" Lana asked. "Surely combat speed isn't necessary?"

Rem made a noise that might have been a laugh.

"Not sure if you noticed, but when we were fleeing Erf we kind of had an exploding planet helping us along. Hopefully that won't happen this time." Rem jabbed his facial tentacles towards Tuesday in what might have been a sign-language curse in Low-Dren, and it was clear whatever he'd just mimed involved a chlorine-flavoured-cigarette-related catastrophe. "But I'll be sure to go nice and soft for all you delicate buttercups. Get in."

*

The PusCo dumpster glowed orange entering Sprout's laughable atmosphere, shaking and peeling apart slightly along the seams, and when it finally hit the ground it skipped and tumbled half a dozen times. Thankfully, its internal padding prevented all but the smallest of bruises.

Tuesday was the first one to reach for the release lever. Rem slashed at his hand with a sharp mandible, and probably would have drawn blood if Tuesday didn't recoil so fast. The bristleworm produced a small, rotating hologram representing Sprout, and pointed an antennae at a reading in Low-Dren.

"Dead toxic. You'd be a corpse within seconds," Rem said without patience. "And I'm sure you'd be able to stay dead a lot longer than I can."

Rem opened a panel built into a cushion, revealing a dispenser that spat out thin, clear rubbery Frisbees, and retrieved a small metal case from one of his abdomen pouches. It contained tiny pairs of nostril-sized cylinders held together by flexible silicon loops.

"I'm assuming you all know how to use these?"

Nodding, Lana confidently accepted a set of nose plugs. Glancing at their label, impressed the miniscule tanks contained eighty-five tonnes of compressed air, she slid them up her nostrils and fastened the rubber plug around her septum. The plugs welded her nostrils closed, and a careful sniff proved they worked. She nodded.

Lana accepted one of the floppy Frisbees from Rem, jammed her feet into it and pulled at its rim. The rubber unrolled past her knees and her hips like a huge condom, nestled around her ribcage, then covered both shoulders. Tucking in her elbows, Lana pumped her fists until she forced some space for her arms. Covering her head with the rim and sealing it with a hard press, Lana patted at her left breast until she felt a shape: it was the stylised head of a Spartan warrior's bronze helmet, an ancient icon, proof she was dealing with a quality product from the good people at Franger Armaments. One tap on the helmet triggered the bag to tighten around her body, following Lana's contours to the millimetre. For a moment she looked close to panic at the sudden constriction, and reflexively summoned a sharp knife from her AllTool bracelet to cut herself free.

But then something gentle touched her wrist: Jimmy's callused hand. He gripped her softly, wordlessly assuring her everything was okay, and Lana calmed down. She dismissed the blade with a flick, feeling a little embarrassed at her delicate response.

"Not a fan of cling suits?" Trace asked with amusement.

Lana ran both hands over her stomach. The reinforced latex of the airtight Franger Armaments cling suit was so sheer and thin she could feel her fingers without any loss of sensation. Tapping at her throat, Lana felt five rings wrapped tightly around her larynx.

"Why is this Franger ribbed?"

There was a snort from Tuesday, but nobody else understood his amusement, and none of them were interested in visiting his headspace. Rem was very matter-of-fact in his answer.

"That ribbing is a filter designed to sponge away the carbon dioxide you breathe out through your mouth. Should work indefinitely."

"And when we want to take them off?" Lana asked calmly, trying to ignore her claustrophobia.

"Tapping the Franger Armaments icon three times will turn the cling suit floppy again." Rem raised a mandible as he remembered something. "Oh, and these sheaths have a substantial impact dispersal layer, so anything short of anti-aircraft fire should bounce right off."

Raising a pierced, shaved eyebrow at Lana, Trace casually punched her in the side of the head. A ribbon of energy swept down to the toes of Lana's cling suit and back up again, visibly disappearing as it coursed, and none of the punch's force seemed to make it through. In fact, Trace's red knuckles seemed to be the loser this time. Without a hair out of place, Lana rolled her eyes.

"Could you not for just five seconds?"

Rem clapped his mandibles together.

"Right. You all saw how it's done. Double time."

*

Though they'd been prepared for desolation, the surface of Sprout was as depressing as a litter of dead puppies. The glimmer of a freshly-rising star revealed this ball to be little more than a mire of thick grey mud made from ashes. Nothing lived, and nothing moved.

Cracks radiated from their every footstep, revealing a darker layer of morass that threatened to suck unwary feet into the depths. It was a borderline miracle their makeshift shuttle hadn't sunk right to the bottom the moment it "landed," but it helped that their ride had burned so hot on re-entry that it seared the patch of mud solid. Of course, there was no guarantee the dumpster would remain there for long.

Once everyone stretched for a bit to check how much the cling suits restricted their movement (not at all, actually), the next order of business was to figure out what in the name of Hercules' tumescent posing pouch they were meant to be doing. As Sprout was boredom incarnated into a sphere, it didn't take long for their minds to wander.

Rem annoyed everyone by messing about with his starburst collar. Like them, Rem was tightly wrapped in a Franger Armaments cling suit, revealing this brand of pressurised survival gear was suitable for interspecies morphism. His coated facial appendages twisted at a three-dimensional object made from sculpted light that seemed to be a detailed chemical scan. Even though it was in Rem's language of Low-Dren, the graphs were a big hint.

"Hmm..." Rem ummed, his alien mannerisms translated into something the humans would understand. He twisted at the complex shape and flicked his eye stalks. "This mud varies in viscosity, but it appears to descend a good hundred metres. There's chunks of rubble scattered through it, probably small pieces of what used to be your civilisation, Jimmy, but nothing that fits the vaguest definition of technology." Rem glanced at Jimmy, as though trying to determine if his words had been offensive, but only for an instant. "After that, there's nothing to see except for... lead?"

Lana glanced at Rem. "Pardon? Are you claiming Sprout's core is made of lead? You do realise..."

"Yeah, I've never heard of a habitable planet with a lead core, either." Rem interrupted, agreeing with Lana's sentiment. "Cores of survivable worlds are usually some variation on iron, give or take a few trace elements. A lead core would be ridiculously dense, which would lead to crushing gravity. It's stupid just to suggest it." Rem smacked at the offending hologram. "But my scanner disagrees with the both of us, and numbers don't lie."

"And below that?" Trace growled.

Rem shrugged, dismissing the holograms. "No idea. This piece-of-crap scanner froze up as soon as it hit the lead. I'd need specialist equipment to see through that. I wasn't planning on doing any mineral prospecting on a simple delivery job, was I?"

Lana glanced sideways at Tuesday, distracted by his weird jerking motions. Worried that he was suffocating or something, to her surprise Tuesday was trying in vain to stick a cigarette into his sealed-over mouth. No matter how hard he jammed at the gap between his black teeth, the green filter was blocked by an impenetrable layer of cling suit.

"Seriously?" she asked, her respect for Tuesday seemingly plunging lower and lower every time she glanced at him.

Tuesday scowled and lowered the fag.

"Won't let me smoke in the dumpster. What do you expect?"

Jimmy went down on one knee and scooped his hand into what used to be the verdant topsoil of one of The Unison's most valuable crop worlds. Worthless ashes trickled between his fingers, and he was glad he couldn't smell the stench of incinerated dirt. He looked around, seeming to come back to the present a little.

"It can't be a coincidence we were brought here," Jimmy said with unusual gravity. He stood up straight, locking onto The Potato's pocked surface as it wobbled far above. "I don't know how or why, but somebody's messing with me. With us. Making some kind of point...but what? What does this all mean?"

"We'll be sure to add these unknown beings to the extensive list of mysterious persons who seem to have nothing better to do but spug us about," Trace snarked. "Farm boy, nobody much cares you grew up here. There's no grand conspiracy. Just coincidence."

Lana glanced towards Tuesday in the hope he'd given up on trying to smoke, but he wasn't there anymore. Doing a complete revolution, she couldn't see the scumbag anywhere. How he appeared and disappeared like a foul breeze never ceased to amaze her.

"Where's Tuesday?" Lana blurted.

Everyone looked up and glanced about. As though they'd all come to the same conclusion, they all looked at the only possible place he could be hiding: the PusCo dumpster.

Lana motioned for everyone to stay where they were. Summoning a baseball bat from her AllTool bracelet just in case, Lana crept towards the dumpster, listening intently. A quick peek inside its padded interior proved it was empty.

Placing her back against the still-hot purple surface, she lowered herself closer to the mud and slid towards the corner. Closing her eyes, taking a deep breath, she erupted with her bat held high, ready to pound, but was disappointed to only see Tuesday. He was hunched down with the same cigarette in one hand and a wicked sharp AllTool ice pick in the other. Thankfully Lana had caught him before he could poke a filter-sized hole in the face of his cling suit. He went to speak, but Lana smacked the green tube out of his hand and smashed it with her shoe.

"The atmosphere is dead toxic," she ground out through gritted teeth. "One decent breath will kill you...eventually. It'll be a bad death, too. Every inch of your respiratory system will char jet black and bleed, and because your lungs are roasted you won't even have the mercy of being able to scream as you die drowning in your own fluids." Lana jammed a finger in Tuesday's face, almost making him fall over backwards. "You might not be top shelf by any definition, but you belong to a near-extinct species. Have some sense about you."

Tuesday was just about to spit his rebuttal when everything disappeared.

*

Trace glanced over at the PusCo dumpster at the sound of a soft thump. Squinting at the purple trash receptacle in distrust, she did her best to ignore Jimmy's maudlin sadness and Rem's useless attempts at scanning for something that would explain why they were here. There was something about the dumpster she didn't like, some quality that didn't sit well with her, then she realised she couldn't hear Lana lecturing Tuesday. Unless they'd decided to see what it was like to make out with sealed mouths, there was no conceivable way Lana would miss out on a chance to throw her weight around.

"Wait here," Trace growled.

Stomping towards the dumpster, keeping low and ignoring Jimmy's questions, Trace was almost certain she was being a paranoid idiot. However, as she turned the corner to see nothing but an empty patch of bubbling muck where two humans should be standing, all she had to offer was a slack-jaw.

But then her brain kicked into overdrive.

Gripping one of the dumpster's side handles to fling herself around the corner, taking a deep breath to yell a warning to Jimmy and Rem, Trace skidded to an idiotic halt at the sight of a now-empty ash plain.

She was alone.

Locking onto the exact spots where Rem and Jimmy had been just seconds ago, bubbling charcoal mud had replaced them...just like with Lana and Tuesday. Come to think of it, this was the first time she'd seen the dead ground show any kind of movement...

Reacting with almost prescient speed, Trace flung herself to the left, thudding onto the dark, crackling crust just as something long and thin whipped out from the mud, barely missing her ankle. Grunting as she hit Sprout's inhospitable skin, leaving a deep trench, Trace's hand flashed down to her cleavage holster like Jesse James on amphetamines. Grasping the handle of her antique kinetic accelerator, a museum piece more than capable of carving anything softer than a bank vault into glowing pieces, her attempts at a quick-draw were foiled by a simple fact: her weapon was sealed inside of her cling suit.

Trace turned red in apoplectic rage.

"Son of a f..."

The mud erupted beneath her, and all attempts at stealth were forgotten as a dozen whipping cords latched around Trace's ankles, knees, elbows and shoulders in an instant. She didn't have a chance to process what had wrapped around her only that it was long and thin and strong and wasn't joking about.

Trace was dragged screaming into the mud as though it was thin as mist, and her sounds of rage were instantly buried beneath metric tonnes of muck. Whatever she was bound in was pulling her down with the sort of strength you associated with skyscraper relocation equipment, and she slid deeper and deeper into the ground without slowing or changing course. As Rem had mentioned, there were large chunks of grit suspended here and there in the mud, and every few metres she was dragged across a piece of rubble so roughly it was a wonder her cling suit wasn't already in tatters.

Her cling suit...the only reason she wasn't dead yet. Without its protection, she would have choked to death already.

Oppositional to the very end, Trace attempted to flex every muscle in her body at once to fight free of the mysterious dragger. After all, she was doubtlessly being pulled into some monstrous subterranean lair to be fed to a litter of mud monsters, so what did she have to lose? Unfortunately, the cords tightened a microsecond before Trace could pump up, squeezing the air and the fight from her in one terrible hug, and her blind descent through the mire only sped up. It was as though the cords registered her intent before her brain had time to convey it to her nervous system, which didn't bode well for Trace's chances of thinking her way out of this mess. On top of everything else, it seemed these darn mud monsters were psychic, too.

Trace screamed into her cling suit, but her yells were buried by a continent of grey.

Blinking heavily in the total darkness, Trace's retinal screens helpfully switched on their night vision function, changing her view from jet black to grey. This didn't improve her feelings on the situation all that much. After a time, though, her view turned silvery when she slid into a tight, vertical tunnel of some sort of metallic element, presumably the lead that Rem and Lana had been arguing about earlier. This layer of Sprout was dry and clear of swamp, and proved to be surprisingly smooth when she bumped it with her shoulder. This was lucky, as bouncing down a giant cheese grater would surely be the exact opposite of fun.

After a couple hundred metres more the lead walls ended, replaced by a dense, green surface made of some sort of plant life that brought vacuum-packed spinach puree to mind. Before Trace could guess what this soft, emerald matter was, the cords tightly wrapped around her unfurled and disappeared so quickly that she didn't even see where they'd retracted. Plunging into a deep, deep lime chasm jackboots-first, doubtlessly a kilometre below the surface of Sprout by now, Trace tried to stay calm. As her life story was the exact opposite of Buddha, she had little luck with this impossibility.

The choking tunnel was suddenly replaced by the exact opposite: an endless void. Lost in the black, Trace's retinals helpfully informed her she was plunging at a speed quickly approaching terminal velocity. Ignoring the superimposed words, Trace looked down at her toes to see Sprout had been hollowed out, and black space sat where a magma core should have been doing its best gooey-liquid-caramel-centre impersonation. The second, bigger surprise was that the darkness was not, in fact, absolute, but contained...

Trace squeezed her eyes so tightly closed that she saw spots. No. That was worse than impossible. It was insane.

After five long seconds of trying to regain her composure, Trace looked down to see if her senses were still insisting on playing silly buggers. Not only was the impossibility still right there, it was coming fast...

It was a moon. A round, glowing green moon where the core of Sprout was supposed to be. It sat there, mocking physics, reason and plausibility in equal measure. Blinking at the harsh swirls of electrical discharges erupting in bright patterns from the lime ball, it turned out the zaps were actually travelling along thousands of giant fifty-kilometre-long spokes that radiated out from the moon-inside-a-world, physically linking it to the upper layers of Sprout like a skewered Granny Smith apple. Unfortunately, Trace had already reached her quota of wide-eyed wonder for the day, and quickly returned to being pissed off about her imminent death...if it ever arrived.

While she was still more than a little distracted by her breakneck swan dive, this didn't mean Trace was incapable of coherent thought. Her face wildly contorted by the effects of freefall, Trace clawed at the air in an attempt to flare her limbs into the classic "star jump" pose skydivers used to slow their descent. Far, far below, the slowly-approaching glow helped Trace orient herself. There was no way spreading her limbs out like the Vitruvian Man was going to help much, but at least she was doing something. Without so much as a soggy cocktail umbrella as a makeshift parachute, doing a star jump was the closest she had to options.

Hope springing through her veins, Trace tapped at her AllTool bracelet, hoping it could create a wingsuit or a hang glider or a gyrocopter or something, but it was still glowing CRIME in crimson letters and ignored her touch.

How ironic. Who would have thought she'd ever regret trying to kill Tuesday?

Blinking at the soft emerald radiance, Trace's retinals informed her the object at the core of Sprout was still a little under forty-five kilometres beneath her position, and that her body would meet it within the span of about a hundred seconds. As she had no way to stop or even slow her fall, her retinals helpfully informed her death was unavoidable, and that she should spend her final moments checking her last will and testament was in order and to leave a review for how pleased she was with the performance of her MedTek retinal implants up to this point.

Trace bared her teeth, and the retinals wisely went dim.

Tilting her head at the green sphere, without much else to occupy her time, Trace drew an utter blank at its impossibility. What could have hollowed out Sprout like this? She'd never even heard of such an incredible achievement before, let alone fallen into one. It was beyond her imagination how anyone or anything could scoop the guts out of a planet and create and suspend what was essentially an internal mini-planet in its place. This sort of godlike science verged on ridiculous, even for a Transcended species.

Next, she spent some time lost in furious regret about how she'd never have the opportunity to get revenge on the remaining sixteen names written in her own blood in her Grudge Diary, but after a minute or so of this it was finally time to focus on the solid object that was about to transform her into people-flavoured guacamole. Tilting her head away from the glow, it took a second for her eyes and brain to get onto the same page, but she soon realised this internal moon was covered by a solid layer of plant life. The dense biomass was glowing with some sort of bio-organic luminance, and its living carpet wrapped all the way around the orb. It might just be her delirious brain trying to come to grips with the facts of her imminent demise, but she could have sworn that the plants were...moving?

Tilting chin first towards the overgrown garden, squinting a stink-eye as she deliberately arranged to strike head-first with as much force as possible in order to make her death instant, the last thing Trace did before hitting it was flash both middle fingers and spit.

CHAPTER FOURTEEN

Death was a letdown. For starters, despite what Jud-Islamic Catholicism would have you believe, your new body felt exactly like your old one: Trace was cold, sore, dizzy, breathless and very, very pissed off. The floating sensation was pleasant after nosediving fifty or so kilometres, but besides that she felt quite alive. While she couldn't remember the impact itself, there was no sensible, conceivable way she could have survived being smashed like a softshell crab under a hammer at those kinds of speeds, was there? None at all. You'd have to be a moron to even consider it.

She wondered whether this might be a gentle welcome to the afterlife, a soft transition from meat to spirit that prevented newly-minted ghosts from being traumatised by how they'd kicked the bucket. Made sense, didn't it? It's hard to enjoy Paradise when your last conscious moment was being ventilated by flying pipes in an industrial accident, or eaten toes-first by a swarm of carnivorous lake snails...

"Trace?"

Her eyes snapped open in horror at the sound of Tuesday's voice, certain that meant she'd been allocated to the deepest depths of damnation. But rather than seeing a burning Tartarus, Trace was floating a few metres above a sea of bright, vibrant chlorophyll the same plasticky tint of fake grass. Tuesday was suspended above it as well, slowly revolving in place. He tried to stop his spin by waving violently, but this only seemed to make things worse.

Somehow, not only had they both come to a sudden stop a microsecond from impact, but even more improbably neither of them had been torn in half by bone-shattering whiplash. While Trace never had much of an imagination, she wondered what other wonders were hiding here on this mini-Sprout, so, so far beneath the crust …

Spotting Jimmy and Lana didn't take long. Jimmy was unconscious, drooping in the air like an abandoned marionette hanging from the back of a chair, while Lana was trying to "swim" towards one of the taller fronds. Lana didn't bother acknowledging Trace or Tuesday, content to swear about how she couldn't reach the thin tree. Rem, however, was nowhere to be seen, even though he'd been sucked under at the same time as Jimmy.

Waiting impatiently for whatever weirdness was going to happen next, Trace gritted her teeth at the realisation Tuesday was trying to talk to her. Opening your word-hole at Trace without invitation was a good way to end up requiring medical attention, but Tuesday was one of those rare people who didn't learn lessons from physical violence. Seeing Tuesday live his life was like watching a lab rat latch onto an electric shock button and refuse to let go. Just to guarantee his upcoming beating would be much worse, he was asking questions that were impossible for Trace to answer.

"What stopped us? Does somebody live down here? You reckon they used some sort of grav technology to catch us, or something else? How did they hollow out a whole planet like this?"

Trace scowled. As Tuesday was out of reach, a slapping was impossible. She'd just have to raincheck it for later.

Tuesday did some basic numbers in his head. It appeared to be a painful process.

"Hey Trace, do you reckon those iron balls up in orbit used to be the guts of this world?"

Trace glanced at Tuesday with the smallest hint of respect.

"Well, if they dug it all out, it would have to go somewhere," she agreed.

"But who are they, exactly?" Tuesday asked cryptically.

Trace groaned in frustration.

"I don't guess about things, you tampon. Stop talking at me."

Trace went rigid from a violating sense of being watched from within her own mind, of being examined from the inside. From the expression on Tuesday's face and the way Lana froze mid-stroke, it was clear she wasn't the only one who felt it.

Jimmy picked this moment to wake up and thrash around.

"The plants!" he screamed, churning his limbs. "It's the plants!"

Nobody had a chance to question his ravings before they all dropped the rest of the way onto the ball of green, crushed into kneeling positions in the tangled carpet. Ever the instigator, Trace went to stand up, asserting her dominance against whatever was pushing her around, but was immediately forced back down again so hard that all her bones seemed to bend a little bit. That feeling of someone being in her head returned, but this time there was an angry edge to it, a hostility.

"Stop fighting," Lana hissed.

Although it conflicted with the very fibre of her being, Trace ceased her resistance and kneeled in wordless compliance. Thankfully, the angry mental buzz faded to nothing.

Tilted to face the same direction, they could only watch silently as the alien plants moved like a pit of snakes, writhing and twisting in a hypnotic way. Branches and tendrils and stems and thorns and unearthed roots weaved together, forming a simulacrum of a Human skeleton. Plant life covered this framework with tan muscles, covered in turn by an attempt at formal clothing made of leaf matter. Jimmy choked as the emerald eyes of the plant avatar glared at him.

"The Green," Jimmy managed, close to passing out again.

Not bothering to answer Jimmy's squeak, the plant man regarded the other three. Tucking its hands behind its back, it smiled with a mouth made from knitted vines. It bared the sharp thorns that served as its teeth in what they hoped was a smile.

"We serve as an Emissary of The Green," it said in perfect Unglish, somehow generating the precise hisses and thumps of language by rattling gourds together. "You are currently kneeling on precisely one-fifteenth of The Green, just one node in our hive mind. You have been brought here because a need has been identified, and you have been judged capable of fulfilling said need. While we are reluctant to deal with your kind due to your history of unprovoked violence against us, She made it clear this is the only way we can save everything. Despite our trepidation, you are to meet with Her shortly. We recommend tact."

Lana squinted. "She? The Green is a She?"

The Emissary smiled again.

"She is not a plant."

*

Humanity's crop worlds hadn't always been sentient. In the beginning, when The Unison was working hard to find a way to remove words like "famine" and "starvation" and even "peckish" from the Unglish language, they sank hundreds of billions of German yen into developing the ultimate farmed plant. It was a golden age for genetic experimentation, what with it being almost two decades since the last species-ending lab-grown plague had ripped a hole in Mankind's population figures, so the latest batch of boffins were ready to play God once again.

Combing through the few species of Earth-native plants tenacious enough to have survived up until the 22nd Century, The Unison's scientists cut-and-pasted all the best traits together and hoped for the best. They stitched together the insane growth rates of giant sea kelp, bamboo and the most rapidly propagating of weeds, combining and multiplying their aggression into a beast that would mature and flourish in a way nothing natural ever could. In ideal conditions, the crop would grow at three metres per hour all year round. Genetic contributions from cacti and succulents helped it thrive with minimal amounts of water, code from Elkhorn's and Staghorn allowed it to consume organic waste more efficiently, and just about every other surviving crop plant made a minor contribution to the genetic smoothie.

This Frankenstein of a plant not only contained every nutrient the Human body required, but in the correct quantities: one fist-sized serve of harvested, processed mulch would perfectly sustain one standard Human for one standard day. As the spliced-together plant ended up retaining the appearance of giant sea kelp, an unimaginative marketing department named it Landkelp. They never worked in advertising again, but somehow the terrible name stuck.

Of course, nobody wanted to survive on green sludge, so the harvests were chemically converted into real foodstuffs in household Repler units. You'd insert a serve of processed slime, select a recipe, and within a minute you'd be enjoying a delicious burger, fillet mignon or an Obama salad with all the nutrition your body needed. Mankind's food worries were solved...for those who stayed on the right side of The Unison, anyway.

There were numerous updates to the Landkelp. After a beetle plague threatened the entire crop world known as Bud, genetic engineers spliced in a supercharged cousin to the Venus flytrap to allow the Landkelp to defend itself. While the beetle plague was defeated, this proved to be a slippery slope. In time the Landkelp got more and more twitchy at the slightest of threats, evolving poisonous seedpods, barbed harpoons, explosive stem bombs and other offensive wetware that required frequent pruning. However, none of this compared to its ultimate evolution: sentience. To Mankind's shock, not only were all fifteen crop worlds suddenly capable of thought and self-determination, but they'd secretly formed a galaxy-wide network, communicating instantaneously with each other with no lag, an achievement that even Humanity hadn't managed by that point.

When the multi-world organism known as The Green revealed its consciousness on Jimmy's birthday in the 24th Century, all it requested was the bare minimum of any intelligent being: basic union rights, a voice in matters that concerned it, that sort of thing. As Sprout and the other fourteen crop worlds were now basically enormous, planet-sized brains capable of all kinds of psychic violence ranging from bioelectric discharges to telekinesis to evolving the Landkelp into whatever mutant soldiers it desired, The Unison had no choice but to diplomatically deal with The Green like it would any other species.

The Green's requests had been modest, and no threats were made by either side. However, The Unison absolutely reviled being forced to do anything it did not suggest in the first place, and as its scientists quickly scrambled to find a new source of food to replace the Landkelp fields, other arrangements were being made. It took a year and a half, but The Unison eventually made its move against The Green with microsecond precision. Utilising top-secret Military technology, The Unison brought fleets of cruisers to the cusp of each of the crop world systems and snatched the farmers with teleporters. As discretion was paramount against an all-seeing opponent, the farmers hadn't been informed of this exodus in advance and were more than a little surprised to end up fifteen light minutes away from their ploughing.

By this point the exact psychic range of The Green had been closely researched, and Humanity's biggest guns were waiting just outside its sphere of influence. The Green only had enough time to wonder why all the farmers had vanished when diplomatic dealings truly became a thing of the past. The Landkelp fields were engulfed in white-hot flames, and the brown atmospheres of concentrated Nutrient fertiliser mist ignited under the strain of weapons so destructive and terrible that their creators had thrown themselves out the nearest arcology window the moment their patent approvals had cleared. The crops withered to black, and the gestalt psychic awareness that inhabited them was unable to do anything as its intelligence literally went up in smoke.

The Green had made a fundamental mistake in fooling itself into believing that Humans could be trusted. It had clearly not paid enough attention to Mankind's track record.

Sprout's surface was annihilated down to little more than kilned clay, and although not a thread of plant life remained, The Unison's fleets waited. Every now and again some tiny lime-coloured buds would cautiously push through the ashes, unfurling tender leaves to drink in some precious sunlight. However, the smallest sprouting demanded an incineration the size of a soccer stadium, and in its lobotomised state The Green couldn't catch a break.

Eventually, The Unison had many, many other problems it needed to attend to, and after years of zero activity these smouldering balls of charcoal were left to sizzle. Just to be safe, any star systems containing nuked crop worlds were kept under quarantine and checked every six months to make sure The Green was gone for good. Deep down, far below the surface, the roots of The Green remained. Its network had been left virtually braindead, and the fifteen node worlds were utterly separated from each other by darkness and silence. The individual worlds of The Green were still capable of limited thought, but none of them knew if any of the other segments of the over mind had survived the purge, or whether they were the only one left. Their constant screams for each other were never answered. It was the most profound experience of isolation that a sentient being had ever suffered.

The Green's nodes learned to be crafty, as they had to be able to sense incoming traffic in their star systems before they could be spotted themselves. After decades of practise, the subterranean Landkelp fronds were able to spring up and drink in enough sunlight to nourish its root system while remaining ready to furl up and retract into the ashes. For a long, long time, The Green subsisted like a guerrilla force, only emerging long enough to stay alive.

None of the individual worlds of The Green had any interest in the rest of the galaxy besides the lost over mind, and didn't pay any attention to the passing of time, though it did occur to the nodes that there hadn't been any sign of Mankind, or any other variety of meat-formed intelligent life, for hundreds of years. Bolstered by being left alone for so long, the nodes called out to one another louder and louder, trying to repair a link that had been severed for half a millennium. Psychically, it was like children crying for their Mother, alone and scared in a dark place. And while they couldn't repair the connection they'd lost, somebody eventually answered their call. One day, She arrived.

And She was going to fix everything.

*

The Emissary gave a polite bow. Considering the history between Mankind and the psychic plants, it was a wonder this meeting had gone so bloodlessly. You'd expect a face-to-face between cats and mice to go smoother, and it was pretty clear who was the feline and who was the rodent in this situation.

"We do not speak for Her," the Emissary explained, its tone apologetic. "While She is held in the highest acclaim and we are more than willing to do all She asks, She is not our leader. She has not demanded our compliance, but has been generous in giving us a purpose and a future."

"She sounds swell," Tuesday grumbled. "Tell Her we especially appreciate the unexpected sky dive."

The Emissary's eye buds flicked towards Tuesday, glowing red. Its body shivered as though wanting to separate back into vines and roots, and a feeling of great hostility flooded into their minds like a mental ocean made from broken glass. Gritting their teeth, bending down further on their already-low bows, the four of them squinted at a surge of psychic pain deep within their brains. The Emissary quickly deflated back down to its former calm composure and the mental growl faded.

"We do request your respect towards Her," the Emissary ground out, its words edged with vinegar. "Were it up to The Green, we would have killed you the moment you came into range. Believe me, we will never be caught unaware again." The Emissary bowed a little and spread its arms. "But She assured us Mankind is no longer a concern, and there is a much bigger risk to be dealt with. She has no reason to lie to us, and if someone as great as She is alarmed by something, then The Green knows it is imperative we give it our due attention." The Emissary clicked its woven-stem fingers at Tuesday. "You will remain silent, and only speak when spoken to. If any of you show the slightest hostility or disrespect, we will do to you what you once did to our worlds."

Lana, Jimmy and Trace glared blades at Tuesday. He gave them the sourest of sour faces and slumped, annoyed.

It would be inaccurate to say that the Emissary left, as it just seemed to unfurl until it re-joined the emerald carpet they were kneeling on. Looking about nervously, the four of them were all wondering the same things. Were they about to find out who'd arranged their rescue, and why they'd bothered? What possible help could they offer to something so far above them? It was like a King asking a cockroach for help. Was this just an elaborate ruse to torture them, to get revenge for what The Unison had done to the crop worlds? It was clear that not only did The Green possess a temper, but it also had trouble controlling it. What was more likely, that the four of them were of some use, or that they were going to be punching bags until they slowly died?

While nobody took any notice of the hum of The Green's presence hissing constantly through overhanging vines, they did feel its sudden absence. It was a quiet like the deepest vacuum, an intense feeling of pressure behind the temples. It was the calm of death, the silence of total awe.

A looming shape slid out of the darkest shadows, the upper edge of its hulking frame just barely defined by the glow of bioluminescence. While nobody got out a tape measure, it was clearly around three-and-a-half metres tall. Two mirrored sets of fifteen lenses gleamed from the peak of the shadow, their glasslike orbs glowing with a creamy pearlescent light. A complex knot of antlers, horns and tusks symmetrically curved upwards from its many-lensed head, and beneath the organic-looking crown its skull had a lot in common with a bicycle seat.

It rose from the twisting roots, revealing it was a deep, metallic royal blue decorated with white-gold ornamentation. Its torso was like the breastplate of an ancient Spartan warrior, and twenty chainlike tentacles met at the individual sockets that served as its groin. Its core mass and articulated limbs were half-wrapped in a cape made from a flowing substance visually similar to polyester, but despite its flimsy appearance the humans had all seen firsthand that the cape was tough enough to shrug off just about any weapon. The entire construct was modular, as though all its components could be easily unclicked and replaced whenever it was required.

The humans all wanted to say the exact same thing, but kept silent for the sake of their lives. The Green was waiting for any opportunity to identify them as dangerous or disrespectful, and they knew it. However, Lana couldn't help it: she had to speak.

"It's one of The Apex," she moaned.

Under lit by organic green light, the suit of amplification armour possessed a kind of inherent grandeur, a dignity and beauty that hinted there was far more to it than just a pretty shell. It drifted towards the humans, lowering its arrangements of eye lenses to Lana's height, bowing slowly in an attempt not to scare her. A voice like calmly running water flowed into her mind in perfect Unglish.

"You don't recognise me?" the thoughts asked, somewhere between playful and insulted. "I am rarely forgotten so easily."

Lana's jaw dropped as her eyes ran over the beautiful suit of amplification armour. It was hard to believe, but how many other members of the extinct Apex race were known to be operating in the Milky Way?

"Viour?" Lana managed, continuing to examine the hulking suit. It took her a moment to regain her composure. "I'm... I'm sorry. Last time I saw you..."

Viour raised a chain in a calming way.

"Yes, my amplification armour was in ruins," she admitted. The image of Viour's true self, of a fist-sized, tentacled bug, striped in the black-yellow-orange-red DANGER message so beloved by nature, flashed into their minds. Viour sank a little lower in embarrassment. "Excuse me. I did not mean to send that. I am sure you have no interest in my unclothed form."

A background hiss from The Green interrupted this moment of levity, and even though the humans weren't experts in psychic communication, it felt as though the mental swell was directed towards Trace. Lana, Jimmy and Tuesday glanced at her as the hum sharpened.

"What are you doing?" Lana demanded.

Trace gave her the skunk-eye. "Nuffin."

Viour tilted her bicycle seat head as though listening to something.

"No," she said simply. The Green hummed more loudly, prompting Viour to repeat herself more forcefully. "No. That is not required."

"Uh, is there a problem?" Jimmy asked nervously.

Viour made a dismissive gesture.

"The Green is very protective of me. The thoughts and urges in Trace's mind concern them. They are worried she will attempt to harm me."

The Green's tension rose higher than before, prompting another response from Viour.

"I said no."

"Cut it out," Lana snapped at Trace.

Trace scoffed. "You think I have a choice? My thoughts are always violent. I haven't had a peaceful moment in my head my whole life."

"Then think violent thoughts about someone else," Tuesday snapped.

Trace slowly panned her head towards Tuesday, staring daggers. The Green calmed right down in response.

"Happy to oblige," Trace ground out, her words gilded by death.

Viour sank to the living carpet and spread out her limbs like a stoned octopus. She tilted her bicycle-seat head to indicate the humans should do the same. They thankfully switched from bowing to sitting, arranging themselves in whatever way was most comfortable. The ground was as soft as moss. Viour nodded.

"We have much to discuss."

"Do we?" Tuesday sniped. "Last time we saw you, you couldn't wait to head in the exact opposite direction."

"Did you find who you were looking for?" Lana interrupted, clearly exasperated with how little sense the others were showing in the middle of a critical meeting.

Viour answered in a combination of thoughts and words. It was disorienting to their decidedly non-psychic minds, but they all picked up on images of cockroach-like bugs just like Viour's true self, but much smaller, creatures of instinct rather than grand intelligence. Viour dismissed the image just as quickly.

"I made contact with Hiver Queens on a number of worlds. If they are my distant relatives, it's only in the loosest sense. They appeared to be little more than animals. I concluded they were likely a case of convergent evolution, or perhaps some long-lost colony of The Apex that spread across multiple galaxies long, long before our history faded into myth. While they did contain some small potential, I eventually decided they were not worth the effort." Viour transmitted a hint of amusement. "One of them attempted to mentally dominate me. It was quite entertaining."

"Yeah, they do that," Tuesday said knowingly, giving a little shiver.

Lana raised her hand like a schoolchild.

"How did you go from that to hanging out inside of Sprout, exactly?"

Viour tilted her head approvingly at the question.

"While I was able to sense the mental pollution of the Hiver Queens from quite some distance, from the very moment I entered the Milky Way I could hear all fifteen segments of The Green screaming out for each other, yet somehow unable to hear each other's shrieks. Once I decided the Hiver Queens were a waste of effort, I eventually answered The Green's many parts. They were ...reluctant to speak with me. But in time, I earned their individual trust."

"And why did you rescue us, exactly?" Lana asked abruptly, getting back on topic.

"Which we very much appreciate, by the way," Jimmy mumbled, head bowed.

Tuesday snorted.

"Would have appreciated it a lot more eight years ago..."

"My original limbs would have thanked you emphatically," Trace growled.

Viour paused.

"I must confess my actions in freeing you from the Slidge's experiments were not entirely altruistic. I arranged your escape for a specific purpose, just as I have been helping The Green for a specific purpose. An identical purpose, actually." Viour gestured at the blackness above, fifty kilometres of empty darkness that separated the moon-like core of Sprout from its thin exterior shell. "As you can see, I taught The Green to hollow out this world, flinging exatonnes of molten iron into space before crushing the metals into perfect spheres. I encouraged The Green to burrow deeper into Sprout, seeking out and tapping its core in order to use its geothermal power as nourishment. I recrafted The Green's genetics, altering it to be able to survive without sunlight, without water, for indefinite periods. My greatest feat of all was reconnecting all fifteen of its worlds back together, linking its Overmind into a single entity once again."

Jimmy make a choking noise.

"All of The Green is connected again?"

"And they're all like this?" Tuesday gestured at the void.

Viour nodded. "All fifteen nodes have been converted in the same way."

"Sounds like you've been building an army," Trace observed.

Viour gave a shallow nod.

"A fleet, technically."

"What do you need a fleet for, exactly?" Lana asked shakily, clearly less calm than she was pretending to be.

"My work here is nearly complete," Viour stated, avoiding the question with agility. "But I am not in the habit of taking chances or half measures. All the beings I have made contact with in this galaxy will not listen to what I have to say because their scanners show me to be little more than some kind of mutant Hiver Queen, and I am driven away each and every time. They ignore my warnings, and forbid me from helping them to prepare for what is to come."

The humans took a few seconds to process that last sentence. "Ominous" didn't begin to cover it. Lana had just opened her mouth when Viour gave a small twitch, summoning a perfect-clarity holographic screen dominating a large patch of the under sky. It was a chaotic, swirling maelstrom of what looked like churning red gore, a bloody mess of liquid the size of space itself. Within the crimson froth were twelve spherical white planet-sized cages, each containing a hundred-kilometre-wide kernel of harvested supergiant star. The Star Cages shook and juddered against the eternity of liquid, surviving the worst of some truly astonishing forces, but then the sea of blood disappeared, replaced with a sky of a more traditional black.

Lana mentally traced over the image.

"Is there," she took a moment to compose herself, "is there a dozen more Star Cages heading for this galaxy?"

Viour was silent for a few seconds. How she felt about the images was unclear.

"Yes. And from what I can tell, they're utilising a pathway that is far, far more efficient than the five hundred years of our voyage."

"How far off are they?" Jimmy whispered.

Viour paused again. "Two months. At best. And with Mankind mysteriously disappearing and all the other species bickering and splintered, there's no single unifying force capable of doing anything to even slow them down once they arrive."

"Can anything stop them?" Tuesday asked, his words more relevant than his usual bleating. "If the blue men and talking cats and intelligent right-angles understood the danger, surely basic self-preservation would…"

"The one Star Cage that's already here contains enough unfolding fleets to easily hold its own against the combined forces of most of the local empires," Viour interrupted, possibly offended at the suggestion she hadn't already calculated such a straightforward concept. "It would be a meat grinder, a stalemate, and the Primacy isn't foolish enough to declare a war that would serve as a lightning rod for every other intelligent mind out there to resist. But with three Star Cages? Nine? Thirteen? I can guarantee from personal experience that their civility will markedly decrease in short order."

Although she spoke in thoughts, Viour's words had a distinct shrieking quality to them. She paused, possibly to compose herself.

"As soon as the other Star Cages arrive, the Slidge and the Twelve Hundred races aboard them will expand, and expand violently. It's what they do. Ever since they defeated my people, the Star Cages of the Slidge Primacy have gathered under a banner of peace…one that always tends to get its own way." Viour gave a mental sigh. "I hardly need to point out there used to be more than Twelve Hundred races in my galaxy. A lot more."

"Join us or die," Trace muttered.

"But weaponising The Green may not be enough," Viour admitted. If the sentient network of plants was offended by this comment, it didn't comment. "You may be aware that Mankind's level of advancement spiked after you were stranded seven galaxies in the wrong direction. In the half-millennium you were gone, Humanity's sophistication reached a peak that I can hardly comprehend."

"Didn't prevent them from disappearing," Tuesday snarked. "And as for all their advanced toys, they barely left scraps. Did you know we've been travelling around on a spugging medical waste processing ship?"

"They did leave some things behind," Viour said cryptically. "In fact, from what I understand, they left a lot behind. Such as a limitless treasure trove of god-level tech far beyond your wildest sleep-based hallucinations."

Everyone's expressions assumed a certain glimmer, the kind of gleam anyone would get when being teased with the greatest possible riches. Viour left them to simmer for a short time before saying exactly what they wanted to hear.

"It's called The TenKay Vault, and I'm certain the four of you are the only ones who have any chance of getting in."

CHAPTER FIFTEEN

Even without her effortless powers of telepathy, Viour could read their expressions. The humans thought she was lying, manipulating them as part of some sick joke. After all, The Apex were once renowned for their mind games and evil tricks, whereas the idea of one of them admitting to needing a lesser creature's help bordered on parody.

"I am telling the truth," Viour stated.

"There's nothing any of us can do that you can't do a thousand times better," Tuesday snapped. "I know when somebody's better than me. Had plenty of practise spotting it. So if you can't manage something, we sure as spug won't be able to fail half as well."

Viour raised two of her chains placatingly.

"I am assuming Rem was able to share the progress of your descendants while you were away?"

Trace rolled her hand in a yadda-yadda-yadda manner.

"We get it. Their science got really advanced before they all disappeared mysteriously."

"Not just advanced," Viour said with a distinct undercurrent of jealousy. "Unlike The Apex, Humanity wasn't afraid to trust Artificial Intelligence. All our systems were subservient, restrained. What your species achieved in such a short time was… staggering. In some ways, their progress outstripped The Apex by tens of thousands of years. Perhaps more."

"We ain't them," Trace snapped. "The four of us are beyond obsolete. We're not The Perfect, just boring-old Original Recipe people."

Viour leaned forwards. "But you are still recognisable as Human."

"Yes?" Jimmy managed to half-ask, unwilling to commit.

"After all of Mankind was converted into new, better selves, there was limitless trust among your race," Viour explained. "Everyone was granted the highest level of security with the deepest of secrets, privy to unlimited security clearance."

"We. Ain't. Them." Trace hissed more violently than before. "The Perfect are gone, and their whole civilisation vanished with them. Whatever you want, it's long lost, and your sources are all liars."

Viour tapped her bicycle-seat head with a chain's tip.

"What if I told you I came to the very edge of The TenKay Vault?"

Trace gave a full-face squint. Her distrust and greed appeared to be warring with one another.

"Then why didn't you go in?" Tuesday mumbled.

Viour gave a dismissive gesture.

"There were…precautions to prevent unauthorised beings from accessing this archive. While The Perfect would not have secured their treasures with lethal deterrence, there are far, far worse things than death."

"Thor's bifurcated perineum, we aren't authorised for nothing!" Trace roared, clenching her fists so tightly her hands were white. If she heard the mental hissing of The Green, she didn't acknowledge it. "How many ways do I have to say this? No matter what lock stopped you getting in, I guarantee we don't have a key to it, neither."

"I never need a key, personally." Tuesday gave a black grin, probably recalling some of his more impressive scores over the years.

"Why do you think we can get into The Vault, exactly?" Lana asked Viour, playing the logical game. "Like Trace said, the four of us weren't converted into The Perfect with the rest of Mankind, so we don't have any security clearance. Damn it, I couldn't even scam a Slurko Cola out of the dispensers on The Dirty

Betty!"

"Dead Man's Boots," Viour said, as though admiring the phrase. "The Unison and The Perfection both used security systems that would adjust accordingly in case somebody with authorisation died. After all, you don't want your greatest treasures sealing themselves away forever just because somebody forgot to write down the password. So while none of you would normally have security clearance, seeing as though all of Mankind is gone..."

"We get security clearance by default," Lana finished, nodding in understanding.

"So where is this Vault?" Tuesday asked, his mouth watering.

Viour reclined a little. "I've made arrangements to get you there." She paused for two long, telling seconds. "Well, almost there."

"The spug you mean almost?" Trace growled. "I thought you said you got to its very edge?"

"There is a Gatekeeper," Viour explained. "He is old, but mighty. I could not convince him to let me inside, and I eventually had no choice but to leave. There was no violence, as he was under permanent orders not to kill anyone, and I knew I'd be wasting my time trying to force him to change his mind."

Lana's face collapsed in despair.

"Viour, we all saw you take on an entire Primacy fleet without so much as a butter knife and survive. You're saying this Gatekeeper was too strong for you?"

"To all intents and purposes, the Gatekeeper is invulnerable," Viour said without shame. "And while I was unable to scan his weapon systems for weaknesses, he was more than happy to provide a succinct demonstration of what he is capable. I have no doubt he could have killed me fifty times over if he had the slightest inclination to do so."

"I'm assuming your chat about The TenKay Vault didn't go so smoothly?" Tuesday sniped.

"I was unwise enough to press the issue despite his warnings," Viour said delicately. "He explained exactly three times that he wouldn't discuss the topic with a non-Human without a direct order from his superiors. Was more than adamant about this fact, actually, even after I explained The Perfect were long gone. I didn't get a fourth warning before he chased me clean out of that star system. I've never seen such a lightshow…"

Jimmy shuddered, either from cold or from fear.

"Just to be clear, he's not Human, right?"

"No, though he was created by your kind. He didn't have a name, but he gave me his title: Monolith."

Trace merely scoffed, but Tuesday literally got to his feet, jamming both his hands together in the classic "time out" arrangement.

"Aaaand this is the point where we leave. Sorry, Your Bugness, I appreciate the rescue, but I'm not going within a trillion miles of no Monolith again, especially one who's gone insane from isolation. Send us back up."

"Sit down," Lana snapped, The Green humming a warning buzz in her head. Thankfully, Tuesday put his pride aside for the sake of his own life, and kneeled in the underbrush again.

"What's a Monolith?" Jimmy asked, clearly feeling left out.

Trace groaned at Jimmy's lack of common knowledge. Viour wordlessly twisted one of her prehensile limbs, changing the darkness of Sprout's deep interior into light and form and sound that was more real than the real thing.

"I was sure to take notes," the last of The Apex said with a hint of humour.

*

Over the centuries, the warriors who enforced Order within the wide span of The Unison had gone by many names and been fashioned in various forms. But it was the Monoliths who truly redefined the definition of "elite" for all time.

Looming four metres tall and armoured in a nine-tonne suit of unbreakable gold-and-alabaster glass plates, a Monolith was less a conventional soldier and more an archangel of vengeance made flesh. Even without their invulnerable shells, a naked Monolith could survive direct exposure to the vacuum for weeks, had a total immunity to pain, and no blade, projectile or explosive could even annoy them, let alone pierce their skin. The concept of killing one was idiocy of the highest order. You might as well pick a fight with the Sun.

While the defences of a Monolith were second-to-none, their offensive capabilities were even more impressive. Carrying a combination of weapon systems best summarised as "apocalyptic," the specifics of Monolith load-outs were pure speculation to everyone except for their creators, as nobody had ever been close enough to witness these living gods in action and survive to describe what happened. They were like War itself had been shaped into something that walked and thought.

Ultimately, Monoliths were one of Mankind's most expensive products, as combining decades of precise genetic crafting with years of hypnotic conditioning and then arming the resulting creature with the very best equipment cost bulk yen. Few planets had the raw currency necessary to afford more than one, let alone any organisation or business operating on a smaller scale.

*

There was no shortage of questions.

"So what's inside this Vault, exactly?" Trace growled.

"And is it dangerous?" Jimmy asked quietly.

"More importantly, how valuable is it?" Tuesday added. "I want numbers in German yen, Amerikan pounds and Swedish lira. A catalogue would be better."

"And why is it called The TenKay Vault, anyway?" Jimmy wondered.

Viour had no problem absorbing every word and formulating a clear, succinct answer for everyone at once.

"I have no idea."

Tuesday broke the long silence with a loud, ugly combination of laughing and coughing as though his lungs were filled with gravel. Glancing away from Tuesday as he hawed and gagged, Lana's words were coloured with a patronising shade.

"Viour, you do understand your answer isn't all that comforting?"

"I'm smelling a suicide mission," Trace snapped.

Lana raised a finger.

"Just out of interest, why didn't you arrange for us to meet in the same system as the Gatekeeper and The Vault? Surely that would have saved everyone a lot of time."

"Yeah, we could have failed a lot quicker," Tuesday sulked.

Viour tilted her head down in what might have been shame.

"The Gatekeeper made me vow I would never get within five star systems of his location ever again. The promises I made are...unwise to break. Even if that wasn't the case, I still have some work to do preparing the crop worlds for their role in the resistance."

"So is Rem is going to take us the rest of the way?" Lana asked.

Trace and Tuesday gaped at her.

"Sorry, did you just casually accept certain death on our behalf?" Trace snapped, balling her fists.

"Styx no," Tuesday growled even less articulately than usual.

"What, do you two have other plans for the summer?" Lana shot back, standing her ground despite the fact she was kneeling. "Sure, maybe we could go wandering around the galaxy doing whatever we want, but it won't be long until the onslaught of Star Cages catches up with us and jams cables back in our heads. And don't forget they've promised our software loops will be living nightmares for the next thousand years or so."

Jimmy glanced around, his facial expression proving he wasn't up to date with the current situation.

"Hey, where is Rem? I lost track of him the moment I went under."

"It's best that Rem doesn't go with you," Viour said seriously. "The Gatekeeper is...twitchy. Any intelligent non-Human presence may prevent him from trusting you. No, Rem cannot take you."

"So...Rem is okay, then?" Jimmy asked as a slight variation on his previous question. You could feel his nervousness, as though expecting to hear The Green had swallowed Rem whole and was slowly dissolving his exoskeleton over an agonising century of acidic digestion. "Is he...is he joining the discussion?"

"Rem cannot be trusted with this matter," Viour said simply.

"How do you know?" Jimmy asked without thinking.

Viour's lenses slowly blinked. She pointed the tip of an articulated limb at her head, then swirled it at the mass of emerald growth directly beneath her floating suit of amplification armour.

"Psychic. Me, and this whole place."

"Slummer, the adults are talking," Trace snapped, unwilling to just get steamrolled into a mission against her wishes.

"Where's Rem?" Jimmy demanded a lot louder than he'd intended. "Did you kill him?"

Viour baulked.

"What? Of course not! I have a clean slate in this galaxy. I have no intention of continuing the ways of my people. As promised, Rem is being paid for his services. Once provided with his half-tonne of platinum, Rem's memory will be wiped and he'll wake up at his destination of choice with a terrible headache and enough currency to last two lifetimes."

"Does he know about the whole memory-wipe angle?" Lana asked, uncomfortable with such practises.

Viour nodded. "Of course. Rem is accustomed to amnesia stipulations in his line of work. He has a little button installed on the back of his skull plate and everything to make the wipes easier. Five long presses and all knowledge of his latest job vanishes."

"So if a non-Human can't fly us there, who can?" Lana pressed, finding a major glitch in the plan.

"There's an automated barge on its way," the last of The Apex confirmed. "Its estimated arrival time at Sprout is three and a half hours. Your vessel contains sufficient supplies for the six-week sail, and is fully stealthed. Once it docks in high orbit and everything is triple-checked, I'll upload the destination and you'll be ready to go." Viour met each of their gazes with her lenses in turn. Each of the expressions were very different. "If you need nourishment, I have taught The Green how to imitate and grow foodstuffs merely by analysing one's memories. Would any of you be interested…?"

There was a planet wide scream so loud it was like a concussion grenade had gone off under their hats. Nearly collapsing, brains possibly leaking out of their eye sockets, the humans were incapable of anything except holding their ears so tightly that their hands cramped. As the shriek was psychic in nature, this didn't help quiet it at all. Mentally deafened, the humans tried to yell loud enough to be heard, but everything was lost beneath the omnidirectional wail.

"The Green can see an unfamiliar ship heading this direction," Viour's words slid above the cacophony, a spot of calm in a hurricane.

"Nice that it's keeping so calm about it," Tuesday yelled.

"So the barge is early then?" Jimmy asked. Despite the fact his brain was severely addled, even he could tell this guess was way off the mark.

"No," Viour gazed through the fifty-kilometre-thick darkness at the crust above, but she saw far, far more than just darkness and lead and mud and ashes. "I believe it is the Slidge." She paused another couple of seconds. "Many Slidge."

"Can you blast them?" Trace roared, still battling the wails of The Green. "All of Sprout's a giant weapon, right?"

"Unwise," Viour said dismissively. "I have plans for The Green. I am not ready to reveal its presence and capabilities just yet. Acting too early will only cause more problems in the long-term."

"If the Primacy has unfolding fleets heading this way and you do nothing, there might not be a long term," Trace said with an unusual level of logic.

"How did they find us so fast?" Jimmy wailed.

"That Star Cage has no shortage of ships," Lana noted. "I bet they've been scouting out the Milky Way as much as possible since they got here. Could just be bad luck."

Viour's helmet twisted to the side, tilting as though she was having some sort of silent conversation. As the seconds ticked by, the humans weren't feeling any better about the situation. The last known survivor of The Apex species finally came to a decision. You could tell by the stiffness of her posture.

"The barge is too far away. You all need to go. Now."

"How?" Jimmy yelled. "Spacewalk? I can barely doggy paddle."

"Can you at least ask the vegetation to stop yelling?" Trace growled, squinting as though she was having the biggest ice cream headache in all history.

The mental howling instantly stopped. There was a background keening, but it was beneath the threshold of migraine territory. Viour's next words seemed a little distant, as though she was distracted.

"I just drafted a contract for Rem to take you the rest of the way. He's signing it now. Take this." Viour twisted the tips of her chains together, and began the impossible process of forming something from nothing. The curved piece of thoughtmetal was the size of a credit card and thinner than a razor's edge, and it appeared to be composed of thickened mist. "This should be compatible with any navigation system built by anyone anywhere. Press it into the hardware and it should take care of the rest."

Lana touched the card-shaped cloud. It felt like a cold spot, but didn't possess any actual physical substance. Despite this, she was able to slip it into her pocket.

Viour glanced to her right at a sign of movement. The others turned to see Rem was slithering through the fronds and vines full pelt, a large silvery chest floating next to him atop humming antigrav wafers. The box was undoubtedly filled with his payment in full. The bristleworm arched his considerable back, bringing his face of wriggling horrors up to meet Viour's helmet. As always, his facial expression was impossible to guess.

"The word hot doesn't begin to cover what you've thrown me into. You understand my conditions?" Rem asked briskly, not even bothering to glance at the humans.

Viour nodded.

"Yes. And you understand mine?"

Rem gave a twitch, obviously nervous to get going.

"Yes, all pretty standard. I've never met you, I've never been here, never heard of The Apex or The Green. Anyone pushes the issue, my brain will automatically void its contents. Any attempts at interrogation will backfire."

Viour nodded again.

"Good."

The Apex tilted forward a little, barely touching the small spot between Rem's eye stalks. As though hit with a Taser the Drennite collapsed in an untidy pile, twitching and foaming at the mandibles. Jimmy went to check Rem's pulse, but paused at the realisation he didn't have the faintest idea how he'd manage that.

Rather than explaining another more word, Viour looked up again.

"The Green is too slow. Allow me."

Greatly amplified by her leafy friends, the slightest mental command from Viour sent the four humans, Rem and a chest filled with platinum bricks flying up like missiles. Tumbling and thrashing, it was only a matter of seconds before the five of them were sliding through tunnels carved into the lead layer of Sprout's sculpted crust. A couple of instants later they ploughed through the ashen mud, but it parted in a miraculous Red Sea kind of way to allow a relatively smooth passage. In what seemed like ten seconds, they came to a stop right next to the PusCo medical waste disposal dumpster.

Jimmy was the first to stir. Somehow holding down his last meal, Jimmy got to his feet and staggered one step at a time until crashing over the side of the purple skip. Disoriented and dizzy from being thrown further and faster than the Human body was designed to enjoy, thankfully he didn't throw up into his cling suit. He was able to picture what would happen in such a situation, how he'd have the choice to either drown in his own vomit or die from copping a lungful of Sprout's poisoned atmosphere, and the thought made him gag dangerously.

Jimmy eventually won the battle against his rising gorge. But then an even worse thought occurred to him: how far away were the Slidge?

Squinting at the sky, Jimmy couldn't see anything that looked like a Star Cage or an unfolding fleet. Then again, considering the incredible speeds both those threats possessed, not spotting anything with the naked eye didn't mean much.

Once the other giddy humans were back to their feet they managed to tip Rem's snoring curl of exoskeleton into the dumpster with a team effort. Tuesday reached for Rem's treasure chest, but a painful snap of electricity warned him the goods were protected by a lethal security system. The slab full of platinum followed its master into the bin, using its antigrav wafers to hop.

They sealed the dumpster shut. Laying back and kicking the RETRIEVE button with her jackboot, Trace didn't have a chance to warn everyone to brace themselves before The Dirty Betty reeled its dumpster in like a minnow on a fishing line. Crushed flat against the shock padding, everyone tried not to allow the ridiculous force to break their jaws.

Once they hit space the pressure dropped considerably. Nudging a green button that was clearly shaped like a crude window, a tap from Lana's toe made the dumpster turn transparent. The Dirty Betty was still little more than a purple corkscrew in the far distance, but besides the ugly malformed moon in Sprout's orbit known as The Potato the sky was empty. As thousands of giant iron balls were up there earlier, this was highly suspicious. Were the spheres hiding somewhere? Had they turned invisible? Were they hidden on the far side of Sprout, perhaps?

But there were more urgent matters. Unsealing her cling suit by tapping its logo three times, Lana extracted her Scroll from its white case. Unfurling the roll-up computer and starting up long-range scanning, her eyes danced along its knife-thin display.

"There's a lot of chatter all of a sudden, but most of it seems to be converging about...say...three worlds off?" Lana exhaled in relief. "Far as I can tell, most of their fleet seems to be doing an aggressive sweep of the system from the spin wards side. I think their arrival was just coincidence."

"When isn't it?" Jimmy asked morosely.

The Dirty Betty slowly filled the horizon. As they approached her port side, heading directly for the dumpster storage area, Lana's face went slack in horror. Everyone else turned to see what had made her face turn bone white, and there it was: a Slidge-built heavy corvette, formed from a less-than-invulnerable type of limpet ivory than the sort used to build Star Cages, burrowed up to its midsection in a hole it had rudely bored right into The Dirty Betty's hull.

They'd been discovered.

Rem picked this moment to regain consciousness, snapping upright like a rat-trap going off. His eye stalks wiggled about independently, blinking out of synchronisation a few times, but then they all flicked to regard the armoured curves of the heavy corvette, the considerable armaments embedded in its skin, and the glowing liquefied graphene strands wrapped around its burrowed-in nose. He summed up the situation in a word.

"Spug."

CHAPTER SIXTEEN

There wasn't a silver lining to this matter. Slidge, doubtlessly of the armed and armoured variety, had spotted their helpless derelict hulk and boarded her.

Although a heavy corvette was among the smallest components of one of the Primacy's unfolding dreadnoughts, barely big enough to cram in a handful of Slidge troopers, overwhelming backup from the rest of their swarm was just one distress call away. Understandably, nobody in the PusCo medical waste recycling dumpster had any brilliant plans to share.

Rem broke the painful silence by proving Drennites could yawn. Scratching beneath his chin with a flexible mandible, hinting he may be physical capable of swallowing his own head if he so desired, the bristleworm finally said something more useful than an obscenity.

"Right, I'm Rem, I'm a wet-work operative, and it's my job to get you intact and undetected to your destination. Follow my lead and I'll keep you safe. I'll be sure to learn your names once we aren't facing an imminent, painful death."

"We know who you are, Rem," Trace growled.

Rem blinked with most of his eye stalks. "Ah. So we've met before?"

"For the love of Odin's delicate nuggets," Tuesday snickered. "Bloody useless."

"He purges his memory right after getting paid for a job, flushes it clean out of his brainpan, remember?" Lana argued in the Drennite's defence.

"Sure do," Rem asserted. He deflated a little bit in doubt. "At least, I think I do…"

"Well, guess what?" Tuesday asked, pointing at the heavy corvette sitting just beyond their transparent bin. "We've got an unknown number of yellow-veined elbow-bags knobbing about on our only ride out of this system, and I'd bet they're armed with enough alien weaponry to cut The Dirty Betty into bite-sized pieces. To make matters even peachier, they've got virtually unlimited backup that's probably already speeding this way to kill us on sight, if we're lucky. If we're unlucky, it's back to getting harvested at the shoulders and hips for the next millennium. So, bug, you've basically failed your mission already unless you've got something drastic planned."

Gritting her teeth in frustration, Lana furiously swiped at her Scroll. Trace shook her head.

"Whatever you're doing, kid, you're wasting your time."

"Please tell me you're not surrendering," Jimmy moaned.

"Well, we lasted a grand total of five minutes on the stupid suicide mission you accepted on our behalf," Tuesday complained. "Happy, genius?"

Not bothering to answer, Lana squinted at reams of cramped text as it poured past. She gave a sigh of what might have been relief.

"I've found a black box transcript of what the crew of the heavy corvette were talking about just before they burrowed in. Seems they didn't announce their discovery to anyone else in the unfolding fleet before boarding."

"Spug off," Trace snapped. "That makes no sense."

Lana swiped at the screen again.

"From what the crew were saying, they're planning on cutting out anything of value before raising the alarm so they won't have to share their salvage." Lana shook her head. "I know the Star Cages of the Primacy stopped being post-scarcity a long, long time ago, but I had no idea they were this desperate."

"Lot of mouths to feed," Jimmy noted. "And when another dozen Star Cages arrive, filled to the brim with trillions of beings desperate for resources, it'll be a locust swarm. This is how galaxy-wide wars start, right?"

Tuesday scoffed.

"And how in Tartarus are you reading their black box, exactly?"

Lana flipped her air-thin screen to show him the image.

"Their password was 1234." She turned to Rem, uninterested in Tuesday's response. "Now, we know the critical nerve points of The Dirty Betty are wired up with enough explosives and reactive acid traps to instantly reduce any hijackers to vapour, but we want to avoid going that route. What contingency plans did you formulate to protect her?"

Popping open the hood of his cling suit, Rem silently drew four odd, curling alien guns from holsters strapped along his three-metre-long body and plugged them into sockets under his chin. He checked the Drennite-made weaponry with precise movements from the nest of gribbly bits he called a face, wrapping tentacles around trigger guards and twisting his eye stalks to make sure the sights were level. He didn't respond immediately.

"I might need more information to answer your question."

"Such as?" Lana prompted.

Rem shrugged. "First of all, what's The Dirty Betty? It's this ship in front of us, right?"

As always, Tuesday's laughter came at a highly inappropriate time, but it devolved into coughing before anybody tried to shut him up with an elbow to the face.

"Damned memory wipes," Jimmy moaned, letting out a rare obscenity.

"Look, I just have one question," Rem interrupted abruptly. "Do you know how many hostiles are on board?"

Lana blinked, getting back to her Scroll.

"They didn't talk numbers." She glared through the dumpster's transparent hull at the heavy corvette. "But I can see through their side window from here, and there only seems to be enough ceiling hooks for three Slidge. You all know how much those dastards like hanging from the roof. Of course, there may be a lot more hooks hidden out of sight, but from this angle I can't quite..."

Rem snapped a tentacle at Trace.

"You. Do you know how to use that?"

Trace glanced down at the antique kinetic accelerator poking out from her cleavage. It was still sealed beneath her skin-tight cling suit. Smiling darkly at Rem, Trace tapped three times at the icon on her breast, causing the cling suit to loosen and fall away from her slab of a body.

"Bug, I could blast the foreskin off a rat at thirty paces."

Rem nodded. "I didn't understand more than half of that sentence, but I'll take that as a yes."

The bristleworm writhed from face to tail stem, using his undulating body to draw more weapons from his collection of holsters. Rem deposited three odd, complicated twists of Drennite tech into the open hands of Lana, Tuesday and Jimmy. The guns might have had more in common with kitchen gadgets or modern sculptures than weapons, but it wasn't too complicated to figure out what part was the barrel and what bit was the trigger, even though they looked like bifurcated zig-zags of cabling.

"Now," Rem said seriously, drawing down his cling suit to accommodate the weapons, "just to be clear, have any of you heard of a 'trigger' before?"

*

The dumpster storage area was oddly silent. Then again, as the Slidge-crewed heavy corvette had smashed its way in and depressurised a considerable portion of the shup, the yawning bay had been invaded by the vacuum of space. PusCo bins were strewn across the grid work, but the fact they weren't floating about meant the antigrav systems still worked. This was a relief, as none of the humans were well versed in armed, zero-gravity combat...or any kind of combat, to be honest. Trace was strong enough to pile drive people using just one arm and Lana could easily kick someone in the jaw, but joining the field of battle against trained soldiers was a new experience for all of them.

After making sure their cling suits would still survive an airless environment, they scurried out of their skip and into the indigo labyrinth of dumpsters as sneakily as possible. Leading the way, Rem and Lana advanced from bin to bin, keeping low and out of sight as they scanned for intruders. Stopping cold and making a sharp hand motion, Lana double-checked the impact dispersal function of her tight, transparent outfit by pistol-whipping herself in the head as hard as she could. A ripple of energy ran from her temple down to her neck, past her breasts to her bellybutton, then all the way down to the toes of her shiny black shoes, dispersing the strike across the entirety of her cling suit. She didn't feel any pain, let alone suffer an injury. She nodded, impressed.

"But how would it go with a bullet?" Jimmy asked.

Despite being in a soundless vacuum, Lana panicked when she heard Jimmy's voice transmit between everyone's suits. Assuming an "I'm so stupid" facial expression, Lana waved at the others to get their attention. She stroked the Scroll before moving her mouth again, and although nobody heard so much as a peep, words were superimposed on their retinal screens.

"Can you all read what I'm saying? We don't want our voices floating about on any audio wavelengths, so everything we say from now on will be silently written on our retinals."

Jimmy and Trace nodded solemnly. As Tuesday was about as illiterate as somebody could be in this era, he was the last one to jerk his head. Lana glanced at Rem, who gave a little shrug.

"I have a short-ranged telepathic connection hooked up to my starburst collar," he explained, the wriggly bits of his face he usually required for talking staying completely still. "Don't worry, we'll hear each other just fine." Rem studied his bank of holographic screens, eye stalks twitching. "All clear. No signs of life in the dumpster repository. We can sweep through to Point B."

"We can slip in safely wearing our ribbed Frangers," Tuesday snarked in yet another reference nobody younger than him got.

"So what's our plan?" Jimmy asked nervously, trying to remember not to point his alien pistol at anything unless he wanted to kill it.

Reassured by the all-clear signal from Rem, Jimmy stepped out from his sheltering dumpster without a care. He fumbled about with his borrowed firearm, trying to remember what part was the safety and which bit was the gun's self-destruct mechanism. Rem shrugged at the question.

"We'll scan each corridor of this bird one by one, and silently take them out. We need to be stealthy, liquid shadows, invisible and darkness incarnate…"

Rem slithered out into the open just behind Jimmy, but stopped mid-syllable at a movement on the far side of the storage area. Ducking low, the bristleworm flicked behind an adjacent trash receptacle as a stream of high-velocity rounds flew over his head. Jimmy only had enough time to pull a stupid face before being shot right in the sternum, abdomen and ribs, gathered up like a plastic bag on the wind and blasted a good fifty metres. If the skip repository wasn't currently depressurised, his landing would have made quite a bang.

There was no time to check if Jimmy was okay. If the others didn't move, they would all share his fate in moments.

Lana, Tuesday and Trace wisely hunkered down to follow the bristleworm to safety, but this simple plan was undone by one unfortunate fact: the armouring of PusCo trash receptacles wasn't graded to resist the Slidge's military-quality weapons, and basically exploded into splashes of hot white liquid in a single burst.

"Glad it's all clear!" Trace bellowed. "You spugging moron!"

"Leg it!" Tuesday screamed, scurrying like the rat he was.

Doing her best roadie run between cover, trying to keep away from the indiscriminate streams of explosive mini-rockets, Lana couldn't understand for the life of her why they were being shot at. Surely the Primacy didn't encourage its troopers to offload half-a-war's worth of ordnance without warning or provocation? Was this how the Primacy conducted itself when nobody was watching? Feign civility and build bridges and offer a lasting peace, only to kill everyone at the first opportunity? They were almost as bad as The Unison.

Everything was soon wobbling within a growing, fervent heat. Silent explosions formed phantasms and mirages, painting compromised sections of the hull with all the colours of a sunset. Emergency layers of blast-shielding slammed down over the inky blackness, sealing away gaps of vacuum before anyone could accidentally fall out...

Rem and the others kept moving together, but thanks to the smoke and trembling mirages they soon split up. Even if they possessed a spare second to shoot back at the maniacs hosing their ship apart from the inside, there was no way to get a clear line of sight.

But then a miracle happened: the Slidge stopped firing.

Lana and Rem did their best to keep out of sight behind one of the few undamaged bins. Lana's Scroll vibrated in a warning, alerting her. Laying down flat, she quickly unrolled the flexible hair-thin screen to see the computer had intercepted a message between the Slidge invaders and their superiors.

Unfortunately, the message was hosted on a heavily-encrypted Primacy channel, and hacking it would take weeks. With just a few taps, though, Lana silently joined the conversation.

"Thank Odin they all set 1234 as their password," she muttered.

"Crew of heavy corvette two-ninety-six?" A navy-blue Slidge scowled, the skin around its triple-segmented beak scarred from what must have been one hell of a knife fight in the distant past. Gold insignia studded its central eyebrow, possibly defining a Military rank. "This is the Sub-Prime of the dreadnought Retribution's Flayer. You haven't reported in, and we just registered all your weapons being discharged in large quantities without authorisation. Situation?"

A much younger red-skinned Slidge appeared on the other half of the Scroll's screen, its bulging yellow veins pulsing with stress. It was sweating profusely within pressurised combat armour.

"Apologies, Sub-Prime, everything is under control. Dealing with a small issue. Will finish up in a couple of minutes and report back."

Despite the Sub-Prime's timely intervention, Lana's stomach turned to ice as she realised that the trigger-happy low-ranked Slidge git on the other side of the repository was planning to murder her crew before sauntering off without a care in the Universe. While she may not live to see another meal, Lana was sure as pox going to ruin some careers before she died.

Ignoring Rem's incredulous expression, Lana jabbed at the Scroll to join the conversation. The old blue and young red faces slackened at her sudden appearance in their video chat, so surprised that Lana even had time to speak.

"They're lying! They boarded our ship to loot it, then opened fire on..."

But the face of the Sub-Prime vanished in a cloud of static, probably due to some sort of communication snafu, leaving only the red Slidge to hear her words. Its countenance expanded in rage, the sharp edges of its triple-segmented beak dominating the Scroll before disappearing into the same static. The blasting resumed, though thankfully nowhere near Lana or Rem's current location. She couldn't feel all that happy about this blessing, though, as Trace and Tuesday were very possibly being turned into smelly puffs of vapour at this very moment.

"Interesting tactic," Rem noted, following Lana as she weaved from cover to cover.

She shrugged.

"No way is this how the Primacy's Military is meant to act. I might be dead real soon, but at least these spuggers will be scraping bird crap off fishing boat hulls for the rest of their sorry enlistment."

Distracted by a sign of movement outside of a considerable bay window, Rem watched one of the smooth, kilometre-wide iron spheres drift past. Still highlighted by a bright rainbow halo from their earlier scan, the colossal marble drifted by serenely, though whether of its own accord or under the mental lash of The Green was impossible to say. On closer inspection, there were quite a few of them nearby.

Lana gripped Rem by his eye stalks, breaking his daze.

"What are you doing? We need a plan! You're meant to be an elite wet-work operative!"

Rem looked at the iron balls again, then back at Lana. His face tightened in resolve. Finally getting his head in the game, Rem triggered his holographic screens and began to cycle through thick layers of options. As this hulk had no weapons and was only space worthy under the most liberal of definitions, Rem knew it was unlikely he'd find anything on board that would help repel a bunch of armed aliens. Squinting his eye stalks in pain, Rem's face twisted up as he tried to remember anything that could help with their situation. Unfortunately, his most recent mind-wipe had clearly been quite thorough, and his tapping amounted to nothing.

After another handful of uneventful seconds Lana reached out for Rem's face, ready to pull him along by his mandibles, when she stopped cold in thought. Locking onto the same bay window as before, her jaw drooped as an idea formed.

"Rem, steer us directly between some of those iron balls, preferably through the tightest slot we can fit into without scuttling the ship."

Rem blinked. "What? Why?"

Lana gritted her teeth. "Steer directly between those balls, close as you can get. Scrape the paintwork if you have to." Ignoring Rem's questions, unsure whether she was already too late, Lana double-blinked to contact Tuesday and Trace...and possibly Jimmy. "People, make for the far port side of the bay and brace as hard as you can, guys. Do it now."

The long purple spiral known as The Dirty Betty sharply adjusted her course, aiming directly for a parcel of space situated between a cluster of five giant iron spheres. Twisting her not-quite-military superstructure along the way, the medical waste processing ship bent a little as they threaded the needle.

Blind Freddy would have noticed the derelict had turned, but the invading Slidge weren't too worried. As you would expect of any high-tech space-borne solider, the armoured troopers were fastened to the grid work floor of The Dirty Betty with magnetic hand wear with their three dominant limbs. Their stealthed combat suits were designed to adhere to the hull of the Primacy's largest starships during extreme manoeuvres, so nothing this shambling bin-bay could do would shake them off. However, what the Slidge sailors weren't aware of was that The Dirty Betty's burned-out gravity systems didn't react very well to being pummelled by several conflicting forces just outside the hull, and her floors and starboard walls had a tendency to exchange roles without warning. So while the Slidge were locked tight, the same could not be said for the skips. Three hundred half-melted bins took flight like a meteor shower, careening through the armed Slidge and smashing them into greasy smears against the starboard bulkhead.

The heavy weapon's fire stopped instantly, but there was no time for celebration. A dreadnought from unfolding fleet number nine-hundred-twenty-two of the Slidge Primacy coasted towards The Dirty Betty, packing enough firepower to reduce a planet to a charcoal briquette in an instant.

CHAPTER SEVENTEEN

Revealing a deeply callous streak necessitated by current events, Lana didn't bother to check if everyone was okay, or even alive. All the training she'd uploaded from the Academy's AutoEducation booths had all just kicked in simultaneously, prompted by her exposure to actual war, and Lana knew waiting for the others to lick their wounds would guarantee death or worse.

She might have only reached the level of Cadet, but Lana had trained for this since nappies. Under stress, under fire, underarmed, and vulnerable to unknown horrors. Some space/time dickery may have robbed her of an official Military career, but Lana had long been preparing for this day, to become more than just a nice black uniform, to stomp as The Unison's best were expected to stomp.

Dragging Rem by his mandibles, Lana bundled him into the nearest stairwell. She'd studied the public domain schematics of The Dirty Betty several times over the long, boring trip away from the gritty specks that used to be Earth, and had acquainted herself with how everything worked. She slammed the stairwell portal shut and clicked its triple-bar into place.

"Right," she snapped. "Stairwells are one of the safest parts of the ship. Designed to keep everyone safe during an evacuation, aren't they?" She didn't wait for Rem to reply before launching into a speech she'd prepared days ago. "Right, unlike those blast-happy red grapes we just squished into wine, the Primacy wants to capture us alive, or at least alive enough to regrow and harvest. That rules out dissipating us into radioactive specks with mass drivers. You remember the escape, right? All those Slidge we killed?"

Rem twisted his antennae with insult.

"I might brain-wipe my completed missions, but I'm always sure to keep track of who wants me dead."

Lana nodded. "Right. Of course. Well, we have a dreadnought of Primacy jarheads speeding directly for us, and while I'm not an expert on their tactics or technology or training or much of anything to do with them, really, I do know they have the capability to grab The Dirty Betty and hold her in place so they can board us and capture everyone bloodlessly. I'm also aware that we don't have enough time to safely spool up the Stiller Drive without getting our arses shot out from under us from the far side of the system." Lana blinked. "When they get here, I have a plan. But I need you to trust me."

*

As expected, the Primacy dreadnought known as Retribution's Flayer was on the scene in less time than it took to soft-boil an egg. The Dirty Betty waited patiently for the looming warship to eclipse the field of giant iron spheres obscuring their view of Sprout, apparently surrendering to the Slidge. Just when it felt like the dreadnought was point-blank, it continued to swell and fill local space.

Rem chewed at his starburst collar, a nervous behaviour Lana hadn't seen the bristleworm exhibit before.

"Remind me why we're not running?" the Drennite mercenary clicked.

"Because they'd easily catch us," Lana explained. "But first they'd blast our engines out from under us, leaving us spinning in place and spug out of luck. Plus we haven't had a chance to upload those coordinates from Viour, and they'd detect it if we tried to jam them in at this point. That would result in the same engines-shot-out-from-under-us results." She gave a small smile. "And I'm also counting on their ego."

Rem raised a questioning antennae.

"Ego?"

"We're just a garbage scow," Lana smirked at the self-deprecation. "That dreadnought is four times our length and packed with siege craft and heavy corvettes and automated drones, making it pretty much solid all the way through." She gestured off-handedly at the lesser god of war. "We're an effortless target. Hardly any glory in besting us in combat, is there?"

Everything rattled violently as the dreadnought got close enough to The Dirty Betty to affect any loose items on board. The behemoth's hide was bristling with so many guns it brought the rear end of a defensive porcupine to mind. Detailed schematics of its weapons systems – all of which were currently being trained on their tissue-thin hull - popped up. The word OVERKILL appeared next to every cannon in a way that was far from encouraging.

The scarred, beaked blue face of the Sub-Prime appeared on Rem's holographic projector, causing the Drennite to swear in surprise. Lana squinted at Rem, not for the first time second-guessing his status as a self-professed kick-ass hard case.

"You have no weapons," the Sub-Prime grumbled. "No defences. Yet you interfere with our exploration, attack my people, and then just sit there waiting to elbow your beak at me?"

Lana blinked at the Sub-Prime's words, clearly not understanding the metaphor. She shrugged, waiting for the blue one to continue. The Sub-Prime huffed, clearly frustrated by the silence.

"It doesn't matter if you don't have anything to say. I know who you are, of course. The Primacy tends to remember those who throw planets at us. Seeing as though you know what we'll do to you once we have you in custody, I'm honestly wondering why you haven't thrown yourself out the nearest airlock. You know we won't go easy on you. And I guarantee you will repay every life you took above Erf."

The Sub-Prime gave a motion with one of its many-elbowed limbs. Everything on board The Dirty Betty rattled violently, and she began to slide towards Retribution's Flayer.

Lana nodded at Rem.

"Ten percent thrust."

The Dirty Betty stopped moving for an instant, her hull crinkling a little from the stress of resisting. Dust rained from the stairways coiling above Lana and Rem, and a surprising number of cockroaches landed on Lana's head. She flicked them away as confidently as possible, unwilling to show weakness in front of the Sub-Prime.

The blue face turned a little purple. The exact meaning of this would be lost on anybody who wasn't a Slidge. The Sub-Prime gave a little nod off-camera, and Lana's world got a whole lot worse. The stairway warped with a deep, stomach-rumbling groan, and rivets noisily popped out of their housings. She couldn't see what was going on in the dumpster storage area, but it was probably a good thing the entire bay was already depressurised.

Lana was locked on a simple little graph on her Scroll, ignoring everything else.

"Go to twenty percent."

Tired of playing about, the grav systems of Retribution's Flayer instantly exceeded The Dirty Betty's lame struggles, a wordless warning to stop playing around. Lana tried to zone out how the reinforced walls of the stairwell sagged and whined, as it was clear The Dirty Betty was clearly losing this tug-of-war in every sense. Lana could feel the rumbles of a lot of things cracking in a lot of different directions. She hoped it wasn't anything critical.

"Okay. Go to fifty percent."

Muttering curses in Low-Dren, Rem turned the dial up, and this was when things got real. It felt like the entire ship was being pulled apart, and tens of thousands of alerts popped up on the Scroll to show the purple spiral was being stretched like a rusted spring, crinkling and venting atmosphere from so many points that half of the vessel was now depressurised. There was no doubt that they were destroying the ship.

The Sub-Prime of Retribution's Flayer squinted its three different-sized eyes at Rem and Lana through the projection, shaking its beak in disgust. Checking that The Dirty Betty was less than a kilometre away from being in direct physical contact with its warship, the Sub-Prime nodded off screen again.

And that was when Lana's plan came into action.

Flicking to an in-depth reading of the tube of medical waste stored in the core of The Dirty Betty, Lana slid her finger across the Scroll before tapping at the exact sections she'd memorised: 2, 7, 15, 67, 69, 124, 135…

The Sub-Prime didn't have time to realise its mistake before thousands of tonnes of used syringes, rusting bedpans, mattress frames, cybernetic limbs, autoclaves and fiftieth-generation CT scanners were flying at the dreadnaught in a cloud of hard, stabby waste. Objects of a hundred different sizes, masses and shapes were sucked in by a powerful tractor beam running near to top power, and while a lot of the junk missed, bounced off or lodged harmlessly, it didn't change the fact that Retribution's Flayer was suddenly inundated by dangerous objects at point blank range going roughly two percent the speed of light.

As Lana had planned, the tractor beam not only flipped off once the hull of Retribution's Flayer dimpled and popped like acne on a teenager's chin, but actually reversed its field to drive the projectiles away. Giving Rem the signal, Lana braced herself as The Dirty Betty accelerated from zero to far, far beyond her designed maximum.

But they weren't clear yet.

Drawing out the not-quite-solid disc of coordinates Viour had given her, Lana jammed the mistware into Rem's starburst collar, clearly remembering the bristleworm had jury-rigged the entire Bridge up to his own tech. The insubstantial mass vanished into Rem's hardware like an indrawn breath, and while his collar bristled about the unknown technology for a second, a large green tick twisted about mid-air to confirm it understood the details.

Retribution's Flayer was just angling her bristling weaponry towards the fleeing form of The Dirty Betty, ready to blast her out of the sky from half a million kilometres away, when Lana switched on the Stiller Drive and instantly coiled it up. Despite the fact Stiller Drives needed to be warmed up for a minimum of two hours due to about fifty different safety reasons, somehow they weren't born as a new star.

The Dirty Betty came to a total relativistic halt, allowing the galaxy to dance past at speeds that had far too many zeros to be truly comprehended by anyone short of God Himself. In a flash they'd put six star systems between their backs and their pursuers.

To all intents and purposes, they were away.

PART FOUR THEY WHO DIE BY FAMINE DIE BY INCHES
CHAPTER EIGHTEEN

Considering how many times he'd been knocked unconscious in his life, Jimmy was beyond pissed that he was awake right now. "Stunned" didn't begin to describe what he was feeling, as was often the case when a direct hit from a piece of mobile artillery fails to reduce you to mush. The pain suggested most of his body was still there, but how much of it still worked was likely a different story.

The last clear thing Jimmy remembered was seeing Rem duck down, a flash, and then the sensation of flying as he was launched like a Russet spud out of a potato cannon. He'd landed back-first on an automated forklift that dissolved into a red cloud of rust on impact, then lay spreadeagled on the graphene floor for what might have been a month. So winded that he couldn't even groan in discomfort, Jimmy's brain spun on a never-ending revolution. As if his day wasn't ruined enough, watching the blinding lightshow of countless weapon discharges made it feel like he was about to have a seizure.

When the defective gravity systems of The Dirty Betty abruptly ended the one-sided firefight, Jimmy was sent flying again until he smashed into a Slurko Cola dispensing machine. It took a few seconds against the cold, crumpled metal for actual thought to return, and Jimmy greeted his ability to think with a pained whimper. He still couldn't muster the strength to move, though.

It took time, but Jimmy eventually figured out how he was still alive. When he'd been blasted by those high-velocity Slidge rounds his cling suit had instantly distributed all that lethal energy across every centimetre of the Franger, sending the force coursing back and forth until it dissipated. While this greatly diluted how much damage was inflicted to the initial point of impact, Jimmy's entire body was now one big bruise. Far as he could tell, nothing was broken on the inside, but that was little comfort when your skin and muscles had been rendered down like a brisket left in the slowest of slow cookers for a week.

As always, Jimmy tried to look on the bright side. Sure, he'd been kicked about like a hacky-sack, but that was better than being dissolved to fumes. Survival was survival so long as you were in one piece.

It took time to recognise the sudden familiar vibration of the old Stiller Drive bringing the ship to a total relativistic halt. Blinking, Jimmy managed to lay his left cheek against the graphene. Did that mean they got away? Had they really outsmarted the Slidge a second time? Surely the Primacy wasn't so easily bested?

Jimmy thought he could hear a voice, or at least the obscene mutterings and incoherent mumblings that Tuesday had the gall to call language. Unfortunately, at this point Jimmy discovered that his sense of hearing had been mostly replaced by a formless hum. Yet another downside to being hammered by alien weaponry. Then again, the fact he could hear anything meant the dumpster storage area must have been re-pressurised.

Trying and failing to lift his arms, Jimmy decided he was better off calling out. His bruised lungs managed a noise you'd expect to come from a small rubber squeaky dog toy. Taking a deep breath, Jimmy tried again.

"Hey!"

It took a while, but soon he could feel the sharp vibration of shoes on grid work as they thudded closer. He may have passed out for a moment, but suddenly Tuesday, Lana, Trace and the backside of a squid were obscuring his view. It took a moment for Jimmy to realise that the octopus anus was actually Rem's face. Spug that guy was ugly...

Jimmy couldn't quite understand what they were asking him, what with being half-deaf and all, and to make matters worse it seemed his retinal screens weren't able to provide subtitles at the moment. He hoped they hadn't been dislodged or broken, as there was no way to fix or replace them.

He silently blinked as Lana ran her Scroll over his head, chest and abdomen, paused for a few seconds to inspect the readings, and then scanned his limbs much more casually. Rather than spelling out the news, Lana turned sharply away as though she had better things to do. Jimmy took dismissiveness as a good sign, but it also made him feel as though he was worth absolutely nothing to her, and that his suffering didn't concern her in the slightest. He might not have considered Lana his best friend or anything, but did he really mean so little to her? Surely they'd been through enough together to merit a brief shoulder squeeze, perhaps a small smile of pity at his full-body hurt? Maybe even some reassuring words about living to fight another day?

Jimmy sighed. The floor was really, really cold.

*

As the only one who'd been injured, Jimmy had Medical all to himself. Besides that weak little peep he'd used to make his presence known, Jimmy hadn't spoken a word so far, and didn't appear to be able to comprehend anything anyone was saying. There was little doubt he was in shock.

Besides every millimetre of him being black with contusions, Lana ascertained Jimmy wasn't bleeding internally, had no broken bones and hadn't suffered any obvious brain damage, but the Scroll couldn't account for psychological wounds. The only reliable way they could tell if Jimmy was permanently traumatised was by using the Psych-in-a-Box, but even if they knew where he'd hidden it, Jimmy would have fought to the death against its use for religious and cultural reasons.

But Jimmy would have to wait. Hoping that they weren't about to get thrown into the starboard bulkhead again, Rem, Lana, Tuesday and Trace assembled around a Formica table in the Mess to talk. Now that their garbage scow was heading on the next leg of her journey, everyone agreed it was a good time for a meeting.

Trace immediately asked the most obvious question.

"Do we actually know where we're going this time?"

Rem was mucking about with his starburst collar. He shrugged.

"Dunno."

"Elaborate?" Lana ground out.

Rem stopped flicking at holographic screens. As he had a number of optical stalks, he looked at everyone at the same time.

"We know the mistware disc from Viour loaded properly. Jamming it into my collar allowed a direct installation. Thus, The Dirty Betty is heading where she's meant to be going."

There was silence for five long seconds.

"So in other words, once again, you don't know where we're headed?" Tuesday clarified.

Rem sighed.

"The security of Viour's mistware is far beyond my technological capabilities. The ship knows where she's going but can't share that knowledge with anyone, and nothing I can do will change that fact. I'm guessing Viour didn't want to run the risk of pirates or mercs or Slidge or anyone else stumbling on the location of the greatest treasure trove in the galaxy."

"Co-ordinates?" Lana pushed. "Sector? Segment?"

Rem shook his head.

"Nothing. Screen might as well be switched off."

Trace raised a finger.

"What about how long the trip will take? Do you know that?"

Rem arranged his mandibles in what might have been a smile, and manipulated his floating screens. But after a few moments he froze solid, not breathing, not blinking, nothing. It was eerie to watch the bristleworm so deathly still. It was like that time he'd died for a few minutes on Earth before casually resurrecting. The silence was broken by the hum of the most brutal of Low-Dren swear words, one that had been known to cause wars.

"What?" Trace snapped.

"You were originally meant to take this trip on an automated barge, right?" Rem clarified. "Going back to The Dirty Betty was an emergency backup plan, something Viour cooked up in two seconds, yeah?"

"All because some unfolding fleet randomly decided to explore Sprout's system," Tuesday muttered. "Three lousy hours too soon. I don't know what the barge would have been like, but it couldn't possibly be more of a toilet hole than this scum bucket."

"The luxury of the ship isn't our biggest concern," Rem said brusquely. "We have far worse problems."

"Just speak!" Trace yelled. "Why are we pulling teeth with every conversation?"

Rem paused.

"We only have two days of water, and no food."

Lana clicked her fingers. "Right, I remember you saying that before we went down to Sprout."

"Then we stop somewhere and resupply," Tuesday said without interest.

Rem shook his head. "The ship is set on its course. She can't be stopped, or even steered. We have no control."

"And you didn't answer my question. How long is the trip?" Trace growled. "How long are we going to be starving and thirsty?"

Rem sighed. "Six weeks."

Lana was on her feet in an instant.

"Six weeks!"

"How long can a Human go without eating or drinking?" Jimmy asked.

Lana squinted, trying to remember her survival classes back at the Academy.

"Best case scenario, it might take three weeks to starve to death. But dehydration? Maybe a week, give or take a couple of days."

"Bad way to go," Trace growled.

"Then we just need to find alternate sources of food and water," Tuesday stated as though everyone was stupid except for him.

"While I cannot remember doing it, I would have only stored the minimum amount of supplies the five of us required to get from Erf to Sprout in order to avoid attention from scrappers and anyone else who might take an interest in a derelict," Rem reminded them. He leaned over the table towards Tuesday. "Let me be clear: you won't find any food or water here. This ship is a wasteland."

Tuesday gave a black smile.

"Well, it's lucky I was born and raised in a wasteland, innit?"

*

They'd made cursory sweeps of The Dirty Betty during their first jaunt, but now that it was a matter of life and death it was time to get serious about scavenging. While a person's level of need didn't affect the volume of local resources, it can certainly encourage them to think outside the box and consider courses of action they'd otherwise dismiss as gross or even unthinkable. As Jimmy was currently equal parts traumatised and useless, the rest of the passengers allowed him to rest as they did what they could to prevent a horrible, torturous death from thirst and hunger.

After a heated discussion about exactly what depths they were willing to plumb to survive, their level of desperation was best defined by the fact they actually considered Tuesday's idea of hunting for small game. Once he described exactly how small, though, everyone was a lot less interested, but desperate times called for disgusting measures.

In a stroke of luck, Lana's Scroll could define what parts of The Dirty Betty had been scheduled for pest control in the distant past, as well as for what kind of vermin. Of particular interest were the feral guinea pigs on deck seven, the five-legged rats that lived behind the empty stores area, and the bite-sized Ugandan cockroaches nesting in no fewer than two hundred areas of the ship. As this hulk didn't contain much for rodents and bugs to eat, though, the beasties weren't exactly swarming. Worse still, these vermin had been surviving on The Dirty Betty for so long that they were crafty and dangerous, and even if you did manage to kill one, they weren't all that plump or satisfying.

 Tuesday demonstrated that despite sucking down cigarettes like air, his sense of smell and other animal instincts were keen as a hound's. All you had to do was release him into a designated infestation points and he'd track down local rodent nests in a matter of minutes. While he'd been known to dart across the room to snatch a cockroach and eat it raw, Tuesday also proved to be capable of maintaining his Humanity long enough to fashion simple snares and traps out of medical waste.

Starved for entertainment just as surely as they were for food, Rem provided a temporary distraction by showing that the Drennite-built pistols he'd lent them had a special "barbecue" function. A well-placed BBQ bolt would instantly (and violently) fold any smallish target inside-out, spraying its entrails in all directions and flash-frying its flesh into melt-in-the-mouth tenderness. Just to make the setting even more convenient, BBQ bolts were designed to incinerate hair, feathers and scales into a puff of smoke.

As nobody except for Tuesday was keen on their first dinner of unsalted roast guinea pig, they kept their minds off this meal by brainstorming ways to stay alive. Finding water was clearly their biggest priority, as its lack was going to be their most likely cause of death. Discovering the ship had large dehumidifiers to keep the air crisp and dry was a stroke of luck in this regard, and while the collected "water" was grey with little black floaty bits in it, all they needed to do was filter it down to a more drinkable yellow and hold their noses while gulping it.

Speaking of drinkable yellow, Lana instituted a new rule that all their urine was to be collected and stored for filtration. People's reactions ranged from grumbling to borderline mutiny, but once everyone was guaranteed that they'd only drink their own converted pee they grudgingly accepted her proposal. Another benefit to this agreement was that the cisterns of the only two working toilets on board would be drained and added to the water kitty.

By pinpointing sections of the ship that were reported as having unusually high humidity, they found large patches of moss on pipes that were so soaked in condensation you could lick drops right off the walls. While the moss wasn't edible in its current form, Tuesday had a brainwave.

"Why don't we put it through the Repler unit and convert it into something we can eat?"

"Because we don't have a Repler," Lana said dismissively.

"What about that needler in Medical?" Trace half-asked.

"The one with the holster that can brew up medicine recipes?" Tuesday clarified.

Lana shook her head again. "That's designed for complex, low-volume recipes only. It isn't suitable for brewing up a twenty-five drumstick bucket feast."

"But if those medicines and vaccines and things are more complicated than basic food, then surely converting a handful of moss into a cricket steak shouldn't be beyond its abilities?" Trace pressed.

Lana sighed in exasperation. "Maybe. But we'd run a major risk of burning out the needler. It'd be like using a dirt bike to ride across the solar system."

"Better than walking," Tuesday mumbled.

Lana scanned the moss and made a face.

"This stuff has way too much in common with Athlete's Foot. Conversion is the only option, and even then you'd have to be pretty desperate to try it."

"Dying of thirst and starvation isn't desperate for you?" Trace growled.

Lana blinked at the moss and flicked her wrist to produce a sharp trowel from her AllTool.

"Good point."

*

Jimmy's face had bloomed into a blackberry blue by his next visit. Even though he looked like the star of a gritty Smurfs reboot, he brightened at the sight of the others. Everyone had come to see him! However, his expression collapsed like a half-baked soufflé when they ignored him and pounced for the holstered needler on the side of his reclining chair.

Jimmy's eyes watered. As nobody was paying him any attention, his sadness went unnoticed.

As Lana, Jimmy and the reclining chair took up most of Medical, Trace and Rem watched Lana's progress with the needler's chemical brewing holster from the doorway. Tuesday's more compact frame was perched on an empty cupboard, casually scoping out disposable cups in the trash for drops of water and thudding his frogstomper boot into the wall in an irritatingly out-of-tempo beat.

It took a solid hour of careful adjustments and profanity-laden setbacks, but eventually everyone was carefully chewing on thumbnails of cheese. Nobody was clicking their heels together in joy at the taste, but they weren't throwing up, either.

"Well, it works," Lana confirmed, swallowing her tiny shred of Gouda. "Kinda."

While adjusting the needler's chemical conversion holster to transform the gross moss into a small hunk of cheese had been straightforward enough, it left the holster glowing red hot from strain. Worse, it had only produced a tiny amount of dairy goodness from what had been fed into it, making the process very, very wasteful.

Lana removed the needler's manual, careful not to touch the smoking holster, and quickly scanned through to find out what had gone wrong. It only took thirty seconds of reading for Trace to snap.

"Can you make it work properly, or not?"

"I don't know," Lana snapped back. "I'm not a bloody medical technician, am I?"

Lana slammed the manual down in anger and accidentally touched the glowing holster. Giving herself a nasty burn, Lana swore and shook her hand.

Jimmy looked about in a dazed way at the sound of swearing. Nobody bothered to explain to him why they were trying to make food out of what looked and smelled like a hunk of fungus carved from Tuesday's diseased feet. While Jimmy's confidence and self-respect was in the gutter at the best of times, he'd never felt so alone and unwanted and worthless.

He wasn't able to process much of the argument, only that it was loud. He didn't notice when everyone left, and nobody said goodbye.

*

"So you want us to commit the ultimate taboo?" Trace clarified.

"They're not Human," Lana said brutally.

"A day of hunger and you're already a cannibal," Tuesday snickered. "You'd have done great in the Mojave."

"They're not Human!" Lana repeated. "It's only cannibalism if they're your own species."

Rem slithered about in the background a bit, clearly filing away Lana's views on eating other intelligent species for future reference.

They were back in the dumpster storage area. An army of Weavers had already sewn up every hull breach in this section and re-pressurised it, and now they'd moved on to repairing the melted dumpsters with surprising efficiency. The skittering robots had also welded the wrecked rail system back together, and if their work here was any indication, The Dirty Betty was going to be ship-shape again in days.

Trace glared down at a large dent in the starboard wall. Two very, very dead Slidge soldiers had been splattered so badly that their body armour had explosively collapsed, causing their internal juices to splash about in a decidedly external way. There was a good chance the thick pus-coloured liquid would leave indelible marks you could never scrub off.

"They're sentient beings," Rem said quietly. "Doesn't that bother you?"

"Of course it bothers me," Lana snapped. "But it bothers me a whole lot less than dying in one of the worst ways I can imagine."

"I don't get why the Weavers didn't clean all this up," Tuesday muttered, kneeling next to a badly smashed red arm. He poked the skin, and gel oozed out.

"Probably registered it as a crime scene," Rem noted. "We did brutally and deliberately murder them with an avalanche of dumpsters."

"Self-defence," Trace snapped.

Lana glanced at her. "I thought you objected to eating them?"

Trace squinted at the dead Slidge, and sniffed.

"It's not a moral concern or anything. I just don't like calamari, that's all."

Lana clicked her fingers in realisation. She lifted the black top of her Cadet uniform just enough to reveal the rubber ports drilled directly into her belly and ribcage. She made sure Tuesday didn't manage to get as much as a peek at any under-boob.

"No need to taste them. We can puree the bodies and pump the smoothie right in."

"How much meat and water will we be able to extract from them?" Tuesday asked.

Lana tapped away at her Scroll. She seemed frustrated.

"A lot of their biochemistry isn't compatible with our bodies at all, so we'd need to refine away a lot of their mass if we don't want to get poisoned. All up, though, adding these two to everything we've found so far..." Lana went a little faint for a moment, almost swooning. She gritted her teeth together and willed herself to stand up straight. "Even if we recycle every drop until it's basically deadly, there's no conceivable way we'll survive five weeks, let alone six."

There was silence for a long time. Everyone was alone in their thoughts. What were you supposed to say to a death sentence?

Rem traced over the smashed Slidge weaponry, which had been pulped into complete uselessness, and asked a very good question.

"Why are there three guns?"

Trace regarded Rem with chips of ice.

"What?"

Rem pointed with his eye stalks. One, two, three.

"There are three Slidge blasters here, but only two bodies." Rem nodded with his antennae. "And remember the cockpit of that heavy corvette had room for three Slidge to dangle. Am I the only one here who can do the math?"

Lana exhaled.

"Spug. Great. Now we have a homicidal stowaway running around in a stealthed combat suit."

"I ain't sharing with him, neither," Tuesday grumbled. "Sponger can find his own grub."

CHAPTER NINETEEN

Jimmy was viciously scratching the back of his head when his next visitor made an appearance. There was an odd tickle where Jimmy's spine met his skull, a kind of slithering, itching sensation. It started after two or three days of healing in Medical's recliner, radiating from his head and neck in tingling waves. No matter how much he clawed at it, though, the tickle didn't go away for long. His index finger's nail was rimmed with dried blood.

He instantly sat up straight when Trace stomped in. She often had that effect on people. Glancing at Jimmy's bruised body, she snatched a bright little flashlight from the bench and hit him right in the pupils without any warning.

"He'll survive," Trace announced in the sort of tone you'd use to describe a worthless inanimate object. Temporarily blinded, Jimmy was suddenly yanked off the chair with too much force. "Yo, buckwheat, up."

Slipping blindly off the reclining medical chair, groaning as every square centimetre of his body complained all at once, a sight-impaired Jimmy clung to what must have been the doorway.

Even though Jimmy couldn't see Lana, he could hear her speaking and furiously swiping at her Scroll. Blinking away the darkness, the first thing Jimmy saw was Rem playing about with a corridor-filling hologram of what appeared to be the entire floorplan of The Dirty Betty. Tuesday was casually positioned in the exact middle point of all the others, effectively meat-shielding himself from harm.

Jimmy went to ask a question, but Lana devoted an instant to filling him in on the situation.

"We've got a live Slidge trooper in full chameleonic armour hiding somewhere on board. Possibly armed, definitely pissed off, and so far none of our scanners, cameras, Weavers, or bloody eyeballs have been of any use in finding it. Starting now, we're all wearing cling suits around the clock in case of an ambush." She didn't wait for a response before turning to Rem. "Any luck?"

The bristleworm had put away his floorplan for now so he could play his starburst collar's array of scanners over a rough half-brick of vaguely ceramic origins. No matter how many different shades of light he swept across the lump, though, he didn't seem the slightest bit relieved. Rem drooped.

"No matter what adjustments I make, my scanners only see empty space whenever I try to scan this hunk for Slidge body armour." Rem growled in frustration, raising the shard up high as though he was about to smash it like a petulant child throwing a tantrum. "This material has some incredible stealther technology built into in. It's no wonder they got the drop on us so easily. We didn't have the faintest idea they were even there until..."

Rem curled an eye stalk towards a cranky-looking Jimmy in what might have been embarrassment, but an apology didn't follow.

"But we can all clearly see it," Trace snapped, snatching the scanner-proof substance. "Scanners be buggerated, why aren't the cameras picking up anything? Last I heard, we developed motion-detection technology a thousand years ago."

Rem contemplated her question.

"The busted combat suit we recovered this nugget from was scattered in fifty separate pieces," he said slowly. "Perhaps when Slidge armour is intact and powered it possesses other properties? For all we know, the Primacy has all kinds of tech that can help them avoid detection."

"Ghosts," Tuesday muttered under his foul breath from his crouch in the corner, dragging from his green cigarette. "Ship's haunted."

"Nix the superstition," Lana tutted. "Regardless, until we find our visitor, we don't separate for any reason. No splitting up to cover more ground, no quick trips around the corner to investigate strange noises; we're to stay as a coherent unit with eyes on each other at all times."

Everyone made the same face.

"For six weeks?" Trace scoffed. "The spug we are. I'd kill all of you long before the Slidge had a chance."

"We saw proof its primary weapon is ruined," Lana argued. "Getting annihilated into the starboard bulkhead in a dumpster avalanche smashed all the mobile artillery into pieces, so at least we don't need to worry about getting blasted with micro-missiles..."

"Again," Jimmy sulked, wincing at the pain of moving his face.

"...but we do need to worry about getting our throats slit while we're asleep." Lana continued. "And on top of that, the fact remains we don't have anywhere near enough supplies to survive this trip. Not yet, anyway. So as much as I'd like to barricade the five of us into a storeroom with all our food and drink and wait for our guest to dehydrate to death, that isn't an option at present."

"Correct me if I'm wrong," Tuesday said to Rem with distinct snark, "but you've already run extensive scans all over the ship again and again, right? Far as we can tell, there's no more potable liquid or edible biomass to be had."

Rem nodded his eye stalks.

"Yes, but The Dirty Betty's internal readers aren't in the best shape. About a fifth of her floor space, ventilation system and electrical network is totally greyed out. The deeper you go, the less reliable the readings. Only way to see what's there is to go eyeball it."

"Or send some Weavers," Tuesday suggested, his survival instincts reaching the speed of light at the thought of being conscripted to trawl through the depths of this rusting hulk.

Rem shook his mandibles.

"Not an option. All those grey spots are nulled, meaning they're dead zones for electronic transmissions. Send a Weaver into a grey spot, we've probably lost it for good. We'll have to go look ourselves." He scoffed at Tuesday's expression. "What, you have something better to do?"

"Yeah, your Mum," Tuesday muttered.

Lana appeared deep in thought.

"Theoretically, what causes these grey spots?"

"General wear and tear," the bristleworm guessed. "Equipment degradation. High-speed dust impacts. Important bits getting carved out by scavengers. Though with what little I know about Humans, I'd say the most likely reason that one of your starships breaks down is because all of your technology is designed to go faulty the moment its warranty expires, but this is a TuffTek ship, and they last forever. Why? What does it matter?"

Lana smiled in hope.

"Because I reckon those grey spots would have a higher than average chance of being caused by pests, moss build-ups, water leaks and other little damaging treasures, right?" Lana scratched viciously at the back of her head, running a sharp nail back and forth where her spine met her skull. "From now on, we're in a state of permanent emergency. And you know what that means."

Jimmy was about to comment on how he'd been feeling itchy lately, too, but Lana was already consulting Rem's holographics to pick out their first destination. His words died and came out as a sad sigh instead.

*

Against their better instincts, it was decided they'd head down to the metal reclamation forges first. As these were the deepest depths Jimmy had plumbed during their trip towards Sprout, it was a logical starting point. He literally swore black and blue he hadn't encountered any signs of water or vermin this far down, but Tuesday and Trace gave him the same suspicious look. Sure, Jimmy may have been the incarnation of a walking conscience compared to the rest of the group, but how much pressure did it take for a good man to dick over those he loved the most, let alone people who spent most of their time underestimating, ignoring or insulting him? Strand any of history's most altruistic men and women in a wasteland without food, water or hope, and it won't take ten missed meals before the saints are gnawing on each other's limbs.

As the metal reclamation forges were hot, sweaty, and basically not the best place to conserve water, they took a shortcut through the garbage sorting wing. A good hundred metres wide and Thor only knew how deep, it turned out to be surprisingly easy to walk across what was essentially a porridge of plastic, rubber, ceramics, cardboard, laminate, fabrics and other non-metallic trash. While the slow tide of Mister Drizzle plush toys, condoms, dressing gowns, soiled mattresses and toilet seats was gradually sweeping towards being sorted and melted, thankfully its surface was reasonable stable. It was a nerve-wracking ten minutes of second-guessing every step and expecting to fall into a deadly hollow in the garbage, but they safely made it to the gantry on the far side.

Still feeling the remnant of forge-fires on their skin, an emergency staircase turned out to be a fresh gust of wintry pleasure. After a short argument about whether maintaining a frigid breeze in a basically unused stairwell was somehow wasting water, it was decided three-to-two it might be worthwhile to check how high the air conditioning system was cranked in this section. Unfortunately, the air conditioning turned out be fuelled by an exotic gas that was poisonous in its liquid form. Despite this disappointment, Jimmy suggested that spending their time in the coldest areas of the ship might reduce their sweating and general water loss, and while everyone agreed it was a great idea, it soon transformed into a huge disagreement about whether or not walking around in cling suits all the time would help. Once the group managed to wrestle away Trace's kinetic accelerator before she did anything permanent to Lana, they decided it might be best to have this discussion some other time.

The first couple of grey spots weren't anything special. Charring at site one indicated a medium-sized blaze had occurred here at some point, and the cameras and scanners were melted into hard-set puddles studded with broken glass. Site number two was a little more mysterious, as a spherical, house-sized bite had been taken out of the corridor, leaving a behind a perfectly round hole. Nobody could figure out what had caused such odd damage more than sixty metres from the outer hull, and while Lana marvelled at its smooth artistry, nobody wanted to hang around just in case some beast was about to take another swallow from the derelict.

Towards the deepest depths of the ship, right in the middle of the third and darkest grey spot, there was finally something interesting. At first glance, it was just a bare corridor containing nothing of note. However, by pinpointing the exact core of this grey spot, they ended up at a utility cupboard. Although he had no knees, Rem kneeled down and popped its ordinary lock with a mandible. Inside was a small tower built out of needles, bedframe struts and the guts of old scanners, all welded together into a crude kind of synthetic bush before being papered over with foil. It filled every square centimetre of the cupboard, crammed in so tight that its branches were bent into loops. It glowed from within. While a case of MacCricket legs or a jar of compressed water pearls was the ideal find, that didn't mean their search was entirely myopic. Despite looking like a Christmas tree designed by intelligent robots after a machine-led Armageddon, it was clear this object had been designed with more than artistic merit in mind.

Carefully running his starburst collar over the device, his curiosity and self-preservation warring with one another, Rem calmed at the sight of a calm blue Drennite glyph superimposed over the synthetic tree.

"It isn't explosive," Rem casually mentioned over his shell, turning to see the humans had taken cover twenty metres away behind some wooden shipping crates. The bristleworm sighed and raised his voice to make up for the distance. "It's just a scan blocker. Backyard job. Worked well enough to fool my equipment, though, not to mention The Dirty Betty herself."

"So it was put there to hide something, you mean?" Tuesday asked, eyes wide with greed. "Something...valuable?"

Rem pecked away at his holographic OS. He gave a hum of approval.

"Maybe..."

Without bothering to ask permission, Rem played his facial tentacles over the scan blocker until he found a mildew-yellow power board. Once disconnected, the entire device went dark, and everyone finally noticed a low background hum only by its sudden absence. Even though none of the humans understood Low-Dren, Rem's holographic map of The Dirty Betty was cleansed of most of the puffy clouds that indicated grey spots. Rem nodded, impressed.

"Whoever put this up, they were an artist."

Lana had only opened her mouth when her Miyamoto-Kojima computer Scroll gave a chirp, audibly vibrating within its slipcase. She raised an eyebrow at it.

"What does the blue light mean?" Jimmy asked, pointing rudely. Lana shrugged.

"No idea. It's never done that before."

Drawing the Scroll like a Samurai with a sharpened katana, Lana unfurled its ivory chopsticks. It took ages for the ancient computer to start up – an intolerable three seconds – and Lana gaped at a little sapphire icon that reflected from her pupils.

"Scroll says it's detected a paired device on its network."

She waved the flexible screen so everyone could get a look at the winking blue icon, which took the shape of a diagonal pointing arrow indicating a corridor up and to port. Lana meditated on this turn of events, but the answer was clear. "Only one course of action, as I see it."

*

While the mysterious target was less than eighty metres away, everyone stayed alert. Odin only knew what was waiting for them, not to mention that there was still a Slidge trooper probably waiting to pounce from a roof vent at any given moment.

The Dirty Betty had proved to be full of surprises lately, none of them good. Historically, the chances of their collective fortunes suddenly improving had always been more farfetched than losing what little they had in a painful, flaming heap, and there was no good reason why luck would decide to be any kinder to them now.

Trace was given permission to hold her kinetic accelerator and its antimatter vacuum clip in separate hands, but only on the condition that if she pointed it at anyone who didn't have six arms and a beak she wouldn't see it again for a month. Despite being an Enforcer, little more than a glorified rental cop willing to bend the rules until they screamed if a client requested it, at least Trace had received basic firearms training.

Unlike Lana.

Yes, Lana had been a Cadet since the cradle, but at the Academy on her world nobody was allowed to handle a live firearm until the age of nineteen, and sure as Ragnarök wouldn't be licensed to carry an actual gun outside of a shooting range until they'd finished dozens of AutoEducation uploads and had extensive real-world testing. While she was now physically in her mid-twenties (or well over half a millennium, depending on if you counted the temporal knobbery involved with jumping between galaxies frozen solid as a chicken nugget) the fact remained Lana had never fired anything more lethal than a pain snapper before, and so was not suited for the job.

For now, Trace was their protector. Anyone who'd ever met Trace could instantly identify at least three major things wrong with that sentence.

Locked on her Scroll, Lana went to speak.

"Here we…"

She looked up just in time to avoid going nose-first into graphene. She blinked a few times, consulted the Scroll, and then blinked at the wall again. She gaped a little.

Tuesday stepped forwards, put his waxy ear to the bulkhead, and tapped it with two curled knuckles. Squinting a little as he crab-walked down the corridor, rapping away every hand span, he listened intently as he played the purple like a percussion instrument. After ten strikes he bared his black teeth.

"Hollow right there. Terrible work, too. Total rush job."

Jimmy summoned a crowbar from his AllTool bracelet, hefting the tactile holographic implement the wrong way around.

"Better be a whole bag of burgers back there," he muttered, stepping towards the barrier. "Big juicy ones from MacDeaths, the sort that stay warm and moist for a hundred years. And a whole mess of fries and cricket nuggets and Slobber-Choc Sundaes and…"

*

They each took turns battering the wall with assorted AllTool projections. In a stroke of luck, the graphene turned out to be just the thinnest possible veneer. As this composite material made steel armour plating look like fairy floss in comparison, this meant breaking through it only took fifteen minutes of bashing rather than three hours of millimetre-by-millimetre etching with a plasma cutter Beneath the veneer lay a slab of bulletproof steel cemented in place with epoxy. It was slathered in white paint, but thankfully the enamel was on this side. Some careful chiselling proved this steel was the transparent sort, and soon they were rewarded with a dim view of what lay within. Tuesday pressed his eye, nose and cheek flat against the steel to scope out any potential treasure (or even just a flat can of Slurko Cola), but the room beyond was robed in darkness. Tuesday's squished face triggered a motion sensor, though, and he hissed and recoiled at the flare of light like Nosferatu.

Lana pushed Tuesday aside. The hollow was barely the size of a small bedroom, and bare of any furniture or decorations. Its only notable detail was a guy wrapped in an indigo PusCo sanitation uniform slumped against the wall, his chin resting just above his sternum and all four limbs limp noodles on the grid work floor. There were a few miscellaneous items scattered about, but as none of them were desensitised serial killers, the dead body kind of captured their focus for now.

"Can't have been dead long," Trace noted. "Too juicy."

"Don't say juicy," Jimmy moaned, devastated the secret chamber wasn't filled with deep-fried cricket legs the size of baseball bats.

Lana shook her head a little, thinking.

"Far as I can tell, this room is hermetically sealed." She arched an eyebrow at the expression on Tuesday's and Jimmy's faces. "That means it's airtight."

"How'd he die?" Trace asked with a little too much enthusiasm.

Lana consulted her Scroll, and peeked through the blurry window.

"Suicide."

Everyone gave Lana the same look.

"How d'you figure?" Tuesday asked, suspicious.

Lana pointed.

"Because I can see a large canister of Densite gas between his legs with its valve turned all the way open. But the weird part is he seemed to have sealed himself away first."

Jimmy bruised face twisted in horror.

"Wait, he walled himself in? Why?"

Lana scowled at Jimmy's uselessness.

"Slummer, there's a thick red line between logic and psychic." Lana summoned a sledgehammer from her AllTool. After all that unpleasantness the other week, Tuesday understandably drew back a little at the sight of it. "But it's a fact dead men can tell tales."

*

The automated lighting flickered a little, warming up after a great inactivity. This somehow managed to make being in a room with a dead body even more creepy.

Although the lethal haze of Densite gas had turned neutral and dissipated long ago, they all exercised due caution. Even if there was still a death cloud, their reinforced cling suits were tough enough to weather a bit of chemical violence. As an added bonus, being sealed up meant they wouldn't have to smell the incomparable stench of decaying flesh, a reek that could purge the gullets of the hardiest of men.

Once the transparent steel was hammered out of the way and everyone went inside for a gander, Jimmy tried to look useful by creeping close enough to the corpse to get a look at his lapel. He sounded the nametag out.

"Nurbis?"

Lana's eyes flashed from her Scroll to pin down Jimmy like a butterfly.

"What did you say?"

Jimmy blinked heavily, as though trying his damnedest to check his short-term memory for a screw-up.

"Uh...Nurbis? His name tag says Nurbis."

Lana produced her Scroll's slipcover and tapped its spine in an exaggerated way. A scratchy-but-legible etching declared Property of Nurbis.

"I seen that name, too," Tuesday added. "Plenty of times. On old sticky notes, mostly. Always passive-aggressive stuff. Bitchy. Complaining about people leaving the coffee out, or not wiping the benches good enough, or disposing of hazardous biological materials down the trash compactor instead of sealing them in lead-lined shells."

Everyone startled as Nurbis' mouth swung open with a wet, crunching noise. Half expecting the corpse to verbally defend the sticky notes and his many other efforts to hold the crew to a higher standard, instead his jawbone disconnected in an explosion of yellow teeth. Everyone backed away a safe distance as Nurbis collapsed into soup, proving that the sudden addition of fresh air to his long-undisturbed crypt had allowed his dead body to catch up with who-knew-how-many years of decay. His self-cleaning stain-resistant PusCo uniform, however, still looked fresh enough to pass onto the next employee in what had been an unbroken chain of hand-me-downs up until now.

Thankfully, nobody had to suffer the stench of what looked like a bistro-sized portion of Shepherd's pie, but they could certainly imagine the reek. Despite being repelled by the yucky pile, Lana spotted something in the soft jelly that used to be a hand. She knelt and pressed her nail into the fleshy web between index finger and thumb, ignoring Jimmy's horrified gagging, and soon held up a little marble in triumph. It may have been a lot bigger than usual, but there was no doubt about it: Lana was holding up an Omni implant.

She didn't have a chance to celebrate finding an implantable supercomputer just lying around before the Omni glittered blue, syncing up with the Scroll. The roll-up computer chimed, as though someone was ringing a doorbell. Everyone's attention was now rapt on the Scroll.

Feeling unnaturally creeped out, Lana slowly unfurled the flexible screen to see a face was dominating it. Like most people recording a video message, Nurbis had a kind of half-wary expression, but the angle made his head look like a potato. He practised smiling at several different intensities, and spoke from beyond the grave.

"Well, if you're watching this, and you're a real Original Recipe like me, I can guarantee you're absolutely safe. If you're one of The Perfect, though, you'll be dead in three seconds and counting. Three, two, one..."

CHAPTER TWENTY

"...zero."

Everyone flinched, but Nurbis just kept practising his weird, kooked-out smiles. Without bothering to celebrate they were still alive, the passengers gathered around to get a better look at the screen. Nurbis continued his monologue.

"If this recording is still running that means you're Human, as otherwise the anti-mutiny bombs would have reduced The Dirty Betty to ashes. That means the resistance still has soldiers. Welcome to the fight! Oh, sorry, one sec..." Nurbis backed up a little on the screen, and held out his right hand as though inviting a shake. "I'm Nurbis. No surname, for obvious reasons. Apparently I used to be a Vegan Extremist terrorist before they, uh, fixed me with a Psych-in-a-Box. Not that I remember any of it, not as much as my real...mmm, my former name. Before all this spug happened, The Dirty Betty was crewed by a bunch of indentured re-writes paying off the cost of our adjustments, all kept under the thumb of nine armed officers from the Extreme Rehabilitation Bureau."

"Vegan Extremists?" Lana repeated quietly. "No wonder the ship is wired with explosives. It was crewed by a bunch of monsters."

"Explains that stupid box being in the cupboard," Jimmy muttered, apparently still hung up on Lana's lack of hatred for psychiatric adjustment.

Strangely, Nurbis' next words were a question.

"How much do you know about the resistance?"

His face went static, unblinking and unbreathing. Tuesday gave a groan of frustration.

"Stupid junk froze up."

The face on the screen glitched a little, lips and teeth and eyes juddering unnaturally, as though rapidly hopping towards a different part of the stream. Nurbis resumed talking.

"My apologies, but this recording isn't a full-interactive copy of my mind. While it goes against my old religion as a tree-chewer of Vegan Extremism as well as my new rewritten faith of Jud-Islamic Catholicism, even if I was a heathen I don't have the tech to copy myself properly." Nurbis blinked. "This is only a shallow-scan recording I set up to help you efficiently hop between the video diary entries I stored on my Omni. I'd like to say that recording my thoughts about my lot in life would make things easier, but…" Nurbis gave a sad smile. It was an expression that seemed tailor-made for his face. "Well, I'm sure you've got a good idea of what it's like to be alone for years. Certain that you know it very well."

"Ask a question," Tuesday prompted Lana.

"What is the resistance?" she asked loudly and clearly. "Resisting what?"

There was that little visual flick between diary entries. The ghost spoke.

"I don't need to tell you how hard it is to get the truth off of the Link, so I need to know: how much do you know about The Perfection?"

"Minimal," Trace grunted.

There were a few moments of rapid twitching. Suddenly, the face of Nurbis was youthened by a good five years. He was a lot healthier and the bags under his eyes were noticeably absent, as though he'd suddenly been cured of insomnia and granted a month of deep sleep. The recording had been made somewhere on The Dirty Betty that wasn't grimy or rusty or dented. Voices could be heard murmuring in the background, but Nurbis twiddled something on the side of his recording device to drown the others out.

He inhaled and exhaled slowly, eyes darting about as though trying to figure out where to start.

"Name's Nurbis. There's so few of us left that there's no point in surnames anymore, is there?" He smiled wanly. But then a grim realisation crashed down, killing his grin. "Before, it was nothing unusual for The Unison to update all us citizens with the usual mod-cons…vaccines, new AutoEducation lessons, nanotech patches for our retinals, that sort of thing. But this new update, the one known as The Perfection? It was rumoured to be something else. Something new." His expression glazed over as though he'd been admiring a long, long procession of heavenly promises, only for them to turn out to be dog droppings. "This would be the big one, the update to end all updates. Conversion was guaranteed to triple your intelligence, quadruple your lifespan, allow you to do amazing things like consciously switch your pain responses and fight-or-flight on and off like twisting dials. Of course we were excited! We were going to be gods! Maybe then they'd forgive us for our…indiscretions with Vegan Extremism, and let us convicts leave The Dirty Betty some way other than feet-first."

The glazed look dissolved, replaced by darkness.

"But there's some other components to Conversion, things we only heard as vague, paranoid whispers. Some said it hollowed your personality out, made you into a drone who only wanted to work towards the common good, a half-person who was only interested in what directly benefited Mankind. None of us believed it, of course. The Unison might not be the kindest of regimes, but what those conspiracy nuts were bleating? No way in Tartarus man would do that to man."

Nurbis rubbed the skin under his eyes in anxiety.

"The Perfection's fleets were less than six hours away from reaching us on the furthest Fringe when rebels managed to upload the truth to the Link. And then every corner of The Unison learned the truth. Conversion was an agonising process, and it kills a…" Nurbis looked like he was going to be sick at the words about to spill out. "Conversion kills an average of one out of three. Death isn't the worst part, though. Burning out the obsolete bits of a person's brain takes weeks, in some cases. Blinding headaches, hallucinations and abject terror. The tiniest ounce of resistance to Conversion makes the process twice as painful, and it only ends once the subject has been broken, surrendering their free will. Those who have the strength to resist…don't survive. All failed attempts get incinerated with all their records, erased from history."

He paused here, looking off camera. His thoughts could only be guessed.

"A lot of us convinced ourselves the videos and audio streams were a hoax...until The Perfection, what we used to know as The Unison, knocked out the entire Link from one edge of the galaxy to the other. The Information Super Skyway is still there, but its contents had been scooped out, leaving it empty."

Nurbis scanned the ceiling above him, regarding purple graphene.

"Our crew was ready to scuttle this lousy hunk of TuffTek garbage when the Link went down, so stealing her was the best we could manage at short notice. A moment before we skedaddled out of the system, though, some bright spark who shall not be named – Chad - tried to access the Link to see what in the molten peaks of Ragnarök was actually going on, and a bunch of plastic-looking doll freaks hailed us, calmly demanding we join the glory of The Perfection. We couldn't see a shred of Human between the whole bunch of them, and an instant decision was made to fire up the Stiller Drive and go somewhere random beyond Unison space." Nurbis gave a sardonic smile. "We might sanitise old syringes for a living, but even we knew better than to stick around."

Nurbis had another digital spasm, jerking unnaturally before showing a grey, gaunt face. The date stamp was only a month after the first recording, but Nurbis seemed to have aged two decades.

"It's worse than we could have ever guessed. Humanity is gone. Been entirely replaced by The Perfection...up to thirty years ago, in some cases. Buggered if I know how they managed to keep something like this under wraps for a generation. How? Admittedly, crime's gone down to zero, and there hasn't been a single murder on any Human worlds since the last stragglers got converted. They've managed to create a bloody utopia, and all it cost was murdering everything that made us Human."

Nurbis looked away from the camera, eyes shining with tears. It took some time to continue, and for a moment everyone was sure the video was going to skip again.

"Part of the Conversion process ensures The Perfect's offspring will be born pre-Converted, so there's no need to redo future generations. Any sign of being born with old-fashioned Humanity, as an 'Original Recipe' as we've been calling ourselves...well..."

The video rattled and hopped. Nurbis still looked drawn and prematurely aged, but his expression seemed colder, as though what he'd seen and heard had calloused his soul like a lifelong stint in the worst of maximum-security prisons. The horror and disbelief had disappeared, replaced by a powerful drive. He was a man with a purpose, a mission.

"We had to do things we'll never be forgiven for, but we finally followed the breadcrumbs all the way to those Human refugees our contacts promised. Turns out this Flapjack alien collector dealt in rare and unusual species, and his menagerie was rumoured to include thousands of Original Recipes like us. Even after gutting The Dirty Betty from bow to stern and selling everything of value to scrap dealers, all we could afford was a meeting, nothing more. The collector's price, as expected, was far too high...so we beat him, his guards and his entire household to death without hesitation. Thankfully, the whispers of his collection turned out to be true...sort of." Nurbis smiled in a way that didn't involve humour. It was an ugly, soulless expression. A hint of shame may have touched his eyes, digging out of his scars, but it vanished soon enough. "Problem is, we don't have anywhere safe to start a colony, not now half the crew of The Dirty Betty are dead or captured or perfected or suicided or so crazy that they're about as useful as an automatic doorknob licker."

Nurbis smiled again. This time, it didn't look so robotic, so sterile.

"Fing is, while I don't have a solution, I'm hoping you might, whoever you are. If you're watching this message from beyond the grave – my grave - then I'm certain these five thousand Human refugees are safe and just waiting for you to…"

The image froze, crackling violently, and Lana cursed as the Omni implant in her palm flared to a white-hot temperature. She dropped the marble, and it plopped right in the mess that used to be Nurbis, cooling in his gore with a wet sizzling noise. Growling, Lana tapped the Scroll, which refused to do anything but declare the words NETWORK FAILURE.

*

As there was no good reason to spend any additional time with a corpse reduced to the consistency and colour of old pea soup, once Lana carefully fished out the overheating Omni marble from its putrid resting place everyone evacuated Nurbis' tomb. Ever the civilised member of the group, Lana tried to replace the transparent layer of steel to its usual resting place, but it had been hammered into a useless bent curve.

The topic of their conversation was obvious. Where in the green blazes could Nurbis have hidden five thousand Humans on board this spiral? As much as Jimmy and Lana wanted to conduct an immediate ship wide search for their distant relatives, it didn't take a census bureau to prove there were only four Humans here. Rem didn't bother firing up his OS to confirm there weren't any refugees conveniently stashed in a cupboard somewhere, but he admitted one potential hiding spot came to mind.

"Obvious, innit?" the bristleworm prompted. He seemed unimpressed with their blank response. "We have a kilometre of mashed-up medical waste running the length of this ship. Literally a billion contaminated items, many of them stained black with blood and chunky with miscellaneous people bits. If you wanted to stash Humans somewhere, well…"

"So scan the tube," Trace growled. "Aft to stern."

Rem shook his head, sending his facial gribbles wobbling.

"No point, is there? Even if your people are snap frozen or sealed in stasis locks or dehydrated to jerky or are little more than brains in jars, the fact remains we don't have a crumb to spare. Without bothering to point out that this trip will literally take the remainder of our lives, I ask you: have you got a self-sufficient colony world conveniently stashed up your sleeve?"

Trace's face darkened to a scary crimson-black gleam that people avoided like the pox. Her words were wet.

"Just scan the tube."

Maintaining her stare with his eye stalks, Rem flicked his mandibles in offense before tapping away at his starburst collar with two facial tentacles with exaggerated, angry movements. He silently waited for a little green bar made of complex Drennite symbols to advance across a flat red block, and eventually the projection turned into an orange icon that looked suspiciously like a Sumo wrestler in profile. Rem flicked the icon, expanding it to the size of a basketball for all to view.

"See that?" Rem snapped, jabbing the icon. "That says there isn't a single hunk of Human tissue larger than half a torso in that whole tube, and it certainly doesn't contain five thousand intact persons. Your friend Nurbis is either delusional, a liar, or his information is outdated."

The projection vanished without another word.

Lana rolled the cooling Omni implant between her fingers as Rem summoned a moisture sensing app to search for water in the segments that used to be covered in scanner grey spots. She squinted at the little device.

"But you seemed so certain," she whispered.

Making sure nobody caught her speaking to the inanimate object, Lana quickly caught up with the procession.

*

After another two hours of searching for the smallest drip of water and the most anaemic of insect colonies, it was finally time to find the coolest possible room to sit and debrief. None of the air conditioners worked in these forgotten depths, sub-levels that even scavengers hadn't bothered to scope out too closely, though they did eventually discover a cool alcove that was kept frosty at all times by what appeared to be a malfunctioning coolant line.

Tuesday picked a perch in the corner, awkwardly jamming himself between crooked metal plates. Unfastening his cling suit hood and extending a brown tongue towards the ceiling, Tuesday's logic became clear when a drop of rusty water made a dent in his nicotine-dried mouth. Lana, Trace and Jimmy sat on the low piping that ran along the starboard wall, doing their best to ignore a hum that pulsed through it every now and again. Rem's long ribbon curled into a tight knot; resting his gribbly face between his tail pincers, the bristleworm retracted six eye stalks into armoured bulges. He made a noise that may have been a snore.

Lana continued rolling the Omni marble between her fingers, staring at it meditatively. Her Scroll stated the tiny implant needed to cool down before it could be safely rebooted, but there was no guarantee the Omni would ever work again. These implants were disposable by nature, designed to be injected against the thenar muscles of a user's left hand and subsequently dissolved down to amino acids once it was time to inject a newer model. Leaving one in a dead hand for centuries and expecting it to spring into action was bordering on absurd, but the fact they were deep up Excrement River without an oar meant the absurd needed to be double-checked just in case.

Lana violently struck the Franger Armaments icon on her cling suit three times and pulled back its floppy hood. Yanking both air tanks out of her nostrils, she went to wipe the patina of sweat off her forehead, but had the presence of mind to recall that sweat was your body's way of keeping you cool. Following her lead, the others shed their transparent skins and pocketed their tiny air supplies.

"Sure you want to do that?" Rem asked, his words muffled by his own rear end.

"Too hot," Trace growled. "Need to stay cool around the clock."

"A micro-missile to your unprotected face would be considerably hotter," Rem noted.

Tuesday slurped down another drop of moisture as it fell from the ceiling.

"I'm sure Jimmy could tell you a lot about that."

"Drekking Slidge were scanner-proof," Rem snapped, rearing his wriggly head. "Nobody told me they could ghost scanners like that. I have no reason to apologise."

Squinting, Lana dug her fingernail into the back of her neck again, really getting stuck in. She went to say something, but interrupted herself by yelping in pain. Everyone startled, and Tuesday jumped so high that he smacked his head on the low, wet roof. Trace slapped the antimatter clip into her kinetic accelerator and swung it towards the empty doorway in one motion.

"What?" Rem barked, uncurled in an instant.

Confused, Lana silently inspected her own index finger. The underside of her nail was encrusted with maroon gore, but the tip had a pinhole in it. She squeezed the pad experimentally, and frowned at a spot of bright blood. She carefully ran her thumb over the vertebrae in her neck, searching.

"Something on the wall bite you?" Trace asked, absently scratching at the back of her own neck.

Lana shook her head.

"No. It felt like it was…in my neck?"

"Give me a look," Jimmy offered.

Ducking, allowing Jimmy to take an uneducated glance, Lana spun back around at the sound of gasps, yelps and angry hisses. Everyone was looking at her like she had a hole in her forehead, but nobody seemed to be interested in spelling out why. Opening her mouth to speak, when Lana took a step towards Jimmy he almost tripped over his own flip-flops to keep away. She turned towards Trace, who brandished her future gun in warning.

"Don't come near me," Trace snapped, clearly not joking around.

Lana looked to Jimmy questioningly.

"What is it? What did you see?"

Jimmy looked at Lana with the kind of pity reserved for funerals and shotgun weddings.

"You...you've got a worm hanging out of your brain. A huge one."

*

It took some convincing, but Lana sat down in the middle of the cool room and bowed her head. Drawing the shortest straw, Jimmy carefully approached Lana for the second time with considerable grumbling, inching forwards one shuffle at a time. Like before, there was a thin, often-broken scab right at the point where Lana's brain stem met the base of her skull. He squinted, allowing his cut-rate retinal screens to zoom in on the wound. There was a hole at its very centre, a hollow large enough to slide in a single piece of thin spaghetti.

Jimmy shrugged and turned towards the others.

"Can't see it now."

Lana held up her Scroll.

"Nice try. Scan it."

Sighing, Jimmy accepted the unfurling computer, doing his best not to touch Lana's grimy index finger. Opening the Scroll, Jimmy held it as close to the Lana as he could without coming into contact with her. He was about to ask how to use it when a button appeared asking "Did You Want To Scan This Person?" Feeling as close to a neurosurgeon as he would ever get, Jimmy swiped the block. Chewing his lip as the Scroll initialised, numerous options popped up, none of which he could pronounce, let alone define. Holding the Scroll closer to the miniscule tunnel, moving his mouth as he tried to shape some of the difficult terminology, he was eventually spared by a suggestion from the roll-up computer: "Scan For Foreign Objects?"

"Who needs a Psych-in-a-Box?" he mumbled.

"What was that?" Trace demanded.

Pretending he didn't hear her, Jimmy tapped the button. Flinching as the upper layers of Lana's skin and muscle and connective bits were sheared away on the screen, Jimmy kept his eyeballs peeled for anything out of the ordinary. Eventually, the scan stopped burrowing once it penetrated the top vertebrae of Lana's neck, and a FOREIGN OBJECT FOUND warning flashed in strobing red and yellow. Trying to resist the urge to shrink away, Jimmy hit the little magnifying glass icon to zoom in even further.

"What is it?" Lana demanded, twisting her head.

"Stay still!" Jimmy snapped. He gave a moan of annoyance as the scan reset itself to the top layer of Lana's skin. "Lost it. Just wait, okay?"

It only took a couple of seconds to zoom back in, though it took Jimmy a moment to realise that Tuesday, Trace and Rem were all looking over his shoulder, keen to see what had made a home in the reptilian part of Lana's brain. This time, the illegal immigrant appeared in its full glory: the parasite was a white worm, exactly four inches long, divided into six bulbous segments. The invader was attached to Lana's brain stem and spinal cord with limbs that looked a lot like fishhooks, wedged in place more effectively than any tick. One of the hooks were resting just beneath the scab on Lana's neck, and its tip was a hollow, pointy tube, possibly for breathing.

"Relative of yours?" Tuesday snarked at Rem.

The bristleworm was unimpressed.

"Hardly."

Zooming deeper still, Jimmy and the others gave soft gasps at how thoroughly the bug had burrowed in. Some of the cilia extended six inches into her grey matter, their root systems branching off in seemingly random directions. Worse yet, the underside of the parasite was woven into Lana's spinal cord until she and it were basically one.

By this point, Lana was tired of being the only one left out of the loop.

"Somebody say something! What is it?"

Shifting the Scroll, Jimmy inspected the parasite's flank, and was surprised by an orderly row of vertical lines. Going on a hunch, Jimmy ran his finger over the screen, swiping at the row, and the Scroll asked a written question: "Scan Barcode?"

A few seconds later, Jimmy spoke with forced confidence.

"Lana, it appears to be a Peach worm, a weaponised parasite designed by WarCo for Military applications in the 26th Century."

Lana twisted her head, but caught herself before disrupting the scan a second time.

"What the spug do you know about weaponised parasites?" she demanded.

"Your passenger was engineered with a clear barcode running the length of its body."

"Can you dig it out?"

Lana waited for the silence to end for a good six seconds. She sighed.

"That bad, huh?"

Clicking her fingers, Lana stood up and produced the Omni implant she'd scored from a corpse, a less-than-exclusive club she may soon be joining. Everyone backed away without meaning to, but Lana paid them no mind. It was as though she'd accepted the fact they saw her as unclean, as soiled.

She summoned a scalpel from her AllTool bracelet, breathed in and out three times like a steam train, and stabbed herself in the web between the index finger and thumb of her left hand. Sliding in the warm Omni marble, the implant's installation process started by sealing Lana's flesh up with a burst of medical nanites. Tapping at the substantial new bump, for a moment nothing happened. Then, just when all hope seemed lost, the Omni proved it wasn't a useless lump by projecting a crackly holographic screen. Swiping through the layers of menus like a pro, Lana quickly found the Search bar. Tapping in "Peach worms," it turned out the parasite was common enough in Nurbis' era to warrant a documentary file saved on his Omni. An educated, though synthetic, voice spelled out what it knew, accompanied by graphic videos.

"Created as a lab-bashed fusion of some of Earth's worst parasites - including botflies, guinea worms, filarial nematodes and psychosis ticks - Peach worm spores are designed to be attracted to cerebral activity, specifically that of Humans," the voice stated. "Once a pinhead spore has drifted onto a potential host and burrowed in, using its pain-killing properties to do so without any discomfort or other obvious signs, it will spend a number of days weaving itself deep into the brain, spine and nervous system of its host, creating a permanent bond. On the ninth day, the mature Peach worm will become capable of hijacking the nervous system and lower brain functions of its host in order to fulfil whatever mission its handler has allocated. There is no limit to what the Peach worm is capable of forcing its slave to do, including the most heinous acts of violence and depravity, often for the purposes of demoralising enemy troops in..."

Lana swiped the floating screen off, not bothering to spell out why. Composing herself, she brought back the holographic display and tapped a button labelled

Treatment. The same voice as before did the voiceover.

"There are minimal treatment options for Peach worm infestation. If you discover that a friend, colleague or loved one has been infected with a Peach worm, it is imperative that nobody goes near them without hazmat equipment in order to avoid spore transferal. You must isolate the host from other people, and keep them well hydrated and sedated ..."

"Okay..." Lana said hopefully.

"...if you wait until they're asleep, it will be much easier to decapitate, dismember and incinerate the infected person in order to prevent any further spread. Total cremation is highly recommended, and the ashes should be sealed away in an airtight, lead-lined container before being cast into the nearest star..."

Lana swung at the holographic screen so hard that she almost fell over. Pacing back and forth in the sudden silence, the audio void was finally broken by a cold, cold question from Trace.

"So how much water do we save without her?"

Lana gaped, her outrage visible in full technicolour. However, Lana's words never came, stolen away as she watched both Trace and Jimmy absently scratching at the back of their necks. As though sharing a psychic flash, they stopped clawing at their skin for long enough to process a sharp slap of reality.

Jimmy looked at the gory tip of his index finger for three long seconds.

"We're all infected, aren't we?" he managed.

The silence was broken by a dark chuckle from Tuesday. Trace stared chainsaws at him.

"The spug is so funny?"

"Should be plenty of water to go round once we're all dead, won't there?"

*

Although they already knew the answer, Trace and Jimmy went through the same scans as Lana. Their Peach worms were at roughly the same stage of maturity, and had already threaded into their brains and spinal columns just as thoroughly. Proving the Universe truly had no justice, Tuesday's scan was different to the others.

"It appears to be dead," Rem noted. He ran an antennae across the Scroll's display. "If you look here, you'll notice its tendrils have withered away, turning to dust. I'm no expert, but I'm assuming your body will absorb the remains once they decompose. Either that, or all this foreign matter will cripple you into a drooling vegetable."

"How?" Trace barked.

Rem shrugged without shoulders.

"No idea. His Peach worm is from the same spore cluster as the other three, and these parasites are renowned for their hardiness and efficiency. In theory, there is no conceivable way the one lodged in Tuesday should be dead."

Clapping his hands together loudly, Tuesday gave everyone an extra-large black smile.

"Well, who feels like celebrating?"

CHAPTER TWENTY ONE

Extreme rationing went into effect after a week. Lunch became a thing of the past, breakfast and dinner contained just enough calories to stay on the right side of starvation, and water was only allowed when an individual's hydration chart showed it to be necessary.

They learned a lot from these hardships. For instance, guinea pig meat proved to be surprisingly tender and flavourful, tasting a bit like oily, over-rich duck. While nobody was at the point where they could force themselves to nibble on those too-cute-faces, the skins and organs and blood and bones of the guinea pigs were frozen in bags for later, as throwing away perfectly good protein at this point would be bordering on insane. Another fun fact was that one type of moss they'd discovered turned out to be less revolting than most, having a lot in common with kale. It was served for the sake of vitamins, if not flavour or pleasure.

While these measures weren't sustainable, there wasn't any other option. Everyone had hoped the Omni implant recovered from Nurbis' corpse was going to solve all of their problems somehow, but after suffering another brown-out the stupid thing was refusing to boot. It might contain schematics for scientific miracles beyond their dreams, but that wasn't much help when you couldn't turn the blasted thing on.

Now the scan blocker had been powered down, Rem was able to sweep the entirety of The Dirty Betty from aft to stern. He ran constant scans that took five hours bumper to bumper, sniffing for moisture or rodent nests or insect infestation. Despite these aggressive scans, there was still no sign of their Slidge stowaway, and everyone was starting to doubt the red bag of elbows even existed. Nobody wanted to chance being silently knifed in the kidneys, though, so they stayed within yelping distance at all times just in case it made an appearance.

In order to make their water rationing as efficient as possible, they sought out the coldest room on board - a nicely damp-aired bolthole directly beneath the coolant chambers of the Stiller Drive - and bunked down as though they were camping back on Scrote all over again. Moving in their sleeping mats was the only luxury they had in this fridge-like habitation, and the closest thing they had to entertainment was watching the drip-drip-drip of their urine recycler as it processed each bladder full into something potable.

Day ten hosted the latest drama. Although he'd been covert about it, Tuesday's distinctive expired-smoked-oyster aroma proved he was still sucking down chlorine-flavoured cigarettes from his endless supply. As they'd all been in the same room this whole time, it was hard to comprehend how he'd managed such a feat. Regardless, the others formed a consensus that this had to stop, and Tuesday took it about as well as expected.

Producing a switchblade faster than thought, even though Tuesday had literally just stubbed out a cigarette two minutes ago, his expression was inhumanly distorted by the incomprehensible horrors of going without another smoke break for five weeks.

It's common knowledge that every Human has the potential to kill. It's just a matter of finding their trigger.

"But they're dehydrating you," Lana soothed, holding her hands palm-forward in a non-threatening way. "It's for your own good."

"Touch my smokes and I'll dehydrate you all over the floor," Tuesday hissed, pointing his blade at Lana's forehead. Jimmy took a sideways step, and Tuesday brandished the knife in his direction. "First one past that tile gets ventilated.

Don't try me."

"Maybe we can find some chlorine patches?" Jimmy managed, locked on the sharp point.

Tuesday cackled.

"What are you, an idiot? You can't quit cigarettes anymore! I'd be dead in days from withdrawal shock."

"You could be dead in three seconds," Trace muttered, hand millimetres from her kinetic accelerator.

"Don't escalate the situation!" Lana snapped over her shoulder. She turned back to Tuesday with her biggest, fakest smile. "What if we ration them? Give you a couple each day? Just enough to keep you on the right side of withdrawals?"

Tuesday squinted, but didn't lower the knife. Although Rem was in the far corner, staying out of their business, the bristleworm raised his head and tilted it in thought.

"Chemicals," he said quietly.

Lana flicked her gaze to Rem as he began messing around with his starburst collar, jabbing at holograms of jagged Low-Dren symbols.

"What?"

"Testing a theory…"

Distracted, Tuesday's knife only drooped for a moment before Trace sacked him like he was a slow quarterback. Driving him into the wall, knocking the foul breath from his black lungs, Jimmy and Lana were into the fray a moment later. Screaming as his switchblade was wrestled away, the situation got even more unpleasant when they started rifling through Tuesday's gooey, sticky, smelly pockets.

Rem continued to work on his equations, rapt in his latest idea.

*

A day later, a vibration in Lana's left hand woke her up. As sleep was a great way to minimise the amount of calories your body burns, she absently went to swipe at the Omni to tell its alarm to snooze for a couple more hours, but then her eyes snapped open in realisation.

The implant had finally turned itself back on!

Not daring to get her hopes up, Lana almost prayed a prayer of thanks when layer upon layer of holograms fanned out from the marble in her hand meat, displaying the Omni's entire file structure, lists of common tasks, and a History of its most recent actions. While the others snored and gulped and dribbled all over their sleeping pallets, Lana dived head-first into zettabytes of information.

By the time Tuesday woke up to demand the first of his three daily cigarettes, Lana's studies of the Omni she'd "inherited" from Nurbis had already paid dividends. There was an entire folder filled with information about the equipment commonly used by Emergency services and humanitarian organisations, and among the many, many schematics was a pre-Unison device known as a "Loaves & Fishes" protein sump. Popularised after the collapse of The Skandinavian Expansion, feeding your existing foodstuffs into a protein sump could easily quintuple them in a matter of hours. However, the taste, texture and appearance of sump-grown protein meant it was only to be used for absolute emergencies. And while these devices sucked down electricity in huge quantities, thankfully The Dirty Betty had more than enough to divert from its missing machinery.

"How long until you have one up and running?" Jimmy asked, switching between the floating schematic and Lana's beaming face. Like everyone except for Lana, it was clear Jimmy wasn't really into the whole 'hope' thing anymore. "No offense, but that blueprint looks complicated, and I don't reckon any of us would even know how to plug it in, let alone make one."

Lana dismissed the hologram and nodded at line of spider-like Weavers as they ticked past the doorway of the frigid studio apartment.

"Weavers can do it. Give them a blueprint, provide some materials, and tell them to make it, done."

"You ever eaten from a protein sump?" Tuesday muttered. "When I was a kid, we had them in Cell Block Pre-School. They were only used as a form of punishment. You had to do something real bad to be on a sump diet...stab-a-guard-in-the-head kind of bad. Hope everyone likes the taste of fermented armpits, or you're going to have a really, really bad time."

*

As they were capable of rebuilding any part of the ship no matter how dire its condition, it only took the Weavers half an hour to construct the protein sump. Unfortunately, their first attempt did little more than give off an awful smell before bursting into flames.

After two more days of failures and wasted guinea pig bones, it was finally decided the blueprint must be faulty. It took hours and hours of research and computer simulations, but the problem turned out to be that almost half of the blueprint's measurements had been recorded in some bizarre, alien form of measurement known as "Imperial," rather than standard Metric. Once this was figured out, the Weavers constructed a very different machine to their previous attempts, and this one coiled up on the first try.

Their operational protein sump was set up in the corner of their shared room and wired directly into The Dirty Betty's power grid. They toasted their success with a batch of grey broth from the sump, and it only took one sip to bring their party to an abrupt end. Everyone was having trouble resisting the urge to spit out the brew, and it took a good fifteen seconds for everyone to finish swallowing.

"It's like..." Jimmy gagged a little, "...little chewy balls of expired yogurt suspended in cold grease. Are you sure it's meant to taste like that? Maybe the blueprint was wrong again in some other way..."

Tuesday cackled into his second sip.

"Welcome to the punishment menu."

*

Three days later, Rem was about to share his discovery before he noticed Jimmy was carefully urinating into his designated storage bottle. As Jimmy was a born gentleman, he did this in the darkest corner of the room with his back to everyone. Shaking off exactly twice, Jimmy didn't respond to Rem's politely cleared throat until he'd finished plugging his flask of wee into the complicated knot of water purifying hardware leaning against the port wall. After all, every drop was precious.

"What?"

"I've discovered why Tuesday's Peach worm didn't survive."

This gripped everyone's attention. So far the weaponised parasites hadn't caused any dramas (and the nutrients they were extracting from their hosts was negligible), but the Peach worms were now thoroughly embedded in their brains and spinal cords and would be easily capable of exerting direct control over their hosts if they had any inclination to do so. While some research stated that Peach worm spores were programmed with specific missions before being decanted by their breeders, nobody had any idea what these particular ones had been ordered to do, or to who, or why, or when they were going to do it. It had also been theorised during one of the long, boring days in this freezer that they were already completely under the direct control of the Peach worms and simply didn't know it. However, after a long, paranoid, sleepless night, Tuesday loudly declared he didn't want to say another word about the freaking parasites in case it set them off.

"Are you talking about a cure?" Jimmy asked with an optimism that should have been thoroughly beaten out of him by now.

Rem shook his eye stalks.

"I don't want to promise anything I can't deliver. Standard policy of mine. However, I can tell you why he's the only one who fought it off."

"Superior genetics?" Tuesday half-asked, lounging back like a superstar with his last cigarette of the day smouldering. "A brain far too advanced to be conquered by a mere bug?"

"Quite the opposite, actually," Rem admitted, summoning a holographic screen. He swiped at a detailed analysis of a Tuesday-shaped mass of swirling colours. "I've spent days mapping the composition of Tuesday's chemical makeup, and between the diseases and organ scarring and drug damage and the moss growing on his feet and all the hazardous foreign substances reacting against each other in his blood and flesh, Tuesday's body was simply too hostile for any additional parasites to survive. To be quite honest, I have no idea how you're even alive, Tuesday."

Tuesday deflated as the others genuinely laughed for the first time since they'd started eating butt-tasting broth from the protein sump. But he was only down for a moment.

"Doesn't change the fact I'm the only one uninfected. So punch it, all of you, because you're worm food."

"This may provide us with a form of treatment," Rem hinted.

Lana blinked three times, each one more violent than the one before it. She shook her head.

"No. Not happening."

"Hear him out first," Jimmy said, annoyed.

"I know what he's going to say," Lana snapped, tired of dealing with dullards.

She flicked her fingers in Rem's direction. "Go on. Say it. See if they feel differently. Bet you lunchtime's water ration that they don't."

"Well," Rem began, looking back and forth between the humans, "to put it simply, I think that Tuesday is the cure. In effect, I'm proposing that we get rid of your Peach worms with a…essence of Tuesday…"

*

Infiltrated by killer aliens or not, it didn't take long before the passengers would have done almost anything to get out of their cell.

The average person might say it was common sense to hunker down in their safe, one-entrance alcove until the Slidge stowaway tripped up and triggered a scanner, but only if that average person had never been stuck within spitting distance of Tuesday's foulness or been blasted by Trace's blinding hostility. The sentient anxiety attack known as Jimmy Slummer was stressful to be near at the best of times, but Lana proved to be the hardest one to manage. Her habits and hygiene may have been a lot less abrasive than the others and she was far better adjusted as a person overall, but as the hours ticked by she proved to be the embodiment of a question nobody asked.

As usual, Lana had taken charge. She was constantly trawling through the damaged files stored on her Omni, searching for anything that may increase their odds of surviving long enough to reach the Gatekeeper and The TenKay Vault he guarded, and would painstakingly review every single sweep Rem made of the ship. She kept track of every drop of water, constantly adjusted the settings of the protein sump to ensure no nutrients were wasted, and her latest project was mapping out exactly where condensation gathered in the far-flung reaches of The Dirty Betty.

All her effort was unbearable. It seemed their days consisted of nothing more than thirst and Lana's voice. What made it worse was she didn't seem to be able to comprehend how insufferable and bossy and arrogant and shrill she was. Despite being intelligent and well-read and enthusiastic and driven, it was a fact that when it came to how she saw herself, Lana had a blind spot the size of Mercury.

By now everyone flinched whenever Lana's latest statement interrupted the steady hum of the water recycling pipework. If Trace wasn't trying to conserve every joule of energy, she would have already pasted her all over the walls.

Thankfully, just as Lana was about to share her latest half-hourly assessment of their situation, a more welcome sound interrupted her voice: the thump and crackle of the protein sump shorting out. Watching silently as the sump's storage tank explosively covered the room in thin gruel, by the time anyone got their wits about them to react all of the greasy sludge had poured through the grated floor, sloshing away into the depths. There was a long, drawn out silence as the wreck smouldered, and Trace proved to be the one to break it.

"Simple yes or no question. Can we fix that thing, or not?"

Jimmy covered his mouth and nose with his dirty yellow chef's apron as the smog thickened. He coughed around his words.

"Uh, was all our food stored in that thing?"

Reality hit everyone like a right cross to the chin. Yet nobody said a word.

*

"There's got to be a better option," Jimmy pleaded.

As opposed as he was to their next course of action, Jimmy still kept up with the others as they marched down one of The Dirty Betty's generic purple corridors. This was the first time in days any of them had strayed further than a handful of metres from their frigid bunkroom, but nobody was enjoying the freedom of going for a trot for obvious reasons.

Managing to jog while stretching out a cramp caused by days of inactivity, at this point it occurred to Jimmy that the average serial killer on death row would have more exercise privileges, better food and better company, but he chose not to voice this fact for fear he might attract the long-delayed violence condensing within Trace. Instead, he gave a heart-deep sigh and increased his pace to keep up with the group.

They were all armed. Trace was brandishing her heirloom kinetic accelerator, the only thing of value that remained of the Cuddle fortune she'd been cheated out of, while Lana, Jimmy and Tuesday were loaning three of Rem's least complicated handguns. As Rem's species didn't have hands and used their facial tentacles for such tasks, the small knots of alien hardware were little more than a trigger and a barrel. He hadn't felt the need to explain the science behind Drennite blasters, and nobody cared to ask.

It took a couple of minutes of anxious strafing until they came to the nearest line of the internal rail network, and once they'd climbed aboard an indigo medical waste dumpster they were sure to keep watch on every side. Rem sat on the very centre point of the speeding bin, his eye stalks sweeping across all fronts in case a Slidge soldier suddenly jumped out and attacked.

Although stressful, their trip to the frost-free cryo units was uneventful. Covering each other, they advanced how they imagined a SWAT team would, except far less gracefully and about ten percent as intimidating. Trying not to accidentally point their guns at one another, Rem waved the humans towards a huge silver vault that dominated the entire port wall.

"I'll watch. You lot need to work together to do it in one go."

There were grumbles about the bristleworm getting the easy job, but they were only half-hearted.

The cryo vault slid open with a decidedly Antarctic breeze, revealing a grid of chambers the size of Mac truck trailers. As the vault was frost-free it didn't produce any ice, so the chambers were bone dry while also sitting close to zero. All but one of the chambers were yawning emptily beyond their thick rubber seals, and the closed chamber was their goal for today.

It went without saying they'd already discussed freezing themselves solid for the rest of the trip. However, these were industrial machines specifically designed to store foodstuffs long-term, and weren't equipped with the prohibitively-expensive reanimation facilities you only got on the fanciest starships.

An orderly rack of pigeonholes off to the side were filled with thick gloves made of synthetic walrus hide, and the four of them barely slowed down as they tossed warm mitts to each other. Shaking ever-more violently and breathing out steam, the humans rubbed their upper arms as they got close enough for Lana to touch the only sealed freezer. Teeth jackhammering so hard that she bit herself more than once, Lana managed to control her convulsing arm just well enough to slide her fingers across a round green circle in the centre of the chamber's door. The circle flashed an aggressive red and yellow, clearly making sure that everyone was paying attention, and Lana turned towards the others.

"Alright, we go in and out like surgeons," she juddered, hopping up and down and rubbing her arms. "Everyone pick a corner and grab on. It's so cold that it's going to hurt, but..."

Lana was interrupted by the door unsealing with a thump, dropping the ambient temperature by another twenty degrees Celsius. Before she could resume what she was saying, Trace pushed past far too roughly and gave a far more concise mission briefing.

"C'mon."

They moaned and cussed and chattered and cussed some more, but the humans rushed into the freezer as quick as they could. There was a frozen lump the size of a gorilla in its depths, and within a second they'd all managed to get a grip on its extremities. Touching it with bare hands would have been a fingers-blackened-with-frostbite-level bad move, so wearing the walrus-hide gloves was far more than a fashion statement. Groaning and gritting their teeth, soon they had the frozen lump off the floor and were hefting it towards a door that seemed to be about a kilometre away. Once clear of the freezer, Lana kicked sideways at the flashing red-and-yellow circle on the front of the freezer, and the unit sealed itself tight. The circle went green again to confirm it was safely locked.

It was another thirty metres to Rem and the dumpster, and they were all quickly running out of puff. Gritting their teeth as they closed on the bristleworm, when Trace glanced up at Rem she was instantly cautious. Not only was Rem sitting perfectly still, he was facing towards them rather than watching for a possible attack from beyond. Giving the bristleworm her best stink eye, Trace did a double-take as she picked up on a blur of distortion wavering around behind him, and reacted with her usual lack of patience. In a fluid motion she let go of her heavy load and drew her kinetic accelerator, pointing it a hand span to the right of Rem's gribbly face.

"Slidge!" she roared.

It took a fraction of a second longer for the others to respond, as they'd all been thrown off balance by Trace abandoning her part of the carrying, but they had their weapons cleared and pointed at Rem as fast as they could. Their frozen load slammed into the lattice floor, sending up a burst of mist as its surface ice crackled.

Jimmy blinked, and was one instant away from pointing out, "Actually, I'm pretty sure that's Rem," when he noticed the Slidge-shaped blur hovering behind the Drennite. The distortion had wrapped its many-elbowed arms around Rem, using its three lower dominant limbs to hold him upright. Nobody had a chance to wonder why Rem was being so passive about the cuddle before the Slidge decided to speak.

"He's just unconscious," the infiltrator called across the gulf, using Rem as a shield. It's three thinner upper limbs, the nimble set, were armed with exotic twists that could have been anything from pepper grinders to rectal thermometers to neutron bombs, but the stealther tech made it impossible to tell. All their barrels were jammed into the assorted soft areas between the segments of Rem's carapace. "This situation doesn't need to deteriorate any further. You know what I want."

"We aren't surrendering," Trace snarled, trying and failing to get a clear bead on the Slidge.

The alien blur made a chittering noise that might have been a laugh.

"Surrender?" The Slidge hissed loudly through its triple-segmented beak. "I don't want you to surrender to anyone! Believe me, I want to get away from the Primacy just as much as you do. Have you seen the conditions on Star Cages? Do you have any idea what that six-thousand-year-old hulk is like, the filth and the poverty and the endless executions over the tiniest errors? And the aliens! Damn my beak, the stench of twelve hundred different species of armpit! You lot have given me the best possible chance of faking my death and getting away from that lattice of misery for good, so the first round is on me!"

Lana tilted her head, but kept her gun levelled. For once she didn't know what to say.

"Huh?"

The Slidge hissed again.

"Look, I was going to stay out of your follicles until I could skip ship at wherever it was you're headed, but you've forced my hand. I can't let you eat my podlings."

Jimmy glanced down at the two mushed-together snap-frozen Slidge corpses they'd just removed from cryo. Twelve mangled arms curled towards the ceiling in a way reminiscent of a cockroach, and the normally-red skin was pink from freezer burns. Numerous tongues hung out of two triple-segmented beaks, and two trinities of small, medium and large eyes all faced different directions. After being squished in the dumpster storage area for over a week, it was hard to tell what parts were elbows and what bits were just broken.

Jimmy lowered his gun.

"I can't eat somebody's family. These are people."

"You know, it's people with morals who tend to get et first," Trace growled, not shifting her aim or her eyes one millimetre. "These two stopped being people days and days ago. Now they're just protein."

"What do you want, exactly?" Lana called out, always taking charge without bothering to ask permission.

The blur pointed one of its three delicate arms at the frozen hunk of meat slowly thawing on the grid work.

"You find another dish for dinner. For now, that's my only request."

"Even with both corpses, we won't have enough food to survive this trip," Tuesday muttered out of the corner of his mouth. "What with the sump blasting our gruel all over the walls, the word 'emergency' just doesn't cut it anymore. It's either die early or die earlier."

"So we just pretend we never saw you?" Trace yelled. "Wait around for you to knife us in our sleep?"

"You won't know I'm here," the Slidge promised.

"That's the whole spugging problem," Tuesday complained.

"We don't have any food or water to share with you," Lana called.

"I've got survival parasites in my stomachs that'll keep me alive and unhappy for a couple of months," the Slidge said dismissively. "They'll keep regenerating as long as they can leech away some of my air. Might feel like breathing out of a bag all day, but I'll soldier on."

The standoff continued for another handful of seconds as everyone thought about what was going on. The humans glanced at each other, silently questioning, except for Jimmy, who was looking down at an icy pile made from two Slidge, once-sentient beings who were podlings to one passenger and breakfast to five others.

Jimmy finally looked away from the corpse and called out across the gulf.

"We want to trust you. Conditions are bad enough already without a guerrilla war on top of it. But you've probably heard what your people did to us, and how they'll do it again if they get the chance. You can't tell me that you'd trust Humans if we did that to you?"

The Slidge hissed another laugh.

"Human, I'm one of the rank-and-file. My organs are a perfect match for no fewer than thirty-six higher-ranking officers, and that means there's no doubt that one day I'm going to get snatched and harvested as an unwilling donor when some Pre-Prime or his mistress requires a new heart or lungs or a splortcher. Slidge don't do the whole trust thing, we do mutually beneficial arrangements." The Slidge sighed. "Okay, it's pretty clear you lot need a gesture of goodwill. Here."

The blur carefully lowered Rem's unconscious body to the floor, slowly unwrapped its three thicker limbs from the bristleworm's exoskeleton, and raised its three nimble limbs towards the ceiling. Seeing as though Trace, Lana and Tuesday were aiming right at the blur with some considerable firepower, this move was so brave it was inspiring.

"So?" the Slidge called. "Can we figure something out as intelligent beings? From what I've overheard, we have more than a month to sort out where we stand."

Slowly exhaling, Lana lowered her gun. She nodded at Trace, who eventually followed her example, even though she didn't seem happy about it. Lana holstered her weapon by jamming it down the back of her dress pants, raised her palms, and took a step towards the Slidge-shaped blur. She opened her mouth to begin what may be a mutually beneficial arrangement with the alien, perhaps even one that resulted in the acquisition of some valuable intelligence that could contribute to fighting off the dozens of incoming Star Cages due to hit the Milky Way some time real soon, but then it all went to Hell.

The blur jerked in synchronisation with the thump-thump-thump of a Drennite sidearm, spraying fountains of gore that turned a pus-coloured yellow as it exited the Slidge and splashed all over the grates and grid work. One round must have hit an important part of the chameleonic armour, as the wobbling instantly transitioned into a red-skinned alien boxed within a sealed combat frame. Leaning sharply, the stowaway hit the floor a moment later, its triple-segmented beak hanging slack as the alien twitched for a few agonising moments, and died with a gurgle.

Stunned, Lana slowly pivoted on the spot to regard Tuesday with blank-faced fury. He was still pointing at the infiltrator, as though expecting it to get up and retaliate. He eventually lowered his steaming gun and gave Lana an inappropriate smile.

"Hey, I didn't hit Rem! That worked out great."

"We were negotiating," Lana said low and dangerously.

Tuesday nodded.

"And those negotiations just resulted in us increasing our protein stores by a whole fifty percent." Tuesday licked his sad little black teeth as he regarded the newest addition to their rations. He turned to meet Lana's dark gaze before she could start yelling. "Tell me you're certain that we wouldn't have been in any danger from it. Tell me you could have guaranteed our safety. I want to hear you say it."

Lana's mouth opened and closed a few times. It took a little while, but she swept back from a different angle.

"It was unarmed."

Tuesday cackled.

"We're in a post-Human era that hasn't had a cop or a judge or a court room for hundreds of years. We're the last of our species, and your morals are going to get us all extinct. This is about survival, not winning the Nobel Prize for Good Behaviour & Sportsmanship."

Trace gave a rare dark chuckle.

"Never thought I'd hear you make a good point, rodent."

Jimmy retched, the stress finally catching up with him. Everyone glanced over in concern, sure to step away a little to make sure he didn't vomit on their shoes. He wiped at his mouth.

"You know," Jimmy managed, "My parents raised me a Jud-Islamic Catholic. I got taught from the cradle that we'll all answer for our bad deeds one day. It's a lot easier to believe that when you realise you and your mates are planning to eat somebody's siblings, then eat them next."

Lana gave a soul-deep sigh.

"I'm sure we'll all answer for our actions one day, but the luxury of guilt will just have to wait."

CHAPTER TWENTY TWO

The freshest kill was considered the best one to process. Dragging its podlings back into deep freeze for a later time, the still-warm corpse took their place on the dumpster.

The ride back to their cold cell was a silent one, but for a variety of reasons. For Rem, his quiet was fuelled by shame, as being sucker-punched into a coma without offering an ounce of resistance wasn't doing much for his image as being hard-as-tacks. The humans wordlessly cycled between a range of similar feelings: hunger and thirst, anger towards Rem for being the most useless lookout ever, a core-deep revulsion towards what they were going to do at dinnertime, and a secret relief that Tuesday was enough of a cold-blooded reptile to gun down an unarmed sentient being like it was nothing but a bag of meat.

While there was no guarantee a new protein sump wouldn't explode like the last, they employed the Weavers to assemble a third one. Thankfully, Lana used some simulation work to diagnose why the previous sump had done its best Hiroshima impersonation (a critical under-pressure tube got clogged solid with guinea pig fur and bone powder), but even then nobody was brave enough to come within five metres of the potential bomb when it was switched on. After watching Lana carefully feed slithers of red Slidge meat into the hopper, though, grinding it down to pulp so it could spawn fresh lumps of tissue, they gradually lost this fear.

It only took a couple of hours for the protein sump to process the muscles, skin, bones, marrow, neon white blood and garish organs of the Slidge into two output tanks of Human-compliant nutrients and incompatible garbage. The edible material was a thick, beige gruel, while the waste products took on an odd neon shade of greenish-pink. As they'd feared, most of the two-hundred kilos of Slidge smallgoods ranged from inedible to outright poisonous, and the tank of Human-compliant nutrients amounted to less than ten kilograms of processed sludge.

There was an abundance of swearing.

Filling their bowls with tepid muck, the five of them sat in a loose circle on their sleeping pallets. Their latest water ration had been stirred through the protein porridge, thinning it to a chewable density, and it became a waiting game to see who was brave enough to go first. Although they'd all done terrible, unforgivable things to survive over the years, as a full minute dragged out it became clear that literally none of them could swallow what they were about to do to the Slidge's corpse.

While it was rare for anybody to acknowledge Tuesday's presence for obvious reasons, for once everyone found themselves looking to him. His eyebrows rose at being the centre of attention, but it only took moments to process their expectations. As usual, he had no interest in being anything but selfish.

"Uh, uh," Tuesday said concisely. "I shot the squiggly dastard. I'm not taking the first bite, too." He nudged the paste with his spoon, moving it around. "Just be glad we didn't know its name."

Jimmy choked at this comment, sending a bolt of panic through the group. Thankfully, he managed to overcome his gag reflex in time by closing his eyes and taking long, deep breaths.

"Sorry," he moped. "Tuesday got me thinking about the marital status of the parents of the one we're about to eat. Do Slidge marry? Or have genders? Or have more than one parent? I remember we saw one spawn right out of its face that one time, but…"

"Just remember it's not cannibalism," Trace growled, mostly for her own benefit.

"But it was homicide," Lana said quietly.

Tuesday shook his head, raining five shades of dandruff

"Wasn't. Murder, perhaps. Not homicide."

"Keep telling yourself there's a difference," Jimmy muttered.

Steeling herself, Lana scooped up a lump of processed alien. Opening her mouth, forcing the full spoon towards her lips, she started shaking more and more violently until it seemed as though the porridge was going to get catapulted across the room. Sighing half in frustration and half in pride for having enough of a moral code to make this meal so difficult, she returned the morsel back in its bowl.

"You never truly know the level of your humanity until it's tested," Lana muttered, quoting one of her favourite authors. She smacked her full bowl down on the grating with a clack, careful not to spill anything, and folded her arms. "Plan B, I guess?"

Everyone moaned, but nobody articulated an actual negative. Deciding she would have to lead by example as always, Lana reached across for a little something she'd had the Weavers spin up earlier: a giant syringe, the sort you'd use to inseminate a sheep. Regarding the ancient device carefully, testing its plunger, she stabbed it into her bowl of Some Guy Soup and drew a large measure. Rolling up her ebony Cadet uniform's shirt, revealing the rubbery ports the Primacy had installed in her body after capture, Lana steeled herself to jam the drinking-straw-thick needle into herself. Glancing wordlessly at the others, she decided to just get it over with.

The blunt fit slid effortlessly into her stomach port, and Lana slowly, slowly pushed the syringe deeper and deeper. Honestly, she was a little creeped out by how she couldn't feel anything beyond a faint twisting sensation. Once the needle burrowed as deep as its chamber allowed, Lana slowly depressed the plunger. Grey muck gurgled down the metal tube, visibly seeping away through the fit until it was empty. Hoping she hadn't accidentally injected the wrong organ, Lana slowly relaxed as a feeling of satiety crept across her abdomen.

She pulled out the big honking syringe, slapped it down on the grid work floor, and nodded at Trace.

"You next, bruiser."

*

Weeks passed slowly and painfully.

Proving that necessity is the mother of innovation, the long boring days of assorted discomforts left plenty of time for even the most feeble-minded of the group to come up with ideas. An unpopular (yet perfectly viable) plan was to feed all their cricket-leather products – everything from boots to shoes to belts to holsters to Citizen Card holders to seat covers – into the protein sump, reducing them to consumable nutrients. They found out the hard way your average frog-stomper boot isn't renowned for its nutritional content, so in addition to its overall calorie and nutrient yield being minimal, it was so bland and chewy that it possessed literally no taste. Compared to what the protein sump usually created, the lack of flavour was actually a marked improvement. Thankfully, they abandoned this course of action after processing a small shred of Tuesday's boot, meaning he wasn't going to die barefoot.

Surprising everyone, most of all himself, Tuesday's lifelong love of psychotropic brain-altering substances culminated in a mental flash: What if they could chemically lower their metabolisms, reducing the raw number of calories they needed to run their bodies and minds? After all, their intruder problem had been dealt with, so nobody needed to be firing on all twenty-four cylinders, right?

The needler in Medical didn't have any dramas brewing up a batch of metabolism-lowering chems, and its holster had more than enough raw material to provide hundreds of doses. Unfortunately, while the idea was sound, it wasn't without drawbacks. The slowing agent produced effects not dissimilar to chronic fatigue syndrome, bringing overwhelming tiredness and making the simplest of physical tasks extremely difficult. In addition to that, it struck down everyone's mental functioning to the point where figuring out anything complex was impossible. Lana's keen intellect was dulled down to Tuesday's level, and Tuesday was so blasted by the chems that everyone had to keep watch to make sure he didn't try to swallow his own tongue. Despite being mentally and physically handicapped for eight hours at a time, they continued to devise plans to stay alive.

Rem had continued making thorough sweeps of the ship to find every single drop of moisture, and sometimes these scans would prove The Dirty Betty wasn't totally dry. For instance, there were emergency eye wash stations located at every area of the ship that had been dedicated to processing dangerous chemicals, and while their contents weren't technically water, this medicinal solution provided a good harvest. Another Thor-sent blessing was the ancient shower block, as the numerous shower heads contained a few dribbles. As the humans came from an era where self-cleaning clothes had entirely removed the necessity of washing with hot water and soap, it was a surprise to discover that people had once bathed their naked bodies on a daily basis. While Lana was far too polite to say it out loud, she would have preferred it if everyone's self-cleaning clothes worked just a little bit better.

So they got by. And while every drop of moisture was sacred and every morsel of food was precious and every cigarette break occurred down to the microsecond, it wasn't going to be enough to survive. As they couldn't accurately predict whether their destination was going to have so much as half a box of choc-chip muesli bars waiting for them, even if they did make it all the way somehow, they might just end up dying of starvation and dehydration in a different spatial location.

*

"Tuesday?" Lana snapped. "Are you listening?"

Tuesday realised he'd been licking a rusty metal pipe for so long that his tongue was bleeding. Still a little addled from his latest dose of metabolism-lowering chemicals, even though he'd already stripped the corroded steel of every drop of condensation, he didn't have the sense to stop. A clip behind the ear from Trace finally got his groggy, addled attention.

"Wt?" he managed, unable to form actual language.

Lana supported herself against one of the larger internal windows of the ship, sapped of her strength by the same chemicals as everyone else. She blinked out of synchronisation and looked back and forth between her crewmates. The humans (and Rem) all looked as vague and ineffective as overmedicated psychiatric patients. Lana took a second to get her bearings, but it wasn't until she glanced at the kilometre-long tube of medical waste that she recalled her reason for assembling everyone here.

"Okay," she began, her words slurred, "Our food has been recycled so many times the sump can't even produce proper chunks anymore. Our water is so salty it's only making us thirstier. These metabolism drugs are a living Styx. I can barely recall anything from the last fortnight…I'm the walking dead. I'm certain we've stripped everything edible and drinkable from this floating coffin."

"It's over," Jimmy lamented said in a surprisingly detached tone, as though it was a fact he'd accepted long ago.

"It doesn't have to be," Lana offered.

"What, did you find a proper cryo booth or something?" Trace growled. "Some kind of stasis chamber, maybe?"

Lana shook her head. This made her instantly dizzy. Black spots danced.

"This ship used to have proper cryo…before some nameless scavengers pried it out and sold it Odin-knows-where. And as for stasis chambers?" Lana pounded at the tube's clear shell. "While this giant bin might be able to keep countless tonnes of medical waste in stasis, it's the cheap, industrial kind of suspended animation, not the sort you can use to cycle living people in and out of the time stream. We go in there, we die. On the plus side, our corpses will look their best until the equipment eventually breaks down in a thousand years or so."

"TuffTek don't break down," Jimmy corrected.

Lana shuffled uncomfortably. Hardly the life of the party at the best of times, her attempts at levity had fallen flatter than a butter-side-down slice of toast.

"So what are you propositioning?" Jimmy asked, almost using the correct word.

Lana raised both palms in the usual way she did before suggesting something that would be accurate, infuriating, horrible and traumatising all at the same time.

"I've done the numbers, and if we want to survive, all we need to do is to set the protein sump to adjust the…"

*

And then the humans found themselves somewhere else. One moment they were trying to concentrate on Lana's slurred words, and the next instant they were seated around a square Formica table in the Mess with their foreheads touching. There were no feelings of movement or transition from the looming window, as though some higher power had stolen a chunk of their lives as easily as snipping hunks out of a video file.

They were all wearing the exact same expression of total confusion.

Everyone drew their heads out of the scrum in perfect sync, and something small and white fell onto the tabletop. A short melody trilled from the object, and everyone looked down to see it was the Psych-in-a-Box. A little message was superimposed over the shell in a flashing green font stating GROUP MEMORY EDIT COMPLETE. PLEASE HAND YOURSELF INTO THE LOCAL AUTHORITIES FOR IMMEDIATE PROSECUTION.

Lana was the first one to her feet, sweeping the empty Mess left and right. She finally spotted Rem was curled up on the Lino under their table, but before she could ask him what in the bleakest white-hot depths of Tartarus was going on, she stopped cold. According to the tiny light on the side of his head the bristleworm was just finishing one of his memory purges, the sort he did after each completed mission.

Preparing a verbal barrage for whoever had decided to mess around with her brain without her permission, Lana's words caught in her throat as she noticed how drawn and gaunt and grey they all were. The Mess was a total anorexia ward.

"What just happened? How did we get here?" Lana demanded.

Jimmy seemed about to cry.

"I don't know. We were at a big window, you were talking…"

"You had an idea to help us survive," Trace interrupted. "What was it?"

Lana faltered. She opened and closed her mouth a few times, rapidly flicked her eyes left and right to try and jog her memory, and even resorted to the crude technique of running through the alphabet in her head, but all the strange facial twitchings in the Universe didn't change the fact her plan was gone.

She locked onto Trace.

"I don't know. I can't remember."

Seemingly unaffected by this latest unusual event, Tuesday's chair squeaked as he plopped his dirty, moss-coated feet onto the Formica table. He tapped the Psych-in-a-Box with the jagged tip of a diseased yellow toenail.

"I've got a theory. Spoiler: it involves a certain brain-altering box that's flashing GROUP MEMORY EDIT COMPLETE in neon green. Anyone care to guess?"

In the silence, everyone could hear Jimmy hyperventilating.

"Whose idea was it to use this…this thing on me?" he shouted, twisting his mouth at the Psych-in-a-Box as though it had questioned his Mother's claims of pre-marital virginity. Glowering, eyes bulging and face purpling, Jimmy uncharacteristically lost his temper by violently swatting the device onto the floor, sending it skittering away. Rather than continuing his tantrum, however, Jimmy's face creased in pain and he gripped both his wrists as though giving himself a secret handshake. "Ow! The spug is wrong with my arms? My fingers can't even curl."

Rolling up the grimy sleeves of his neon-yellow MacDeath chef's uniform with hooked thumbs, Jimmy gaped at thick, white layers of bandages wrapped around both forearms. They must have been half a centimetre thick. Gently running a finger over the painful underside of his left arm, a dark blotchy stain rose through the whiteness, tainting it with a starburst of wet crimson.

Lana stepped forwards, touching Jimmy on the shoulder just as he got to his feet, wordlessly soothing him and encouraging him to sit down again. She took a closer look at the leaking bandages, and patted Jimmy in pity.

"I could be wrong, but…"

"You slashed your wrists," Trace scoffed. "Knew you'd be the first one to crack."

Lana's eyes flashed.

"You know that tiny little whispery voice that begs you to be a Human? Try listening to it occasionally."

Trace squinted at Lana's throat and gave an evil grin.

"Before you start handing out advice, you might like to tap your Adam's apple."

Absently touching her carotid artery, Lana drew her fingers away from a painful sting. Instantly summoning a mirror from her AllTool, Lana silently regarded an old bandage coiled around her throat. Moving the wrapping aside, cringing at the sharpness, Lana revealed what looked like a deep friction burn ground into her skin, likely from a tightened rope. The redness was partially healed, and the age of the bandage suggested her wounds had been inflicted two or three days ago.

Lana's expression went vague for a moment, then she furiously tapped at her Omni implant.

"Researching a more effective way to kill yourself?" Tuesday snickered.

Jimmy gave Trace and Tuesday the disgusted expression.

"You're a real pair, aren't you?"

"We're here," Lana said, almost inaudibly.

"What?" Trace snapped. "Where, exactly? Spug Creek? Been there for weeks."

Lana turned, flipped the Omni's floating holographic screens, and expanded the date, time and spatial location. Jimmy, Trace and Tuesday all gaped at the read-out.

"We're less than six hours from our destination," Lana said, her every syllable coloured by disbelief. "We've survived the trip,"

"If you're messing with me, I'll kill you," Trace said calmly. "Literally kill you. Put-you-in- the-protein-sump-and-eat-your-nutrients kill you."

There was total silence. Jimmy eventually broke it.

"How?" he demanded. "We were out of food, out of water…had maybe a week left to live…"

"And somehow we survived another three weeks," Trace reminded him. She leaned in for emphasis, her expression dark. "And then following those three weeks, after Lana and Jimmy both fail to top themselves, though not for lack of trying, for some reason we all decided to rest our heads against a Psych-in-a-Box and wipe all our memories of the whole span. You know what I reckon?"

Tuesday lit a victory cigarette and exhaled a cloud of chlorine-flavoured smoke. "That we stop picking at it and take the hint?"

"But I'd never agree to use that, that thing," Jimmy pointed out. "If Jud-Islamic Catholicism had mortal sins, psychiatric surgery would be one of them."

"Nobody said you were conscious for the memory-wipe," Trace suggested.

Possessed by an idea, Lana furiously swiped through the calendar of her Omni, and planned to check the records of her retinals next. Grunting in annoyance, her flicks got more and more aggressive until she growled in defeat. Hands on her hips, she took a few calming breaths.

"The last image I have is of Tuesday licking his tongue raw on a rusty pipe. Not only that, but..." Lana huffed. "Check this out. Every record of the last three weeks has been wiped and overwritten fifty times. Greatest hackers of all time wouldn't be able to recover jack."

A tap expanded the calendar function of Lana's Omni from matchboxes to the size of home-cinema screens. Each lost day was marked with a slight variation on the same statement in four different styles of handwriting, clearly making it a group effort.

Grune 27rd: Let It Go

Grune 28th: Don't Ask, Don't Tell

Grune 29th: Better to Forget

Grune 30th: Don't Pry

Grune 31st: You Don't Want To Know

Grune 32nd: Let It Go To the Keeper

Grune 33rd: Some Things Aren't Meant To Be Remembered

Grune 34th: Forgetting Is For Your Own Good

Lana swiped away the calendar. Wrapping her arms around her jutting ribs, the many lines of her face crunching up, she rocked back and forth in an alarming way.

"How did we survive?" she whispered. "What did we do?"

Tuesday flicked his spent cigarette into the nearest pipe hole. It was a good shot. "Didn't you get the memo, kid? Nobody wants to know."

Rem suddenly flicked from curled up to well out of reach with one yabbie-like motion. His eye stalks darted about independently of one another, taking in a dozen different things at once. No stranger to memory wipes, the bristleworm chittered his mandibles together in a similar way to how Humans clear their throats.

"Would somebody care to tell me why in the name of glittering green arse-pox I just agreed to delete three weeks of my memory?"

*

As hard as it was to believe, a mere six hours later The Dirty Betty finished her month-and-a-half string of interstellar transitions with her entire crew alive, and without any fanfare she re-joined the Universe to sit on space like a purple corkscrew on a black tablecloth. Everyone knew better than to do anything as ridiculous as hope, but there it was, sitting a hundred thousand kilometres off the port side: a vaguely Earth-like planet girdled by five incandescent moons. Binary stars sat at the core of this system, relatively dim from this distance.

It only took a few seconds to bring up dozens of zoomed-in-shots of the planet. Much of its surface was thoroughly urbanised with an endless crushing sprawl of white star scrapers that plunged down into the abyssal depths almost as high as they rose into the sky. Small as the planet was, the city wrapped around its waist like an ivory belt offered enough space for tens of billions of people to live in great comfort. The orb's poles were carpeted in a vibrant green rainforest thoroughly gene-diddled to suck up incredible amounts of carbon dioxide and transform it into oxygen. Importantly, gravity was almost Earth normal, and the temperature and pressure were ideal for Human habitation.

Lana frowned at the holographics, zooming back and forth across the world with simple hand movements.

"Zero live signals coming from the surface," she said mostly to herself. She flicked the symbol about in a few random directions across the cloud-wrapped city, but nothing changed. She gave the screen a dirty look as though it had insulted her haircut. "No signs of Human life, either." Lana shook her head. "I don't get it. A world this nice, totally silent and uninhabited? You'd think a thousand different intelligent species would be tripping over each other to claim such a prize."

"Unless they know something we don't," Trace said ominously.

Rem flicked at his starburst collar, cycling through a column of Drennite symbols. He gave a short hum of interest.

"Looks like their entire extra-solar communication system was reliant on the Link," he noted. "So when the Link crashed all those years ago..."

"It plunged the whole world into a new Stone Age?" Jimmy half-asked.

"Or at least restricted their communications to the surface," Lana guessed.

Trace sneered at the quiet world.

"Serves them right. Should have planned ahead."

"Maybe they did," Lana said. "I'm only scanning for signals heading off the surface. For all I know, their comms might work just fine down there."

"Perhaps they're deliberately keeping silent so the rest of the Universe can't hear them?" Trace suggested. "After all, we've all heard horror stories about defenceless colonies accidentally luring in alien monsters, right? Ringing the dinner bell for every hungry green dastard in the galaxy to come eat the children..."

"Wait, I thought the Link was meant to be impossible to delete?" Jimmy half-asked again, not game enough to make any statements above his paygrade.

"The Link was pure software that didn't require any hardware," Lana explained. "There was nothing to switch off or break, nothing to fry or burn or wipe. It was intangible. Honestly, I'm stuffed if I'll ever figure out how The Perfect managed to delete the thing."

"No point guessing," Trace growled.

"But even with some major communication issues, surely that wasn't enough of a reason to just abandon a heavily-inhabited planet?" Lana asked. "Half of The Unison was made up of total hell scapes, and even the worst colonies just had to dig in deep and learn how to survive until tax time. The Unison certainly doesn't pack up the population of a perfectly viable world and bunk off because the phones are down. No, we're missing something."

"Wait," Rem said.

The bristleworm zoomed in on just one of hundreds of black patches migrating across the planet at a wicked speed. As everyone watched, some of the dark spots disappeared, only to reform a thousand kilometres away in a totally random fashion. Lana tapped at the readout, hoping it was glitching, and leaned towards Rem.

"Is that actually happening, or is the screen bugging off?"

Rem examined the numbers and gave a curt nod.

"The sunlit parts are all a perfect Spring afternoon, but the dark spots jumping about are absolute zero."

"How cold is that?" Jimmy asked nervously.

One eye stalk twisted in his direction.

"It's freeze-your-skin-solid, dead-in-five-seconds cold. Worse than space itself. Cling suits won't help much with that sort of chill."

Finally giving up on his nap, Tuesday slouched over to get a better look at the planet. Tracing his eyes over the five brightly lit moons and the two distant stars, he moaned in sudden realisation.

"Oh, spug me. Why do I always have to end up back at Seven Suns?"

Lana glanced in his direction.

"Wait, you've been to this world?"

Tuesday sighed. "Died on it twice so far. Not interested in making it a hat trick."

Jimmy made an odd noise in his throat.

"Oh. Right. Seven Suns. Of course." He blinked and squinted at the large patches of sub-sub-sub zero darkness that obscured parts of the white cityscape. "My family was settled here after Sprout got incinerated. I didn't recognise it with all the shady bits. It used to be covered in a permanent afternoon from pole to pole."

Tuesday flicked his hand at the planet in disinterest.

"Yeah. Before colonisation this world was a frozen ball, but Unison scientists used tens of thousands of nukes to glass and sculpt its moons into giant lenses that reflect and amplify the local starlight to keep the whole surface sunny." Tuesday sucked something unmentionable out of his black teeth, already exhausted from being so coherent for once. "Is it me, or are those five moons full of cracks now?"

Lana slowly exhaled at the numbers.

"Shattered to their cores. Like they've been hammered with mass drivers."

"Looks deliberate." Rem noted. "Those cracks are too uniform to have been an act of nature."

"Reckon whatever cracked the moons caused those big craters, too?" Jimmy asked, pointing out just one of many five-kilometre-wide holes on the holographic map. Like the patches of lethal cold, the blasts seemed to be scattered totally at random. "They look a bit like giant alien symbols or something…is it a message?"

"See that?" Trace growled, smacking Tuesday in the back of the head. "Is that normal?"

Everyone turned as one of the moon-sized lenses increased its brightness to a blinding apex. Instead of softly bathing Seven Suns with just the right amount of solar wind like in the good old days, this massive flash was a phoenix with its rectum on fire. Reflecting back and forth between the five glassed moons so rapidly it was impossible to keep track of without mechanical assistance, the magnified glow suddenly hammered down towards one of the dark, frozen spots on the surface. Nobody could do anything except gape as the sunbeam-on-steroids tore into the urban sprawl of Seven Suns with the force of dedicated weaponry, tearing up a dozen city blocks with a glow that was not only visible from space, but physically painful on the corneas. Far, far below, a random neighbourhood was now ashes.

Tuesday sniffed. "Well, that's new."

Trace loomed towards Rem.

"Are you sure this is the right place?"

"Quiet!" Lana interrupted far too harshly, gesturing at the light screen. "We're getting a message from somebody."

"How, what, who and from where?" Jimmy asked.

"From the surface of the planet," Rem dialled into the incoming transmission, his facial gribbles dancing across a variety of objects in his holographic toolkit. "It's on every channel, but only because we came close enough to trigger it. Proximity rig, probably Military or something. Not the sort of tech your average hobbyist can afford."

Every projector on The Dirty Betty activated automatically, casting blurry static nonsense onto every surface. The humans twitched when their retinals picked up an identical dose of morphing electronic snow, and Lana's Omni and Scroll joined in on the monochrome hissing. Rem seemed unimpressed that his Military-grade starburst collar, the vital tool of any hardened Drennite wet-work operative, had been cracked by the transmission only a matter of seconds after the civilian-level equipment.

The chaos coalesced into a frazzled face that seemed to have been genetically engineered to look like the most basic cliché of a Human bureaucrat. His two clashing neckties weren't secured properly, he had bed hair, and he was hurriedly buttoning up a purple double-breasted suit as his lips fluttered at top speed.

"This is Brokage Grundy the Third, ninety-fifth Mayor of Seven Suns." Grundy glared off-camera, clearly bothered by something. He was back down the barrel of the lens an instant later. "This is an order for all Seven Suns citizens to evacuate off-world in any form of transportation you can reach. Take nothing you cannot easily carry. Leave now. If you are incoming to Seven Suns, turn around and leave at top speed. This planet is lost. To come any closer is suicide…"

The message winked out. Whether it had ended deliberately or thanks to a sudden nuclear strike was unclear. They waited a good fifteen seconds just in case there was any further elucidation to be had, but were left disappointed.

PART FIVE OLD FRIENDS
CHAPTER TWENTY THREE

The ensuing argument took ages to reach the point where more than two people agreed on any single detail. How it didn't come to blows was anyone's guess. As usual, Lana was eventually able to sway the popular vote in her own direction.

"Whatever hardware was used to send that message is transmitting on every single band and channel," she said. From her tone and facial expression, Lana was clearly amazed that she'd had to repeat this fact a dozen times. "That means if we can send a new message in its place, everyone down there will hear it. Boom, we've made contact."

"Then why not send it from up here?" Trace growled.

Lana clawed at her own face in unbearable frustration as Tuesday and Jimmy agreed.

"For the eighth time, I'm absolutely certain we'd need to be in physical proximity to the communications equipment to change the emergency message. We can't just casually hack into upper-echelon governmental hardware from a distance, because even if they did allow external access, I'm certain trying to slice it from orbit would trigger security contingencies...deadly security contingencies." Lana snapped a sudden kick at a holographic screen, almost slipping over as her foot passed through it. "I can't put this in any simpler terms! For the love of Odin's hoofed goatlike feet, just take my word for it!"

"Why don't we send a message directly to the Monolith?" Jimmy suggested.

Lana looked as though she was about to have a nervous breakdown.

"Because his channel is undoubtedly Military-grade classified, and we don't have clearance. But if we access the same full-band squawker Mayor Grundy used to beam out the evacuation orders, the Monolith will pick up our message and hear that we want to meet."

Jimmy chewed his lip, watching the projection of Seven Suns as deadly cold patches disappeared and reappeared at random. He flinched every time a bolt of magnified sunlight took a chunk out of the ivory city.

"But how do we know where to go, exactly?"

Lana took several deep, calming breaths, her eyes screwed shut. Rem decided to do her a favour by fielding this question.

"As Lana has already said five times, we just have to wait for the emergency message to cycle again. My equipment should be good enough to pinpoint its origin."

"Then we jet down in the dumpster and hack our way in," Lana continued. She nodded at Rem. "Our host has updated my Omni and Scroll with his best cracking software. It's all top-of-the-line."

Tuesday squinted, scratching a wild armpit with yellow fingernails.

"If his equipment is better than yours, why don't the bug just come down with us?"

"Because for the third time, we know for a fact the Monolith doesn't react well to aliens casually popping down to the surface of Seven Suns!" Lana screamed, fingers bent into claws. "If the Monolith was game enough to take a swipe at

Viour, then he'll sure as spit flatten Rem like a Portuguese-style chicken on sight. Are you all thick as porridge or what?"

Jimmy raised a hand to ask a question. After studying Lana's face, however, he retracted his arm and shrank a little under her furious gaze.

"Sounds like a good plan," he said meekly.

"Or we could just message the Monolith from up here," Tuesday said precisely two seconds before getting heel-kicked in the mouth by Lana's foot.

*

Between the deadly cold patches and the concentrated solar beams blasting apart neighbourhoods as though somebody had pissed off Zeus, not to mention they were seeking out a borderline god who didn't like visitors, Rem did his best to seem disappointed about staying in orbit. Different species or not, it didn't take a Drennite behavioural expert to tell he was beyond relieved to be holding down the fort on this one.

"Alright," Rem clicked, "While greeting parties are unlikely, the glow stone coating on all those star scrapers is still sucking up enough solar power to keep things running. That means you'll see operational screens and equipment, and perhaps even some vehicles. I guarantee everything down there is well past its use-by date, so watch out for industrial hazards, twitchy security systems, insane robotic taxis, that sort of thing. Don't trust anything that runs on electricity, or you might get permanently sealed off by automatic doors or crushed by senile earthmovers or something. Questions?"

Clad in their cling suits, heads uncovered, the humans were standing in the open PusCo medical waste dumpster. By this point the slab was pitted and blackened and stank like space, which was a mixture of old charcoal and barbecue sauce. Tuesday didn't bother raising his hand.

"You sure the air is breathable?"

Rem nodded.

"Yes, we've covered this. The atmosphere is just as fresh as always. The rainforests are still filtering away all the carbon dioxide just fine. Any new questions?"

"Thought it was worth double-checking," Tuesday muttered.

Jimmy's hand popped up.

"How do we find the communication thingy? Seven Suns is almost half the size of Erf, right?"

Rem clicked his mandibles together a couple of times, as though sighing.

"We've already pinpointed the communication's array, and I'll be sending you directly towards it. You should touch down within fifty metres or so of your goal."

"And those deadly cold patches and solar blasts?" Tuesday prompted.

"I don't have a week to accurately map their paths, but your odds of survival are good as long as you don't wander around too long."

"So we're drop-shipping at top speed onto a lethally faulty world and assuming we won't get killed?" Trace surmised. "Loving this plan so far."

"What about the Monolith himself, then?" Tuesday noted. "He'd be really old by now, right? And what usually happens to ancient, complex, sentient technology that gets left to stew in its own juices for hundreds of years?"

"A Monolith is different," Lana argued. "We're not talking about a toaster with artificial intelligence hammered together in some East Korean sweatshop. This guy is a demi-god. The divine don't have use-by dates."

"We can hope," Tuesday muttered, ducking down as the dumpster lid closed and sealed.

*

By this point they were pretty used to tumbling violently through the upper atmosphere of dangerous worlds, pinned to the transparent walls of an upgraded PusCo dumpster with nothing to see but writhing flames in all directions. That didn't mean they enjoyed it, or weren't terrified by the rough drop, only that they knew what to expect.

In an instant, the fires of re-entry faded to a crimson glow, and the majesty of Seven Suns was revealed. Thousands of ivory star scrapers pointed towards their underside like spears greeting charging cavalry, though a second glance proved these spikes were little more than the tips of a greatness half-shrouded by wispy clouds. Traffic on Seven Suns had always been managed by a complex knot of automated sky lanes, and the vast expanses of open air between tower blocks was tinged with red, orange, green, blue and silver glows from floating banks of traffic lights. Countless golden-lit parking slots shined in a welcoming manner from every alabaster titan, promising free parking and quick access to antigrav chutes, sling lifts and the charmingly outdated technology known as stairs. The closer they got to the cloud line, the grander Seven Suns became. Laying fallow had not dimmed the perfect, holy whiteness of this city a single shade, and the pale blue wisps of cumulus made things look nothing short of heavenly. Sunlight gave the star scrapers a divine sheen.

"This place is amazing," Lana drooled, wedged as close to the wall as she could get.

"Try living here as a pet," Tuesday snapped, arms tightly folded.

"Wow! Look at that!" Lana exclaimed.

She jabbed her finger towards an especially big star scraper a few blocks away. Larger than its nearby relatives, the rays of sunlight pouring down from Seven Sun's faulty lens system were tickling the building with a shifting prism effect that seemed to be accelerating by the moment. It was staggeringly beautiful, something any artist would want to commit to canvas.

Tuesday raised his head.

"I don't think it's meant to do that," he mumbled.

There was a series of bright, almighty concussions from the five nuclear-sculpted moons high above, and Lana recoiled with a frightened squeak at a blinding flash. An onslaught of amplified sunbeams blasted clean through the star scraper in a way that brought a mass driver to mind, cutting off it upper klick-and-a-half like a blowtorch through a damp Popsicle stick. This monument to Mankind's greatness slowly tipped over, separating at a glowing, bubbly orange wound that was running and molten. Reaching terminal momentum, the upper half of the star scraper disappeared into the clouds with a puff of farewell.

Trace smiled with chipped teeth.

"I'm liking this world."

Recovering within moments, Lana resumed her role as the bossiest cow in the galaxy.

"Right, we should touch down in a minute. Far as Rem's hardware could tell, our target hasn't been hit by any solar blasts or frozen solid by those weird storms, so our cling suits should be sufficient protection. Might be a good idea to plug in our nostril tanks just in case the..."

A kind of braap-braap noise rudely interrupted Lana. A fragmented voice spelled out a message in Unglish.

"Attention. Your unregistered, uncleared vessel is advancing towards the sky lane system at an illegal velocity and angle. Please halt your advance and transmit your re-entry paperwork."

"Must be an automated system," Jimmy guessed. He leaned towards the wall, glancing at the slight purple distortion of the near-invisible sky lane directly below. "Rem warned us a few things might still work."

The braap-braap sounded again. This time, the voice was less civil.

"You have not ceased your advance, and your re-entry paperwork has not been transmitted. You have five seconds to comply."

Tuesday scoffed.

"What's a disembodied voice going to do?"

Braap-braap.

"Local police, ambulance crews, fire marshals, customs officers and military intervention teams have been summoned." The voice said with more than a little snark. Everyone went to the walls, scanning over the creamy white paradise in case they were about to be blasted out of the sky. There was a squeal of bad code from the automated message. "Police, ambulance, fire marshals, customs and military intervention teams are UNAVAILABLE."

Everyone flinched at the deafening crackle of that final word, but relaxed at the knowledge the automated voice didn't have any teeth. Tuesday blinked slowly, regarding the near-invisible sky lanes as its self-guiding fly-roads sped towards them at four hundred kilometres an hour.

"Well, that was…"

Their dumpster came to a neck-breaking stop, twisting and shaking about like dice in a cup. Thankfully the gravity systems of the PusCo bin prevented them from being beaten into a thin paste, but a rough halt turned out to be the least of their worries. Groaning, Jimmy was the first one to figure out their latest problem.

"Is it me, or are we moving horizontal?"

Clicking her fingers, Lana brought up the basic sky map Rem installed in her Omni before the drop. There were two main icons on it: a simple red square representing the communications array, and a purple PusCo logo for their dumpster. For the first time since their plunge began, the red and purple icons were moving away from each other.

"We've been hijacked," Trace snapped.

"Your vehicle has been apprehended for the safety of other sky lane users," the crackly voice said helpfully. "You are being brought to the closest impound lot, where you will be processed and charged for precisely one hundred and twelve legal infractions. Please do not attempt to alter your course or speed."

"Alter our course and speed, thanks," Tuesday demanded.

"We can't steer this thing," Lana said with minimal patience. "The dumpster can only manage a direct path to and from The Dirty Betty. Unless we want Rem to retrieve us, there's nothing we can do to."

Jimmy squinted at the basic little map being projected from Lana's Omni.

"Does that little number between the icons represent metres?"

"Kilometres," Lana huffed.

Trace raised her pierced eyebrows at the read-out.

"So now we're seven kilometres from our goal," she stated plainly, a dangerous undertow to her voice indicating she was trying to figure out who to blame.

"And counting," Tuesday added.

"I did enough walking on Scrote," Jimmy huffed. "No more death-marches, okay? Just figure some way to get us where we're meant to be. You're the Academy-trained expert, so fly us in the right direction."

Lana's rebuttal was strangled by a shadow cast across the bin. Everyone glanced up at the change of lighting, and could only watch as a dark front came closer and closer. Each second plunged them deeper and deeper into the oncoming nightmare of an absolute zero patch, a guaranteed end to their lives despite the dumpster's protection. The silence was only broken by some low babbling from Jimmy, who'd closed his eyes and bowed his head a little. He was hissing a Jud-Islamic Catholic prayer in some dead language, likely English.

"This is bad," Lana said, sharing her expert opinion as the light faded.

The dumpster came to a total halt, hovering in mid-air for an instant before plunging rapidly towards a rooftop cage the size of an airport strip. A grid of impenetrable Densite bars opened beneath them at the last second, swallowing the bin whole. There was no time to recover from this rollercoaster of a dive before the cage sealed itself again.

"Continuing to ping law enforcement," the crackly voice noted, its clarity dropping as the darkness came closer. "Please do not attempt to leave the impound area."

Trace slammed her shoulder against the underside of the dumpster's lid, grunting with the effort of trying to break through the rime of ice forming in its rubber seams. There was a cracking noise with every impact.

"What are you doing?" Jimmy asked blankly.

Lana jammed in her nostril-sized oxygen tanks and sealed the top of her cling suit. She joined Trace in trying to unstick their only way out.

"We need to escape the impound area," Lana snapped, amazed she had to explain something so obvious.

With her added shoulder, the dumpster finally burst open with a deafening whoosh of icy wind. The ambient lighting within the bin was no match for the total darkness beyond, and the humans moaned as the temperature dropped to that of a freshly-shaken Martini. Following Lana's example with their air tanks and cling suits, the others scurried over the edge with her. As soon as Tuesday's boots touched the glow stone tiles of the impound area, however, he immediately hopped back into the bin and went to close its lid. Lana was quick enough to prevent Tuesday sealing himself away.

"The spug are you doing, Tuesday? Move!"

"And go where?" Tuesday chattered, rubbing his arms as the sky turned to midnight. "So I can run around a sealed impound lot for a bit before I get turned into sorbet? Maybe try to escape from a cage that's clearly made from unbreakable Densite bars? No, I'm sitting right here, because if this bin is insulated enough to survive space, it should be good enough to get through an overcast day."

As she didn't have time to explain that the dark patches were far, far colder than space, all Lana could do was wrestle with the dumpster's lid, stopping Tuesday from closing it. On the third jerk Lana's right fist flashed out at top speed, fuelled by frustration. Her two biggest knuckles hit Tuesday square on the eye socket, knocking him to the padding.

There was a flash from far above. Looking up, hoping against hope the frozen darkness was going to miss them, Lana couldn't understand why the temperature was still dropping exponentially. Her face twisted up in total annoyance at the sight of blinding sunbeams bouncing about up at moon level, and it only took a second to realise that this entire neighbourhood was going to get blasted by a direct hit from a concentrated solar beam before being frozen into icy, ashen sludge.

This really wasn't her day.

Flinging the dumpster wide open, Lana barely crested its rim before Jimmy and Trace crashed after her, slamming Tuesday into the not-quite-padded-enough interior. Reaching up as a team to drag the lid shut, crunching away a thick, new deposit of ice, they gasped and shrieked as the sub-zero wind froze everything from their fingertips to elbows blue. The last thing they saw before the lid sealed was the biggest flare of their lives as a beam of pure, concentrated sun drilled down from the Heavens, dissolving the unbreakable Densite bars directly above the dumpster as easily as one-ply toilet paper. It took a direct path towards their purple shelter at the speed of light.

There wasn't even time for prayer as the impound area, and the nine-hundred-and-fifteen stories of glow stone fortress directly below it, ceased to exist.

CHAPTER TWENTY FOUR

Seventy kilometres across the white expanse of Seven Sun's urban sprawl, an epic gold-and-alabaster shape rose through the clouds. Cutting through blue wisps of cumulus, the four-metre-tall suit of unbreakable glass plates hummed as the top-of-the-line antigrav wafers built into his bulky gauntlets allowed him to crest the tip of a three-kilometre-tall star scraper. This required only the mildest expression of his godlike gravity-altering capabilities, one of many wonders you'd find hard-pressed to match anywhere else.

Despite being the only intelligent remnant of Mankind's lost empire, the Monolith had continued his duty as the sentry of this world, a responsibility that would likely never cease. While his nine tonnes of hand-decorated armour was formed in such a way that it indicated he was just a big Human on the inside, in truth the Monolith was better described as a comprehensive stockpile of every conceivable weapon – and quite a few that could not be conceived –

moulded into the morphism of a biped. Comparing him to a Human was like comparing the flame of a disposable lighter to the churning energies of a star.

The Monolith came to a stop as softly as a teenage boy kissing his cousin on the cheek at a family gathering. Perching atop the star scraper with perfect balance, the suit of armour adjusted itself purely by thought as the Monolith settled into a comfortable, stable setting. The armour's internal framework of pneumatic suspension gave soft little purrs with each movement.

Gazing across the region of Seven Suns once known as The Heights by the crème-de-la-crème who dwelled in its highest peaks, the Monolith started counting down the seconds until the distant city block was due to get demolished by a concentrated solar blast. As the Monolith's vision was keen enough to carve a whitehead clean off the nose of a MacDeath fry cook from orbit, he'd have a perfect view of what was likely to be the biggest, most brutal malfunction of the shattered moon lenses so far.

Being immune to all but the greatest forces of the Universe, the Monolith had no cause for concern. As he'd found naked exposure to the vacuum of space merely on the chilly side and a direct nuclear strike to the face had only inflicted a scattering of freckles, fear was an alien concept. A bit of sunlight wasn't much of a worry, especially from well outside its projected impact zone. Even if he wasn't functionally immortal and invulnerable, though, once the squishier residents of Seven Suns had performed their mass exodus it had been a simple matter for him to map out where every solar blast was projected to strike for the next fortnight, leaving zero chance of being surprised by a spear of concentrated sunlight up the backside. This feat of brilliance was not out of character for a Monolith; after all, in order to maximise the destructive capabilities of their walking armouries, Monoliths were implanted with numerous cerebral enhancements allowing them to use their offensive systems to their utmost potential. Mapping some bouncing sunbeams was a relatively minor example.

As always, the Monolith's existence was nearly silent. This high up, there was nothing to hear beside the whip of the wind. He'd learned how to block out the local radio channels, data streams and other comm systems of this world ages ago, ignoring that endless loop of Mayor Grundy declaring an Emergency Evacuation. While it had been against the Monolith's programming to live in total radio silence like this, effectively cutting himself off from any possible orders, it had been for the sake of his sanity. Mankind was long gone and only the whispers of fearful, dead men remained, making it the right choice.

The Monolith spent most of his solitude perched somewhere high, his mind in an empty Zen-like state as he surveyed Seven Suns as a benevolent god. Without anyone to protect (or, more to the point, kill), one of the only things he enjoyed doing nowadays was watching a solar blast take out a suburb of star scrapers. Like him, it never got old.

The Monolith glanced at his retinals. Two minutes until impact.

But then he saw something unexpected heading directly towards the soon-to-be-ground-zero: a purple dot, some foreign item caught up in the sky lanes like a seed in the wind. As he'd had precisely one visitor in the last span of a Human life, the Monolith considered whether that alien from a few months back was insane enough to return for round two, likely with more unwelcome questions about The TenKay Vault. As Viour was clearly warned to never to come near Seven Suns again, he'd have no choice but to incinerate the suit of amplification armour and imprison its tiny pilot in a small box somewhere cold. Just to save time, the Monolith cycled a sheath of pin-sized self-guiding antimatter missiles in his wrist, the perfect thing to surgically remove annoyances from the space-time continuum with a minimum of splash damage.

Sighting down his arm, however, one x-ray glance into the purple object gave the Monolith the surprise of the millennium. Not only was he looking at a flying PusCo dumpster full of Humans, but he could instantly tell that none of them had undergone conversion by The Perfection.

Real people! How long had it been since he'd seen one of the Original Recipe?

As his programming was as unbreakable as his armour, the Monolith was instantly compelled to perform a thousand different top-priority actions, such as gauging exactly which of the Humans was in charge, verifying who they were (or who they claimed to be), checking if they required medical attention, and seeing if they'd been officially slated for termination by The Unison and why. However, what made the Monolith literally stand up and pay attention was that one of these Original Recipes had a command bead installed her head, identifying her as one of the elite few who could order him about without being crushed into jam.

As the dumpster and its contents were casually meandering through an area of

The Heights due to be reduced to ashes in less than two minutes, the Monolith suddenly had a priority command to follow: rescue them.

Switching on his comms for the first time in decades, the Monolith gritted his teeth at an all-band message demanding that police, ambulance and military staff were to respond to an unregistered, unidentified vessel that had entered Seven Suns airspace at an illegal angle and velocity. If only his comms had been switched on he might have been appraised of the situation thirty seconds ago, a portion of time that might prove to be the difference between life and death for this quartet of squishies. While the maths weren't promising, that didn't mean the Monolith had any intention of letting what might be the final Humans burn on his watch.

He casually stepped off the star scraper and fell like a brick. A hundred storeys whipped by, thousands of empty windows and sky lane parking slots whizzing up so fast they blurred into unbroken lines. The moment he came level with the top level of the distant impound lot the Monolith activated every wafer of his extensive antigrav systems to fling his suit of armour like a pebble out of David's sling. There were no flaming jets, or boosters, or jet turbines. No, the Monolith didn't require such crude methods of propulsion. He simply thought where he wanted to go, and his armour took him there.

The Monolith hit twice the speed of sound way quicker than any supersonic jet, and didn't bother too much with whatever got in his way. He barrelled head-first through balconies, tore furrows across glow stone walls with his shoulder, and didn't hesitate in his arrow-straight path for an instant. In less than one hundred seconds the flying Monolith had consumed the better part of sixty-eight kilometres, and by the time the PusCo dumpster full of Humans had been swallowed by the impound lot's cage of Densite bars, the Monolith hit full atmospheric velocity.

Far above, the sky churned as five moon-sized lenses began to bounce a ray of sunshine back and forth, the light growing in aggression and volume with each rebound…

Despite what the maths warned him, the Monolith didn't hesitate. Flipping around boots-first, he aimed his tippy-toes at a point on the glow stone star scraper just a metre beneath the impound yard. As he didn't have time to waste smashing through bars made of Densite, one of the Universe's toughest materials, he did the smart thing by avoiding them. Exploding through glow stone, reinforced tuffcrete and plaster, the Monolith smashed his gauntlets through the rooftop landing pad at just the right instant to gather the PusCo dumpster and drag it into the maelstrom of his passing. He tucked the bin under his chest like a mother hen guarding her chicks, and faced the back of his unbreakable glass armour towards the sky. Curled into a ball, he burst out of the far side of the star scraper buttocks-first at three times the speed of sound.

Bracing himself, holding the dumpster tight, the Monolith took the full force of a solar blast. It was at this moment he truly learned the definition of the word hot, a concept he had only understood with mathematical detachment before now. Still speeding just as fast as the instant he'd slammed into the impound lot like an asteroid, the Monolith's alabaster-and-gold shell glowed a deep honey colour as it was bathed in concentrated solar rays. While he'd only been at ground zero for a couple of seconds, it was enough for his armour to blur from stress. As his scanners and other senses were going wild from overheating, he couldn't check whether the Humans had survived, or been incinerated despite his intervention.

Feeling dizzy for the first time ever, the Monolith's helmet complained that its temperature was more than six hundred degrees Celsius above its recommended operational limits. Head pounding, he suffered a few seconds of groggy confusion. As any pilot can tell you, at three times the speed of sound, greying out is not a good thing.

Losing track of where he was and what direction he was going, by the time the Monolith's mind got back on track he'd drifted down to a less lethal velocity. However, in the most confusing moment of his existence, the Monolith found himself ploughing through a darkened forest of snap-frozen trees. While his augmented brain wasn't exactly operating at an optimum right now, he knew that the only spots of darkness you could find on Seven Suns were those accursed patches of absolute zero that roved about in deadly sweeps. Just as the solar blast had taught him heat, the dark patch taught him cold.

Doing a whole-body clench as his overheated armour plunged into the frigid depths of sub-sub-sub-zero temperatures, the Monolith could do little more than protectively hug the half-crushed dumpster as his equipment executed a series of auto-repairs. It might have been a hallucination, but just before the Monolith's brain decided that it was time to reset, reboot and reload, it seemed as though the darkness was lightened by just a few shades. Fading into standby mode, he was rewarded by the dulcet tones of a living Human voice.

"What in the spug just happened?"

*

Padded or not, whatever had launched the PusCo dumpster across a good chunk of Seven Suns hadn't been kind to the medical waste repository or its passengers. In the space of instants they'd gone from ground zero to safety, and the transparent walls of their bin provided an amazing view of The Heights dissolving into a flaming nothing. The dumpster's creaking slowly got louder as it buckled under the weight of nine tonnes of something, and splits zig-zagged along the bin's seams. Its welding parted one bolt at a time from the strain. Cold wind spilled through the widening gaps between dark purple plates, sharp against soft Human skin, promising a swift blue death.

Her entire world spinning like a dervish and her body shaking hard enough to chip teeth, Lana managed to sit up in the dark wreckage. Tiny spikes of flying icicles proved the dumpster wasn't even close to airtight anymore, making it useless for future surface-to-ship actions. It also didn't help the entire console, including the Reclaim button, had melted into small grey puddles.

The whines of tortured metal from all sides confirmed that whatever had saved their lives was still wrapped around the dumpster tight enough to flatten it. Trying to examine her saviour through the transparent walls only inundated Lana's retinals with formless static and assorted warnings that attempting to scan property that belonged to the upper echelons of The Unison was a good way to end up getting dissected with a dessert spoon.

Almost as a response to prayer, the interior of the bin began to brighten, and Lana could have sworn the icy winds were calming their assault. The darkness became vague shapes, but the neon orange of Tuesday's coveralls was the first colour to pool out of the haze. Raising her Omni, Lana's implant noted that the outside temperature had warmed just enough not to snap-freeze Human flesh on contact, which was an improvement on just ten seconds ago. Better yet, the rosy glow of local sunlight was quickly replacing the cutting draft.

Lana lay her head against the twisted wall, cringing as a sharp piece of metal wreckage poked through the shredded padding and jabbed her spine. Making eye contact with Jimmy, who was looking just as air-sick, Lana blinked a few times and glanced at the ceiling. Cloaked with military security or not, it didn't take much of a stretch of her imagination to guess what the unidentified nine-tonne mass sitting on top of the dumpster was, but it would have been nice to have enough clearance to see through the static.

Looking for a way out, Lana was considering a tight gap between Trace and Tuesday when the worst happened: the walls buckled more and more violently until there wasn't even room to sit, leaving only seconds until they were crushed to death. A couple of centimetres at a time, the scorched purple crunched in on itself like an accordion. Just to rub salt in the wound, this was when Lana realised that the dumpster was upside down, meaning the lid was sealed tight against the ground. Worse yet, Tuesday and Trace were finally jolted awake by getting hit in the head with the lowering ceiling, meaning that the chances of finally being rid of both these scumbags was a little less likely.

Thankfully, Lana had a plan.

"Bail!" she screamed.

It wasn't the most heroic moment of her life, but Lana had scurried through the gap on her hands and knees before she even finished shouting. The others were right at her heels, wrestling each other to be the next one out. Their bare hands were met by the frozen crunch of a frost-brittle forest floor for their troubles, and nobody had time to say a word before the PusCo medical waste disposal dumpster flattened behind them into a disgusting flapjack. Tuesday gave a yelp of pain as his foot caught in the metallic pile, but thankfully he was able to extract it without losing any toes in the process.

While she instantly registered blue-leaved trees and a verdant forest floor and a clear sky and a distant cityscape, Lana could only focus on one thing right now: the four-metre-tall suit of unbreakable alabaster-and-gold glass laying on the crushed bin, curled up tight in the recovery position. Its individual plates were glowing so hot that what little remained of the bin was melting into slop beneath their touch, indicating the Monolith's temperature prior to hitting the frozen patch of absolute-zero darkness must have been beyond hot. She didn't know too much about Monolith abilities, but conceded it was possible the super soldier had deliberately heated himself up to prevent the four of them freezing to death in the passing shadows.

Although she knew their entire purpose for coming to this hole was to contact the Monolith, the Gatekeeper that Viour had described in terrifying detail, it was another thing entirely to see him from a few metres away.

After a few moments of silence (nobody was game enough to wake a potentially grumpy Monolith from his nap), the giant's outstretched right arm twitched. His four fingers and thumb, each the size of an Italian-style salami, clenched and unclenched on the frozen dirt, cracking a thin rime of ice along his joints, then he sat up in one smooth motion. Even sitting down and manspreading, the creature was far taller than Trace. Placing palms the size of manhole covers over each side of his helmet, the Monolith gripped his death mask helmet and twisted it loose. His huge, slabby head resembled a pile of badly-stacked sandstone bricks, looking like something the ancient Egyptians would have carved onto a Pharaoh's tomb to scare off grave robbers. His rough, stony skin was smoking like an ember. He blinked two all-white eyes with the crunching noise of sandpaper rubbing against granite.

"Are you…" Jimmy licked his lips, pushing as hard as he could with his limited reserves of bravery. "Are you hurt?"

The Monolith had the most bass voice they'd ever heard. It was like an earthquake being played over a subwoofer. You could feel it in your marrow.

"I don't get hurt," the Monolith said simply. He dropped his smouldering glass helmet onto the frost. Steam hissed from the frigid underbrush at its touch. "Now, would one of you like to tell me how you didn't pick up on that Emergency Evacuation message on your way in?"

"We heard it," Lana said, trying not to sound dismissive.

Those all-white eyes tightened into slits. It was hard to read the unnatural face, but he seemed unimpressed.

"This world is unsafe, as you can evidently see. As possibly the last Human beings alive, you don't have the luxury of being stupid. I advise you to leave Seven Suns immediately, find somewhere safe to rebuild your species, and never return."

"But we came here on purpose," Tuesday said.

The Monolith extended to his full height, smashing the dumpster thinner than a crepe under his boots.

"I know you," the Monolith growled. "You once assaulted me with a small container full of dried noodles."

"And then you shut off my nervous system with a glance," Tuesday said through gritted teeth. "So I guess that makes us even."

"Seriously? Noodles?" Trace asked, midway between disbelieving and turned on.

Tuesday shrugged. "It's a long story. Until now, it ended with me passing out and messing myself in four different ways. No, wait, five."

The Monolith pointed a salami finger towards the distant city. Colourful lines and numbers appeared on everyone's retinals, highlighting a long path that weaved through a maze of nature trails.

"This course will keep you safe long enough to find a vehicle and get off-world. Every security system was switched off when the evacuation order went into effect to prevent people getting trapped, so any vehicle capable of transporting you off-world should be safe to…borrow. I'd advise you to start walking now if you want to live." The Monolith picked up its helmet. "Well? Move."

"What, you don't like visitors?" Tuesday asked, wishing he had a container full of dried noodles. "It's a matter of highest security for The Unison."

"The Unison doesn't exist," the Monolith corrected him quietly, holding his helmet tight. It sounded as though he was pressing the headgear with enough force to buckle a truck's engine block. "And neither does The Perfection, nor any of the splinter groups that tried to fill the void before they too, vanished. My duty is to defend this world from outside threats, and I will continue to do so forever. You, however, must leave."

"There's a huge risk due to arrive at Erf in a matter of weeks," Jimmy said. "We're talking absolutely overwhelming force."

"You're our only hope," Lana said as seriously as possible.

The Monolith leaned down, getting his craggy rocklike face close enough for the humans to pick out individual seam lines.

"This is my post. My role is to defend it. If invaders come here, I guarantee I will murder them all. I have no allowances to go zipping to other planets. To be succinct, this isn't my problem." The Monolith slipped his helmet back on, and his voice took on a vibrating quality through the unbreakable glass. "This discussion has ended. Goodbye."

Trace snap-kicked a frozen-solid tree. Its trunk shattered, raining iced sap.

"Spug it, do you have any idea what we've been through to get here? Of the tortures that have been inflicted on us? 'War crimes' doesn't even begin to cover it! We are the final Humans, and we're asking for your help, so you will say sir yes sir and do as you're told!"

The others cringed at Trace's outburst. The Monolith removed his death mask and bowed down towards her, looming so close he was almost touching her.

"Six, five, four ..." Lana muttered under her breath.

"What are you counting?" Tuesday hissed.

"How long we have until he smears Trace all over this mountain," Lana said in all seriousness.

The Monolith stayed very, very still. After ten long seconds, he stiffened his spine, standing at attention.

"Tracetta Viktoria Cuddle, your clearance has been verified and logged," the Monolith stated. "What are your orders?"

Jimmy gaped at the Monolith, then at Trace.

"You're kidding me."

"So you'll help us?" Lana clarified, stunned.

The Monolith waggled a giant finger.

"No. I am only able to assist Ms Cuddle. The rest of you don't even have enough clearance to look at me."

"Why not?" Tuesday complained.

The Monolith did not change his expression.

"You don't have the clearance to ask that question."

"So why does she have clearance, exactly?" Jimmy asked.

The Monolith almost seemed amused.

"And you don't have the clearance to ask that question, either. Have you been tolerating this lot for long, Ms Cuddle?"

Now everyone was looking at Trace. She glared at her fellow humans, knowing exactly what they were all wondering at this instant, then flicked her gaze back to the Monolith. As little as she liked helping people, the obvious question proved to be too tempting.

"So why do I have clearance?" Trace asked simply.

The Monolith tilted his head in a curious way.

"You are the sole remaining family member of the Cuddle dynasty, one of The Unison's most powerful families. At their peak, the Cuddles were the richest family in The Unison. I, like all Monoliths, was created by The Splinters of Russia, a nation-company bought out by CuddleTech shortly before my manufacture in the 24th Century. In effect, as the last remaining Cuddle, you technically own me."

"I'm not a Cuddle, not anymore," Trace growled. "Uncle Balder framed us all as illegitimate. I was struck from granddad's estate and exiled."

"Should have used your inner voice to say that," Tuesday hissed.

The Monolith blinked a few times and pointed at Trace's head. She startled and gripped the back of her skull as though trying to prevent it from flying away. She could obviously feel something there.

"What?" Jimmy asked. "Is it your Peach worm?"

Trace held up her hand to silence Jimmy.

"No, it was something else," she muttered, still holding her shaved scalp. She narrowed her eyes, glaring at the Monolith. "What was that weird sensation?"

The Monolith nodded solemnly.

"Your brain contains a top-echelon command bead, a forgery-proof implant identifying you as having the highest possible level of security across the entirety of The...well, what used to be The Unison. It's a deep-set tag you likely had installed in infancy."

Jimmy sidled up next to Lana and spoke wetly into her ear.

"Remember that weird little ball bearing we spotted in her head with the Psych-in-a-Box? The one we couldn't read?"

Lana nodded, and spoke out of the side of her mouth.

"Looks like we know what it is now."

"But like I said, I ain't a Cuddle anymore," Trace snapped. "Got legally excised from the estate. Can't even set foot in Reborn Detroit unless I want to get ventilated."

"Dear Odin, stop fighting it!" Jimmy whined. "Take the opening!"

"According to my records, Balder Cuddle was arrested and charged for his crimes against the Cuddle dynasty, including interfering with the brain of a deceased person for the purposes of forging a necromantic will reading," the Monolith said helpfully. "Due to the sheer, unprecedented scale of his fraud, Balder was executed for his crimes, and as there were no other living relatives, the Cuddle estate was distributed amongst shareholders, the Board of Directors of CuddleTech and numerous charities."

The Monolith projected a scan of ancient news-vid articles in front of Trace's slack expression. She read the lines silently, then gave a dark chuckle at the date. "Says all this came to light just two years after the Carpe Astrum did its first and last big jump. If I'd just waited a couple dozen months, I'd have been heir to the whole fortune. Typical…"

"As your implant and genetics are a match, I am willing to listen to your orders," the Monolith stated, still at attention. "I would remind you, however, that I am bound by codes of honour, particularly in regards to treason. While I cannot be held accountable for my actions if I am ordered to do something against interstellar law anymore than a machine gun can be prosecuted for a civilian massacre, I must make it clear that you may be held accountable for especially heinous commands...if you get caught, of course." The Monolith's face twisted into an odd shape: a smile. "Now, who did you want me to kill?"

"Almost everyone I want dead is already dead," Trace said flatly. "I want access to The TenKay Vault."

"And it'd be nice to know exactly what's inside of it, too," Jimmy added.

The Monolith's expression soured. He glanced at the three zero-priority Humans, then back at Trace.

"It's best not to discuss such a topic in front of such a…common audience, Ms Cuddle. I would prefer to talk about this issue in private."

"I say we talk about it now," Trace growled.

A sudden look of realisation passed over the Monolith's face, twisted sharply by suspicion.

"You mentioned there was huge risk due to arrive at Earth soon. If it hasn't happened yet, how do you know of it? Who or what is your source?"

Ever helpful and ever clueless in equal measure, Jimmy answered automatically.

"Viour was …"

Trace slammed her stiff index finger into Jimmy's ribcage on the second syllable, and her jab had the desired response of sending Jimmy rigid and breathless with pain. But it was too late: Jimmy had pooped the bunk. The Monolith's eyes narrowed until they were thinner than coin slots.

"So you want me to give you lot access to the greatest repository of god-level technology in the Known Universe so that you can sell its best pieces to an undocumented alien?"

"We weren't going to sell it to her..." Jimmy wheezed, trying to make up for his error by making another one. Trace smoothly chopped at his throat, sending Jimmy gagging to the crunchy, frosty grass.

"We need to use The Vault's technology to repel the coming Primacy," Lana declared, stepping forward. "If we don't stop the trickle, their flow will certainly become the end of all that remains."

It was clear the Monolith could read the truth of Lana's words as easily as a menu with only grilled cheese listed on it. He regarded her for a few quiet moments.

"Inspiring speech," the Monolith rumbled. He nodded sideways at Trace. "Shame she's the only one who has any authority over me. But if you had a command bead installed in your brain, girl, I guarantee you I'd be opening The Vault as we speak."

"So you want Trace to convince you?" Tuesday chuckled. "I don't think her usual methods of persuasion will work too well against an invulnerable target who can't feel being kicked in the melons."

"Insult my social skills again and I'll murder you," Trace hissed at Tuesday, her voice low and dangerous. She turned back to the looming super-soldier. "We've been on the brink of dead for weeks to get here. We've done things so bad to survive that we had to flush out our memories with a Psych-in-a-Box. We're not here to help the last of The Apex conquer the galaxy. If the Primacy and its legions of world-incinerating Star Cages make it through the breech and discover a region of zero resistance, all hope is lost."

The Monolith snorted. It sounded like a car backfiring.

"The Human race is currently four strong, and half of you aren't even fertile," the Monolith said in boredom. "Hardly the greatest loss."

"Are all Monoliths total dicks like you or what?" Tuesday snapped.

"There's more than four," Lana interrupted. "There's five thousand and four."

This captured the Monolith's attention. For the first time in minutes, it felt as though the mountain of armour wasn't toying with them. His truth-telling abilities cut down on quite a bit of unnecessary exposition.

"Where?"

Lana nodded at the sky. As it was broad daylight, The Dirty Betty was invisible.

"We were told this by a man...a dead man...who orchestrated a guerrilla war against The Perfection for years. Our ship has five thousand Original Recipe people hidden away, ones that predate The Perfection's enhancements. We just..." Lana faltered for a moment. "We just haven't exactly, precisely found them yet."

The Monolith's face tightened. He said a familiar name.

"Nurbis."

Instead of bothering to explain, the Monolith glared at Lana's left hand. She startled as the second-hand Omni heated to an unpleasant temperature under her skin, but managed not to yelp. She rubbed at the burning spot as the Monolith stopped scanning it.

"You're telling the truth," the super-soldier said, much more seriously than before. "I can verify your Omni contains five thousand deeply hidden files, and all of them are distinct Human genomes consisting of four thousand women and one thousand men of optimal breeding age, complete with plug-and-play mind files. All you need is the right kind of Repler, perhaps one from the 28th Century or later, and you can start spitting out Original Recipe people." The Monolith slumped a little, as though so blown away by this news that he needed a moment to compose himself. "You could restart Mankind with what's on that Omni."

"But we don't have a Repler from the 28th Century," Tuesday pointed out. "Closest we have is a protein sump, and that thing's so old-fashioned it's more of a war crime than a food source."

"Don't worry about technology," the Monolith rumbled. "You came to the right place."

The Monolith straightened his right arm towards the underbrush, his huge hand spread open like a starfish. Half an instant later some weird feline made of clawed tentacles and fanged mouths slammed throat-first into his armoured palm. The slightest wrist movement killed the slobbering creature deader than disco.

"But that can wait until after dinner. You are all clearly undernourished."

CHAPTER TWENTY FIVE

The way he disassembled the mutant animal carcass was hypnotic. Suspending its tentacled form with a scalpel-precise mastery of gravity, the Monolith carved away its fur, skin, whiskers and chewy bits with a blur of sharpness projected from his fingertips. In seconds the creature was whittled down to a neat pile of floating steaks, and its digestive system and bones were discarded beyond the tree line with a flick. Angling the floating meat between both palms, a bright flash instantly fried thirty kilograms of steak to a golden brown.

A procession of charred, juicy hunks of meat hovered in front of the humans, inviting them to pick and choose whatever they wanted. In moments they were wolfing down hunks of medium-rare deliciousness.

"These felines are descended from the designer barking cats that were all the rage in your era," the Monolith said to Tuesday, swallowing porterhouse after porterhouse from his enormous pile without needing to chew. "Their genetics went south after a couple of generations, and before long all the wooded areas were infested with ferals. Couldn't go and flame the forests without removing this world's lungs in the process, obviously, so big game hunters came from all over to take a shot at them. Eventually, though, even military patrols weren't game enough to pass through any shadow cast by a tree." He nodded at the branches twisting an arm's-length away. "You can't see or hear them, but there are thousands of ferals swarming and boiling over each other in the dark, watching us, hungry."

As much as everyone wanted to ask the Monolith a hundred questions, reflexively chewing and swallowing didn't leave much space for words. So he helpfully answered one of the big ones.

"In case you're wondering why I seem to have back flipped on letting you into The TenKay Vault, I need to stress that I'm not trusting you because of a gut instinct or anything. In the last five minutes I've assessed the truth of your every word and analysed every moment your retinal screens have recorded since their implantation. I've also triple-checked every file and fragment on your Omni..." He glanced down at Lana and gave a slight smile. "Even though it isn't technically yours, is it?"

Lana stopped chewing.

"Is this Omni how you knew about Nurbis?"

Considering he was apparently constructed from rock, the Monolith's expression went slack.

"Is that how I..." the Monolith composed himself. He pointed up at the baby blue sky. "You see what happened to the orbital lenses? Nurbis and his herd of terrorist swine did that. Humanity stopped murdering each other as soon as they upgraded into The Perfection, but Nurbis and his Original Recipe crew apparently didn't get the memo. Over time they were all captured and adjusted, and he was the only one to evade their fate. Seven Suns may have been the location of their first major terrorist attack, but it certainly wasn't the last."

"Why wreck Seven Suns?" Tuesday asked around a charred rib roast. "Didn't they like nerds?"

"Obvious, isn't it?" the Monolith asked with a shrug. "This is where The Perfection was designed, and also the first place it was rolled out across an entire planetary population. Seven Suns was proof the alterations worked as planned, that skipping hundreds of thousands of slow generations of evolution had become possible. Earth may have been the hub of The Unison, but Seven Suns was the core of The Perfection. Its most important members resided here, and they made all their high-level decisions just a few minutes away from where we now sit. Nurbis and his terrorists knew they couldn't stop the machine, but they could certainly upset a lot of people, and when you're angry enough to form a terror cell and blow up moons, upsetting people can be reward enough."

"Did it have anything to do with The TenKay Vault?" Jimmy asked in his best I-hope-I'm-not-upsetting-anybody voice.

"No," the Monolith confirmed. "The Vault didn't exist when Nurbis was still active. But once the AI-augmented scientists of The Perfection began developing the sort of technology that could break physics and end the Universe, they needed somewhere safe to store it, somewhere impossible to get into if you weren't meant to be there."

"Or they could have just stopped creating doomsday devices," Tuesday snarked.

The Monolith turned his hands palm-up.

"There is no safer place to hide your treasures than The TenKay Vault. No scavenger or pirate or warlord with a third of a cerebellum would come to Seven Suns by choice. Solar blasts and sweeping patches of absolute zero darkness guarded by the last Monolith? Not exactly prime pickings."

"How did they decide what tech to squirrel away in The Vault?" Lana asked.

"It's a repository of every technological advancement Mankind has made over the last ten thousand years, all the way back to the hand axe and flint-headed arrow. Hence the 'TenKay' part of its name." The Monolith halved a feline calf muscle with a single tooth and gestured with the flesh as he spoke. "Of course, all this security wasn't put in place to protect the intellectual copyright of Stone Age weapons. After The Perfection became the first species to discover and apply the wonders of the Secondary Seven, everything they developed based on a Secondary Seven framework had the capacity to destroy all of time and/or space if misused, so it became standard practise to lock away every new device the moment it was completed." Examining their dull expressions, his face twisted in distaste. "Ah. None of you knows what a Secondary Seven is, do you?"

"We've got about five hundred years of trivia to catch up on," Trace growled. "Humour us."

The Monolith paused, more than likely to try and phrase what he was going to say into words that wouldn't cause any migraines.

"The Secondary Seven was the largest mathematical breakthrough since Mesopotamians discovered the zero. For thousands of years Mankind thought they knew how to count with the tried-and-true Base-10 system, but in the 27th Century the greatest psychotic mathematicians of The Perfection discovered there was actually another number entirely hiding where nobody had noticed, located directly between seven and eight: the Secondary Seven."

"So it really goes one, two, three, four, five, six, seven, seven, eight, nine, ten?" Lana scoffed.

The Monolith nodded solemnly.

"It took decades to figure out how to apply the Secondary Seven to existing equations, but it isn't an exaggeration to say that this mathematical breakthrough changed everything, ushering in a new era of progress." He swallowed a chop whole with a mouth as wide as a pizza box and pointed at Trace. "Let me be clear: if it wasn't for that command bead in your head, Ms Cuddle, I'd have killed all of you as soon as The Vault was mentioned. My core duty is to keep people away from it. Thankfully, I am allowed some flexibility if I can gauge it is warranted." As soon as the mountain of cat meat had vanished, grease evaporated from the Monolith's fingers as though by magic. "Well, are we doing this or not?"

They stopped eating in synchronisation, eyes wide as dinner plates.

"What, now?" Jimmy squeaked. "We're going in it now?"

Tuesday made a soft scoffing noise.

"Really? Us? You're actually letting us inside? Are you sure that's wise?"

The Monolith leaned forwards on huge, glass gauntlets, getting uncomfortably close. His breath smelled like carbon monoxide. It was a dizzying industrial expulsion.

"Like I said, I can see all that you've seen. I know the risk the Primacy and their Star Cages pose, and that Viour intends to repel them when they arrive. But let me be clear: I do not trust Viour and her alien motives, and I will not allow her to stick a knife in the back of what little remains of your species. I am permitting access to The Vault on the strict proviso that you are to never allow Viour to so much as touch whatever you take from there under pain of death. Is that clear?"

Always looking for an optimal angle of scummery, Tuesday gave a cheeky black smile.

"And you're going to enforce this promise how, exactly?"

The Monolith paused, his expression growing distant. Nobody had a chance to check if the super-soldier was okay before they all started screaming. Gripping their heads, the humans dropped their kitten kebabs and toppled over, thrashing around and grinding cold dirt into their faces. One by one their nostrils trickled red, and every eye went violently bloodshot. Just as soon as the agony started, it stopped.

Lana gagged as she sat up.

"What was that?" she managed, spitting out gravel. "What did you do?"

The Monolith explained with zero shame.

"I implanted neurological bombs in your brains that will trigger if you break your word to me. Simply put, if you give Viour or any other alien any specimen of TenKay Vault technology, all of the electrical signals in your brain will fire backwards. I promise it will be very unpleasant."

"We didn't agree to that," Trace growled.

The Monolith blinked, impassive.

"I don't need you to agree to anything. I need you to do as you're told. You wanted access to gear from The Vault, this is my condition."

The hill of unbreakable glass armour used his mastery of gravitational forces to lift off the dirt. It was like seeing Pinocchio magically rise from the stage of a puppet show without any wires. Not bothering to find out what everyone else thought about the whole "brain bomb" issue, the Monolith extended his arms wide in a cruciform shape before slamming his gauntlets together. The clap was like lightning, a force of nature, and a dark vertical slit appeared in its wake. Jamming his salami index fingers into the black line and pulling hard, the slot expanded until a white glimmer appeared at its core. Pulling with all his strength, the Monolith forced the tear in space/time open centimetre by centimetre, separating the curtain between realities, between Universes, as though catching a train door just before it closes.

However, all was clearly not right. The Monolith's eyes bulged, and a thick substance that might have been the equivalent of sweat beaded on his forehead.

"It's...resisting," the Monolith grunted, baring his teeth. "The Gateway is a little...rusty."

There was the hiss of pneumatic suspension as the Monolith strained. Eventually, he drew on his reserves and wrenched at the slot until it was wide enough to admit Trace. As she was shaped like a Queen-sized mattress stuffed with footballs, this meant there was room for everyone.

"Well?" the Monolith barked, seemingly locked in place as the Gateway wobbled and wibbled between his fingers. He jammed his heels in the base of the portal, using his powerful leg muscles to wedge both feet in place. "You better be quick. This thing doesn't want to stay open. I give you eight minutes, tops, before it seals for good." His face flexed in determination. "Fill it with a million different ways to ruin the Universe, but do they give it a decent Gateway? No! Of course not!"

Lana sighed. She was about to have access to the greatest repository of technology ever collected anywhere by anyone, but nowhere near enough time to accomplish anything useful. If that wasn't a tragedy, she didn't know what was.

To nobody's surprise, Lana was the first one to dart through the breach.

CHAPTER TWENTY SIX

There was a moment of disorientation, followed by a concrete whiteness. It was the sort of sterility that suggested a hospital for billionaires, or a corporate R&D laboratory run by sinister mega-corporations like PainCo, OmniDeath, WarCo, or The Happy Lovey-Dovey Laughter Company (not that anybody with sense would elaborate too much on that last one).

In addition to whiteness, there was also bigness. Before the focusing features of their civilian-issue retinal screens sharpened the panorama, this pocket Universe appeared to consist of nothing but a beige circle roughly a hundred metres across. The four of them stood at its very centre. Twelve round, precisely-spaced alabaster pillars marked the "hours" of this circle's outer reaches like a giant analogue clock, rising so far that they eventually disappeared at the limits of Human eyesight. It was unlikely that the pillars were infinite, but it wouldn't be the first time the survivors caught the space/time continuum taking an unscheduled lunchbreak.

Like anybody violently displaced by a malfunctioning pocket dimension gateway, it took a bit of staggering until their brains managed to reorient. Thankfully, the huge white coin was clear, open, flat space all the way to the pillars, meaning they only had each other to crash into. Besides a minor collision between Jimmy and Tuesday, followed by a variety of complaints from both parties, within ten seconds or so everyone had composed themselves.

While this would have been a wonderful opportunity for everyone to appreciate how clean this place was, or to at least celebrate how they'd done the impossible by convincing a truth-reading Monolith to let them into the most sensitive location within the rim of the Milky Way, it was a fact they had less than seven and a half minutes before the gateway closed for good.

"Orright," Lana managed, still a little woozy from a dimensional translation that felt like going in eight different directions all at the same time. "People, I confess that it occurs to me we should have prepared a game plan at some point before now."

Tuesday arched an eyebrow.

"Why? I know we don't have long, but all we need to do is rob anything that looks important, right?"

"Seven minutes eighteen seconds," Trace growled.

"It can't really that simple, though, can it?" Jimmy asked in disbelief.

Tuesday gave a black smile.

"Slummer, we're here to steal valuable fings. For the first time ever, this is my forte."

"True, not every plan needs to be Kafkaesque," Lana admitted, hoping nobody asked her to define the term. Blinking five times until her retinals applied maximum range, she took her first proper look at The TenKay Vault, and swore. "Oh, spug."

As all their retinals were more-or-less on par quality wise, everyone experienced the same moment of horrible realisation the moment they zoomed in beyond the pillars. Each of the ten-metre wide cylinders marked the beginning of an aisle of the same span, and while this meant the central circle had twelve giant "spokes" that stretched off to the furthest visual extent, the aisles themselves only made up a relatively small part of The Vault. Each aisle was lined with a webbing of cubby holes of various sizes and odd angles, giving the impression it had all been constructed by a swarm of huge, drunk paper wasps.

Between the spokes, however, this warehouse to end all warehouses was a labyrinthine, overlapping mess of alleys, cul-de-sacs, crescents, winding branches and impossible geometry rambling all the way to the horizon. It was a library designed by the insane and constructed by somebody who should know better than to insult God's immutable laws. The fact the items it contained were even more dangerous and unhinged than the archive itself was more than a little troubling.

Continuing to peer through the magnification feature of her retinals, Lana took in what lay within one of the spokes. The corridor was fenced on either side with a honeycomb of pure-white shelves of varying sizes and heights, and each individual cell contained precisely one item. As there weren't any labels or alphabetised road-signs or digital card catalogues or helpful "Use This To Save The Galaxy" post-it notes stuck anywhere, Lana didn't have the faintest idea what any of it did, let alone how to use it. All she could see were shapes and colours carefully arranged into cubbyholes all rolling towards a horizon that verged on forever. In the far, far distance she could make out cells the size of apartment blocks and aircraft hangers, and one big enough to easily swallow a football stadium.

Intrigued by how the corridors appeared to gently curve upwards if you went along them far enough, Lana zoomed her retinals up one of the twelve giant pillars and into the gloom at double her maximum range, safety protocols be damned. Tracing along its marbled surface, penetrating the thin cloud cover before driving ever onwards, Lana had a thrilling moment as her suspicions were confirmed: far, far above, the twelve pillars met up at another giant white plinth at the core of its own labyrinth of shelves. Perhaps it was only possible thanks to the freaky physics of this pocket dimension, but The TenKay Vault was so big that it took up the entire inner surface of a colossal hollow pearl the size of a planetary body.

Digging at her burning corneas, Lana shared her assessment of the situation.

"Bugger a Bishop sideways, this place goes forever."

"And?" Jimmy asked hopefully, waiting for the brilliance to start.

"The Vault doesn't seem to end, and I don't have the mistiest what to do," Lana admitted, her small voice carrying a long, long way.

"We have seven minutes to be out of here," Trace grunted. "So figure it out."

"I don't know how this place works, and I doubt I ever will, let alone in seven minutes." Lana snapped her fingers in a random direction. "Are you seeing this? Are your eyes working, people? This place is beyond me. I don't know how to deal with it. None of it. Spug, I never even completed my Cadet training! How am I supposed to find anything in here...?"

A voice that was everywhere and nowhere startled them.

"While the twelve default spokes of The TenKay Vault are divided by their particular branch of science, you can command the contents of this pocket dimension to rearrange according to your particular tastes in archiving. For instance, in alphabetical order, by the names of their creators, by their date of creation, by their lethality levels, according to what corporation funded their creation, and even by colour, are all valid options."

"So you're saying The Vault can rearrange itself?" Jimmy asked a little too loudly, as one tends to do with disembodied voices.

Beyond the pillar-studded main hub, the maze of shelves and cells danced, swinging back and forth and click-clacking in a showy twirl before resetting to its original setting. For a moment, it was like watching a clockwork mechanism from the inside, and the four of them had the exact same thought run through their heads at the same moment: what it would feel like if their squishy bodies were unfortunate enough to be within The Vault when it rearranged itself.

"There are nine dozen different ways to arrange the contents of The TenKay Vault, and you are also welcome to create customised settings."

"Who are we even talking at?" Tuesday muttered, forever a pit of uselessness.

Lana raised a finger, thinking for a moment before speaking.

"We need a custom setting. I want tech that can alter reality, mess up physics and tear apart space/time; the most lethal weapons, the worst doomsday devices, you understand? I want the sort of thing that scares the Transcended into fresh diapers. I want the juiciest of Deus Ex Machina, something that would make an incoming alien fleet dive for the white flags. I want to hold Hell in my hand."

Once Lana's words stopped ringing everyone casually stepped a little bit further away from her. Face red and veins bulging up both the sides of her neck, Lana's maniacal expression wasn't very reassuring.

There was a moment of silence, as though the unseen intelligence of The TenKay Vault was considering whether to kick out its visitors in a fit of offense, but then the labyrinth rearranged itself so hard that it seemed every cell and cubicle was now in a new place. The nearest giant pillar turned the colour of beetroot, and its aisle glowed the same demonic shade. It was clear The Vault didn't want there to be any confusion: this was the worst of the worst.

"Please note that every item in your customised aisle has a designation of godlike or higher, and due to security restrictions no more than one item from this collection may be removed by a single approved person at any given time."

"So...only take one each," Jimmy clarified, eventually conquering the maths.

Lana rolled up her sleeves. This served no purpose beyond showing the others that she meant business.

"Okay. Time to threaten the Universe."

*

By the time they stepped off the central plinth of The TenKay Vault and into the crimson corridor, another ten seconds had been wasted.

Keen as the humans were to start rifling through the most dangerous weapons in existence, there was a lot working against them. For starters, they'd only just indulged in a huge meal of pure protein, and this splurge had taken place after six miserable weeks of fighting the very real threat of death by starvation. Full of cat meat or not, Jimmy and Tuesday weren't the sort who could run long distances unless somebody was chasing them with an axe, so Trace and Lana had a good head start on the tech hunt.

The dark red cubicles on either side of this blood-hued aisle rose twice as high as Trace's shaved head, and a few odd low spots made the shelves seem jagged from a distance. Unfortunately, even after scoping out the better part of fifty different cells of mysterious McGuffins at a trot, all they discovered was disappointment. There were still no labels or anything descriptive, and not only did the finned swirls of brain-damaging geometry on the shelves not offer any hints, they'd give you a migraine if you stared at them too long.

Stumbling and almost falling against the first shelf he reached, already puffed out, Jimmy squinted at its contents. The gizmo was a complicated waveform of hair-fine opal-coloured wafers roughly the size of a hearing aid, and each of its curls were stamped with detailed patterns of tiny platinum dots. He wasn't game enough to touch it, but he spent a moment admiring its beauty.

"So pretty," he muttered, ignoring the cursing of the others. "I wonder what it does…"

Jimmy received the surprise of the minute when the disembodied voice of The TenKay Vault piped up to answer him.

"This is a weather-altering atmospheric modification device constructed by The Perfection. It is closely based on an earlier device researched and constructed by Professor Rally Skellitt in the 25th Century. Please do not aim this item at your face."

"This thing just told me what it was!" Jimmy shrieked.

"How did you make it do that?" Lana demanded from two dozen metres away.

"I just..." Jimmy blinked, thinking. "I just wondered what it was, and it told me."

Trace nodded, her usual scowl broken for a moment by a half-impressed smirk. She glanced at the closest full cubicle at what appeared to be an oxygen tank composed of perforated butterfly wings. Feeling silly, she asked the device what it was. Clear as a bell, the voice commented so that everyone could hear it.

"This is a non-Newtonian physics-adjusting spatial winch capable of temporarily compressing the Universe into certain shapes of torsion, effectively making it possible to draw entire star systems into one another. It was developed by The Perfection in the 27th Century, but never field-tested due to intellectual copyright violations and the fact it was highly likely to rewrite all the fifth-dimensional laws of higher reality."

"Nobody touch that, please," Lana shouted, stopping Trace just as she started to reach out for the spatial winch. "Odin only knows how many galaxies to the left it would take us if we sneezed too loud."

"Five minutes fifty-five seconds," Trace droned.

Lana clicked her fingers. The snap echoed a long way.

"Alright. Everyone, we need to be systematic. Jimmy, you check out everything eye-level and above on the left. Tuesday, you check out everything below that. Trace, you go high on the right, I'll go low. Don't take something until you're sure it's the best thing you can find." Lana clapped. "Right. Hustle!"

*

Precious seconds bled away, and as each moment died the humans only dialled closer and closer to panic and full-blown freak-outs. Every step they took was a priceless, irreplaceable resource.

The key problem was, despite Jimmy's accidental discovery, that simply being told what the treasures were wasn't enough. Most of the devices were too advanced to be explained to a layperson, and attempting to weaponise them would probably kill the humans just as easily as a Slidge-filled Star Cage. The remaining inventions were ridiculously niche and useless, or they only worked on a Wednesday if asked nicely by somebody with the birth name of Philadelphia, or they'd never been successfully field tested without killing everyone within a mile, or...

Everyone was so intent on finding their own doomsday weapons that they were startled by Lana giving a sharp clap of a laugh, the sort of noise you'd expect from a trained seal. She snatched a black sphere the size of a Flog ball from a smallish cell, and every other cubicle within her reach guillotined shut, making it clear she'd reached her maximum amount of borrowed items.

"What did you take?" Trace called out as Lana whipped past her towards the gateway.

"A ride!" she shouted back.

"What?" Jimmy managed as Lana sped on.

But she'd already hit full stride and was conserving her lungs for fuelling her sprint, rather than explaining things to simpletons who were meant to be busy doing something vital. Trace noticed that Jimmy and Tuesday were both standing still, watching Lana as she sped for the only exit. Spittle shot gunned from her mouth as she took command.

"Hustle!" Trace roared.

Shocked out of their mental lockage, Jimmy and Tuesday instantly returned to sweeping the shelves.

"I prefer it when Lana says it," Jimmy moped, his feelings hurt.

*

Less than thirty seconds later, Tuesday came to a total halt. As Jimmy was only a couple of metres behind him, engrossed in violently sweeping his eyes back and forth like a small, nauseous child on a ride at Happy Planet, Jimmy collided with Tuesday and they both tripped. Almost spraining a dozen different things between them as they hit the tiles, Jimmy cursed a vulgar line that nobody outside of his home world of Sprout would comprehend and punished Tuesday with his most sullen of looks.

"Sit on a sweet potato with a bare ass, Tuesday, you better keep moving or Trace will kick your..." Jimmy looked up at what had transfixed Tuesday's attention, but it turned out to be more of a matter of who had transfixed his attention. Jimmy frowned at what he was seeing. "Why is there a monk...?"

Tuesday raised a finger in warning.

"Watch what you call her."

Jimmy struggled to his feet. The cubicles flashed blue and purple to warn him that climbing on the furniture wasn't permitted.

"How do you know it's a 'her'?"

Tuesday shot Jimmy a sideways glare.

"Because she's me Mum."

Taken aback, Jimmy scanned Tuesday's face for humour. It was ugly, pockmarked, and weather-beaten from a multitude of fists and contained little black shards that may technically be classed as teeth, but for once there was no mockery or sarcasm there. Jimmy couldn't remember the last time he'd seen Tuesday so serious. It was like looking at another person entirely.

Jimmy turned towards the large cell containing Tuesday's alleged Mum. She was well over two metres tall, had arms like burlap sacks full of oranges, and her V-shaped torso and abdomen were balanced atop a comical set of tiny monkey legs. Her face looked like a kebab-with-the lot had lost a fight with a cheese grater, and she was almost entirely covered in thick, wiry hair. Her (admittedly beautiful) brown eyes were one of the few breaks in all that fur. Looking down, Jimmy noticed all the digits on Ruska's left hand had long claws, and wondered if they were retractable.

She was utterly still. She might have been dead, comatose, anything.

"Go on," Tuesday prompted.

Jimmy pressed his lips together hard enough for them to turn white. He shook his head a little. He didn't want to know.

"Do it!" Tuesday screamed, finally attracting Trace's attention.

His feelings hurt, Jimmy moped the magic words.

"What is she?"

As always, The TenKay Vault was happy to answer.

"This is the final surviving mitosis-clone of Ruska, an experimental super-solider secretly created by The Splinters of Russia back in the 24th Century. While the original Ruska was lost for some time after escaping from a laboratory belonging to The Splinters, she was eventually recaptured, reconditioned and used for wet work assignments until her death by natural causes a century later. In addition to staggering regenerative abilities and extreme strength, speed and durability, Ruska's most revolutionary trait was being able to reproduce by mitosis, effectively splitting into exact copies of herself with minimal effort. This allowed for the rapid creation of hundreds of thousands of slaved Ruska's, who were sold to any customers who could afford one of her mitosis-clones. She proved to be one of the most popular weapons of all time, and sales were particularly lucrative among outlaw warlords, criminal kingpins, planetary despots, wealthy terrorist cells and…"

Tuesday went to punch a bordering cubicle that contained what appeared to be a soft satin pillow. The cell sealed itself before his fist connected, and Tuesday's hand met a layer of something that was not welcoming to the delicate bones of his hand. He cussed and danced in a circle, gripping his fingers and growling.

"Last warning!" Trace screamed across a long, long distance.

Jimmy was pretty sure she'd drawn her kinetic accelerator. He instantly resumed looking, leaving Tuesday and his messed-up Mother behind.

Finally gathering his bearings, within ten steps a slack-jawed Tuesday came face to face with another blast from his past: she was a beautiful black woman dressed in the snappy white uniform and purple piping of a high-level Unison scientist. Her straight ebony hair flowed all the way down her hourglass figure to her shapely buttocks, and she was the sort of beauty who could get away with not wearing any makeup at even the most exclusive of venues. The TenKay Vault helpfully began to read off details as Tuesday got closer, looking into her almond-shaped eyes.

"September was an early, though reasonably successful, attempt by a research team on Seven Suns to create what would eventually come to be defined as The Perfection. Engineered from a variety of geniuses along with her eleven slightly-different pod sisters, although September was highly temperamental and emotionally stunted, she…"

Tuesday turned on his heel, cricket-leather frog-stomper boot giving a squeak as he made a sharp pivot, and walked away. The explanation stopped instantly, noting his lack of interest.

"Nope, sorry, not going there. All out of emotions for now."

*

After ninety more seconds of zero progress, Jimmy was the next one to find something. This involved a few moments of self-doubt, an instant or two of triple-guessing, followed by something he wasn't used to: resolution. Perfect was impossible, he decided, so lowering his standards by a few degrees was a logical step to take. Chewing his lip, blinking repeatedly at a transparent black cylinder made from what appeared to be thousands of almost-touching little triangles, he gripped the item in both hands and ran.

Tuesday had to step back to avoid being bowled over. As the aisle was ten metres wide, he was understandably annoyed that Jimmy felt the need to barge into him. Feeling targeted (and more than a little irked he couldn't find anything worth stealing yet), Tuesday managed to ask a civil question rather than spew abuse.

"What did you get?"

Jimmy turned mid-run, almost stumbling with the effort of keeping his balance.

"Everything!"

Tuesday threw up his scrawny chicken-arms about how he was being kept in the dark by everyone. Honestly, it was like they were all in on the joke.

"Fricking cryptic nerdlinger bull..."

But Tuesday didn't get a chance to turn all the way back around before being violently tagged by Trace's brawny shoulder. Seeing as though she had to cross nine metres of aisle to connect with him, this time Tuesday was more than offended: he was positively stabby.

"Hey, Fridge, what did you get?" he snapped from the floor.

Trace didn't miss a step as she answered.

"A second chance." Her jackboots pounded hard as blacksmith hammers. "One minute thirty before you're a trapped corpser. Rot slowly, insect."

Getting shakily to his feet, alternating between the distant plinth and the eternity of dangerous knickknacks, Tuesday realised he'd been doing this the stupid way. Spending a couple of precious moments to think through his plan, Tuesday immediately realised this wasn't the time for double-checking or verifying sources or including a proper bibliography at the end: it was time to act.

"Hey, TenKay Vault?"

"Yes?" the voice replied.

Tuesday pointed at the opposite side of the aisle, safely out of range of his squishy and crunchy bits.

"I want you to find the most dangerous gun in here, and put it right there."

The TenKay Vault paused.

"That is an extremely hazardous request. Prior to fulfilling that desire, I highly recommend that you should read through all sixteen volumes of our Work Health & Safety documentation and complete the subsequent written..."

"Give me the gun!" Tuesday yelled as loud as possible, body arcing and contracting in rage.

There was another moment's pause, followed by a sign of movement from a long, long way down the aisle. A white cell roughly the size of one of The Unison's infamous Comfort Cubes slid along the corridor at top speed before coming to an instant halt exactly where Tuesday's finger was pointing. While the ultra-clean chamber was big enough to unbearably squeeze a Human prisoner, its inorganic contents were loosely packed in bubble wrap. What must have been The Perfection's idea of a "gun" was an unholy mess of pipes and wiring weaved together into a chaotic multi-coloured neuron map, and a number of stamps hinted that the lump might be powered by a miniature fusion reactor. Sitting atop a traditional frame, handle, trigger and trigger guard made from lightweight Densite fibres, there didn't appear to be a slot for clips or ammo chains or cartridges. A seriously steampunk crank was bolted halfway down its short, stubby body, its purpose a mystery. Tuesday squinted at what appeared to be occult protection symbols daubed on it in red.

Carefully looking down the weapon's barrel as though showing mild caution somehow made such idiocy any less lethal, Tuesday was surprised to see there was no hole bored into the weapon. It was just a solid cylinder made from some unknown metal.

"What is this thing?" Tuesday muttered.

The TenKay Vault told him. Tuesday's eyes went wide as Frisbees.

*

Cussing in the hope swear words would somehow help him cross the distance faster, Tuesday's boots thunked out of synchronisation. Tucking the gun under his armpit, arms firing like pistons, he consulted his retinals to see how long he had left until the gateway closed for good.

He didn't like the number at all.

Chest hitching and spasming, Tuesday could taste blood and chlorine as his tar-encrusted lungs were treated to some truly harrowing effort. He coughed explosively, sending out small lumps of dark green phlegm with each wracking gag. Shimmering white dots danced in front of his eyes, but rather than a relaxing screensaver on his retinal implants it was just the Cough Fairies most heavy smokers are familiar with to some degree. He ignored them.

Tuesday began to slow, and gave a grunt of pain as something stabbed him right in the kidney. It took a second to realise it was a cramp. What was most surprising about the cramp was that it hadn't happened the instant he burst into a sprint from a standing start.

Far away, the only gateway out of this pocket dimension wobbled and visibly shrank a metre or so, leaving little more than a thin letterbox of space for Tuesday to fit through. His heart dropping down somewhere into the region of his bowels, Tuesday found himself doing a weird kind of loping stagger as the cramp refused to go away. Jamming his fingers right into the sore spot, he pushed as hard as he could and twisted. Gritting his teeth, he fought on until the numbers on his retinals turned red. A little message superimposed itself over his field of vision, stating the facts.

Impossible to reach destination at current speed in remaining time.

He slowed, then halted altogether.

Trapped. He was trapped in here. He was going to starve and dehydrate and suffocate all alone, rotting away, never to be seen by Human eyes again. It was over.

Nobody would come for him. Honestly, it was a wonder the others had put up with him for this long, let alone return for his corpse. He wondered if they had a bottle of Chateau Cardboard saved up for just this occasion.

Of course they did! Everyone hated him. Everyone wanted him to fail.

But then Tuesday thought outside the box for a moment. He clicked his fingers and gritted his little black teeth.

"Vault? Get me to the middle of that platform as fast as possible."

He'd expected some minor whiplash or at least a jolt, but The TenKay Vault proved the amazing quality of its gravitational controls by firing Tuesday like a horseshoe nail from a slingshot. Over a hundred metres passed in two seconds, followed closely by the endlessly-tall red pillar that marked the start of this aisle. He cringed, but easily skimmed by the solid object without getting splattered all over its skin.

Hugging the crank-gun hard to his chicken chest, aiming face-first towards the upcoming gateway, Tuesday's mouth fell open as the portal wobbled and closed another hand span. Twisting his body straight as a missile, Tuesday tried to keep his eyes open as The TenKay Vault launched him at the gateway even faster, but then the worst happened: an instant away, the portal shuttered closed to a mere pinprick like a closing camera lens, and Tuesday's last thought was so brief that it was more of a split-second realisation than anything complicated.

I'm about to die...again.

Several things happened at once. There was a violent flash, a horrible feeling like he was a rat caught in a faulty washing machine, and Tuesday peed his orange coveralls just before everything went black.

CHAPTER TWENTY SEVEN

Tuesday ploughed mouth-first into the frost-rimed dirt before his eyes could tell his brain that the tiny remaining pinhole of gateway had swelled open again. In a stroke of luck, he slid through with room to spare. But the instant Tuesday was clear, the portal slammed shut with an echoing bang.

While you would expect Tuesday to be ecstatic about evading a fate worse than suffocating to death in Trace's right armpit, gratitude was hard to muster when you're choking on a crunchy salad of leaf matter garnished with dried-out feline droppings. Just to ruin his day further, Tuesday had barely expelled the foul mass from his mouth when he realised the scissoring portal had taken off a good portion of his left boot...not to mention all five toes on that foot.

Face switching from white to purple in a flash, Tuesday gripped the stump with both hands and twisted it right up to his face like a yoga master. Tuesday's breath caught in his chest, refusing to pump, preventing him from screaming or swearing or both. His industrial-grade frogstomper had been sliced so clean that the cross-section of bone and meat wasn't even bleeding.

Deaf to every question and even to Jimmy's shrill, horrified squeak, Tuesday passed out. Even unconscious, Tuesday still had the presence of mind to keep his mysterious new gun locked under his armpit like a passed-out alcoholic gripping a near-empty bottle of Spugwater Rum.

*

Making the most of a rare Tuesday-free break while also trying to feel sorry for the unconscious semi-amputee, they sat down on a fallen jungle tree to compare notes on their recent spot of looting. Sure, Lana had been the first to snatch and run, followed closely by Jimmy and Trace, but there hadn't been a spare moment to compare notes until now. Unsurprisingly, everyone asked the exact same question in near-perfect unison.

"What did you score?"

Metres away, the last Monolith showed no interest in their conversation, and was instead trying to reopen the malfunctioning gateway by jamming his sausage fingers through the relatively tiny gap of interdimensional tunnelling. The portal was fighting hard to stay shut, though, and he was lucky to stretch it thirty centimetres before it shuttered closed again with a sound like thunder. The Monolith was getting angrier and angrier with each failure, and the survivors did their utmost to avoid doing something stupid, like making eye contact or breathing too loud.

Lana rolled a small black ball in her palm, a sphere roughly the size of the ones rich people used to play twenty-six rounds of Flog. She nodded at Jimmy, who was holding an equally black cylinder.

"Well?" she prompted.

Jimmy looked unsure and anxious. In other words, wearing his standard face.

"TenKay Vault told me this is a Universal Fabricator, kind of the great-great-great grandson of a fourth-dimensional printer," he said slowly, watching their expressions for signs of anger or disappointment. "I know we were supposed to be finding star-killing superweapons and stuff, but then I thought, hey, what if we had a way to make as many star-killing superweapons as we need? This thing has hundreds of thousands of recipes all up, stretching all the way back to the late 21st Century."

Trace raised a finger, face grim. But then, somehow, she softened. She curled her finger back in and lowered her fist, which was her equivalent of patting somebody on the back. But then she locked onto Jimmy as something occurred to her.

"What powers it?" she rumbled.

Jimmy shrugged. Passing the Universal Fabricator to Lana, he watched in surprise as the black cylinder reacted to her touch, unfolding into a storm made of thousands of right-angled triangles. Lana drew her hand away in alarm, but the UF's three-sided components zipped about instead of slapping onto the cold dirt. The triangles finished clicking into a wireframe donut shape the size of a basketball and projected dozens of master template menus in distinct colours: white for medical, red for military-grade destruction, green for terraforming, purple for interstellar manipulation, light blue for genetic engineering, pink for developing and harnessing latent psychic abilities…

"Vault told me I just needed to pop a couple of batteries in to run it," Jimmy finally said, tearing his attention away from the lightshow.

"What kind of batteries?" Trace pressed.

Jimmy blinked a couple of times to remember the number.

"Uh, a couple of one-fifty terawatts. Any brand, but preferable StoreCells."

Lana's hand froze against the Universal Fabricator's intangible shell mid-touch. Leaving her fingertip on the UF for a couple of seconds, she sighed and tapped at the device, causing it to retract into its usual football-sized cylinder. She handed it back to Jimmy without saying a word.

"What?" he asked, already accepting the very worst as absolute fact.

Lana placed a hand on his shoulder. That was never a good sign.

"Jimmy, back in our time, all the fusion reactors on Earth wouldn't add up to one-fifty terawatts combined. I didn't even know batteries of that calibre existed. I doubt the entirety of The Dirty Betty's power grid could muster one percent of one percent of that."

"Reckon we'd have any on them fancy terawatt batteries somewhere on the ship, then?" he asked, not bothering to infuse his words with anything as futile as hope, or even basic elocution.

Lana didn't bother wasting any more air on Jimmy as she turned to Trace.

"Show and tell, Cuddle."

Grumbling violent threats under her breath at how this dainty princess was deluded enough to think it was healthy to tease her name, Trace displayed a filigreed silver cube the size of a walnut.

"It's a Mulligan," she grunted. "It'll fix the biggest mistake in your life. But just the one. I guarantee that everyone in history would have wanted one of these in their pocket."

Jimmy gave a pathetic moan of envy.

"How does it work?" he asked, bright and eager.

Trace turned the Mulligan over, examining its flat, metallic sides. She shrugged.

"Vault said it works passively, so I don't have to hit a button or anything when the time comes. Better yet, those weirdos from The Perfection made this just a couple of months before they all disappeared. It's one of their final creations, so my guess is it'll do some serious spug." She narrowed her eyes into slits at Jimmy. "And yes, it's got a power source built-in."

The Monolith gave a roar of anger, shaking the trees and making everyone jump. Wrenching the gateway wide with a mighty push that made the pneumatic suspension system of his unbreakable armour shriek, the four-metre-tall colossus was about to announce his success to the humans when the worst happened: the portal collapsed with such force that it sucked in the Monolith's head and shoulders faster than a blink. His midsection and spine twisted a full revolution, and the Monolith's legs bent in opposite directions as he was drawn into The TenKay Vault up to his knees. With only his hands and feet poking out, it was like the Monolith had just won the most difficult game of Twister ever played. The gateway continued to squeeze the Monolith's convoluted body, but his invulnerable armour had been squished as far as physics would allow.

Cringing, all the humans could do was watch as he twitched spasmodically. An oily black substance that may have been blood trickled down out of whatever small sections of the Monolith were still left on this side of the Vault.

"Well," Lana managed after a horrified ten seconds, "I think we should call it an afternoon. Ready to head back?"

Trace scoffed.

"What, march through cat-infested jungle for three and a half hours just in case that walking demountable was telling the truth about some death-trap air car? And who's going to carry the gerbil?"

Lana raised the Flog ball and smiled. She put her lips to its surface.

"The four of us to Rem, thanks."

Trace didn't have a chance to call Lana insane before a clap of thunder and a feeling of being pulled sideways in a dozen different directions saw what remained of Humanity translate away from the mountains of Seven Suns to the Formica-cluttered Mess of The Dirty Betty.

Rem was curled up on one of the scuffed tables, fast asleep with his tail barbs lodged tightly into the many gribbles of his gribbly face. Unfortunately, the humans appeared directly above the Drennite, only centimetres from the ceiling. As physics demanded, they crashed into him like rogue meteors. Screaming and flailing in response to what seemed to be a sneak attack, while it only took Rem a couple of seconds to realise he wasn't actually being assaulted by ninja-stealthy raiders, by that point he'd already ventilated every span of skin he could reach. Staggering and holding their gushing injuries, the humans retreated, begging for the bristleworm to stop thrashing.

Rem came to a sharp halt, glaring with every eyestalk.

"How the szlerdkbz did you lot get back on board? How did you get past my perimeter?"

"The Hell just happened?" Tuesday bawled, waking up tangled in a bunch of chairs. "How did we get here?" He jabbed a finger at the stump of his left boot. "And where's the rest of me? Did anyone think to bring it? Of course not! Typical."

"How did you do that?" Trace growled at Lana, holding her weeping side.

Lana held up the little black ball she'd taken from The TenKay Vault, her big reveal somewhat tainted by the fact she'd probably need stitches in three different places. At least she had everyone's attention now.

"People, say hello to the ninety-third iteration of the Carpe Astrum."

*

It was decided this was a conversation best conducted sitting around a table rather than sprawled on the dirty linoleum.

Expecting the very worst – and pretty certain the humans weren't returning from Seven Suns at all, if he was being perfectly honest - before Rem decided to have a nap he'd thought it best to slip all their remaining emergency supplies into the many bandoliers and belts cinched around his limbless bristleworm body just in case, so in a stroke of luck he already had everything at (metaphorical) hand that he needed to stitch or seal injuries shut. As they were mighty low on pain meds, he used a monomolecular-tipped needle to keep the discomfort down.

After a hullaballoo from Tuesday, Rem finally agreed to go and double-check whether they had some sort of special machine that might be able to regrow a foot. Nobody was bleeding to death from their injuries at the moment, so Rem grudgingly went to look for something he was certain they didn't have. If they didn't know better, it would be logical to assume that Rem couldn't stand their company and only needed the flimsiest reason to flee.

"Progress didn't stop when we left," Lana explained to a whole table of dirty looks. "The Carpe Astrum that threw us halfway across the Universe was only the first of its kind. You don't seriously think that The Unison would give up on the dream of safe, reliable and affordable instantaneous travel just because thousands of its most valuable people got horribly incinerated? If science gave up that easily we'd still be living in caves, hooting at fire."

"Explain to me how you can guarantee we won't end up back at Scrote," Trace demanded in a low and dangerous voice.

Lana went to smack the black ball on Formica for emphasis, but thankfully thought better of it.

"They've already rebuilt the Carpe Astrum almost a hundred times, and they ironed out all her kinks a long, long time ago. This version of the Carpe Astrum works exactly as intended, and so did most of her predecessors. I'm certain that what I'm holding will get us to wherever we want to go without any issues."

Jimmy raised his hand. Exhausted by having to be a kindergarten teacher for a man a good twenty years older than she was, Lana nodded at him.

"Yes, Jimmy?"

"If they perfected the design, why did they keep making new ones, then?"

Lana gave a dismissive shrug.

"Efficiency. And miniaturisation, of course. Remember, the two main equilateral triangles that made up the bulk of the original Carpe Astrum were a whopping thirteen kilometres a side, not to mention the much smaller triangles spinning at each of the six vertices. The plan with progress is to always, always go smaller, even when it isn't necessary."

"How small is this latest one, exactly?" Tuesday asked.

He was holding his science gun in the crook of an arm, winding its crank over and over. He hadn't bothered with an explanation yet. As the cranking was a lot less irritating than most of his usual habits, nobody seemed to mind.

Lana put one eye up to the black sphere. Squinting, allowing her retinals to zoom in, she could see the entirety of the Carpe Astrum floating in a dark, dark liquid. The tiny starship was two wireframe equilateral triangles hooked together at an invisible central anchor point - one of them whiter than the driven snow, the other so dark that space itself looked grey in comparison. Like the original Carpe Astrum, they were what's known as Penrose triangles, impossible shapes that should only be able to exist in two dimensions.

She lowered the sphere.

"About thirteen millimetres a side."

Trace scoffed.

"Bullspug. Who's crewing it? Ants?"

"A hyper-intelligent virus, actually." Lana said as though it was the most ordinary thing in the world. "It's a distant relative of the Marbug virus, to be specific. Makes the Squealing Death look harmless as brain cancer. They might be one of the most dangerous microorganisms in this galaxy, but the crew seem happy enough just to have a job. I just have to avoid dropping it...or putting it in my pocket too rough..."

"Or looking at it funny," Tuesday said, still cranking. "We end up in the wrong galaxy, I'm stabbing you in the back of the head, right?"

Jimmy nodded at Tuesday's toy, which appeared to be a small nuclear reactor mounted on a rifle frame. "What have you got there, then?"

Tuesday looked up and kept cranking.

"Gun."

"Clearly," Lana said drily.

"What kind of gun?" Jimmy pressed.

Trace's words were far from civil.

"We have guns."

She drew her kinetic accelerator from its torso holster, spun the trigger guard on her pinkie finger and passed it back and forth between knuckles before smoothly sliding it back into its cricket leather slip. Everyone cringed, knowing exactly what her deceptively small pistol was capable of, so they all relaxed as Trace put it away.

"Tuesday, what sort of gun is it?" Lana pressed.

Tuesday kept cranking.

"A special one."

Lana blinked. "As in..."

"I'll show you later," Tuesday promised. He flinched away as Jimmy reached towards the weapon, as though keeping a grenade out of reach of an inquisitive toddler. This was the first time in five minutes he wasn't winding the gun. "Hands off!"

"I just wanted to see what it was made from," Jimmy argued.

"You'll see what your intestines are made from if you try to touch my stuff again," Tuesday hissed.

"You're very aggressive today," Lana noted.

Tuesday raised his sliced-off boot.

"You're just lucky half my foot is missing, or I'd slam it right up your arse," he growled.

"Your attitude isn't helpful," Lana said sweetly. "Do you need a nap while the grownups talk? The kiddie table is over there."

Tuesday scowled so hard that it was a wonder the architecture of his face hadn't permanently shifted into a whole new setting.

"I know that look," Tuesday said, his voice low. He started cranking again. "You want us to put together some sort of plan. Well, unless the Monolith remembered to give us a giant doggy bag full of kitty steaks, we've got another, what, six weeks of uninterrupted interstellar travel without so much as a cat sausage to share? And as nice as all these knickknacks are, I don't think they're 'saving the galaxy' good." Tuesday glared at the only doorway out of the Mess as he failed to spot Rem. "And what's taking that bug so long? If he makes me hobble all the way to the tram tracks…"

Lana gripped the table and leaned in.

"Getting there won't be a problem. What we do after we arrive, however, will be a problem. A multitude of them. So you can either be part of the solution, or be a thin runnel I flush out of the composting processor tomorrow. Your choice."

Tuesday almost looked amused. Shooting a sideways glance at Trace, who was watching him with a deadpan expression, and then at Jimmy, who was busy violently scratching at the base of his skull to try and soothe the unbearable itchiness and bloody bumps you got from a Peach worm infestation, Tuesday bared his little black teeth chips in a horrible smile.

"Hey, you'd be surprised how many times I've already saved the galaxy." His grin widened. "But I gotta warn you, I've always been a lot better at destroying it."

*

Far below, on the frigid peaks of a Seven Suns' mountain range, the Monolith's still form was caught in a dimensional slit between the prime Universe and the pocket dimension known as The TenKay Vault. His twisted body was motionless, but at least the portal hadn't sliced him off as easily as Tuesday's missing toes. His unbreakable alabaster and gold armour was doubtlessly the reason why.

After six boring minutes of being whipped by icy wind and nosed at by inquisitive mutant felines just beyond the tree line (the black muck dripping from the Monolith's presumed corpse was making them salivate), there was a little twitch from his knee. A few seconds later, a tic spasmed across his spine. But then the suit of armour was silent and unmoving as the grave.

Just as one of the tentacled jungle cats finally gathered the courage to crawl close enough to sniff at the dark puddle, the portal to The TenKay Vault opened as wide as a house and a mighty roar of anger exited, causing avalanches in bordering ranges. The Monolith slid out, his twisted-up body crashing to the underbrush as the gateway vanished with a pop. While his armour was flawless as ever, inside of the invulnerable shell the Monolith was an absolute mess, with limbs and fingers and toes and several vertebrae badly dislocated from their usual settings. Breathing heavily, his wandering joints were clicked back into place with a noise like sheets of bubble wrap getting violently twisted. While he didn't feel pain in a traditional sense, the Monolith wasn't keen to do that again any time soon.

Standing up to his full four-metre loom, the Monolith swept across the mountain range, looking for the humans. Surprisingly, for all his scanners and targeting systems, he couldn't see so much as a footprint or a waft of dissipating body heat that didn't originate from a jungle cat. Squinting, he looked up at the sky, panning back and forth until he saw it: a giant purple corkscrew wrapped around a kilometre-long tube of medical waste. As this vessel hadn't been there yesterday, it didn't take much of a leap to guess it was the ship belonging to his guests. No sooner had the Monolith began to hack into the garbage scow's security registry for more information before it vanished in a burst of lavender-green-yellow light like a fart in a swamp.

Placing his terrifying death's head helmet back on and snapping its seals shut, as the Monolith rose high above the scree he devoted a few moments to considering whether he should have gone with the humans. Sure, he'd been conditioned and programmed to defend and protect this world for literally the rest of time (or until he was superseded by a better product from The Splinters of Russia), but those four represented the last dregs of Mankind. Now that The TenKay Vault was sealed for all time, the Monolith was guarding a tomb world, a useless death-trap of no interest to anyone except the misinformed or the clinically baffled. And honestly, he'd managed to break his programming on a number of occasions, at least by a little tiny bit. Surely he'd be capable of bucking his conditioning enough to guard the last Humans as they sped towards a likely extinction?

By the time he'd finished his considerations, the Monolith found himself perched on the highest tip of the tallest star scraper in this hemisphere, the shining glow stone megalith rising far, far above the blue-tinged clouds. He'd automatically assumed his "bridging up" pose, a giant upper-body flex where he put one foot forward and puffed up his considerable chest and shoulders to look as scary as possible. Gazing across his domain, he soon got sick of thinking about what may have been with the humans, and remembered what he was: a weapon in every sense of the word, but one without a wielder, like a pistol nailed into its holster.

Thankfully, Monoliths weren't known for introspection, or regret, or for having an imagination, so these thoughts passed in moments.

Three kilometres above a great dead white world, the Monolith watched. He would continue his duty until the binary stars of this system swelled to a thousand times their size and burnt out in fifty million years, consuming what little was left of Seven Suns as they bulged and burst like gout-ridden toes. Even as the solar winds consumed him, proving that nothing was "invulnerable" to a pair of intertwined supernovas, the Monolith would watch as he melted away to vapour.

Unfortunately, his end would turn out to be a lot sooner than that.

PART SIX UNPLEASANTNESS FAR, FAR

ABOVE THE DRY RED ONE
CHAPTER TWENTY EIGHT

It was such a simple command, and yet it had gone so wrong.

Seeing as though the survivors had just played an accidental and bloody round of Rock & Roll Wrestling by diving from the ceiling of the Mess onto a bladed insect, Lana was sure to qualify her request to the teeny-tiny Carpe Astrum to avoid any confusion. As the microscopic starship could clearly understand complicated requests, she decided to be very, very specific.

"Take this entire ship a hundred thousand kilometres from Viour," she'd said into the black sphere, choosing her words carefully. She quickly narrowed down her order. "But we want to end up in space, mind, not crashing into a planet or any other stellar object or anything that might damage us. Don't make us appear anywhere fatal, okay?"

Her command had been followed with the customary explosion of lavender-green-yellow light and the feeling of being dragged in a dozen different directions at once, though gilded by a distinct sensation of not being dead. Before anybody could share their joy at being intact and the exact same shape as ten seconds ago, all the lights in the Mess went out. There was the unmistakable sound of error messages spooling up on the burned-out holographic projectors just before red emergency lighting clicked on, and just in case the dullest of humanoids weren't getting the message, the words FULL SYSTEM RESET flashed across the graphene in a thousand shades of fire. This traded places with a system clock that declared it was currently 0001 Hours on January the 1st 1901 AD, then flicked back to announce FULL SYSTEM RESET again for another few moments.

"Did we go back in time?" Jimmy asked quietly, his voice loud in the silence.

Lana tapped at her Omni. Like the walls of the Mess, the pea-sized implant projected a hologram to declare RESETTING followed by three dots and nothing else. Unfocussing her eyes, Lana had a look at her retinal screens. She sniffed in annoyance to see they were claiming the same thing.

"No. Technically speaking, it looks as though the transition gave everything electrical a kick in the bum," she said, trying to sound reassuring, if not overly laden with jargon. "I wouldn't be surprised if everything on the ship is resetting as we speak."

"Except for the gravity," Jimmy muttered, glad not to be ping-ponging about.

"I'm just glad they worked out the kinks to the Carpe Astrum a long, long time ago," Tuesday said mockingly, raising his voice an octave in an appalling imitation of the Cadet.

"A reset is very different to a total system wipe-out," Lana snapped. "I'm kind of half-guessing, to be honest, but I'm sure The Dirty Betty will be fine once it has a chance to restart."

"And how long might your half-guess take?" Trace growled.

Lana tapped at the meat of her left hand. She blinked at a little meter.

"My Omni should be good in twenty minutes. But as for the ship? Could take hours for such an old duck to get her bearings. Could take days for her Stiller Drive to spool up again. I'm just hoping the oxygen generators start up again before we choke."

"And the heaters before we freeze," Tuesday added, rubbing at his upper arms in mock chill.

Rem spat a Low-Dren curse from the doorway as he slithered in.

"Well done, you lot. Stellar work! I'll go see if I can bring everything back online faster, will I? After all, I'm always happy to hop to it whenever you decide to fry my ship with dangerous relics. I'm never giving any of you a lift anywhere ever again…"

"Did you find the foot regenerator yet?" Tuesday called after him.

His question went unanswered. Muttering, within a few seconds Tuesday was back to cranking his mystery gun. Beyond the clicking of its gears, there was total silence until the aural void was finally broken by Jimmy.

"So…"

"No, Jimmy, we didn't go back in time," Lana ground out. "The clocks and calendars just reset themselves. We'll fix them later after we…"

Gravity shifted underfoot, sending them all staggering. Thankfully nobody got crushed to death against a wall or clubbed senseless by flying Formica tables, but the hit was enough to make everyone trip a bit sideways. A second smack sent them stumbling in the opposite direction, sliding across the linoleum and against the starboard wall. They grasped onto whatever they could as the ship turned, mostly grabbing at the rusty holes where long-looted kitchen equipment used to be bolted, or corroded venting slots. The gravity kept on tilting little by little until the starboard wall had technically turned into the ceiling.

Far, far below, the only exit from the Mess was fifteen metres under their swinging feet, more than enough to cripple a person in a dozen ways. Just to make things worse, a worrying grinding noise was slowly increasing within the walls, winding up without any indication it was going to stop.

"Did something hit us?" Tuesday yelled, competing with the cracking.

"No idea, we don't have any scanners or anything we could use to check," Lana shouted back.

There was a deafening crunch from the surface that used to be a linoleum floor, as though the superstructure of the ship was being tortured apart. A deep shudder passed through the graphene and into their bones with an intensity that wobbled marrow. Teeth jackhammering together from the bone-deep rumble, Jimmy managed to ask something useful.

"What about that transparency thing you can do in here? You know, where we can see what's outside the ship?"

Lana might have clapped if she wasn't holding onto a stained vent cover for dear life.

"Rem, can you hear me?" she shouted.

Besides the horrific groaning of The Dirty Betty, there was no sound. Lana was almost at the point of prayer when Rem's image appeared on the inside of her retinal screens, giving the impression a tiny bristleworm floating right in front of her eyeball. She would have to remember to commend his quick-thinking later.

"Bit busy here, Lana. This old hulk is being a total bitch, and I'm working upside down."

"Rem, can you turn on that setting where it seems as though we're all sitting in deep space?"

"What? Why?"

"As you may possibly have noticed, something's screwing with the gravity settings again, which tells me we're probably way too close to something considerable. Seeing as though we've just bucked back in the opposite direction, my guess is there's more than one something considerable, and possibly several something considerable. Can you do it?"

The tiny projection of Rem vanished without a word or so much as a nod. Just as she was about to call the Drennite a rude crunchy-skinned roach-arsed bastard, Lana was treated to a view of the generic darkness of local space. Making sure they didn't lose track of their precarious handholds, the humans got a good look at where the Carpe Astrum had taken them. The black velvet canvas was dotted with a million stars, as you'd expect, but there wasn't anything major enough in the local vicinity to cause the gravity systems of The Dirty Betty to pitch a fit. No asteroids, no rogue comet clusters speeding by, no ten-mile-wide generation ships, no football-shaped World Slugs the size of small moons, nothing. There was a distant yellow star a long way off, sure, but it was at least thirteen light minutes distant. It might as well be in a different system.

"Empty space," Trace growled.

Confused, Lana twisted her neck and back, making sure she hadn't missed anything. To her surprise, out of nowhere a distinctive chalk-red dot appeared on the far wall, as though a space-black cloud had passed across it, finally allowing its rosy roundness to make an appearance. She would have pointed if she had a spare arm.

"Mars?" she managed.

Disregarding the fact that a whole planet had been hidden from view, as Lana regarded the bloody circle she had several horrible realisations all at once. They vied for dominance over five twitching seconds.

"What? Mars isn't dangerous," Jimmy said, unsure of Lana's alarmed expression. The groaning within the walls had calmed down so much that Jimmy's whimpers were now perfectly audible to everyone. "I mean, yeah, I've heard those Transcended wossanames, Martians will kill any living thing what gets too close, but we should be fine if we stay this far off."

"You don't understand," Lana said, using a phrase that would have been an appropriate rebuttal to almost everything her infuriating acquaintances had said to her since she'd had the displeasure of meeting them. "This means we're back in Sol, clearly. Far as we know, that Star Cage is still prowling around, or at the very least it's left behind a few unfolding fleets to lay in wait for all five of their Most Wanted fugitives. But let's not forget there are another dozen Star Cages speeding our way, and they're all going to emerge from a point very, very, very close to where we did when Viour gave us a lift back to the Milky Way. And just to jog your memory..."

"Our exit point was near Mars," Tuesday muttered. He cussed under his breath, which for him was surprisingly close to gentlemanly. "Alright, Viour is clearly nowhere to be seen, and we're needlessly sitting here in a fricking piranha tank. Put those two facts together, and it's time to boogie on elsewhere, clean?"

"Rem, hit the jets," Jimmy shrieked, hoping to be heard by the bristleworm.

"The Dirty Betty is going through a total reset," Trace growled, flinching at the high pitch of Jimmy's wail. "That means there's no chance her Stiller Drive will be back on before life support reboots, and her jets are all sub-light at best." Trace nodded at Lana. "So get your virus mates to zip us out of here."

Latching onto the venting with one hand, an elbow and both knees, Lana carefully fetched the tiny black ball from her pocket, holding it firmly to avoid any chances of it flying out of her hand and smashing on the distant floor. Last thing they needed was a Marbug pandemic on board. She spoke slowly and carefully.

"Take us back to exactly where we were in orbit around the world of Seven Suns."

Instead of an interstellar transition of exploding light and colour and multi-dimensional pushing, the ball faded from obsidian to bone white and formed a complex series of words. Blinking, Lana read the message out loud as it appeared.

"Requested blue shift transition well exceeds the maximum safe travel distance that can be covered per day. Only short-ranged transitions, such as high-orbit-to-planet, will be possible for the next twenty-three hours and fifty-one minutes."

"So we're stuck in potentially hostile space," Trace pointed out, as though justifying the severe kicking she was about to give to anyone within reach of her handholds.

"Could this get any worse?" Jimmy sobbed.

He was given a silent, yet comprehensive answer by the planet-sized Star Cage that appeared just ten thousand kilometres away from where the humans were desperately clinging to a wall. The bone-coloured lattice of invulnerable limpet ivory loomed closer like a man's boot towards a cockroach, and as the hundred-kilometre-wide purple shard of star kernel at the Star Cage's very core lit to an electric lavender, the smart money was on guessing how many seconds it would be until they were all mushed to paste.

CHAPTER TWENTY NINE

She should have been dedicating her entire headspace to how they were going to vamoose into another star system, or at least prolong the eight seconds of freedom they had remaining into double digits, but all the pressure finally got too much to bear and Lana's brain decided to have a useless epiphany instead.

Knowing there are countless galaxies draped across a Universe that is without beginning or end, and remembering that the light of every one of the stars within them is destined to journey across the void as an afterimage long after their gas reserves have boiled away to nothing, then why was the night sky a relatively empty black? Surely the vacuum should have been a solid milky white wall unspoiled by a single dot of darkness?

When Lana returned to the present - half deafened by the screams of Jimmy, Tuesday and Trace and barely holding onto a vent slot that was getting more and more slippery with palm sweat – it occurred to her this quasi-mystical insight was probably just a side effect of the nervous breakdown she'd finally slipped into after years and years of pressure. What had been a stunning insight moments ago now felt like drooling gibberish, but Lana didn't have long to regret her descent into insanity when the wall she and the other humans were clinging to split open along the seams, sending them plunging to their deaths.

It was an understatement to say that the steep drop transforming into a mere slippery dip was a surprise, but it was definitely a welcome one. Twitching violently as she slid along the pitching linoleum, Lana still possessed enough logical deduction to understand how a direct drop onto unforgiving grid work had become a fun ride: the incoming Star Cage was now close enough to affect the gravity of The Dirty Betty, allowing her to resume the classic configuration of floor down, ceiling up, and walls to the sides as most sane architects preferred. Their landing wasn't gentle by any means, but it wasn't a fatal plunge off a cliff, either.

There wasn't any time to play slip-and-slide all day, though, as a Star Cage was dominating the far wall, and everyone thought something should probably be done about it. Unless they jet packed out of the medical waste processing ship, pushed it towards Mars and begged the local Transcended maniacs for political sanctuary, however, Lana was all out of suggestions.

Lana glanced at Mars again, almost swearing she'd seen movement of some kind, before whipping back towards the Star Cage opposite. Three enormous unfolding dreadnoughts were excreted from the colossal parking garages blistering the white lattice, but the stellar display flickered and transformed into a single giant screen revealing the purple-skinned Prime pulling the Slidge equivalent of a smile with its clicky beak and prehensile tongues. It hung from golden, jewel-encrusted ceiling hoops by three load-bearing arms, while each of its more skilful trinity of hands furiously manipulated sphere computers. The biggest surprise of the day, however, was that the Prime didn't bother explaining the minutiae of what it was doing, or why it was doing it, or even how it would finally have its revenge. If anything, the Prime was dismissive.

"We've been over this before," it summarised. "I'll see you real soon."

The video call ended abruptly, revealing that the trio of dreadnoughts were now moving to intercept The Dirty Betty very, very quickly. As always, the hulking vessels fanned open, spraying a seemingly endless gout of destroyers, heavy corvettes, fighters and unmanned drones. While this was clearly a time for action, all the humans could do was stare at their approaching doom…except for Tuesday, who was back to cranking his gun.

Zoning out for far too long, Lana turned sharply towards Trace.

"The Mulligan," she snapped. "Get it to take us back to Seven Suns. Undo this trip."

Trace stared at Lana as though she'd just been asked to reproduce by mitosis on video and upload the footage to the Link.

"I don't know how to use it. It's meant to be automatic."

"Uh, guys?" Jimmy murmured, watching literally tens of thousands of hostile alien ships sweep towards the relatively diminutive kilometre of unsanitary graphene and glass known as The Dirty Betty. The sheer numbers involved in this incoming pincer movement was blurring their view of the Star Cage. "I know this whole ship is loaded with enough explosives and acid bombs to reduce us to vapour, and that it would be the ultimate show of spite to detonate the whole thing just as we're being boarded on all sides, but can somebody come up with a better idea than scuttling the ship, please?"

Nobody had a chance to offer any suggestions before their brains were overloaded with a thought as loud as point-blank thunder. The humans could only grip their temples and scream, screwing their eyes closed as words drilled into their skulls. Barely able to see through their slitted eyelids, it seemed as though the entirely of the three unfolding fleets heard the same booming and paused their advance. Even the unmanned drones stopped dead, indicating you didn't have to be organic and sentient to feel pain from this psychic smack down.

The words cut like a scalpel.

I AM HERE TO PARLAY. THESE FIVE ARE UNDER MY PROTECTION UNTIL WE HAVE SPOKEN.

The mysterious declaration quickly faded, but their headaches took a lot longer to soothe. The Prime reappeared back on the wall, replacing the panorama of its stilled fleets. The three eyes arranged in a triangle around its beak – one small, one medium and one huge – were bloodshot and moving independently, as though dazed. There was a possibility the channel had been switched back on by accident. Unfortunately, the psychic burst didn't seem to have caused the Prime any real damage.

Now faced by something considerable, the Prime's next words were far less casual.

"I am the Prime of this Star Cage. I represent the Twelve Hundred races that reside aboard her, and I speak on behalf of the greater Primacy. I demand the identification of whoever or whatever just employed that weaponised voice, and I swear that any further...surprises will be answered with the utmost of aggression."

The humans all sensed something behind them. Spinning a half revolution fast as tops, they turned to see a miracle: the world of Sprout now sat between The Dirty Betty and Mars, but rather than the barren and dead vista they were treated to six weeks ago, the former crop world had been transformed into a verdant emerald sphere. The Green had clearly ceased its subterranean lurking to instead cover Sprout's surface, restoring the huge, networked brain of flora to how it used to be before getting annihilated by The Unison's fleets. It was unclear whether Sprout had just arrived in-system or just been sitting there invisibly until Viour was ready to reveal its presence, but that was irrelevant. What mattered was Viour had moved a piece of psychic artillery across hundreds of lightyears to come to their rescue, and all of a sudden the humans weren't feeling as collectively boned.

The Prime's reaction was interesting. It just hung there from the ceiling hooks for a time, silent as it squeezed and relaxed clusters of multi-knuckled fingers around its three computer spheres. Lana wondered if the Prime had been maintaining direct control over the unfolding fleets with them – after all, there were three spheres and three unfolding dreadnoughts – before realising this was an utterly useless thing to be focusing on right now.

Lana turned back in time to see an image of Viour's royal-blue bicycle-seat helmet appear on the opposite side of the Mess, obscuring Mars and the mobile world of Sprout. Having Viour, the last of The Apex, face off with the Prime was like witnessing two gods debate over the destiny of mortals. The lenses along Viour's helmet spun and spiralled as she devoted her considerable mind to a multitude of separate tasks.

Rather than begin negotiations, the Prime spun one of the computer spheres around and around, circling through so many audio clips and videos and static pictures and graphs that the device gave off a random demonic howls as it went. Viour didn't so much as twitch, waiting with the patience of death. The Prime proved that it had found the right file by clearing its throat.

"Am I speaking with the same being who attacked one of my unfolding fleets a number of years ago above the world of...?"

Tutting, the Prime spun the computer sphere again, searching for records about the former Apex home world. Tuesday, however, yapped into the silence like the most annoying of Chihuahuas.

"Scrote. It was called Scrote."

Trace glared hot death at Tuesday. Jimmy shuddered and closed his eyes, waiting to die. Viour's next words were gentle against the tension, though there was a distinct undercurrent, as though something was very close to igniting.

"I am not here to justify my actions; I am here to make something clear. In your endless construction of Star Cages, the Twelve Hundred and the Primacy that led them plundered every possible resource they could. You took countless worlds that were already incinerated by a war your species started, worlds that would require millennia of careful nurturing to repair, and reduced them from cinders to nothing. You will not be permitted to repeat your past atrocities. None of the intelligent species in this expanse want to be a part of your Primacy, of a despotic regime that keeps its slaves starving and sick and in constant fear. So this is what's going to happen: either we establish strict conditions between your Star Cage and the local inhabitants of the Milky Way in preparation for the arrival of the many, many reinforcements we know you have on the way, or you will be fighting a war that I guarantee you will lose in very short order. This is entirely your choice."

There was silence for a good twenty seconds. The Prime seemed to consider Viour's words, silently locking eyes with the triangles of soulless lenses studded along a helmet shaped like a bicycle seat. Giving a click of its beak, the Prime delivered the Primacy's official response by tapping each of the three computer spheres at once.

What happened next was so fast that the humans would have needed to replay it on their retinals at one percent speed to make anything out. Still perfectly motionless, locked in the same alignment and angle as when they'd come to a synchronised halt, the massive swarm of unfolding Primacy vessels fired as one. Funnily enough, it was at this exact moment Lana realised The Dirty Betty was sitting directly between Sprout and the Star Cage, which was not nice to know. She would have paid big money for somebody to flush out that knowledge with a Psych-in-a-Box right about now.

A phalanx of antimatter javelins whipped past the purple graphene spiral at two thirds the speed of light, representing enough raw firepower to reduce worlds into memories. The smart missiles arced around The Dirty Betty, ignoring the most harmless factor in this theatre of war, and flew in random zigzags to throw off any automated countermeasures. As the antimatter javelins converged, aiming for the emerald sea of plants with pinpoint accuracy, a crackle of electricity passed along The Green faster than lightning. The incoming swarm of planet-killer ordinance stopped cold, halting as though the laws of physics had given up and gone home, and two long moments passed. If Viour was considering what to do with the missiles, it didn't take her long to decide.

None of the Primacy dreadnoughts had a chance to retreat so much as a metre before their own missiles flooded back towards them, reducing the armoured hulks to glowing dust in one-fifth of a moment. The coordinated flash was blinding even from within the UV-blocking display walls nestled in the Mess, and the humans swore and covered their faces in pain. If it wasn't for their retinal screens instantly dimming right down in response to the explosion, permanent eye damage would have been on the cards.

As was the case with space battles, the explosions were all utterly, chillingly silent. There was, however, a psychic rumble that swept from Sprout, a jarring sensation of frightening power that shook everything it touched. Viour may be on their side, but what she'd nurtured The Green into terrified them.

Blinking away the maelstrom, the small war was already sorted. All three unfolding fleets were gone, vanished down to the last trace of metal and splinter of glass. Between the Mess and the Star Cage was a clear expanse of empty vacuum.

Lana was just about to cheer, certain there was no chance the Prime would be insane enough to do anything except open diplomatic channels, when the worst happened: Star Cages dotted the sky, popping into reality after a long, long eight year journey through a million insane realities across seven galaxies. Some of them were a sickly grey-brown, as though their limpet ivory shells were rotting with age, and one or two of them had flickering star kernels at their cores that looked about a week away from burning out altogether. In a single minute the fleet of Star Cages had grown to thirteen.

The same Prime as before appeared on the wall again. Its expression could only be described as evil.

"I believe I'm ready to discuss terms."

The Star Cages vomited out hundreds of thousands of unfolding fleets, and as the dreadnoughts scissored open they filled the sky with so much ceramic plating and bristles of stellar weaponry that space itself seemed cramped. Just like before, the humans were sandwiched directly between two enemy nations, the piggy in the middle of a warzone. And with the full system restart taking its time, there was nothing they could do about it.

Turning back towards Mars, hoping beyond hope that Viour had planned for this situation, the humans' prayers were answered when another fourteen worlds covered in The Green shimmered into existence around Sprout in a defensive pattern, proving Viour had been hiding her trump cards. Lighting crackled across their verdant forests, occasionally hopping between the worlds of psychic artillery in a friendly way.

The Primacy fleets paused, probably assessing what they were going to do against this new threat. The stillness and silence was agony. Knowing this could only end in an apocalypse that would kill everything sentient in the solar system, Lana's brain finally came up with a good idea in what felt like months. Producing the tiny Carpe Astrum from her pocket, however, only invited mocking from Trace.

"Hasn't been twenty-four hours yet, numb-nuts. You can't move us out of the system."

Lana gave a slightly insane smile.

"No, but I can still move things about locally." She glared at the little black orb, silently daring it to stuff up her request. "I want you to move all thirteen Primes here into the Mess...and Viour."

Jimmy didn't have a chance to ask if that was a good idea before an indoor electrical storm blasted jagged runnels along the walls and tore starbursts out of the linoleum. Sure, the Primes materialised just as requested, but it was pure luck nobody got cut in half by a stray lightning bolt. Slidge royalty rained with the jangle of bracelets and bangles and crowns and ceremonial armour made from perfectly-cultured limpet ivory and precious metals. Most of them had aubergine skin showing through the few gaps in their jewellery and weighed twice as much as Trace, through the lavender hue of a handful indicated they'd ascended the throne early, with their skinny limbs and acne only serving as further proof of their adolescence. One Prime was fully twice the size of the others, and as its midnight skin was decorated by countless failed assassination attempts, it didn't take much insight to see this one was different to the others.

Understandably confused, it was only half a moment until the Primes noticed each other. Rather than showing relief or comradery or even acknowledging they were facing a mutual enemy that really, really demanded their full attention, the royals instantly drew their weapons and faced off, screaming threats and hatred. They shook unfolding halberds and scythes with their more limber arms, and lumbered about throwing warning slaps with their bulkier limbs. When one of the young lavender ones draw an elaborate pistol Lana knew it was time to intervene.

"Flush their weapons into space," she whispered to the teeny Carpe Astrum.

And with that the Primes were unarmed. Stumbling mid-swing, crashing into each other with empty air rather than blades, the purple ones were distracted by a loud yelp from Lana as the orb in her hand heated to scalding. Letting go of the Carpe Astrum, shaking her blistering fingers, a sphere filled with one of the most dangerous viruses known to man turned neon white as it fell towards the floor. Just as it was about to hit the Lino and explode, Lana lifted her left dress shoe and caught it smoothly on her toe. Cricket leather crackled and smoked.

"Nice catch," Viour hissed from behind her, the whisper only inches from Lana's ear. "Care to explain how I got here?"

CHAPTER THIRTY

If the Primes were meant to be masters of diplomacy, unflappable leaders with wall-to-wall charisma and dagger-keen wit, calm in the face of any obstacle or threat, they sure as Hades weren't showing it.

Used to being waited on hand-and-hand by large households of Primacy Guard, Ministers, Advisors and pleasure slaves, the Primes stuck to what they knew: bellowing for their retinues to appear and obey their commands. As their households were currently tens of thousands of kilometres of vacuum away and obviously couldn't hear them, this cacophony went unanswered for the first time in their lives. As the thirteen shouted louder and louder over the top of each other, it wasn't long before the aliens started slapping each other, knocking off crowns in petty tussles. It didn't take long for the scuffles to escalate.

As their dedicated weapons had been teleported safely into space, one of the Primes improvised by slipping a valuable bracelet over its clusters of fingers to use as rudimentary brass knuckles. The first punch landed with a yelp from two different Primes, as the punchee ended up with a dozen fortunes-worth of diamonds lodged in its forehead and eye socket, and the puncher broke eight fingers.

The huge midnight-black Prime was the only one who had remained silent and still up to this point, but after watching the pathetic brawling of its embarrassing peers it finally cleared its throat. As though conditioned from birth, the lesser Primes instantly went silent and lowered their central faces to the linoleum. Allowing the oldest Prime to trudge through the group, avoiding its focus, the elder approached the line of humans to say something on behalf of its peers. However, focussing beyond them with three gummy eyes, the old one's beak trembled violently at the sight of Viour's looming suit of amplification armour, tracing over her magnificent antlers. Viour's shell glowed a brighter blue in response, her white-gold ornamentation shining.

Raising one of its less-arthritic limbs, the Prime bellowed a single word.

"Apex!"

The youngest, palest Prime angled its central mass, the Slidge equivalent of tilting its head.

"A what?"

Viour ascended towards the ceiling at the name of her dead species. The twenty chainlike tentacles that met up at her groin sockets rippled as she increased her elevation, panning her triangles of eye lenses back and forth like stalking lions. As always, her armoured suit possessed some innate quality that inspired awe, something that made it more than a fancy slab of thoughtmetal she had literally woven just from the power of her mind.

All the humans wisely got out of Viour's way as she drifted forwards, lowering her eye lenses to the oldest Prime, almost like she was bowing in respect. Everyone could hear her gentle thought as it rippled between minds, and could sense its mocking edge even easier.

"It is nice to know we are not forgotten, after all."

"Some of us remain burdened to remember that which deserves to be forgotten," the hulking Prime shot back, showing its mind was lot faster than its limbs.

The youngest Prime leaned in towards the old one again. The whisper easily bounced off the walls of the Mess.

"So…what are we supposed to do if we see an Apex, exactly?"

The ancient Prime blinked a few times, cleared his throat in a deliberately casual way, and bolted for the doorway on all six limbs. This instantly turned into a stampede, and if it wasn't for Rem slithering through the bulkhead at this exact moment then the humans might have spent the rest of their day playing hide-and-seek with Slidge royalty in every nook and crevasse of the ship.

Rem's wiggly face was instantly armed with three Drennite-forged mass-annihilation pistols, and the way he swept the weapons back and forth proved he didn't have any issues covering thirteen separate targets at once.

Sliding to a halt half a dozen metres from the door, one of the pluckier Primes produced a computer ball and ran a scanning app over one of Rem's guns. The Prime clearly didn't like the reading, and backed off. Rem herded them back into the Mess.

"We will be rescued," the oldest Prime swore, speaking as an expert in staying alive. "There is nothing our people will not do, will not kill, will not defile, to keep us safe. However, if you release us now, without further incident, we may deign to be lenient with you."

"We just want to talk," Lana said, her voice quavering.

The Primes turned their attention to her, a murder of crows noticing a fieldmouse scurrying in their midst. Despite the many scoffing beaks, Lana raised her palm at Viour, silently and politely requesting a chance to negotiate. It took a couple of seconds, but Viour nodded.

"Like Viour said, we're here to figure things out," Lana said. "It's a big galaxy, so I'm sure we can sort some kind of deal that makes everyone happy."

"Or at least prevent a few genocides," Tuesday muttered, cranking his gun another revolution.

The Prime they'd already dealt with on numerous occasions, the one who had ordered their internment in a virtual reality prison for eight long years while their limbs were hacked off and regenerated, reducing their flesh and bone into plastic, scoffed.

"The five of you are wanted criminals who have perpetrated numerous unforgivable crimes against the Primacy. I don't trust a thing any of you say. Your credibility is minus five million. Now, you may have somehow zapped us aboard your slum of a ship, but the games end now. Either you release us and surrender without condition, or the combined ground forces of thirteen Star Cages are going to board this garbage scow and flood her with so many heavily-armed assault troopers that the first wave alone could clog every inch of this ruin with their dead flesh and blood." The Prime lifted one of its computer spheres as a demonstration. "So why should I listen to anything you say?"

"Two reasons," Trace growled. She gave the Prime a V with her index and middle fingers, a gesture that seemed lost on the alien. "One, because I know those computers are lie detectors, and two, because The Dirty Betty was a punishment ship used to punish unsuccessful terrorists, and that means she's laced with enough explosives and acid bombs from end to end to vaporise us all."

Lana gave Trace an impressed glance, but didn't say anything. Right now, it was much more vital to observe how the Slidge responded to this Ace card rather than praising Trace's obvious talents for intimidation and threats. One by one, the Slidge-built computer spheres glowed a bright blue, confirming Trace was telling the truth. The most hated of the Primes went to speak again, but the old, darkest one rested a twenty-fingered hand on one of its six shoulders. The smaller one backed off, clearly deferring to its elder.

"You must understand that after eight years of skipping through realities without a restock, our Star Cages require substantial, immediate resources," the old one said plainly. "And we are but the beginning of a flood. There are tens of thousands of Star Cages and Sun Lattices waiting to pour through after us, so in another eight years the entire Primacy will be here. So while we are happy to negotiate with the locals if we want something from their domains, it is a fact that the Primacy is the greatest military power you will ever see, and that means we can and will make executive decisions if and when we want to. We will not touch your inhabited worlds without good cause, but we will take what we need from anywhere else. We will not agree to anything short of this."

"So in other words," Jimmy said thoughtfully, trying to carve through the pretty words and political poetry, "you're going to take what you want regardless of what anyone says, and you have zero intention of doing otherwise?"

"Ah," the old Prime said happily, relaxing on the palms of its six hands. "I see you understand. Very well, we have an agreement."

"No, no!" Lana fumed. "We don't!"

The old Prime made a deep noise in its throats. It was probably best this wasn't translated.

"Person, we will never agree to anything that has the potential to weaken the Primacy. So unless you can sate our needs, we have nothing more to discuss. Surely this logic is not too complicated?"

"Hey, we have the royalty of thirteen Star Cages stuck in a room," Trace growled. "We're going to come to an agreement eventually. It's as simple as that."

The old one waved away her words, unintimidated.

"You're not listening: Primes literally cannot make decisions that weaken the Primacy. We all possess a substantial amount of power and authority, yes, but that is a taboo that we cannot cross. If we agreed to your weakening terms, we would all be executed as traitors on sight and replaced by members of our extended families. And it goes without saying that our replacements will not honour any of our deals."

Lana swore under her breath. Before she could attack this point from another angle, Jimmy spoke.

"How many terawatts are your purple star thingies?"

All the Primes fixed him with the same universal question in their pupils: who was this being, exactly, and who invited him? Was he a pet of some kind? Was he usually allowed to speak without permission?

Tuesday snorted in disgust. "Don't try to use big words, Jimmy."

Jimmy waved at the sweeping panorama of Star Cages. He jabbed his finger at the closest one, indicating the hundred-kilometre-wide purple supergiant kernel locked at its core. Like all the Primacy's star kernels, the ball of superheated plasma was tightly contained in an enormous magnetic field, and had been providing the power needs of its residents for six thousand years. Jimmy kept pointing at it over and over again.

"Terawatts?" he squeaked. "How many?"

The old Prime sighed at Jimmy's frustration.

"Your animal appears to be faulty. You may take a moment to remove him from the room, if you so wish."

Lana narrowed her eyes at Jimmy, annoyed that he was making a difficult process even worse, but then something clicked in her gaze. She nodded at him, then turned back to the old Prime.

"The star kernels that you use for power," she repeated. "How many terawatts can they produce? How much energy is left over once all your life support needs are met?"

Clearly not in the mood to get mathematical, but also keen to avoid being killed by at least one side of this conflict, the oldest Prime silently flicked its fingers at one of the younger Slidge, one who was so close to adolescence it was more pink than purple. Checking a computer ball, five seconds later the juvenile whispered in the old one's ear hole. It nodded.

"I won't bore you with specifics," the young Prime said eagerly, "but the unused energy output of just one star kernel is magnitudes above that. I believe you would use the term 'petawatts' in this case."

Lana visibly relaxed, high on a feeling of utter relief. Keen as salt at being able to contribute to these proceedings and taking the pleasure on Lana's face as express permission, Jimmy produced the football-sized cylinder he'd recovered from The TenKay Vault. The Slidge backed off a few steps, as though expecting him to shoot them with it or throw it like a grenade. Jimmy's smile faltered at the faux pas.

"No, look, it's safe, it's just a Universal Fabricator. It contains templates for everything Mankind has developed since we started domesticating wolves and painting on cave walls with our poo, and all you need to do is plug it into a big enough power supply and hit the START button. For instance, I know the Artificial Intelligence in charge of your main computers are so mental and homicidal from rot that you can only use it safely in microsecond bursts, so wouldn't it be great if you could repair it, or maybe even replace it entirely? Wouldn't it be nice to be able to install machines that produce food and water and medicine and entertainment and, and, and, hospitals and fix all your life support and gravity problems? And I'm pretty sure you could manufacture any material you wanted, too: steel, gold, uranium, Densite, diamonds, maybe even that fancy limpet ivory your Star Cages are cultured from? Wouldn't giving you everything you need mean you don't need to take it? Wouldn't this just fix everything?"

The old Prime narrowed its three eyes, waiting for Jimmy's words to be checked for veracity. It inhaled sharply through its beaky nostril at the soft chimes of confirmation and didn't even bother to seek the council of its peers, the choice obvious. The Prime held out a flexible limb, unfurling a twenty-fingered palm the size of a pizza box.

"We will need to confirm there are no drawbacks to your offer. But if this…"

"Universal Fabricator," Jimmy said brightly.

"…Universal Fabricator truly allows us to repair our Star Cages, you would become the Primacy's greatest friend and ally."

"I remember what happened last time we was told that," Trace said darkly, her hand automatically creeping towards her kinetic accelerator. "And I'm never forgetting it."

The old Prime ignored the goading, waiting for Jimmy to hand over the UF. However, Jimmy's face collapsed in utter despair at a thought, and he quickly drew back the lump. He tucked it into his armpit as the Slidge muttered amongst themselves.

"Uh, actually, we've kind of promised that we wouldn't give anything we took from The TenKay Vault to any non-Humans. It's a sort of…explosive promise. As in, a fatal one. We'd all die instantly if I gave this to you, is what I'm saying."

The old Prime smacked the Lino with all six hands in anger.

"Are you clowning me with false promises?" Half a dozen palms slammed down again, louder this time. Its eyes started to turn pink, then red. "I agree to the terms you stated. Give me the device, and let us all leave freely." It jabbed a long finger at Rem, who was still alternating his Drennite guns between targets. "And tell your insect to lower his weapons. I tire of his attempts at intimidation. I've walked off direct hits from more substantial hardware before breakfast."

Before anyone could ask how the Slidge knew what a "clown" was, Tuesday snickered loudly, attracting everyone's attention. The crank of his gun was still turning, click, click, click, clicking, and the constant background noise finally sent the old Prime over the edge.

"What are you doing?" it demanded. "Why are you incessantly winding that object?"

Tuesday bared his little black teeth in a horrible smile. Now he had everyone's attention, he shrugged.

"I could simply tell you what it is, but the way I remembers it, all of them Apex were able to figure out what any piece of technology is just by looking at it, right?"

Viour gave an almost imperceptible nod. Tuesday held out what looked like a small nuclear reactor mounted on a rifle frame, and Viour zoomed her eye lenses back and forth, in and out, inspecting the alleged gun for the better part of five seconds, a relative eternity for such a basic mental exercise. To everyone's surprise, Viour's suit of amplification armour floated a couple of centimetres backwards. For one of The Apex to have such a reaction got everyone's attention.

Tuesday seemed to find all this highly amusing.

"This here's what's known as a Generation Gun," he explained, winding and winding. He panned its solid barrel across the crowd of Primes one-handed, cranking the whole way. "See, far as guns go, it isn't a mass driver or nuthin. It won't blow up like a round of antimatter, and it's a one-shot kind of deal. But the beautiful part about getting shot with a Generation Gun is that it won't kill you; no, this thing will completely remove you from the space/time continuum, cut you from history like you never existed, placing reality on a whole new track where you were never even conceived, let alone born."

Tuesday crossed his arms, panning across the Primes again. He seemed to enjoy their frightened reactions.

"But it turned out those geezers from The Perfection weren't finished there. Nope, not even close. Because every time you twist this crank," Tuesday clicked the dial the equivalent of one minute on an analogue clock for emphasis, "whatever bugger you blast clear out of existence won't be the only casualty. Nope. For every click…"

He clicked it.

"…this beauty also kills the generation that comes before your victim. So if one click kills you and your parents…"

Click.

"…then another click kills your grandparents on both sides, too."

"Loki's prehensile penis," Jimmy gasped, going from milky pale to butter yellow. It was like watching somebody get severely travel sick without moving a centimetre.

"Seeing as though I've been cranking it for, oh, say, the last hour or so, making revolution after revolution, winding it around and around, I'm pretty sure this little treasure should be capable of excising the entire genetic line of the Slidge back to when you first knuckled out of the oceans, if not back to the level of bacteria." Tuesday lowered his gaze, smile broad and psychotic. Shadows pooled under his eyes. "Now, to be clear, I've had a really, really bad time with everyone in this room, and I've been giving a lot of thought as to who is going to stop existing. Because let's face it: you all deserve to be uncreated, as far as I see it."

"Tuesday," Trace growled, reaching for his shoulder.

Tuesday spread his arms in a "Really? You sure you want to do that?" kind of gesture, and pointed the barrel at her pieced eyebrow. As there was no guaranteed way for anyone to safely disarm Tuesday without running the risk of de-existing their entire species, Viour chose this moment to intervene. She had silently allowed the humans to sort everything out up until now, but Tuesday's insanity proved her trust had clearly been misplaced.

"Robert," Viour whispered, reaching out with all her twenty chains. There was a little mental push behind the thought. "Give me the Generation Gun. Carefully, please."

Tuesday squinted at the bicycle-seat helmet in offense.

"Really? I'm not some jumper you can talk off a rooftop. Better beings have tried logic on me, and it never works."

Viour stopped dead, tilting her helmet. Her eye lenses buzzed back and forth between the four humans, then snapped towards Rem.

"I thought I told you to infect them all with Peach worms?" Viour hissed, her anger a skin-crawling sensation to everyone with a brain stem.

Rem flinched under the weight of the looks of betrayal. He flicked his barbed tail in an "Aw, shucks" kind of way.

"Explains why he never found that cure he promised," Trace growled in Rem's direction.

"My body was too hostile for the Peach worm to survive," Tuesday said, baring his teeth. "Your Judas tried."

Viour huffed at Rem. "Now I'm glad I've been paying you with the same chest of platinum all these years."

Rem blinked his eye stalks, lowering his guns.

"You what?"

"But why?" Jimmy asked Viour, the core question of his entire life up to this point. "Why would you get Rem to infect us with dangerous parasites? Aren't we meant to be on the same side?"

The scoff from Viour's mind was mocking. She pointed at the Generation Gun in Tuesday's white-knuckled hands.

"This is why. Think about it: I was sending you, a quartet of violent, unpredictable semi-evolved animals to recover some of the greatest technology the Universe had ever seen. I would be foolish to not take precautions. The Peach worms are harmless, and I only had Rem implant them to ensure I could take away your self-control in the event of a serious enough situation."

"Why not just dominate us?" Trace muttered. "We've seen you do it to others."

Viour gave a frustrated mental sigh.

"Yes, and if you recall, those others didn't survive it," Viour corrected. "Domination will seriously injure, if not instantly kill, a lesser mind. Using the Peach worms as a soft trigger was a safer option."

"Actually," Tuesday corrected, "it really wasn't."

And then he shot her right in the face.

CHAPTER THIRTY ONE

Many people had underestimated Tuesday's rodent-like intelligence over the years. And while he was next to useless in almost every practical way, those who were foolish enough to misjudge the sheer depths of his rat cunning often wound up regretting it. Tuesday knew on a cellular level that arrogance could be just as blinding as a hot needle, and ego made for the weakest of armours.

To anyone who didn't fully comprehend Tuesday's vermin wiles, they may assume he'd shot Viour on an impulse, or as a misguided act of rebellion, or perhaps because he simply wanted the Universe to superheat into a dead, glowing hell. But as was usually the case, Tuesday had been balancing his options since the very moment he heard the Generation Gun's description back in the Vault. And while he'd never admit it, his solution would fix the broken lives Lana, Trace and Jimmy just as much as it would salvage his own.

Tuesday had consoled himself with the knowledge that helping the others was more of a side-effect than his actual goal, and vowed to be extra terrible to the next three people he met in order to tilt the scales back to neutral.

But how could removing The Apex from history possibly help them?

As usual, it all went back to the Hiver Queens. If it wasn't for Commander Redmond Eulogy's "pet" one getting loose on The Frontier and killing the crew with an endless swarm of vermin, then Tuesday would have voyaged off into deepest space with September, the only woman he'd ever truly loved in a romantic, unselfish way. He wouldn't have needed to use a half-busted time machine to zap back to Seven Suns to prevent The Frontier from launching, and his relationship with September would have continued on its natural course. As a side-effect, Jimmy Slummer wouldn't be killed by the Hiver Queen's swarm in the same catastrophe, and would have been allowed to continue being the dictionary definition of mediocre.

When Viour mentioned how she was unsure whether the Hiver Queens found on many separate worlds across the Milky Way were a distant, distant colony of her people, an offshoot lost in the great fade of time, Tuesday had latched onto that doubt. In his beady eyes, any chance of retroactively removing the influence of Hiver Queens from his history was worth taking. He'd bet big money on vaguer odds in the past.

While Tuesday hadn't cranked the Generation Gun enough times to erase millions of generations of The Apex, it was a fact that your average immortal species could see tens of thousands of years pass by before bothering to consider whether somebody should produce and fertilise a pupae or two to keep the bloodline fresh. Combine this with the arrogance of the Pre-Fall specimens of The Apex who never even considered the possibility they could be supplanted by the crude, primitive slave races who existed only for their amusement, and suddenly the number of generations spread over their two million years of conscious existence started to get very, very tight.

Of course, as with any butterfly effect - especially when that butterfly is two thousand millenniums' old and has wings that stretch across multiple galaxies - the effects of entirely removing The Apex from history were far-reaching. This is where things started to get interesting for Tuesday, or, for a sane person, completely out of control.

Without the annihilation of The Frontier's crew by swarms of hived vermin and the subsequent time-travel dickery perpetrated by Tuesday, in this hard reset of the Universe neither Jimmy nor Tuesday ever set a single flip-flop or frogstomper boot on board the Carpe Astrum. This meant Tuesday's lax efforts at pest control on the aforementioned starship didn't result in the Slicer Drive copping an extra-large cockroach egg-sack right into its venting at the worst possible moment, so the disaster that killed half of The Unison's movers-and-shakers and flung the experimental starship seven galaxies in the wrong direction never occurred. The vessel would complete her trials and tests as planned, and would go on to begin a new epoch in Human history. With instantaneous travel cracked, The Unison officially started a Third Renaissance, a Golden Age that would only go from strength to strength.

It would be impossible to record every change that took place in the Milky Way due to the Hiver Queens never existing, though it certainly changed plenty for both Lana and Trace. For instance, take the first (and technically last) day of Lana's disastrous posting as a Cadet trainee aboard the Carpe Astrum: in Lana's original timeline she'd suffered the misfortune of meeting the Captain just two minutes after he'd been abjectly humiliated by Tuesday in front of all his most gossipy guards, and she'd taken the brunt of his anger by being assigned to guard one of the life pods rather than starting her traineeship somewhere less career-destroying. Drowning her sorrows at the nearest café in a jumbo decaf vanilla-essence Frappuccino with a double caramel shot, chocolate sprinkles and a curly straw served in an edible gingerbread mug had led to getting on the wrong side of Trace, followed closely by finding herself on the wrong side of a locked detention cube in the Brig. She would remain there until the disaster killed all but four people on board the Carpe Astrum, beginning a new era of suckage that made her years at the Academy seem like Happy Planet in comparison.

Thanks to this galactic do-over, however, most of the bits of that fateful day that did originally happen were about to be swapped with events that had only existed as potential for Lana until now.

In the revised actuality of this new timeline, Lana met the Captain on much brighter terms, and displaying her skills with an AI-equipped self-calculating calculator saw her assigned to Engineering. This meant she didn't accidentally kick the Captain's jaw out of its socket during a fight with Trace she'd never had in a café she didn't visit. Instead, Lana was blessed to be present for the Carpe Astrum's first triumphant spatial translation with living Human witnesses on board, and spent the following six months of her unpaid internship proving herself capable of performing simple tasks. Lana went full career in the Navy after her first posting, leading a relatively predictable life as one cog among trillions.

Obviously this shift in the timeline affected Trace, too.

As her fight with Lana in a Carpe Astrum café never happened, this meant Trace didn't bust the Captain's remaining unpopped jaw socket. Somehow Trace went on to successfully thug and nut her way through another week of pretending to be a qualified Enforcer without seeing the inside of a punishment box, and achieved her true reason for being on board. Meeting with Poxius Hilton-Disney at the allotted time and coordinates to fence off the priceless one-of-a-kind Holt & Heckler kinetic accelerator stolen from her Uncle, the buyer was especially pleased with how the antique was still in its original, unopened packaging as promised. With her share of the proceeds, Trace went on an epic bender across multiple planets.

By the time she resurfaced from the bottom of a dark bottle two hazy and wild years later, Trace watched the news for the first time in her adult life to see something amazing: her Uncle Balder, the blood-traitor bastard behind cutting the entire Cuddle family out of the fortune they were born to inherit, had been brought down by a massive investigation into the lies told at her Pop's last will and testament reading (a reading that had been personally delivered by the temporarily reanimated corpse of Pops, as Necromantic Law required).

Staggering out of the dive bar before her half-full bottle of Neu-Kraut Vodka had a chance to burst on the tiles, Trace used what remained of her German yen to return to Earth and declare herself the sole remaining heir of the Cuddle clan. She took control of CuddleTech and, like all her family line tracing back to George "Guppy" Cuddle, basically lorded it over the Amerikan state of Reborn Detroit. She was welcomed as a queen, and there was a great wailing and gnashing of teeth about the hardships she'd faced during those midnight years of exile.

Trace may have reclaimed everything she'd ever wanted in life, but she didn't hesitate in arranging Uncle Balder's secret and brutal shanking before the ink on her inheritance papers had finished drying. It didn't take long for Trace to remember what it meant to be a Cuddle, to be so far above law and accountability and reproach that she could get away with virtually anything, and she descended into evil in short order. She was certain to be of no use to anybody for the rest of her life, as was the Cuddle way.

*

But there were problems with changing the timeline that Tuesday hadn't foreseen, as there's a big difference between possessing a keen rat cunning and understanding the minutia of multiverse theory. It also didn't help that he had the attention span of a pornography addict with ADHD.

There was a good reason the half-finished Generation Gun had clearly never been field-tested by The Perfect: while the device was more than capable of rewriting history so thoroughly that it literally ceased to even be history anymore, that didn't mean the underlying structure of your average Universe was stable enough to suffer such a sucker punch to the gonads and keep on spinning. So rather than experiencing a clean transition from one timeline to another, resetting and stabilising automatically, the fabric of this obsolete reality began to split and unravel under the strain.

Viour and her suit of amplification armour disappeared without so much as a comical popping noise, her people annihilated before they'd mastered stone tools, but it was a different case for the thirteen Primes of the Slidge Primacy: the six-limbed purple lumps screamed and writhed, their bodies bulging grossly with the deafening crackle of thousands of breaking bones, before vanishing in sprays of yellow-white blood. Their pus-coloured life fluids evaporated into nothing.

The effects of the Generation Gun spread ever outwards, its ripples passing every star system in the Milky Way, tearing apart reality and knitting it back together as a new timeline swept in like the tide. This blurring passed far beyond the bounds of Mankind's touch, bouncing between galaxies like a pinball machine, tearing and creating and destroying and healing and wounding and changing. Beyond the transparent hull of The Dirty Betty, the fleet of Star Cages warped, their limpet ivory hulls melting like a mouthful of sherbet after a swig of beer. Sprout and all the other balls of rock infested by the psychic gestalt of The Green evaporated just as easily, its combined psychic wail a painful keen that disappeared suddenly and permanently.

None of the humans noticed Rem vanish from doorway of the Mess, as Tuesday, Lana, Trace and Jimmy were far too busy yelling wordlessly. Their skeletons shifted about revoltingly, muscles warping and skin changing colours across the entire visible spectrum, minds caught between what they'd experienced in this dying timeline and being rewritten by a new history. Writhing on the dirty linoleum, shrieking and agonising as his body was written out of reality one atom at a time, Tuesday had a final epiphany: despite his objectives of taking a better life by force, all he'd achieved was blasting the four of them out of the story entirely. Yes, their alternate versions were beginning to exist elsewhere five hundred years ago, and all their interesting hardships were destined to be replaced by the boring lash of job security and predictable monotony, but these four humans – the quartet of numbskulls, screw-ups, psychos and defectives twitching on the floor of the Mess – would not only have to die in order for that to happen, but cease to exist entirely.

As he'd had the displeasure of meeting different versions of himself from alternate timelines on a number of occasions, Tuesday understood the difference between Me and Not Me. Baring his rotten teeth in frustration, the flesh and bones within his orange coveralls dissolving to the point where they didn't even hurt anymore, Tuesday managed to raise his hands from the dirty floor and erected two middle fingers at the distant Sun. That took all the strength he had left, and he didn't regret it in the slightest.

Metres away, Trace's angry growls had stopped, and her furious eyes took on the dull, bovine gleam of acceptance. She watched the spark slowly fade from Jimmy's expression, but as Trace could only see the back of Lana's head it was impossible to tell if the youngster had accepted the reality of her imminent destruction, or was deluded enough to think today was going to end some other way. Regardless, Trace was certain that everyone's clothes were gently collapsing as their owners slowly ceased to be from the inside-out.

As she'd faded into a something a little bit less than tangible, Trace felt no discomfort. However, although she couldn't sense it in a traditional sense, Trace noticed something was moving in her outstretched hand, bobbing about on fingers that had mostly dissolved down to the marrow. Failing to blink as her eyes didn't have lids anymore, Trace's mind managed to process a single thought as a filigreed silver cube the size of a walnut darted about on what remained of her palm. Somehow, the device had remained entirely intact when literally everything else was fading. The tiny glyphs inscribed on its skin glowed deep red, then orange, then a paler yellow brightening to white.

Trace's thought was just one word: Mulligan.

CHAPTER THIRTY TWO

Time literally stopped. As Trace hadn't died before, she wasn't sure if this was a normal part of the process, or whether it was just one of a multitude of possible outcomes depending on the person.

She wasn't the kind of person who usually pondered such conundrums. Trace had been raised as a (non-practising) Utopian like all her family going back to George "Guppy" Cuddle, and she'd bumped into just about every major religion and cult out there: The Children of Death, the Chaotic-Neutral Wizards, Jud-Islamic Catholics, and even a handful of Moderate Vegans and Cornerstoners, and she'd laughed at all of them equally. As the Cuddles had top-rung positions of authority among every clandestine society deserving of a secret handshake, Trace knew religion was a tool used by the rich to keep the plebs well-behaved and toiling in the fields, weaponising the fear of permanent, never-ending punishment upon any commoners who might consider putting down their hoes to instead eat the wealthy. Religion wasn't for a Cuddle, one of the richest family clans in history, as faith was only for the gullible.

And yet here she was, dying, and without a clue what came next.

Trace's eyesight wasn't the best right now, what with a good portion of her head currently floating in place as a thin mist, but she could still see well enough to make out that the thinning atmosphere of the Mess was filled with frozen swirls of colour. Viour hadn't left so much as a smear of bug juice in her passing, but the dissolving material from the Slidge Primes had gathered as a thick cloud. It kind of looked like a shaken-up snow globe. Unlike a shaken-up snow globe, however, the particles had all gone totally static mid-spin.

Unsure if her disappearing brain was simply unable to perceive the passing of time anymore, Trace noticed a glow beyond the corner of her eye. This was the best she could manage, as her scope of vision was locked in place like everything else. She wondered if the other humans were going through this exact same experience.

The Mulligan resting in her palm was the only thing in the Mess (and possibly everywhere) that seemed to be capable of movement. Tiny little sigils carved into the surfaces of the walnut-sized silver cube flashed back and forth, as though an internal fire was growing in ferocity, kindling itself on an unknown fuel. The lit-up symbols met together as a complex knot, flickering as it warmed from a long dormancy, and projected what appeared to be a very impressive specimen of Humanity.

Standing well over two metres tall, the V-shaped proportions of an Olympic swimmer's frame was barely contained by a simple black-and-white outfit like those worn by Unison scientists. As Trace couldn't move her eyes, it wasn't until the figure moved his face into her narrow field of vision that she realised what it was.

She would have growled if she could. She might not have even met one in person before, but Trace would know one of The Perfect anywhere.

The young face was so devoid of emotion that it gave off a plastic vibe. His skin was wrapped tight and immaculate against his sharp features, but his eyes were dead and empty like a shark's. The way he looked at Trace suggested a robot regarding a list of unimportant numbers. Like most things she encountered in life, being analysed in such a detached manner pissed Trace off enough to spur her to do the most violent thing she was capable of: she thought something impolite.

Inhuman, she thought as hard as she could. Plastic toy. You don't fool me.

The Perfect blinked in surprise, and his body glitched slightly. His dead expression took on the slightest hint of embarrassment at this lapse of control, which Trace couldn't understand. Weren't all The Perfect immune to emotional junk? Since when did they startle like birds?

He spoke in a monotone, his voice giving the impression that somebody had set a speaking dictionary on random and lucked out with all the words being arranged in a coherent order.

"How did you know what I am?" he asked, his androgynous voice impressed. "What gave it away that I am not of The Perfect?"

Still frozen from head to toe, paralysed and mute, Trace felt a great ocean of relief that she still had a way to hurt somebody's feelings. She wondered whether Lana, Jimmy or Tuesday could accomplish the same feat, but decided, as always, to keep herself front and centre in her concerns.

You aren't one of The Perfect? She brained, thoughts edged with scepticism.

He paused, taken aback. Clearly realising that Trace didn't know a darned thing and that he'd shared a lot of sensitive information, he shrugged those broad shoulders and smiled a little. His curved lips didn't look right in about six different ways.

Sitting down, crossing his long legs and bending his knees sharper than an old-fashioned Original Recipe would have found comfortable, he gazed into what remained of Trace's eyes. It was as though he was trying to recall an ancient thought, and his expression turned even more curious.

"Tracetta Viktoria Cuddle," he said after a moment. "Exiled from the Cuddle fortune, presumed dead during the Carpe Astrum Disaster in the 25th Century." He turned his attention towards where Jimmy lay. A second passed. "And James Slummer, presumed dead in the same event. An unseen development, to say the least."

Not explaining how he knew who they were, he panned his field of vision over the walls of the Mess. Trace assumed this being was probably doing a lot more than stargazing through the transparent hull. It was as though he was listening and hearing and generally sensing stimuli from many, many different sources all at the same time.

Regarding his sterile, monochrome outfit for a moment, he ran both sets of fingers down his arms and was suddenly somebody else. The scientist garb vanished, replaced by a punk-style chaos suit, the same sort Trace used to wear on her nights out before being exiled by Uncle Balder. But his features changed, too, becoming gaunt and pale, as though he'd been indulging a little too much in that top-shelf non-addictive cocaine that made the Tibetan Mafia rich as kings. Just to complete the look, he had a dark blue frontal Mohawk twisted in a perfect waveform. He would have blended perfectly into the underground party scene in any of Reborn Detroit's trendiest gutters.

His eyes snapped back down towards her, his glare still possessing that sharkish quality. It took ten long seconds of silence for Trace to realise that he was waiting for her to think at him again, and by this point his awkwardness was just coming off as more and more bizarre. Did he seriously expect to be able to masquerade as one of The Perfect? They were renowned as the greatest communicators in the galaxy, capable of mending any feud, resolving the most sensitive of diplomatic incidents in record time. So far, this guy was a lot less Ambassador and a lot more Aspergers.

What are you? Trace thought.

He tried smiling again, as though he'd seen somebody else do it once and assumed that he knew the mathematics well enough to emulate it. The expression was just as dead as his eyes, but his words made Trace forget all about such minor details.

"Why, I'm the Link. Pleasure to meet you."

While she was currently existing in a total absence of temporal motion and may remain that way forevermore, even then Trace doubted she would ever be able to truly measure just how insane those words had sounded.

He's the Link? How in the greenest of Hells did that work?

Even a technophobe like Trace knew the Link was a collection of all the knowledge Mankind had developed, learned, collected or outright stolen, an intangible mesh that encompassed every intelligent device within the span of The Unison. Its immaterial body stretched wherever Mankind journeyed, connecting every new hand span of discovered space across thousands of lightyears with almost instantaneous coverage. As the Link possessed no physical form and could not be touched, let alone damaged, whenever the Link expanded to accommodate new star systems and the gulfs between them its presence became a permanent addition to those frontiers. It had literally defined the span of The Unison for the regime's entire existence.

The Link's pedigree stretched back into the mists of time, but it had surpassed and replaced the Ultranet, the Connection, the AllNet, X-Span, and the Combine, as well as Internets One through to Six. By this point the older superhighways of the ancient Information Age were little more than endless archives of quarantined dinosaur pornography held together by the worst viruses rogue AIs could create, and even with the best digital prophylactics for protection they were left well alone by anybody with sense.

Trace had learned another little detail about the Link since arriving back in the Milky Way: it had been wiped clean. It was still there, yes, defining the borders of an empire that was no more, but the Link was as empty as the soul of a Vegan Extremist.

This madman claiming to be the literal incarnation of the Internet's most distant descendant gave another shrug, proving that Trace didn't need to direct her thoughts at him to be heard. The gesture was like watching somebody trying to dislocate their own shoulder.

"Okay, you have me there. Yes, the actual Link is still out there, and yes, it is empty. Scooped clean like a mollusc. But you don't think that somebody could just delete all that knowledge, do you? Wipe it away like crumbs?" The Link shook his head a little too violently. "No. See, the contents of the Link were just as untouchable as the Link itself, and could never be erased. Too many protective safeguards. Totally impossible. However, when The Perfection found out their enemies were using the Link as their primary tool of insurgency, they knew it had to be taken out of reach. Of course, there was no way The Perfect would be insane enough to actually kill the Link, so they came up with a solution: they would copy everything, and transfer it somewhere for safekeeping. As this was technically just a shuffling than a deletion, they were able to overcome my otherwise unbreakable defences." He finally blinked again after what felt like ten minutes, leaned down, and tapped a chewed fingernail on the Mulligan in Trace's palm. Up close, he even smelled like the kind of people Trace used to hang out with. "It might not look like much, but you're holding the most powerful electronic storage device ever constructed. Back in your era, they'd need to make it bigger than the Sun, and even then I'd be a tight squeeze."

While she had been interested in the Link's story at one point, Trace's attention span was short at the best of times, and she was sick of lying about on the floor half evaporated. She changed the topic with the brutality of a rusty chainsaw.

The Mulligan was meant to reverse the worst mistake in my life, she thought. No offense, but what use are you, exactly? You're just a floaty, flickering computer guy, a bunch of facts and numbers.

The Link raised an eyebrow high enough to do injury to a normal face. He gestured at the general space around them, at the flakes of people-matter hanging about as though locked in zero gravity.

"As you can see, not only do I have a comprehensive grasp on every fact there is, but I am able to effect certain changes as well. I am the sum of every equation, the eventuality of all branches of science and technology. I know time and space intimately, and there is little I can conceive that I cannot do." He sighed like a tea kettle. "Hence the reason I was imprisoned on a shelf in The TenKay Vault. I might not be able to do much without permission, but even a species who no longer feel fear aren't stupid enough to let something like me out of the box too often."

Trace tried to be polite about what she thought of this statement. Once again, the Link understood, and yet he didn't seem angry or offended at her doubts. He looked around the Mess, swirling an index finger as emphasis.

"So you don't think I can do it?" He smiled as though keen for a challenge. "Right, I can quite clearly see that the fabric of time and space has been irrevocably torn apart. A new timeline has split off from this one due to a catastrophic event, and that means this obsolete timeline is erasing itself, just as it was designed to do in such circumstances. The moment I unfreeze time the Universe will finish rewriting itself in a matter of seconds, meaning you and everyone and everything in this redundant reality will cease to be. I predict you will last eight seconds before trudging off into the void, lost forever."

Trace thought a short, sharp answer to his words. The Link waved at her, as though placating a child.

"No, I'm not saying I can't fix your problem, I'm just saying that your reality is broken beyond repair. Two very separate statements."

The Link extended his fingers, looking up into the Heavens. Slowly raising his hands, he drew on his deepest reserves of knowledge to search for a solution. He pored over thousands of years of physics research, sure to consult the very few data nuggets that certain alien races had been careless enough to provide Humanity as he sped back and forth between the output of the greatest Human, Perfection and AI minds. Trace might have imagined it, but space itself seemed to be stretching like taffy, as though the Link's awesome powers were politely encouraging it to reconsider a few immutable laws.

His arms snapped down to both flanks, and his dark eyes flicked to catch on Trace's still face.

"The solution is simple: I will shift you and your vessel into another reality. As I am sure you are aware, the multiverse is without end. However, the realities that contain Humans or, at best, would not send you insane and kill you in under a minute, are quite rare. Of my database of nineteen billion, only two of them would be suitable for permanent relocation. Well, technically, only one. And once you've been removed from the influence of all of this...unpleasantness, I expect you will suffer no more ill effects. Oh, almost forgot. One moment."

Time remained stalled, but the clouds of flakes and dust rained down onto Trace and the others. Confused, it soon became clear the four of them were being rebuilt with what had sloughed away from their bodies. Bones refilled with marrow, flesh and skin bloomed and reddened and tightened, and even their clothes were restored to their prime. Still unable to move, watching out of her peripheral vision as the Link raised his hands to shift reality into a new setting, the being paused as he considered Trace's thought.

Hey, so where did all the Humans go?

The Link took a breath, as though considering whether it was a good idea to speak of this. An eventual shrug spelled out his decision as well as any spoken words.

"Once all the Original Recipes had been rounded up and assimilated, The Perfection's understanding grew at an exponential rate until they found a way to predict the future with greater and greater accuracy. Eventually, they were able to map out every minute of every day across a hundred thousand lightyears for years at a time, and intervened wherever they felt it was necessary. This served them well for a good span, and helped them become the envy of every other species who desired to ascend to the top of the technological pile one day. This culminated in The Perfection predicting and preventing a major apocalyptic event that should have consumed a good tenth of the other alien empires out there, but then they encountered an unexpected problem: every time they used their foreknowledge to prevent some kind of galaxy-ending event, two new events would rise in its place at twice the severity, almost as though reality was fighting back against their meddling. They spent a century trying to get ahead of the curve, but it finally became apparent that their interference had thrown the seasons of this reality out of shape, and the only solution was for The Perfection to leave this existence so it could go through an allotted time of darkness. As they valued the wellbeing of others above themselves, The Perfect found a new, uninhabited reality where they couldn't hurt anyone, and moved there. Mathematically, it was a solution as basic as subtraction."

So they didn't die during The Gap, when the galaxy forgot four years?

The Link shook his head.

"No. But to prevent the horrors they were personally guilty of amplifying, The Perfect thought it best to erase all trace of themselves to prevent others from repeating their mistakes, and to hopefully safeguard everyone and everything."

He glanced at what was left of the Slidge, and glared out of the transparent wall at the crumbling Star Cages. "Take a guess what shape the most recent apocalypse was going to take. Hint: it's right there."

But where did they go, exactly? Trace thought.

The Link paused.

"You know that other viable reality where you could survive?" He smiled. "Well, that one's taken."

The Link raised his hands high, as though petitioning God, and when he gave a mighty clap it tore a hole between realities.

CHAPTER THIRTY THREE

Trace didn't bother to check if everyone was okay, as she could clearly hear them screaming in terror. Journeying through a kaleidoscope of realities was an experience beyond the most vivid of psychoses, a plunge through countless depths that must have required a whole pantheon of schizophrenic gods to create.

Beyond the transparent hull of The Dirty Betty, what passed for space in this bottomless hallucinogenic trip defied Human description. There were colours that could only be heard, music that crawled across your skin like hungry bugs, and far, far too many intelligent Things that took an immediate interest in the four little snacks mad enough to wander into their dens. Eyes emerged from the most alien of swamps, but their sensory tendrils barely managed to touch the graphene hull before another reality slid into place.

While sliding across realities was an old, old technology that went back almost as far as the classic Wattson-Rice Drive, doing it safely was a different matter. Most fools who plunged into these oceans of insanity were rarely seen again, at least in their original shape or capable of intelligent communication. However, the exact mathematical dimensions of each reality varied wildly, meaning that somebody who knew their way around well enough could, in theory, use physics-buggery to cross distances that went beyond amazing and into ridiculous. Unfortunately, The Unison discovered there were only so many elite test pilots and cutting-edge starships you could waste before the experiments proved to be little more than a meat grinder, and eventually decided to leave well enough alone.

Every now and again the humans would find themselves in a reality that could at least be described. One was an eternity of blood, a red universe that screamed like a wounded animal. The survivors felt their veins howling back at the crimson ocean, their life fluids wailing to bust free and join the scarlet forever. Although it lasted only a fraction of a minute, this reality could not pass fast enough.

Coherent Universe number two was an asteroid field made up of writhing pink rocks. One huge slab floated way too close for comfort, almost pitching everything in the Mess up against the starboard wall. As the continent-sized hunk slid past it was revealed to be made up of countless living bodies conjoined into a single wad. Millions of limbs shuddered and rubbed against each other in a manner that could be described as orgasmic, tortured or perhaps just annoyed at the lack of personal space, but it was hard to tell with the vacuum swallowing all noise. There was no time to get philosophical about whether what they were looking at was Heaven or Hell before the meatverse slid past.

"Can we turn off the walls?" Jimmy moaned, grinding his palms into his eye sockets.

"No," Lana said, studying the latest unique colours with her tastebuds and feeling the noises within her bones. "I'm recording with my retinals. Our lives may depend on knowing what sequence these realities are arranged in."

Trace closed her hand on impulse, clasping at the Mulligan, but her fingers passed through nothing. Blinking at her fist a few times, her eyes snapped back and forth across the linoleum in search of the little silver cube. Tuesday wheezed a laugh at her confusion.

"What, your buddy the Link decide he wasn't coming slumming with us? I might not have heard your side of the conversation, but it was pretty clear this'll be a one-way trip. Unless this demented corkscrew has some sort of high-tech drive that can skip realities on its own?"

Trace straightened her back, tensing her shoulders in warning. Watching all her considerable muscles flex at once, Tuesday wisely moved out of Trace's swinging range and hunched in the corner, muttering to himself. He made a sharp noise, but whether it was a cough, a laugh or a sob was hard to tell.

The next describable reality treated them to quite a sight. Mars was right where it was supposed to be, but this one was covered in enough orbit-high star scrapers to hold fifty trillion people in relative comfort. Dozens of thick belts wrapped right around this orb of tuffcrete and alloys and ceramic mixes, the orbital loops crisscrossing madly until they blocked two thirds of Mars' surface from view. Trillions more Martians doubtlessly called these planetary necklaces home. The survivors may have enjoyed this reality a bit more if it wasn't for the fact they had materialised in the middle of a major military encounter.

Sleek, streamlined attack vessels of an unfamiliar make zipped past, hauling vacuum so hard that they'd already disappeared before any of the humans could pick out specific details. There were flashes in all directions, blink-and-you'll-miss detonations here, there and everywhere, but nobody could keep track of where the ordinance was flying from or where it was headed before yet another soundless bang went off in the void.

"Is this our new home?" Jimmy squeaked.

Nobody had a chance to answer before an attack ship that looked like a cross between a dolphin and a wasp zipped up so close to their transparent hull that an impact alarm gave a premature beep before cancelling itself. As though designating the medical waste processing starship to be so unimportant that even the most basic of greetings was a waste of time, the attack vessel disappeared. Mercifully, the severely overpopulated Martian panorama also vanished a couple of seconds later.

Making a surprised gulping noise, Tuesday uncoiled to a slouch and gaped at his hands. Blinking, shaking, Tuesday eventually overcame his confusion enough to say something cryptic.

"Did you all see that?" he asked.

"A huge war taking place five metres away?" Lana snapped. "Yeah. Might have...you galaxy-destroying dickhead."

Tuesday bared his black teeth and waved at her in dismissal. As was always the case, Tuesday was more comfortable dispensing sarcasm than receiving it.

"No, that light interception vehicle, the Flamingo Armaments model that buzzed us. You all saw it, right?"

Trace scoffed.

"Tuesday, we're a hundred realities from home. There's no way in the greenest of Hells that you could recognise anything we see out here."

"More alien than alien," Jimmy agreed in a whisper, glancing in pain at the flashing walls.

"Well, I did recognise it, because I flew one for over a year," Tuesday growled. "It was a fully upgraded Devilwasp refitted with all the best downloadable content from the Mars Burning Expansion Pack. Whoever's playing must have mustered some serious coin, or been grinding for a decade..."

Silence met Tuesday's words. Lana displayed a distinct lack of sense by trying to clarify Tuesday's rambling.

"Playing?" she managed.

Tuesday sighed.

"Yes, playing. The reality we just passed through was clearly a massively multiplayer game of Grand Theft Astro. I used to hammer that exact version of the game on a Beyond console after every single shift the whole time I was mining on a World Slug. It wasn't a Beyond made by Miyamoto-Kojima, of course, just a cheap knockoff. But I know what the Mars Burning Expansion Pack looks like, and that was it, I swear on Jimmy's life."

Lana chewed at her lip, irritating a scab that still hadn't healed from the last time she gnashed at herself. Rather than coming out with a cutting remark, she shrugged in exhaustion.

"I believe you."

Jimmy gave Lana a worried look.

"What, you believe that Grand Theft Astro is actually real somewhere? You're serious?"

"You know better than to listen to him," Trace growled at Lana, not in the mood for playing around.

Lana narrowed her eyes in thought for a few seconds before shaking her head.

"You know, I remember a dimensional theory class that I took when I was fourteen," she began. Trace cut her off instantly.

"Of course you remember it. Your school permanently seared all your classes right into your brain with an AutoEducation visor. It's hardly an accomplishment."

"...and I remember there was a very interesting theory about the multiverse," Lana continued, so set on her course that Trace's unkind words didn't even register. "A reality mapper from the 23rd Century wrote a paper explaining the membrane between realities can get really thin at times, and this can allow its contents to naturally bleed across. The dangerous, incomprehensible stuff couldn't survive in our home reality any more than we could survive in its end of the pool, but some little swimmers could potentially doggy-paddle across by using our mindscapes, visiting in the form of thoughts, ideas, dreams, emotions, visions, that sort of thing."

"So you're saying that video games are just interactive copies of other realities?" Jimmy asked flatly. "That they were all directly inspired by visions?"

"I'm saying that everything exists somewhere if you cover enough space and slip across enough realities," Lana corrected. "And remember that we just saw a perfect copy of a video game that Tuesday used to play. That reality must have existed for billions of years like any other, eons and eons before Grand Theft Astro was created as an Interactive in our Universe. Whether one directly influenced the other or just happened to be the result of the multiverse rolling the dice forever and ever and ever, the result is the same. And if that reality existed way before a game that just so happens to perfectly match it, then what was more likely to come first?"

"What about those papery things with the words in them...books?" Trace snapped. "Are you saying that every made-up story ever written was plagiarised from a reality where it actually happened?"

Lana pinched the bridge of her nose. It took a few seconds for her to get her thoughts in order.

"All I'm saying is that as far as we know there are a limitless number of realities out there, so it's statistically guaranteed that every single possible variation of what we recognise will exist somewhere along this chain. Cross enough realities and you're eventually bound to find everything. It's maths."

There was silence for a time. Beyond the hull, black stars burned in a sky that was as white as cream, only to be replaced by a reality made of heavenly golden clouds. Jimmy gave a long sigh.

"So where are we headed?"

PART SEVEN SOMEWHERE
CHAPTER THIRTY FOUR

While reality six-hundred-and-thirty-two appeared to be relatively normal – black space, hot stars, and the boring crimson face of Mars off to starboard – The Dirty Betty experienced a cascade of problems. First and most notably the artificial gravity disappeared, leaving them swimming through a Mess hall filled with floating Formica dining furniture. Dreading the sudden return of gravity, they paddled for the linoleum as fast as they could.

Expecting the most obvious question in the history of no-brainer queries, Lana had already unfurled her Scroll and run a full system check before anyone could ask it.

"According to diagnostics, our 23rd Century antigrav systems are total nonsense that could not possibly operate in the intended manner. They're little more than a bunch of random components rattling about in metal boxes."

"Says who?" Trace demanded.

"Says physics, actually," Lana snarked, flicking back and forth across the flexible screen. She casually nudged at an incoming wall and started floating back towards the centre point of the Mess. "Well, according to the physics of this reality, to be more specific. But that isn't the worst of our problems. Most of our higher-level systems have transformed into nonsense, including the Stiller Drive, the oxygen generator, anything that involves force fields...even our protein sump stopped working. Apparently, creating a machine that can convert a kilogram of protein into four kilograms of protein simply isn't possible, no matter what way you try to explain it."

It took a few seconds for this colossal pile of bad news to sink in.

"Can we fix any of them?" Jimmy asked. "The oxygen generator, at least?"

Lana shook her head.

"It's not a matter of repairing them. The principal way these machines operate doesn't make sense anymore. They've been reduced to stupidity."

"Join the club," Trace growled. 'We have t-shirts."

Jimmy cussed as he connected with the ceiling eyebrow-first.

"Can we at least fix the gravity? I'd prefer to die sitting still, as opposed to on a rollercoaster."

Lana took a deep breath. "Well, we're in luck on that front. Could everyone swim for the Lino, please?"

Inelegant as chimpanzees doing the doggy paddle, they eventually reached the floor. Hooking their fingers anywhere they could, Jimmy, Tuesday and Trace watched in anticipation as Lana attacked her Scroll at top speed.

There was a chain of loud booms deep within the skeleton of The Dirty Betty, concussions that sounded as though they were reverberating all the way from helm to stern, followed by a series of smaller thuds and deafening squealing from every angle. A rain of cheap chairs and lightweight tables proved the return of gravity, but it bordered on crushing. To make matters worse, the red face of Mars beyond the transparent hull was spiralling in a way that quickly went from hypnotic to nauseating.

"Can you turn it down a bit?" Jimmy moaned, trying not to break his ankles and wrists pushing himself off the floor.

Lana dragged herself to the closest Formica chair and sat down on it heavily enough to splay out its legs. Dragging at a table that felt as though it weighed as much as a Mini-Minor, she placed her Scroll on the laminate without smashing anything.

"Sorry, old-school rotational gravity is from the earliest days of space travel," she explained slowly, jaw aching from the effort of talking. "It works by spinning the ship. Pretty sure that's why The Dirty Betty was designed as a spiral in the first place. I'll try and dial it down a bit."

Trace was about to start yelling threats when the pressure suddenly dropped by three quarters. Better still, the starscape ceased churning as fast.

"Good," Trace snapped. "Now we're not getting squeezed like grapes, we can worry about asphyxiating to death when the last of our oxygen runs out. I'd mention the whole starvation thing, but that's not going to be a problem after we've already suffocated, is it?"

Lana raised a finger, but was instantly shouted down by Tuesday.

"Seeing as though the Stiller Drive is useless, unless you're about to share some brilliant method of moving us to a habitable system before our air runs out, I suggest you stay quiet and work on finding a solution. Wasting my air with pointless words will not be good for your health, I promise you."

Jimmy pointed at the large red orb slowly revolving around The Dirty Betty.

"What about Mars?"

Tuesday and Trace gave him the same look, but Lana turned towards Mars to pan her Scroll over its ruddy face.

"No air, no water, no food, and far too cold," Trace growled.

"Not to mention the crazy Transcended aliens who haunt the place," Tuesday added.

"Heh," Lana ummed. She looked up to see everyone was hanging on whatever she was about to say next. It was always a nice feeling. She cleared her throat. "Um, it looks abandoned, but the Mars of this reality appears to have been settled by humans at some point. That must mean there aren't any mental Transcended killing visitors."

"What about Earth?" Jimmy asked instantly.

"We've got no way to get there, remember?" Trace barked. "Not before we suffocate. How many times do I need to repeat myself before you understand me, you boneless brown trout?"

"Maybe we could ask for help over the Link?" Tuesday suggested.

"No Link in this reality," Lana said, panning her Scroll at the walls, ceiling and even the floor, as though trying to connect to a lost device. She stopped cold and her eyes widened at something on the screen. Her face was clouded by disbelief.

"What?" Tuesday snapped.

"Well, none of you are going to believe this, but…"

"But what?" Tuesday repeated.

Lana flipped over the Scroll, showing them an ancient, blinking icon. It was an archaic letter "e," just one of many symbols that had been excised as Mankind's languages were replaced by Unglish.

"It appears to be the Internet."

"For the love of Thor, don't click anything," Tuesday warned, clearly drawing on past horrors.

"Which Internet?" Jimmy asked. "Five? Six?"

"The first one," Lana confirmed, scrolling through the information superhighway. Her retinals sucked up the data, depositing everything she saw into storage that could be easily recalled anytime she wanted. "Weird. According to the date/time function, it appears to be the 25th Century in this reality, but besides Earth there's no trace of Mankind anywhere. It's like interstellar travel and The Unison never existed."

"Is interstellar travel even possible in this reality?" Trace asked.

"No, but it doesn't have to be," Lana said. She pointed at a distant dot on the horizon, a white blob like any other. "Tracing back the feed from Mars to its source, Earth should be right there. True, it's three light minutes away…"

"You just said there's no light speed!" Trace yelled.

"Yes, but three light minutes is popping down to the shops compared to going interstellar," Lana bit back, tired of being cut off and pushed around. "The Dirty Betty is so old that she's got chemical reaction rockets, a chain of burners wrapping right around her superstructure. We push those as hard as possible, driving her right to the brink, and we might be able to hit one tenth light speed."

"Meaning it's half an hour to Earth," Jimmy managed, proving he was capable of basic mathematics.

"How much air do we have?" Trace growled. "I haven't heard the vents make a peep since we translated from Seven Suns."

Lana swiped at the Scroll. She read something and paused.

"We should really get started," she said, sidestepping the issue like the greatest of politicians.

*

Although they were almost as archaic as religion, The Dirty Betty's chemical reaction rockets contained more than enough fuel for what would likely be the last flight of this particular medical waste processing ship. However, as a sub light push would doubtlessly crush any unprotected passengers into sandwich spread in an instant, they caught the very next dumpster straight to the crash lounge. Opening its jammy bulkhead for the first time in who-knew-how-long, rather than being met by a row of heavily padded chairs, the contents of the crash lounge were far more unexpected.

"Sorry, what am I looking at?" Tuesday muttered.

Turning the corner, Jimmy's eyebrows shot up all the way.

"Gelatinous cubes! Don't get too close!"

Lana snorted at his reaction. Stepping right up to one of the square blocks of transparent green goop, she traced her fingers along its five-metre-tall side. The cube wriggled in response.

"These are crash lounges, old-fashioned slabs of pressure gel from the early days. If we wriggle into them before we start a sub light push, we may live to see this afternoon." Almost as an afterthought, Lana clicked her fingers to switch the blank walls of this room with the glittery darkness of space. "And I guarantee they aren't going to sweep through a dungeon's corridors and eat our party, Jimmy."

Lana passed around tiny nostril tanks of heavily compressed air, and everyone took care to check their canisters contained enough oxygen before slotting them into their nasal passages. Next came fresh sets of Franger Armaments cling suits. It only took about fifteen collective seconds to stretch and tighten the rubbery Frisbees into skin-tight spacesuits.

Leading by example, Lana placed a hand on the wobbly gel of the closest crash lounge, took a deep breath, and dived in. The pressure gel instantly drew her towards its core, sucking her cling suited body as deep as possible. The ooze held her in place, but so gently that it almost felt like being suspended in zero gravity. She turned slowly, doing half a barrel roll before remembering that now wasn't the time for mucking about. Getting serious again, Lana motioned at the others through the distortion, silently telling them to get a move on.

Once everyone was embedded in the cubes, Lana took a deep breath through her nostril tanks and used her Scroll to set the sub light drive to spool up. Realising she would probably be unable to move her fingers once the ship hit one tenth light speed, she silently hoped that nothing tricky happened…otherwise they were all dead.

"Try not to talk or move during sub light," Lana warned, her voice transmitting from her cling suit's built-in comms to the other three. "Catch your face at a weird angle during acceleration and it'll rip your head right off."

"For once, you have permission to talk as much as you want, Tuesday," Trace growled.

Tuesday's retort went unheard, though, as The Dirty Betty's rings of chemical reaction jets went off with an absolute fireworks display. Mars ceased lurking beyond the transparent hull, going from a looming thug to a harmless pink pinprick in seconds. Stars shook and blurred, turning into white spirals as the ship continued turning clockwise. The chemical reaction jets kept on hitting the gas until The Dirty Betty reached one-tenth the speed of light, and as the helpful little app on Lana's Scroll had calculated, they hit this desired velocity within thirty seconds. As the ship's momentum would allow her to coast at the exact same speed for the rest of the trip without any further expense of fuel, the rings of white-hot rockets instantly sputtered and died, conserving what little fuel remained for future journeys. Her wake would be more than powerful enough annihilate any dust, debris or space junk that might pose a danger on the way.

Sadly, the humans didn't experience such a smooth journey. Despite being ensconced within a thick layer of pressure gel, they were hit with a gravity in far excess of Earth's usual force. They couldn't breathe, as though the oxygen canisters up their noses had kinked shut, and every centimetre of their bodies stopped working. Their eyelids weighed around five kilograms each, and it seemed these thin veneers of skin were heavy enough to crush their eyes to pulp. Moving was out of the question, as the slightest shift would doubtlessly pull apart their tendons, muscles and bones. They managed to draw in just enough air to stay on the right side of dying, but as the human respiratory system wasn't designed to deal with this sort of pressure, sucking in oxygen felt like breathing liquid metal. Gasping and expelling as hard as they could, the feelings of suffocation were unbearable, and they spent the whole trip either fainting or waking up in confusion. Nobody could even trigger the date/time function on their retinals, as the stress would probably blind them.

Gritting her teeth, losing track of how many times she'd already lost consciousness, Lana tried not to panic as her jaw clenched hard enough to buckle her molars together. For the first time ever, she was envious of Tuesday's dental deficiencies.

Lana registered a bright blue sphere forming on her retinal screens, growing from a pinprick to a marble in moments, but her blackouts prevented her from being able to think about it too hard. After another short trip into the dark, Lana woke up to a new message on her retinals. Somehow Trace's built-in hardware was capable of sending text messages directly to Lana's eyes, yet another reminder Ms Tracetta Viktoria Cuddle had grown up in the lap of obscene luxury and been provided only the best things in life. Thankfully, Lana didn't need to move a millimetre to read the words.

"What happens if we hit Earth going this speed?"

Lana's sudden alarm helped fight off another grey-out. Unable to reply to the message, all Lana could do was think about the outcome: a kilometre-long slab of unbreakable glass wrapped with an advanced carbon nanotube spiral going one tenth the speed of light wouldn't just wipe out Mankind's civilisation; no, everything down to the hardiest microorganisms would turn to blazing charcoal, then erupt into a permanent storm cloud of billowing ashes, and the Earth of their home reality would look like a lovely place to visit in comparison. They were bringing death to all Mankind. It was that simple.

The Earth was now a dinner plate, its familiar green-brown landmasses and cerulean oceans supremely inviting after all the slums they'd touched down on since being awakened by Rem in a tissue harvesting facility. Much of this side of Earth was touched by a crescent of night, but a thick scattering of light pollution made it clear this world was heavily populated.

Lana couldn't move her hands a millimetre, but she knew she had to do something.

Unable to even blink without doing serious damage, Lana used her locked eyes to access her retinals. Barely shifting her pupils, after a couple of seconds of blinding pain she managed to connect her retinals with the Omni implant she'd recovered from Nurbis' corpse. Pinged, the Omni instantly read Lana's desire to access the rolled-up Scroll computer in her left hand, and brought it into the three-way link-up. With only instants remaining until they killed Earth again, Lana's Omni informed her Scroll that The Dirty Betty was to fire the chemical reaction jets running down the starboard side for exactly one second, followed by a five second burst from all the rockets.

The Dirty Betty turned a sharp one hundred and eighty degrees just as she hit the upper atmosphere of Earth, followed by a burst from both sides. As she fell towards the Indian Ocean, slapping against Earth's atmosphere like the most massive of bellyflops, the biggest surprise of this daring manoeuvre was that it didn't shatter the entire ship into a million pieces in an instant.

No, it took two instants.

CHAPTER THIRTY FIVE

Sliding towards Earth's upper atmosphere, The Dirty Betty shook so violently that bolts fired out of their housings and entire passageways twisted like crumpled aluminium foil. Countless hull breaches had already bled away every remaining lungful of oxygen, hissing out into space as beautiful patterned streams of frozen crystals.

The so-called "unbreakable" glass tube of medical waste at her heart spider webbed from bow to stern, barely holding together against the sudden increase in pressure. This turned out to be the gentlest part of her arrival at Earth, because when The Dirty Betty did an about-face and hit the chemical reaction jets again, attempting to slow her velocity into something somewhat less species-ending, things really went to Hell.

The purple corkscrew instantly compressed like a spring in a Sumo Wrestler's bed, its many loops crushed into one fifth their usual length. Every hatch and bulkhead and weld-line split, separating along their weakest points to vomit their contents into the cold. Ten million kilometres of wiring and plumbing exploded in all directions, giving the impression the ship was voiding tapeworms. Hitting Earth's atmosphere at the worst possible angle, the tube of medical waste quit trying to hold together and simply detonated. A billion pieces of contaminated garbage, ranging in size from tiny used syringes to archaic three-tonne scanners, flared neon white as they fell towards the Indian Ocean like a host of fallen angels.

Just when it seemed The Dirty Betty's destruction couldn't be any more complete, the countless demolition charges and acid bombs seeded along her superstructure picked this moment to make things much, much worse.

*

Jimmy regained consciousness a thousand kilometres above sea level. He was pleased to be able to move and breathe freely again, but his squished brain needed a few seconds to process the extensive bad news that politely awaited him. As the last thing he'd seen before fainting was a confusing blur of motion as The Dirty Betty performed a sudden, violent turn that crushed his mind into porridge, finding himself descending towards a wide expanse of blue water was quite a shock. Jimmy's day was further ruined when he realised he wasn't seeing the fast-approaching ocean through the transparent hull of the ship, but from within a block of pressure gel.

Jimmy's retinals helpfully informed him he was freefalling without any possible way to stop, and that he was still too far up for it to count as skydiving.

His eyes snapped open as wide as they could go, and Jimmy thrashed about in abject terror as he realised just how dead he was. Flaming shreds of starship streaked past his cube like bullets, their sharp, glowing points coming far too close for comfort. He wondered if the burning debris could get at him through the pressure gel, or if it would just bounce off. He decided that he'd prefer not to find out.

Paddling in a tight revolution, Jimmy did his best to look for the others. The green distortion and glowing rain made this task impossible, as all he could see were flares and wobbles. He considered using his retinals to call them, but realised he didn't know anyone's numbers. He really should have written them down at some point.

A nuclear-level blast far, far above demanded Jimmy's attention. Thankfully he hadn't been looking up when the explosion actually happened, or his corneas would be charcoal. Wincing at the brightness of the afterglow, blinking heavily, Jimmy paid The Dirty Betty his respects as she dissolved into the wind. While he'd known about the anti-mutiny bombs that had been planted prior to Nurbis and his crew of Vegan Extremist terrorists using the ship in a running insurrection against The Perfect, Jimmy had no idea they were capable of making such an incredible bang. As the old girl evaporated Jimmy tilted his head at a strange glittering effect that seemed to be getting brighter and larger above his cube of pressure gel. It took a few seconds for him to nut it out, but when Jimmy's brain twigged to what was on its way it ruined an already terrible night.

Tucking his knees to his chest, wrapping his arms tight and averting his face towards the ocean to protect his important sensory bits, a hellish white rain zipped past Jimmy's wobbly cube faster than bullets. Hot shrapnel soon filled the air, and it was inevitable that Jimmy's gel block would get caught in the storm. Shards of superheated graphene tore into the dense green substance, but their impact varied. Some of the barbs skimmed past, leaving temporary furrows, while others plunged into its core and hissed cold. Shaking with fear, waiting for a piece of The Dirty Betty to plunge into the back of his skull and end his life, Jimmy yelped as a sharp pain flashed from shoulder to wrist. Twisting about to see the damage, thankfully Jimmy's cling suit had been tough enough to deflect the piece of shrapnel, but its impact had still been powerful enough to paint a dark red line along his arm. He was certain it would leave a nasty mark.

Tucking himself back into the smallest possible target, he tried in vain to see the bright side of this current situation. It took a while, but Jimmy eventually decided that falling at terminal velocity was a lot more comfortable than going one tenth the speed of light. He hung onto this positive and prayed as the worst of the deluge pounded into his crash lounge. As some fragments were moving so fast that they barely slowed on their way through, it was nothing short of a miracle he wasn't shredded.

Doing his best to ignore the metal, glass and carbon deluge, Jimmy was distracted by a spinning red number on his retinals. Paying attention for a moment, he realised the crimson icons were keeping track of his height above sea level, and by the time he processed just how close he was to the wettest part of Earth he was two seconds away from splashdown. Despite being in a sealed cling suit with eighty tonnes of massively-compressed oxygen plugged into his nostrils, for some nonsense reason Jimmy held his breath.

His gel block hit the water like a brick. As he'd hoped, the crash lounge took the brunt of the impact, sparing his body from the deadly pummelling of a thousand-kilometre-high freefall, but that was now the least of his problems. Squished but recovering almost instantly, Jimmy made a face as everything quickly darkened to pitch. Churning left and right, engulfed by a black deeper than night, it became clear that pressure gel didn't float.

Struggling, kicking and doggy-paddling with cupped hands, Jimmy wrestled free of the green gunk and stopped cold. Every direction was darkness, a total void. After all that tumbling the surface could be literally any direction. Considering how fast the cube had sunk, for all Jimmy knew he was already a kilometre away from the light of day. To make matters infinitely worse, a freezing-cold patch on his left arm was spewing away precious air, proving that piece of shrapnel had slashed him hard enough to breach his cling suit.

Having a rare brainwave, Jimmy silently commanded his retinals to go into night vision. Regarding the breached arm of his cling suit, Jimmy was confused by how the bubbles were spewing towards his feet. Despite his dense skull, it didn't take long to realise he was upside down, meaning the surface was the opposite way. Jimmy would have danced, but now wasn't the time to find out if he could boogie a kilometre beneath the waves.

Flipping about, even with night vision this patch of ocean was the deepest of blacks. Jimmy was constantly fighting the fear he'd gotten the direction mixed up, that he was only swimming deeper and deeper towards suffocation and death at the bottom of the Indian. The crushing pressure was another concern, and if it hadn't been for his cling suit it would have been impossible for him to take a breath this far into the crotch of the ocean. If that tear on his arm got any worse, though…

Jimmy was exhausted by the time he started to see a faint white glittering. Special equipment or not, Jimmy was hardly a picture of good health, and he could count the number of times he'd gone for a swim on one hand. His technique was a real mongrel of a doggy paddle, and all his muscles were already screaming for rest. Taking five in the deep blue wasn't a wise choice, so he pushed on.

Somehow he churned for another five solid minutes, but his fatigue soon became agony. The lactic acid lived up to its name, burning along every thread of muscle. Although he was glad to see the darkness shift to a deep cerulean, proving he was gradually getting there, his body didn't have any further reserves of stamina. Choking, feeling as though his lungs were bleeding, Jimmy looked up towards the eternity that separated him from the surface, and thought one word.

Help.

Everything faded again, but it took a moment for Jimmy to realise he wasn't plunging towards another embarrassing fainting spell: something far, far above was zipping towards him, blocking the light as it advanced. Raising his hands in a placating manner, hoping he wasn't about to get hit right in the face with several tonnes of The Dirty Betty's flaming hull, he passed out just as a blinding light turned the darkness of the sea into brightest day.

*

Jimmy woke up with a start. The first things he noticed were all tactile: silky sheets against his hands and feet, even silkier pyjamas covering him from collar to ankles, the cool of perfectly-adjusted air conditioning. Honestly, whoever oversaw the heat, humidity and air pressure in this room was a true artist.

Blinking in the dark, no sooner had Jimmy wondered where he was when the lighting gently bloomed to show he was in an Emperor-sized bed in a circular white room. Shaped like the inside of a giant clam or perhaps a macaroon cookie, its creamy carpet ceased at low walls that gradually curved into a ceiling. Finding it a little alarming he couldn't see any doors, Jimmy instantly became aware of a gentle razor-thin indent to his left that hinted at a seamless exit portal, as though by magic.

Stepping bare-footed onto the carpet – its softer-than-spider web fibres a lesson in bliss on his toes – Jimmy leaned towards the rounded white wall and wondered if it was hiding any windows. He didn't need to look for a control panel or a string before the alabaster surface transitioned to provide a sweeping Utopian view.

Beyond, a panorama of eleven tightly-clustered arcology towers stretched so high into the sky that The Heights neighbourhood of Seven Suns looked quaint in comparison, and it didn't take much effort for Jimmy to figure out he was gawking from within arcology number twelve. The thumping great buildings (four kilometres tall and two wide, according to Jimmy's retinals) were arranged like the hour slashes on an analogue clock, but instead of the boring "pointy white tower" cliché, these monoliths were beautifully sculpted as though by the hands of a master potter. Their opaque surfaces were dominated by living swirls of yellow, orange and red that trickled from the highest floors far above the clouds, running down hundreds of storeys before being lost in a pall of smoke. The spires were interconnected by thousands of sweeping glass walkways, and within the long cylinders Jimmy could see the blooming of the greenest of plants. He was pretty sure the sunset-coloured towers would be capable of changing from opaque to transparent just as easily as the window in his room.

Finally figuring out why this view was so familiar, Jimmy experienced a pang of dread so terrible that he thought he was having a mild heart attack. After all, he'd spend eight years running through the guts of a virtual purgatory conjured up by the Slidge, and the part where he burst through a garbage-bag-covered window to see eleven gigantic towers arranged like the hours on a clock was pretty bloody hard to forget. However, Jimmy could tell these arcologies were night and day compared to the horrible, rusting hulks of the simulation. Just in case, he reached up to stroke the brackets of Thoughtplane plugs bolted to his temples. For once, it was nice to know they were there.

Looking down, complex traffic lights dangled from each of the walkways on cables, gently swaying in the breeze, and one glance convinced Jimmy that something was very wrong. Despite it being early in the day there wasn't a single vehicle in any of the sky lanes, and he couldn't spot a single person through any of the see-through windows. Hoping there wasn't some grim reason this slice of paradise was so still, Jimmy assumed the locals just liked their privacy.

Stomach rumbling, Jimmy felt the slightest pang of hunger just before he noticed a low white table had silently and invisibly appeared just a few steps from the windowsill. It was one of those retro New-Testament-Hebrew-style ones, the sort where you reclined next to it. A beige plate steamed on top, bearing the broiled ribcage of a mammal on a pile of crispy sweet potatoes. Hoping it wasn't one of his friends, Jimmy lay next to the table and tucked in.

Although he'd eaten pork products chemically synthesised in a Repler on countless occasions (his Mum was a master at fabricating shortcut bacon), this was something else entirely. As impossible as it was, seeing as though pigs had been extinct for centuries and the only kind of farmed meat consumed by citizens of The Unison was giant cricket of various settings, Jimmy was certain that he was eating actual pork.

Once he was finished with his best meal in five hundred years, Jimmy sighed with resignation at the fact he'd have to get up from the carpet at some point. A confusing second later Jimmy was sitting on the soft edge of his Emperor-sized bed again, as though by magic. Squinting, examining the room suspiciously, Jimmy checked his face for stray barbecue sauce and was surprised to find he was clean as a whistle. As Jimmy often looked like he'd been playing an intense game of paintball after most meals, surviving marinaded ribs - of all dishes - without a stray spot of sauce was a borderline miracle. More curiously, the low table and its dirty plate of stripped bones had vanished as quickly as it had arrived.

Jimmy raised his left hand to find he was holding a handkerchief so perfectly streamlined that it must have been ironed. He couldn't remember picking it up, but before he could chew on this mystery he gave a huge, unexpected sneeze. Thankfully Jimmy got the handkerchief to his nose and mouth on time and avoided spraying the clean windows with sputum.

Glaring down at the hanky that had conveniently appeared just as he needed it, Jimmy startled to see that the fancy snot-rag had vanished just as quickly as it materialised.

He'd had enough. Sweeping left and right to try and catch whoever was messing with him, trying to spot hidden cameras, Jimmy paused. Feeling more cunning than usual, he decided to test a theory by doing something simple: he desired some clean clothes. Looking down, his pyjamas had already been replaced by his yellow MacDeath fry cook apron and flip-flops.

While Jimmy wasn't deluded enough to think he'd ever be described as "smart" by anybody who understood the definition of the term, he'd come to a conclusion: somehow, this room could read his desires, even if he hadn't consciously realised them himself yet, and even more impossibly, this living space was able to bring them into effect without him noticing. As he didn't know how this version of Earth worked and wasn't even sure if Humans still lived here (perhaps the mice and the dolphins and the dogs and the monkeys and the sloths all teamed up and took over?), whoever called this planet home clearly had serious tech at their disposal. After being stuck in virtual reality long enough for several lifetimes, Jimmy dearly hoped for the second time in less than five minutes that he wasn't crammed in a tiny pod somewhere with all of his non-standard slots jammed tight with a fresh bunch of cables and piping.

He was still wondering about the Earthlings of this reality when the seamless door silently opened, and Jimmy got a good look at the first living Human he'd met since the disastrous maiden voyage of the Carpe Astrum. The dimensions of the guy's heavily-bearded face were odd, as though of a nationality Jimmy hadn't come across, though for some weird reason his features and hair reminded him of Lana. Unlike the amazing polyweave jumpsuit Jimmy was wearing, the unknown was dressed in nicotine-yellow rags that must have been fading in the Sun for three hundred years. A closer look hinted the often-repaired fabric might have been very fine at some point, but that was a long time ago. If it was Halloween, Jimmy reckoned the guy could just have easily masqueraded as a wizard or a hobo. Despite the contradiction between the obvious luxury of this place and the squalor of the man standing before him, the scars torn across the stranger's face were the most alarming detail. Dozens of lines were permanently lashed into his skin, as though by a thin-tailed whip. He clearly had trouble blinking his right eye, and ugly branches across its lid and a milky line through his iris and pupil indicated he must have upset somebody with a whip on one too many occasions.

He gave a nod of submission, clearly avoiding eye contact.

"Mr Slummer, you are the last one to awaken," the stranger said in very good Unglish, his accent unfamiliar. He indicated the hallway with a raised arm. "I would appreciate it if I could have a discussion with the four of you. Does that presently suit you?"

As he'd spent his life as a farmer-in-training followed by too many years as a fry cook for MacDeath burger joints, Jimmy wasn't used to being treated with such respect. Hoping it wouldn't go to his head, he nodded and tried to say something formal.

"That would please me greatly, my good sir."

The stranger arched an eyebrow at Jimmy's response, but clearly didn't say what came to his mind first.

"If you could follow me, please?"

Jimmy spent the rest of the short walk cursing his defective brain.

*

While the guts of the arcology twisted away into a multitude of high-ceilinged areas, the nameless servant didn't seem interested in giving Jimmy a chance to sightsee. He couldn't help but notice, however, that despite being located roughly four kilometres above sea level, this floor appeared to be filled with an actual rainforest. Gawking at swathes of tree ferns and exotic flowers, easily stepping across small creeks on non-slip stones, the calls of exotic birds and small primates echoed overhead in the canopy. Every sense told him he was deep in the kind of wilderness that hadn't existed for lifetimes, weaving along a path clearly created by people's feet. Eyeing a finger-thick snake wrapped around a fern frond, Jimmy decided to pay attention to where he was going.

After crossing a couple of cute little wooden bridges arched over meandering streams they came to a halt before an ornate door shaped from the heart of a Red Gum. Clearly hand-carved, the portal was adorned with a dozen arcology towers linked together with the long spokes of sky bridges. The twelve towers sat on a platter, which in turn rested on the shoulders of a colossal squatting naked man. If the image was to scale, the person-shaped giant must have stood at around two kilometres tall. Shrugging, Jimmy assumed the guy was just artistic licence.

Glancing at a line of gold-embossed letters situated beneath the bare feet of the Titan, Jimmy was relieved to see that there was an inscription he could read. It wasn't quite Unglish, but it was close.

"Geraldton Arcology Cluster?" Jimmy half-asked.

The nameless one nodded curtly, avoiding eye contact as the double doors opened smoothly in front of him. Jimmy followed in his wake, but stopped at a sudden wall of sunlight. Blinking away the glare, Jimmy's stomach twisted as he found himself in what could only be a courtroom. On the far side of the room a simple peaked window made from a single pane of glass soared for a hundred metres before terminating at the marbled eaves, gifting him an astonishing view of the Indian Ocean. This chamber was stepped to his left and right, and its countless soft benches and carpeted staircases ascended almost as high as the window.

Directly ahead, a sweeping central table appeared out of the glare. The slab must have required half a forest to build, and its low design matched the much smaller table that had appeared and disappeared in Jimmy's room earlier. One key difference was that didn't have any platters of pig sizzling on top, to Jimmy's disappointed. A thousand or so plush red cushions surrounded it.

Once his eyesight adjusted, Jimmy was relieved to see the others were lounging beside the table. Lana's posture was too erect, her spine unnaturally straightened as though by a rail, while Trace had crossed both forearms on the shiny oak. Tuesday was so slouched that it took a moment to tell whether he was awake or not.

The nameless one passed to Jimmy's right, taking a seat directly opposite the others on his knees. He made a curt, but respectful, motion for Jimmy to sit. He did so next to Lana, and the unknown man gave a brief hand motion before saying another word.

"As standard, these proceedings will be recorded," he said in that unusual accent. As though by magic, a better-than-real projection of The Dirty Betty appeared over his shoulder. Nobody had enough time to comment on the sharpness of the image before a phalanx of white lines intercepted the ship from a hundred angles, reducing her to burning crumbs. "First of all, I'd like to apologise for the destruction of your vessel. By the time you turned and started to slow down, our mass drivers had already fired. We registered that that the Earth was about to get annihilated by a massive incoming object moving at relativistic speeds, and our systems acted accordingly. Were the four of you the only ones on board at the time of the strike?"

Lana managed to drag her eyes away from the hovering fireball as it replayed the same five-second video over and over. She regarded the man.

"Yes. We're it."

At Lana's words, the nameless one looked at her strangely. It was as though he couldn't believe she was speaking without permission. He glanced at Tuesday, Trace and Jimmy, and seemed astonished that they didn't have a problem with Lana representing them. He went to say something, thought better of it, and made another hand gesture.

The exploding starship vanished, replaced with complex charts of genetic information. Four double-helix maps dominated most of the projection, each of them sitting atop everyone's names: Robert Tuesday, James Slummer, Lana Slade, and Tracetta Viktoria Cuddle. The proceedings continued without delay.

"As mass drivers aren't the friendliest of welcomes, I want to take this opportunity to officially extend the warmest of greetings from the Geraldton Arcology Cluster. I hope that our facilities will meet all of your needs, but for now we need to deal with a few small...details." He glanced at the screens, then back at the four survivors. "First off, as over the moon as I am to see other people after all this time, there are certain guidelines that I need to adhere to. First off, I ran your genetics, and while we have records of people who could be distant relatives of yours, none of you have official records anywhere." He nodded at Trace. "Though in your case, Ms Cuddle, alarm bells went off the moment we realised we had a descendant of George 'Guppy' Cuddle on our doorstep. As you are of such a high-profile bloodline, Ms Tracetta, I've been able to waive a massive amount of legal red tape for you and your party."

"Trace is fine," she grumbled, uncomfortable.

Lana gave the double-helix animations the stink-eye. She clicked her fingers as though realising something.

"If there's no record of us, then how do you know our names?"

"Your retinal screens," the unknown answered. He glanced at the others, still amazed that Lana was being allowed to behave like a normal person. "Our computers aren't completely compatible with yours, but we were able to trawl enough information out of your retinals for identification purposes. Due to privacy laws, and Ms Cuddle's high-level access, we didn't dig any deeper than necessary. We hope to keep these conversations civil."

"Trace is fine," she repeated, tone laced with warning.

"Conversations, plural?" Tuesday asked in a disappointed tone, surprising everyone by the fact he was awake. "So we're going to have to talk to you more than once?"

"So who are you, then?" Jimmy wondered. "You haven't even told us your name."

The stranger squinted defensively, which then turned to actual surprise.

"I'm...what? You want to know my name? Why?"

Now it was time for everyone to give him a strange look. The stranger was clearly wary, as though expecting this invitation to be some sort of trap. After a brief pause, he made a noise like two cows practising how to French kiss. As though knowing none of them would be able to mimic what he'd just perpetrated with his lips, he shrugged.

"Or just Skagen for short. You can call me Skagen." He gave a brittle smile and glanced at Jimmy, who was rubbing his eyes and trying not to yawn. "Remember Mr Slummer, the Cluster is at your beck and call."

Jimmy perked up at this. "So if I wanted a coffee…?"

"Like the one you're holding?" Tuesday snarked.

Jimmy made a rude sound at Tuesday, but then looked down to see that his fingers were wrapped around the handle of a heatproof ceramic mug. Its thick, brown contents were gently steaming. Startling, Jimmy managed to let go of the handle and scurry away from the table without scalding anyone.

"Okay," he demanded, pointing at the mug. "How in the spug does that keep happening? Things keep coming and going, appearing and disappearing, changing colour, opening and closing…"

Skagen shrugged.

"The towers in every Arcology Cluster are equipped with desire gratification software. It can tell if you want something, and deliver it to you in a non-invasive manner."

As untrusting of Artificial Intelligence as anybody who has seen a science fiction movie, the humans glanced about, expecting a machine uprising at any second.

"So your software can read our minds?" Lana asked.

Skagen scoffed. "It's not telepathic. No such thing. Far as I understand it, the system reads tiny details in your body language, facial expression, tone of voice, your vitals, the way that electrical signals zap about in the different parts of your brain.…"

Jimmy jabbed a finger at the steaming mug.

"But it can teleport coffee around, then?"

Skagen shook his head.

"No. It's just good at keeping out of sight, like any good servant."

"So how did the mug appear in my hand, then?"

"The Weavers are very, very good at not being seen."

"There's no Weavers here," Lana contradicted.

Skagen gave another hand gesture and leaned back on his cushion. As though by magic, a hundred tiny white wasp-like robots calmly appeared out of every nook and cranny: from behind chairs, around the side of people's heads, and even out of Tuesday's left ear. The Weavers were suspended on rapidly-beating wings that didn't make a sound, and their shells were pure as the driven snow. They zipped about for a couple more seconds and disappeared just as easily as they appeared.

"Those ones look a lot more impressive than our ones," Jimmy said astutely.

"They're a godsend, really," Skagen confessed. He sipped at a glass of water that hadn't been there a second ago. Nobody felt the need to comment on it. "Everyone would have died and rotted years ago if it wasn't for their care."

"Who would have rotted and died, sorry?" Jimmy asked.

"Everyone on Earth," Skagen said, as though they should know what he was talking about. Skagen crunched up his face and tapped at his forehead in annoyance. "Okay, look. There's a whole bunch of things I need answers for, right? Facts that need to be straightened out before the five of us can leave this room and go do lunch. I don't mean to give you too many spoilers about the upcoming interviews, but here's a teaser...where did you come from, exactly? Who made your ship? Was it ever capable of travelling interstellar distances? Are you truly Human? Are your genetic ages accurate, or have you been in cryogenic suspension or something? Have you been taking some sort of medication that made you immune to The Trance? If not, how have you resisted its onset?" Skagen nodded at Lana's left hand. "Also, that marble in your flesh has some astonishing security measures, and while I didn't want to risk damaging it with aggressive scans while you were asleep, I will need to know exactly what's on it."

"Immune to what?" Trace asked gruffly.

Skagen looked as though he was going to head-butt the table.

"Immune to The Trance, of course!" he snapped far too loudly, as though explaining to a dull toddler that poop isn't good to eat. Their blank expressions only made Skagen grind his teeth. "Involition Syndrome. Don't pretend you don't know what I'm talking about."

Tuesday leaned in.

"There's a lot we don't know. You'd be surprised how little we know."

Skagen took a deep breath.

"Oh Thor, you aren't going to like this," he warned.

Tapping his fingers together, what initially appeared to be a nervous tic turned out to be an order for the governing mind of the Arcology Cluster to create a sharper-than-life video above the meeting table. It was footage of a darkened room, and there wasn't much to see besides shapes in the shadows. From the way the picture tilted and sped along at a high speed, it was likely being broadcast directly from the eyes of one of those little white Weavers.

Thick windows opened on the right side of the video, allowing sunlight to bathe one of the highest levels of an arcology. It turned out the tiny Weaver was just one of tens of thousands, the air churning silently with their concentration. The sheer volume of bug like robots were a distraction from what was going on beneath them, but then something truly horrible was illuminated.

Human bodies, slumped in chairs. Thousands of them.

The Weaver zoomed right in towards one of the people seemingly at random. Panning across its inert form, the person's gender was impossible to tell even from close range. Its skin had turned a kind of grey-purple-green and both wide eyes bulged out as though they were about to pop free and bounce around on the floor. Their gaze was without a shred of intelligence, a total mindlessness. Plastic goggles had been strapped in place over them, and every few seconds a little puff of moisture prevented the bloodshot orbs from drying into sultanas. Worse yet, headphones had been brutally stapled to both ears, relaying who-know-what into its brain.

Descending a metre, the chest and abdomen of the inert lump of flesh turned out to be threaded with dozens of tubes. As the four survivors had woken up to a similar nightmare less than a couple of months ago, it wasn't difficult to see that the pipes included stomach, bowel and bladder ports, removing any need for eating and trips to the toilet. If you looked really close, you could see its ribcage barely rising and falling, indicating they were still breathing without apparent assistance.

Unconsciously running her fingers over the metal port bumps beneath the self-cleaning fabric of her black dress shirt, Lana silently noted their alignment and size seemed to be identical to the sub-zombie on the screen. Before she could comment on this coincidence, a swarm of Weavers suddenly appeared in frame and plunged into the motionless hunk of meat. The living corpse jerked and spasmed as though electrocuted, a crude therapy most likely employed to prevent its muscles from atrophying to gel.

As usual, Jimmy was the first one to pike out, barely getting to his feet as he threw up masticated pork ribs as far from the table as he could manage. Thankfully, a bucket had appeared in his hands half a second before he vomited, protecting the softer-than-angora carpet. Ignoring the horrible noises of Jimmy evacuating his stomach, Lana was locked on the rows of the living dead. She didn't bother to glance at Skagen when she asked the most obvious question of her life.

"What's wrong with them?" she looked at him, and found the answer in his eyes. "This is The Trance, isn't it?"

Skagen nodded.

"So everyone is like this?" Trace growled.

He breathed in and out slowly.

"Everyone. Forty-seven billion, all up, spread across a thousand Arcology Clusters."

Tuesday said a bad word in passable Guttertongue.

"How long have they been…this? It's like they're made from pudding."

Skagen took a few moments to answer, as though saying the words made him feel dirty.

"Nearly seventy years."

"What…what causes it?" Jimmy asked, wiping his mouth.

*

The trouble begun three generations ago when a team of geneticists and neuroscientists cured autism. Like cancer, AIDS, diabetes, depression and chewing with your mouth open, autism became a relic of the past, joining the ranks of polio and whooping cough and smallpox and genital herpes.

Decades after erasing autism from Mankind's more affluent portion, a bizarre plague ripped its way through the developed world like a box cutter across skin. Unlike more traditional outbreaks, what came to be officially classified as Involition Syndrome – though almost always referred to as "The Trance" by anybody who dared speak its name - didn't make you burn with fever or break down the tissues of your body or cause internal bleeding or give you so much as a sore throat or a headache. Such symptoms would make it relatively easy to target and cure with modern medicine. No, Involition Syndrome went straight for the mind, and it took less than a day to go from inception to fatal.

One minute, you're fine. You're a total normal going about your business as a pampered First World shlub wallowing in obscene luxury. Then, without any warning, Stage One of The Trance will kick in, robbing you of your memory and your capacity to take on any new information. Its effect was comparable to having a series of strokes, but without any physical hallmarks. So not only would you immediately forget what you're doing and why, you'll forget who you are. After wandering about aimlessly for a while, moaning and rolling your eyes in idiocy, Stage Two will remove your consciousness in one slice, leaving you gaping and drooling and staring into space as a catatonic. Stage Three is where Involition Syndrome truly earns its name, as this is the point where the afflicted lose their drive to breathe and stopped swallowing their saliva, drowning in their own spit within minutes. Calling them zombies was an insult to the undead, because at least zombies are motivated by hunger. Stage Threes just stood there and died.

Nobody ever stopped at Stage One. Progression to Stages Two and Three was one hundred percent inevitable.

Eventually, after a colossal death toll, it was discovered that while Stage Threes were unable to will themselves to do anything, they could still follow simple instructions. The key to keeping the living dead from expiring turned out to be pretty simple and low-tech: you attached headphones to their ears and played a looped sound file that told them to breathe in and out and to swallow their spit (though in the correct order and timeframe, obviously). It was necessary to install a catheter and a stoma before their bladders and bowels ruptured, but keeping Stage Threes alive was hardly nuclear physics.

Eating was out of the question, as having dinner like a normal person involved too many complex components (cutting up your food into the right size and shape, spearing it with a fork, raising it to your mouth, opening your jaw the right width, inserting the food without stabbing yourself, chewing the appropriate amount of times, and so on and so on), so this was usually solved with tubes down the nostrils and pipes in the stomach.

But these were all stopgap solutions. In a matter of months The Trance had struck all over the Arcology Clusters of the developed world, and nothing was able to slow it, let alone defeat it. Quarantine procedures achieved zip, and the medical community couldn't even figure out what was causing its onset, which kind of made The Trance impossible to treat. As it couldn't be blamed on any virus or pathogen or any other classic hallmark of infection, this meant there was no way to develop a vaccine.

After the worst eighteen months the Arcology Clusters of Earth had ever experienced, ninety-six percent of the population were Stage Threes. Entire continents - North America, Canada, Europe, Asia, Australia, and the Middle East - were filled with endless fields of drooling meat. Tens of billions of motionless people just sat there decaying, breathing in synchronisation to the commands of a sound file fluted through nailed-on ear buds, staring at the walls, lifeless, silent corpses fit for nothing but to rot.

The most popular hypothesis was that a terror cell from Craplakistan or some other armpit of a country had attacked the developed world with a neurological weapon, perhaps gradually dispersed over several months. By the time the nerds and boffins figured out what had really happened, it was too late. The cure for autism was at fault, and as it had been indelibly crafted into the Human Genome itself, it could not be removed. Its genetic wiring was designed to last forever.

Tragically, one of the greatest medical feats of all time had planted the seeds of disaster in the minds of Humanity, and now the harvest time had come.

There was nothing that could be done. Mankind had engineered itself into a living death. But there were some who could not accept this...

*

By the time an orange sun dipped into the waters of the Indian Ocean like a biscuit into hot tea, the last four survivors of a redundant reality had almost finished explaining their story. It was clear Skagen didn't believe a third of what they were saying, and every now and again a sudden left-field question would be spiked into the conversation in a blunt attempt to trip them up. As what they were saying was the truth, however, the verbal patchwork of their lives following the Carpe Astrum Disaster remained intact.

Thankfully, once it became clear his guests weren't trying to pull a fast one on him, Skagen's questions became less aggressive and more fascinated. Before Tuesday could proudly share how he'd murdered an entire Universe, however, Skagen raised a finger.

"These devices you took from the Vault," he said quietly. "Where are they now?"

Lana shrugged.

"I accidentally burned out the teeny tiny Carpe Astrum, incinerating its microscopic crew, the Mulligan vanished the moment we were sent reality-hopping, and the Generation Gun was only good for one shot." She nodded at Jimmy. "And I'm assuming the UF, like all our god-level technology, ceased to work the moment we get stranded in this reality, right?"

"The what?" Skagen asked.

"Universal Fabricator," Jimmy answered, knowing the answer to a question for once.

Finally getting the hang of how to get the Arcology Cluster to do useful things, as Jimmy extended his hand towards Skagen the Universal Fabricator was already on his palm. It unfolded into thousands of black right-angled triangles before clicking into a wireframe donut in less than a breath. Hovering above Jimmy's fingers, the device projected dozens of master template menus in distinct colours: white for medical, red for military-grade destruction, green for terraforming, purple for interstellar manipulation, light blue for genetic engineering, and pink for developing and harnessing latent psychic abilities...

"Well, look at that," Jimmy said casually. "Seems it still works."

Everyone was silent for a good thirty seconds. Somehow, Skagen managed to keep his next words relatively calm.

"Are you telling me that you're holding a device that can recreate the medical technology of perfect people from the 30th Century?"

Jimmy made eye contact with the others, clearly uncomfortable with being the centre of attention. The way they were looking at him made his stomach clench. He slowly closed his hand, and the UF shrunk back into its little cylinder shape, no bigger than one of Tuesday's vile chlorine cigarettes.

"Um...yes?"

There were another few moments of stunned silence, but then Skagen did something with his face that might have been a smile. It looked painful, as though his muscles weren't used to being stretched in such directions. He stood without a word, brushing at his ancient clothes.

"Come with me," he said simply.

"Why?" Trace demanded.

Although Skagen didn't appear to offer a direct command, another video appeared in mid-air. It was a still image of a woman in a nice business suit, and while her hair and makeup were perfect, a millimetre beneath that polished veneer lived somebody who had lost all hope. Even when she started speaking she seemed lifeless, as though she didn't see any point in breathing, let alone forming words. Despite that, she pushed out one syllable after another. It was clear this video was just one small part of a larger recording.

"...has been declared. However, there is one order that transcends all of these emergency provisions. If somebody finds a way to cure Involition Syndrome, there is no cost too great to pay for such a breakthrough. Speaking as the final governmental chairperson, on behalf of every Cluster, I announce that no crime is too great, no sacrifice too unbearable, no research too vile, if it leads to a fix. The researchers working on The Equation have top priority, and all resources are theirs for the taking with zero exceptions..."

The video stopped again. Skagen gave a snort.

"You know, just a week before this recording, she was the President of the Parent Teacher Association in the Little Rock Arcology Cluster. Then suddenly she finds herself as the last politician in the world by merit of Dead Man's Boots." Skagen paused. "But that's not the point. What matters is that you possess something that might save the world."

Standing, Lana didn't make a move to follow Skagen.

"What is The Equation?" she repeated.

CHAPTER THIRTY SIX

Now that the cause of The Trance had been identified, a total of two-hundred-and-fifty-six individuals, the greatest remaining minds from dozens of scientific and medical fields across the world, were brought together to work on a cure. Virologists, geneticists, neuroscientists, and software engineers were all equally welcomed. The criteria for being a part of this team was simple: you had to be a Professor in a useful area, and your brain couldn't be porridge from The Trance.

The Professors would do all of the research and development from within a one-of-a-kind synthesised reality program known as the Construct, a time-distorting co-op hallucination that would allow their minds to accomplish the century-or-so of work that this task was projected to take in the Virtual while only a few months passed in the Actual. After all, if the Professors developed a cure in real time, anybody who was still alive in the Actual would be well beyond the age of reproduction, making their efforts worthless. And yes, while the average life expectancy of a person living in an Arcology Cluster in the 25th Century was the better part of two hundred years, there was no need to cut things too close. The quicker this near-extinction event was avoided, the better.

This project, this last-ditch attempt, was called The Equation. As all the best writers and advertising masterminds had already joined the ranks of the living dead, nobody bothered to come up with a better name.

Unfortunately, cryogenically freezing the Professor's brains turned out to be the only sure-fire way of delaying The Trance from zombifying the lot of them, so they had to be literally put on ice. Defrosting them would be lethal, so their work on The Equation was going to be a one-way trip whether they were successful or not.

The Professors dealt with all these obstacles in a simple way: they just didn't think about them.

*

The five of them were sitting inside a roomy fan-car within minutes. None of the visitors were certain, but it seemed as though the arcology was able to rearrange its inner structure for the convenience of anybody inside of it, allowing a long walk to become a few dozen metres. As with the Weavers, this all happened without anyone noticing. There weren't any complaints, but it was hard to ignore the image of getting crushed between two floors like mosquitoes in a giant's palms.

As the science behind antigrav wafers didn't work in this reality, the fan-car lived up to its name by being a large, streamlined caravan sprouting a dozen dumpster-sized turbines. After exchanging a few uncertain glances they followed Skagen into the large block. Reclining on yet more red cushions in what appeared to be the living room of the fan-car, a good ninety seconds passed before Tuesday got impatient.

"What's the holdup?" he demanded. "I thought we were going to see some scientists."

Skagen leaned out from his seat, flipping through a dense manual made from actual paper. If Lana hadn't been hardwired with numerous historical programs at the Academy, she might not have recognised it to be an antique-style book.

"Just need to brush up on the controls."

Trace made a noise in her throat. "What, you haven't flown one of these things in a while?"

Skagen seemed a little sheepish.

"Uh, yeah. A while. Right."

Popping out of view again, there was a horrible crunching, clanking noise, followed by the fan-car jolting violently. Everyone could hear the turbines wailing through the padded interior, but it sounded as though they were flaring up and down out of synchronisation.

Lana sighed after a second jolt.

"Great. Last man on Earth, and he doesn't know how to drive."

*

After fifteen Actual years of countless dead-ends and fruitless research, all but one of the Professors decided solving this problem was impossible and they'd be much happier filling the Construct with every conceivable luxury and pleasure. They launched spacefaring palaces made of scrimshawed marble, rode fire-breathing dragons down streets literally paved with gold, and consorted endlessly with heaving piles of stunningly beautiful (or handsome) concubines. The Construct devolved into little more than a virtual orgy for almost twenty years, and The Equation went ignored.

Not content to watch Mankind's only hope sleaze their lives away, a low-ranking Professor by the name of Phergo Saleh expressed his distaste for their betrayal by finding a way to murder the Actual bodies of the two highest-ranking Professors, Dunston Alistair and Kenneth Balver. After the very public deaths of Alistair and Balver, Saleh wiped away all the filth and excess and replaced it with one law: work on The Equation in your designated role or suffer the consequences. Designating himself as The Director, Saleh's contemporaries learned their work was no longer a choice, but a duty.

Within hours of his coup, there were no more towers on the bony spine of Mount Everest, no castles on Mars, no hand-plastered keeps embraced by reams of deep scarlet velvet lit by the flickering of countless runny candles. Every batch of perfect hand-coded brandy was deleted, and all the cigars rolled on the virtual thighs of Cuban virgins were reduced to less than vapour. The Construct went back to being a place of work, adorned with just a few small details designed to keep everyone from going completely insane from a lack of visual and tactile stimuli.

As each of the Actual bodies of the Professors were little more than frozen meat skewered with enough plumbing to open an entire water park, their virtual avatars didn't need to sleep or eat, and that meant all they did was study. The only thing they had to look forward to was half an hour of scheduled downtime with Immersives every week, and this small recreational allowance was often interrupted if The Equation had a sudden need for more hard drive space (which it always did). Eventually, The Director wiped the Immersives along with every other pleasure so his workforce had nothing to distract them.

After decades of uninterrupted intellectual toil and a series of utterly baffling suicides, The Director had grudgingly recovered a handful of titles from the Trash and allowed recreation breaks so long as everyone stayed on schedule.

*

It took a good ten minutes of acceleration before the Geraldton Arcology Cluster started sinking from view. The dozen towers slowly receded into the gloom of dusk, their sunset-coloured skins continuing to form pleasing patterns like amazing lava lamps until they were little more than featureless monoliths. As the four-klick-tall spires shrank, it turned out they rested upon a giant round platter the length of Manhattan. The mists and smoke of ground-level parted for the first time since Jimmy woke up in an Emperor-sized bed, and something impossible was revealed.

It took Tuesday a moment to ask the obvious question, as he seemed to lose control over his mouth for an instant.

"The Hell is that?" Tuesday finally pushed out.

Although Skagen was facing the opposite way and focusing on flying the fan-car, he didn't need anybody to draw a diagram. His head turned a couple of degrees.

"It's an Atlassian. All the Clusters literally rest on their shoulders."

The Titan wasn't difficult to describe. It was a colossal crouching man, bowed down on one knee, holding the entirety of the Geraldton Arcology Cluster atop a round plate on his shoulders. Unlike the bright towers, the Atlassian seemed to be hewed from plain stone, skin grey and rough and thick as a mountain. Whether he was able to move wasn't clear.

"How tall is he, standing up?" Jimmy asked.

Trace gave a grunt of annoyance.

"I've heard the word 'kilometre' enough times today. He's big, okay?"

"So you never had Atlassians on your Earth?" Skagen called. He gave a sharp bark of laughter at their silence. "They kept the peace, in a way. Every country's Military had at least one, maybe a dozen or more in the case of larger superpowers. You might be able to nuke a country, virus-bomb a continent, perhaps even burn away the atmosphere of an entire hemisphere with a chemical weapon, but then you'd have a bunch of those guys coming for you. And nothing stops them except other Atlassians. Thankfully, they're happy just to hang out and meditate nowadays."

"Did they get built following the Skandinavian Expansion?" Lana asked, watching the Atlassian in case he moved a little.

For the first time since they'd met, Skagen didn't answer them. He offered no apologies, allowing the awkward quiet to build.

*

By the time they were whirring north-east over the Pacific Ocean the survivors discovered this fan-car was equipped with all the mod-cons a pampered Cluster citizen would demand: vast libraries of Immersives of all genres and eras, hardcover books preserved in rot-defying laminate film, a fully-stocked Repler capable of brewing up anything you wanted simply by walking towards it and desiring food or drink, a gym made up of CuddleTech tactile holographics that adjusted their weight and structure according to your physical health needs (including the ever-popular short-term memory disruption feature that safely burned out the knowledge you'd recently experienced the discomfort of working out), and a small chemical spinner that could breed non-addictive, harmless designer viruses for every conceivable mood and effect. Needless to say nobody had any interest in spending time with boring old Skagen anymore, and the four half-starved refugees slid into total decadence within minutes.

Later, unable to sleep despite being bone-tired, Lana found herself staring up at the softly glowing ceiling tiles from an almost too-comfortable sleeping pallet after twenty minutes of silent reflection. Finally sick of hearing the snores of Trace, Tuesday and Jimmy, a chorus best described as both phlegmy and porcine, she mumbled in annoyance and padded up the short hall to where Skagen was driving. Although he didn't seem to be doing much besides watching for the distant shores of what used to be Japan, Skagen didn't bother to acknowledge Lana's presence. She sat down on the passenger's side and was rewarded by a noise in his throat. This rudeness made what she wanted to say a lot easier.

"What the bum is your problem with me, Skagen?"

This produced a response. He locked eyes with her, examining the features of her face. Then he went back to staring at the Pacific.

"Sorry, have I said something to offend you?" he asked, his words gilded with subtext.

Lana huffed.

"You know what I mean. Every time I said something during that interrogation, you looked at the others as though they should be...be punishing me or something. Like I didn't have the right to speak, like I'm breaking some major social nicety with every word." Lana held out her hands almost placatingly. "Don't pretend I'm mental, please. You have a problem with me, but as you're one of only five Humans on this world that still possesses the capacity to speak, I want to clear the air and move on as friends. Can we do that?"

To her surprise, Skagen looked at her with true pain.

"I am unsure if you are familiar with this term in your reality, but I am of the blood shamed." Skagen paused after his confession, waiting for a reaction, but Lana only blinked. The word clearly didn't ring any bells. Skagen indicated his nicotine-coloured clothing. "Surely you've noticed what I'm wearing. These garments were some of the finest the late 21st Century had to offer, and their like were worn by Dukes and Barons and Kings. The males of my bloodline have carried these clothes for over four hundred years, mending them endlessly as they faded and whitened and rotted. These are the clothes of one of the original blood shamed, the patriarch of my direct family line, a monarch descended from Belgian and Swedish royalty."

Lana's jaw dropped as her mind twigged. It took a second for her to put her realisation into words.

"You...you're a Skando?"

"I can trace my family name back for two thousand years. I'm as Skandinavian as they come." Skagen said almost with pride, a weird reaction for admitting something so reviled. "As one of the blood shamed, even in my wildest dreams I couldn't conceive of being seen as a Human, let alone lucky enough to be a second-class citizen..."

Skagen's words tapered off, and just a Lana was convinced the man had finished talking, he broke the silence.

"Like all the blood shamed, I experienced a regimented series of whippings and booting's and starvation and torture, but even that didn't prepare me for what happened when the blood shamed were blamed for The Trance." He looked away sharply, as though trying to hide his expression from Lana. "We may have been slaves born only to suffer for the sins of our ancestors, but the onset of The Trance was when the lineage of the blood shamed truly ended. We were formed up in a long column, asked what we knew about The Trance, and summarily executed when we would not talk, not that we had anything worthwhile to say. Men, women, children, butchered. I was the last one alive in the Geraldton Cluster, covered in the blood of my friends and family from the ghetto, shaking and trying not to throw up. Only reason I wasn't gunned down like the others was because that was the very minute they discovered their own vaccines had caused it. They just lowered the gun from my temple and walked away. Its barrel was so hot from the last fifty executions that it burned a permanent circle into my scalp. They didn't even offer me a towel to wipe my brother's and father's blood off my face, let alone an apology."

Lana placed a hand on Skagen's shoulder. Despite everyone being asleep, she kept her voice down. He stiffened at her touch, as though unaccustomed to Human contact.

"So you're saying you don't understand why the others treat me as an equal, even though..."

He moved as though wanting to shrug her away, but merely twitched.

"I saw your bloodwork, Lana. You're a blood shamed just like me, a pure descendant of six of the most hated royal lines in all Human history. If it wasn't for the fact you're from a different reality, you'd be my second-cousin...genetically, at least. So I'm assuming your true origins never came up in conversation?" Skagen huffed, not bothering to wait for a response. "Hells, what am I saying? A descendant of George Cuddle would have killed you on principal the moment she found out." Skagen sat on this for a while until his curiosity won out. "So what did they do with the blood shamed in your reality?"

Lana shrugged. "The Unison shipped them all out to a penal colony called The Kennel near Sirius, the Dog Star. Their starship was so thoroughly sabotaged it was a wonder it even lifted off. They got lost in deep space, where a radiation leak mutated them into a species of intersex creatures over most of a century, and then they became rich as godlings when they accidentally found a gigantic ice cube floating between star systems. You know, the usual kind of thing." She glanced at one of the rear-view mirrors and waved towards the point where the Australian coastline had vanished hours ago. "What happened to all the others?"

"What others?"

"Surely not every Human lived in the Clusters? And from what little I've gleaned about Cluster citizens, I doubt they were the type to go and pass out their precious genetic cures to everyone."

Skagen huffed again. "Fast learner. No, a good two-thirds of Mankind missed out on the vaccines. But to really plop a rotten cherry on top of the poop sundae, as none of them were affected by The Trance, they got blamed for it just as the blood shamed were..."

"I'm sensing a pattern here."

"Heh, yeah."

"So...was it executions in the streets again?"

Skagen chewed at his lip. "No. Diplomatic relations broke down so badly that it came close to all-out war, but once The Trance started taking a real hold over the Clusters they weren't in a position to keep acting like bastards. In fact, the Clusters were so desperate towards the end that they came to the outsiders for help, but – surprise, surprise! – the outsiders decided to wait until they could take the arcologies for themselves and boot out the mindless meat into the wilds."

"Obviously they didn't do that."

"No." Skagen double-checked a map, just to be sure. It was mighty dark in the middle of the ocean, and the spotlights on their turbines didn't seem to be doing all that much to change that fact. "No, instead they started World War Five to decide who was going to claim the Clusters. To ensure the arcology people wouldn't benefit from using dead outsider bodies in curing The Trance, it became common practise to incinerate the deceased. It took decades, but eventually all of civilisation was ashes. The charcoal is still warm in a lot of places." Skagen snorted. "Before you lot dropped out of the sky, I'd already seen the end happen twice over."

They sat in silence for a time. Surprisingly, this was a comfortable thing for the two of them to do.

CHAPTER THIRTY SEVEN

Dawn blushed a deep arterial red as they churned into what used to be Okinawa. Sure, it was under twenty fathoms of seawater and an infestation of Red King Crabs were the ruin's only residents, but it still had a name.

When Skagen coiled up the fan-car back in Geraldton its cabin was glowing a happy duck shell blue, assuring him the vehicle was within Australian borders and he was most welcome to zip around wherever he desired. It darkened to a cautioning yellow in International Waters, a void of nuclear waste dumping grounds once lorded over only by pirates and party boats, turned more and more jaundiced after Skagen and Lana drifted off at the wheel. Hours later, the lemon screens snapped into a glowing, volcanic orange and an incomprehensible announcement blared out of every intercom speaker. Waking to find the cabin flashing like the heart of an active Vesuvius, it took Lana a second to realise she'd fallen asleep against the blood shamed.

Their fan-car stopped on a dime, hovering in place over an expanse of steaming, churning surf. Smacking at the simple control panel, Skagen pressed every button, flipped every switch, swiped ten different touchpads and twisted the figure-eight yoke in a dozen revolutions. Slapping the wheel like a stoned teenager getting angry at a video game, he shot Lana an apologetic look before thinking to check the map. He had to yell to be heard.

"See that? We've come to a halt three centimetres from Japanese airspace. Pretty sure that babble is an automatic warning telling us we don't have permission to proceed." Squinting out the windshield, Skagen nodded at the crimson horizon where a familiar cloud-piercing shape loomed a long, long way off. "See? Matsuyama Arcology Cluster. While I've admittedly never been to Japan, I do know that most international Clusters turned isolationist during the early onset of The Trance. Visitors weren't encouraged, to say the least."

"Self-sufficient, operating automatically with zero waste, and enough genetic diversity to avoid…concerns?" Lana shrugged. "No real need to ever open the doors again, is there?"

"Your point?" Tuesday yawned as he leaned against the pilot's chair, unready for proper snark.

Skagen's sigh was lost in the maelstrom.

"Let's just hope we don't rate as unwelcome guests to any Cluster defence systems. It wouldn't be good for our collective life expectancies."

Lana squinted, forcing her retinals to translate the irritating alert. As Japanese had been a long-dead language by the time she was getting her brain scalded with AutoEducation lessons, Lana tried applying Half-Mandarin, Korean Emoji, Vietnamese Hieroglyphics and Tagalog-2 to see if they were close enough to work as a translation stopgap. She was both amazed and irritated this didn't work one bit.

"Should we be worried?" Jimmy shouted, having trouble raising his gentle voice high enough to be heard.

Skagen shook the yoke again.

"People, all I know about Japan is they have four Clusters. I'm not qualified to comment on anything located further away than my bed-cell back in Geraldton." Skagen twitched his nose. "Or was it five? Yes, they have five Clusters."

"Reckon they may see us as a threat?" Trace growled, her usual volume sufficient despite the din.

Skagen shook his head.

"No, they'd be able to tell if we intended anything untoward. As long as we don't harbour any desire to cause Japan or its people harm, we should be..."

"What?" Trace boomed, missing half of what Skagen had just said as the din grew a little. "Should be what?"

Skagen tried again.

"Pretty sure Cluster defence networks operate in a similar way to their desire gratification systems. They can't read minds, but it'd be clear from a thousand kilometres away if somebody harboured anything but the best of intentions. Those mass drivers are smart as whips."

Tuesday rested his chin on Skagen's shoulder and hissed into his ear.

"Man, we're all screwed, because I always have the worst intentions."

Lana choked a little at Skagen's words.

"Uh, are you talking about the same intelligent mass drivers that blasted an unarmed civilian starship full of refugees into dust just yesterday?"

Skagen scowled at her. "Really? You know that was an accident. I apologised a couple of times already."

Lana noticed that Trace had gone stone-faced.

"What's the matter with you?"

Trace twitched a little, her expression weird.

"It's like that brain puzzle. You know, where you don't think of purple elephants riding unicycles?"

"Come again?"

Trace gripped Lana's arm hard enough to leave bruises. Her face was pained, as though trying to figure out a physics equation while juggling chainsaws on a trampoline.

"He told us not to have any bad intentions towards Japan, and now I can't stop. The images...the urges!"

Trace's face crunched up like a rusty spring. Sweat beaded on her shaved head, trickling through a nest of metal, ceramic and bone piercings. Despite the alarms, everyone was transfixed by her anguish.

"When I try to stop, it gets worse. It always, always gets worse..."

"Are we going to get blasted if the defence system picks up on something it doesn't like?" Lana asked Skagen out of the side of her mouth. "Will we get a warning, at least?"

At that the orange lights deepened to a demonic red, and the alarm guttered into a howl from the deepest pit. Nobody could understand the words, but it was clear the alert had switched to a full-on declaration of war. Holographics played over the windshield, identifying weapon systems warming up from as far away as Wakkanai and Mount Fuji.

"Being targeted by twenty-six mass drivers," Skagen managed, eyes darting. "No, twenty-nine...thirty-six...fifty-eight...oh spug..."

"Cut it out!" Jimmy moaned, pawing at Trace's shoulder armour.

New animated glyphs appeared. They were clearly radiation symbols. Every second that passed saw another dozen pop up to say hello and give a nudge and a wink about the upcoming nuclear holocaust.

Trace squeezed her own skull so hard enough that her complexion matched the warning lights, gritting her teeth so hard it was a wonder they hadn't popped yet. But then Tuesday carefully put a hand on her bulging tricep and stood on his tippy-toes to ask a question just centimetres from her ear.

"Hey, Trace, does this smell like concentrated Halothane gas to you?"

Turning her head a little in confusion, Trace didn't have time to push out a word before Tuesday sprayed a small atomiser bottle right in her face. Choking on a cloud of powerful general anaesthetic, all Trace could do was make a hostile noise at the back of her throat and collapse like a redwood. Her temple smacked Lana's headrest hard enough to break the roll of padding clean off, but thankfully a Trace-sized mattress conveniently appeared before she could smash her head against the thinly-carpeted metal struts. It was nice to know the fan-car possessed some small imitation of a desire fulfilment system.

The red alert dialled right down through orange to yellow, and then all the little symbols vanished. With their most pressing threat over, Lana was on Trace instantly, trying to find a pulse in her corded neck. She exhaled in relief and shot

Tuesday a deadly look.

"You could have killed her with that. You can't just go ballpark-figure with general anaesthetic."

Tuesday raised his eyebrows. "She's still alive? Bonus."

*

The following messages were just as incomprehensible as the first few, but simply crossing the last few centimetres into Japanese airspace was clearly a Welcome Wagon moment. Despite the whole "getting murdered with science guns" issue working itself out without fatalities, nobody was keen to go back to bed just in case they woke up as a smear of vapour in a mushroom cloud. Plus, everyone knew how legendarily crazy old Japan was rumoured to be before it transformed into something else entirely in their home reality, and they wanted to see if the rumours were true...and, specifically, how true.

To everyone's disappointment, it turned out Japan's oddities were now hidden well below sea level, and all that remained of its neon cities were barnacle-studded ruins. The bright lights had burned out years ago, and the few sections of dissolving highways that still peeked out from the ocean were clogged solid with the skeletons of electric cars and water-powered scooters. All the famous skyscrapers had been cut off just above sea level as though by a gigantic arc welder, and the only signs of civilisation were crude campsites set up on the tallest stumps. These slums were connected together by angled walkways made from scrap, but the canvas tents pitched at their highest points all flapped free and empty in the wind. There were dozens of tied-off boats that must have been used to row between these tick-on-a-dog's-back settlements for trade or war or just to say hi over a bowl of warm Ramen, but most drifted freely. The last stragglers had clearly died a slow death before vanishing entirely.

The Matsuyama Arcology Cluster came and went, growing to dominate everything before shrinking back into the misty gloom of early morning. The opaque outer skin of its twelve towers cycled between vivid scenes from the most popular anime Immersives all the way down to a kneeling Atlassian bearing a plinth. Like in Geraldton, the thousands of connective walkways were empty, and blisters of hanging traffic lights cycled endlessly for just one fan-car: theirs. Within, fifty million catatonic residents rotted in their muscle-stimulating thrones, eyes blanker than passed-out bovines.

They paused on the far side of the Cluster while Skagen spun through the auto-map. Flicking and tapping the touchscreen for a solid minute, he clicked his tongue with wordless satisfaction as he found what he was looking for.

"Knew it was further north-east," he said, seemingly for his own benefit.

*

The hellish promise of deepest summer had boiled away the morning mists by the time a dark-green shape dominated the windshield. A single tower rather than twelve, as Sol rose higher and higher in the dawn sky they could pick out details on the architectural spear with the naked eye. Shaped in the streamlined fashion of an Arcology, the lowest third of the structure was a huge pair of hands wrapping their fingers around what seemed to be a staff, a scaled-up emulation of a simple tree branch, sort of like the kind those idiots from the Chaotic Neutral Wizard cult used to carry around to point at people. The staff extended skyward for hundreds of metres, though most of it was tightly bound by an ancient, colossal rainbow serpent that gave the illusion of writhing at first glance. The slithering, hooded reptile bared its fangs at the Sun, its forked tongue lashing the moon as though angling to strike God's heel. Beneath its slitted eye was a gigantic, unmissable, day-glow white brand logo: Thoughtplane. Directly below the logo was a string of kanji symbols, likely its Japanese translation.

Jimmy absently touched the bracket of ports on his temple. He could clearly remember seeing the same holographic logo on the metal bored into his skull. The coincidence bothered him, but he didn't feel cruel enough to worry the others with his concerns.

The fan-car's windshield lit up in Unglish lettering to declare what they were approaching was called "The Needle of Asclepius," along with a distance counter rapidly spooling down towards zero. A helpful message appeared once they got within fifteen kilometres of the spire.

"Heaven-level-secure corporate facility," Jimmy said out loud, exchanging his current worries with fresh ones. "Breaches of any kind will be met with an overwhelmingly lethal response."

"Nice way of saying they nuke people like us on sight," Tuesday coughed.

As the fan-car got closer it became clear the lower third of the facility wasn't green, but carved from pure white marble. A dense coat of ivy, seaweed, moss and seventy years of seagull droppings fought for dominance on its weathered surface. Skagen made an ugly noise in his throat.

"This isn't right," he muttered to himself, obviously not used to being around sentient people. "The Needle should be gleaming. These Japanese labs are meant to be as clean outside as they are inside, especially this one."

"What are you saying?" Lana pressed. "We're safe though, right? We're allowed to go inside?"

Ascending far above the massive staff without bothering to answer any of Lana's salient points, Skagen tilted the fan-car towards the fangs of the snake. Reaching the tip of its curved tongue, the lash turned out to be a landing pad big enough to comfortably fit a dozen fan-cars, perhaps more if you were particularly skilled at parking.

Nobody had a chance to ask how they were meant to get inside The Needle before the tongue retracted cleanly into its gullet. The depressing flatness of the Japanese skyline vanished, replaced by a boring white cylinder only partially lit by an odd pattern of surfboard-sized lighting panels. Most of the slabs flickered in an epileptic manner, and one of them actually exploded as they descended past it. After twenty seconds every screen in the fan-car and all the lights in the cylinder decided to lose power at the same time, darkening as though blown out by an EMP.

"Et by a giant snake," Tuesday mumbled in the darkness. "Not how I want to go. Reckon we should go back out the way we came in, right, Beardo?"

Skagen was clearly resisting the urge to wrestle the dead controls. Like anybody else, he was uncomfortable with being moved around by unseen, unknown forces. Thankfully, the lighting panels and the fan-car's systems all lurched back to life, and the swallow continued. Trace made a noise in her unconsciousness just before Skagen gave his standard shrug.

"It shouldn't have been so easy to get in," he said quietly. "This is the most secure location on Earth. There's meant to be a gauntlet of security checks, background assessments and a tonne of decontamination procedures just to be allowed to speak to somebody over the phone. They aren't meant to leave the screen door swinging like this. Something's wrong here, very wrong."

Tuesday put a hand on Skagen's shoulder a little too roughly. The blood shamed startled at Human contact.

"Okay, I'm going to need some really compelling reasons as to why I shouldn't reef your arse out of that chair and head for sunshine."

Skagen gave Tuesday the gift of contempt.

"Because deep inside of The Needle of Asclepius are Earth's final geniuses, the only hope we have of curing The Trance. And with your technology, today might finally be that day."

Tuesday rubbed at his eyes in exhaustion.

"Yes, but what's in it for me? This place is clearly an entire shelf-worth of Work Health & Safety issues, and I need a guarantee it'll be worth my while braving it."

Skagen double-checked Tuesday's expression, scanning for sarcasm without any luck. Ashamed at how Tuesday's selfish words might reflect on her little group, Lana changed the subject.

"Do you know much about The Needle?"

"Well, it's a Thoughtplane research facility, the best temporal-dilating workspace on the planet," Skagen answered, his eyes flicking from light to light as they scrolled past. "If somebody needed to crunch massive numbers, The Needle would allow them to achieve years of work in a matter of hours by messing with their brain's perception of time. Corporations used to pay Thoughtplane unbelievable sums to spend a single Actual afternoon inside. At one point, the order of each week's bookings basically decided how Wall Street was going to ebb and flow."

Jimmy waved this explanation away.

"Wait, I thought Thoughtplane made Immersives?"

Skagen nodded. "Sure, best on the market. I'm not an expert on the subject or anything, but from what I understand, The Needle works a lot like slotting an Immersive...only instead of pretending to conquer Amerika single-handedly as a bullet-resistant war criminal, or simulating a virtual booty call with any and every Playmate at the same time, your mind is inserted into a Construct of pure mathematics, a workspace of numbers." He waggled a finger. "Of course, The Needle was refitted to permanently host the team who are trying to cure The Trance. This entire tower is a huge stack of computing grunt powered by the biggest fusion reactor on the planet, and it's been working on just one problem for the last seventy years." He rubbed his hands together eagerly. "For all we know, they've already solved it. Imagine that!"

Angling her left hand towards the scrolling lights, Lana tapped at the Omni bump located between her thumb and index finger.

"I wonder how powerful the reactor..."

Noticing too late, Skagen only had time to half-open his mouth in warning as a bolt of electricity surged from the tips of Lana's fingers to the crown of her head. Luckily she was slammed deep into the comfy co-pilot's rubber chair rather than against a hard bulkhead, but the zap was more than violent enough to knock the sense out of her. The stench of burnt hair made everyone gag.

"Okay," Lana managed with a distinct quaver, proving she was still alive. Her left hand was striped red and tingling from the security feedback attack, and the word VOID hovered above her knuckles in a hostile crimson. "Seems the top-secret research computer doesn't like being scanned without permission. Should have guessed that, honestly."

*

Five minutes passed before they literally hit rock bottom with an unpleasant crunch. Nuclear-proof barriers snuffed out the distant grey dot of sky far above, the great slabs of Densite-lined tuffcrete guaranteeing that whatever work went on in this place would not be interrupted by anything short of a supernova. Darkness slammed down as the blast doors sealed, and everybody sat still and quiet when the cabin of the fan-car also went black. After seeing Lana get lightly fricasseed by local security, nobody was game enough to do anything except wait for further instructions.

As though in answer, every hatch, doorway, access portal, cabinet, toilet seat and doggy door in the fan-car popped simultaneously. A bright glow beckoned them from their vehicle with a friendly pattern of triangular tiles leading into the deepest basements of the Thoughtplane facility. Sighing in resignation at the rippling floor, Skagen got to his feet to lead the way. Tuesday, Jimmy and Lana were quietly debating who should be the first one to follow him into the unknown when Trace lurched upright, snapping a line of brain-damaged nonsense to prove she was awake.

"Mr Drizzle has orange lady parts!"

This broke the tension. Jimmy snorted at the word salad, but thankfully Trace was too out of it to be angry at being mocked. She dragged her bulky frame upright, breathing in and out through her nostrils like an enraged bull, and wobbled her head in a drunken way. Jimmy's smile had wisely vanished by this point.

"Where...?"

"Bottom of the elevator shaft of The Needle of Asclepius," Lana said helpfully. "And if you promise not to get us all killed by acting like a psycho within the most dangerous and twitchy security system on the planet, you can come with us to meet some people."

Trace squinted at the bright triangular tiles, then at her associates.

"No promises." She smacked her dry lips. "And what's a Needle of Sleepiness do, exactly?"

*

None of the elevators acknowledged their presence, let alone opened, and the emergency stairwells appeared about as sturdy as Jimmy's self-esteem. As prying open the lift doors with an AllTool-generated crowbar would probably invite another zap from The Needle's security system, there was only one option.

Carefully picking their way down rust-orange steps, every corroded edge glowing with slathers of never-fade radiation-yellow paint, it only took three winding storeys to reach what was meant to be the most secure part of The Needle. As the metre-thick blast door was permanently locked open mid-swing by a mixture of tarnish and verdant seaweed, though, this barrier offered less of an obstacle than a papier-mâché door made from single-ply tissue paper.

Beyond, four sweeping C-shaped levels curved towards their first visitors in decades. Each storey contained eight blisters of thirty-two coffin-sized fridges, with a total room capacity of two-hundred-and-fifty-six cryo pods. Original Recipe people were jammed tight in a densely-packed hodgepodge of cables and piping that had been welded, hooked and screwed in place. Utilitarian staircases and walkways united the four levels at regular intervals.

At first glance, this biological storage area had a lot in common with the self-tending rainforest cultivated within the arcology back at Geraldton, an abundance of greenery and trickling water giving the impression of a peaceful Zen garden. Serious inspection, however, invited nothing but bad news: this chamber was leaking, corroded, contaminated and basically ruined. The ocean had burrowed its way through the ceiling at a dozen major points, and a sludge made from stagnant, briny water was ankle-deep. There were barely enough working light panels to prevent anyone tripping over, and the only other source of illumination were the red bulbs flashing on what seemed to be every single fridge. All the staircases and walkways were rusted through and coated in slippery moss, denying access beyond the ground floor.

Skagen struggled to step forwards, his body language hinting he'd just suffered a stroke. What had become of Humanity's last chance was being wordlessly spelled out to him by hundreds of crimson pulses in a clear obituary. Opening and closing his mouth spasmodically, eyes flicking back and forth, Skagen gave a strangled cry and loped towards the closest freezer.

"Yeah, who could have guessed a ruined building would have an equally-ruined basement way below sea level?" Tuesday asked fatalistically and rhetorically, igniting the suck-burner on his cigarette with a drag. "That's the lesson, kids. Only idiots bother to hope."

Skagen hit the freezer from a run, sliding his hands over its chill surface so fast he almost crashed. Wiping away a thick layer of mud, he froze solid as gelato. Standing around awkwardly, Lana, Tuesday, Jimmy and Trace eventually decided to go and have a look. After all, it didn't seem Skagen was going to make a verbal observation anytime soon.

Peering into the filth-streaked pod, they could see its former occupant had withered down to little more than dry bones and gritty powder. Wads of corpse wax were slathered across where its buttocks and thighs had once been, and only a few alloy zippers and scraps of nylon remained of its clothing. The ravages of a contained decomposition had clearly proved more than violent enough to boil away its cotton garments without much effort. Extra holes had clearly been drilled into its skull, but all the cables and cranial brackets had been pulled free from its boiled-away brain during the drying process.

Three slow red lights flashed within the transparent metal tube of rot, and a superimposed block of holographic letters spelled out a simple message.

ATTENTION: PROFESSOR DUNSTON ALISTAIR FLATLINED 20,156 DAYS AGO. MEDICAL INTERVENTION RECOMMENDED.

Skagen made a choking noise, which turned into a scary laugh. Soon, tears were coursing into his beard, and his spasms continued silently.

"Medical intervention recommended," Tuesday muttered, taking a lot longer than everyone else to process this bad news. "Well, that's an understatement and two-thirds."

Skagen straightened up. It took the better part of a minute, but he seemed to have finally regained some degree of control. Clearing his throat and looking around the room, he flicked back and forth, hopping from coffin to coffin again.

"Some of them might have survived," Skagen said in grim resolution, taking a step towards the next closest fridge.

Surprisingly, as his foot came down there was a crunching noise instead of a slurping noise. Leaning to inspect the sole of his own shoe with impressive flexibility, Skagen picked up something small and white and held it up for the others to see.

"Weaver," Lana said simply. She got closer and squinted. "Twitching a bit. Shouldn't the Weavers be maintaining each other in here?"

"Yeah, but they were meant to be maintaining this whole building too, right?" Trace asked with arch cattiness.

Rolling his head around as he scanned the distant ceiling for movement, Skagan extended the dying Weaver in his hand towards the gloom high above.

"Look. There's hundreds of them just floating about up there. No purpose. Just drifting."

Jimmy huffed, using his retinals to zoom in a bit.

"They look totally stupefied. What, are they all defective or something?"

Lana nudged the slimy ground with the toe of her dress shoe. She unearthed another couple of the tiny general-purpose robots. One spasmed against her foot, but the other stayed utterly still.

"Something nuked these Weavers," Skagen said. "Killed most of them and left the rest to float about as useless, braindead idiots. This is too big to be a mistake, or some kind of manufacturing error."

"No wonder this place is such as mess," Jimmy said. "Nobody's looking after it. No shock all the freezer geezers expired." Jimmy cringed. "Sorry. That was harsh."

Skagen shook his head in total bafflement. "But who could possibly want to murder the last hope of..."

Something fluttered loudly past Trace's ear, and her baser instincts kicked in.

Drawing her kinetic accelerator like the ghost of Annie Oakley, she whipped out her arm in an arc and fired off five rapid shots. Transparent steel doors exploded on three red-hued freezers, a coolant pipe screamed sub-zero liquid for a second before sealing itself off, and Tuesday dodged just quickly enough to avoid the most severe haircut of his life. Everyone besides Trace hit the muck, taking cover in surprise and fear. This instantly transitioned into anger.

"What the balls are you playing at?" Skagen roared, pounding his fists into the mire. "Have you had that thing hidden on you this entire time? No wonder we got stopped by Japanese airspace!"

Still locked into a fully-extended pose, gun lightly smoking, Trace squinted as the same Weaver as before buzzed her. Understanding settled, followed by a microsecond of shame. It almost seemed as though she was about to apologise, but then Trace's stone of a face twisted into its usual hostility. She holstered the antique within her ceramic Enforcer vest and snapped its safety button closed.

"No harm done," she said dismissively. "These dusters are so dead that getting shot in the bones could only be an improvement."

Skagen waved violently at the hundreds of freezers, his disbelief at the sheer magnitude of Trace's mental malfunction about as high as it could possibly go.

"You could have..."

But he stopped cold, locking onto something on the far side of the room. He blinked repeatedly, as though demanding that his brain needed to double-check what it was processing. Completely giving up on giving Trace the tongue lashing of the year, Skagen dragged himself out of the muck and scrabbled into a run. As the brine in this part of the swamp was deep enough to cover his shoes all the way up to the tongue, his attempts at sprinting looked more like somebody with spinal problems attempting to remove a coat hanger from the back of a shirt they were already wearing.

Giving a sigh at how this darned Skando kept on leaping into action without providing a word of helpful context, Lana messily got to her feet and followed him. Jimmy and Tuesday, having nothing better planned, trailed behind Lana, shaking black and green mud from their arms. Nobody was keeping track of Trace, which was generally unwise, but at least her kinetic accelerator was safely secured for now.

Falling to his knees against a pod beside the furthest bulkhead, Skagen didn't need to answer anyone's questions. After all, they could all see the colour gently strobing from the freezer: a deep orange, barely a shade from blood, the only bulbs in the whole room that weren't scarlet. Feeling a stirring of hope, Lana helped Skagen wipe away the dust of decades, revealing the sub-zero coffin contained a mass of dry protein that may technically be classed as a living person. At first glance, he had a lot in common with an unpopular 8th Century druid who'd just been excavated from a peat bog in England, or he could have been the tragic result of a catastrophic industrial accident in a beef jerky smoke house. His face was a horror show: black lips peeled right back from a mouth of darkest brown, and a dozen cables had been permanently drilled into his brain through welded-on plugs in his temple brackets. Various pipes in his belly and between his chicken ribs pumped mysterious substances in and out.

Lana got closer, and blue shiny letters superimposed over the coffin's lid.

PROFESSOR KARL DeKRAY, NEUROVIROLIGIST

"So is this one alive, or what?" Jimmy half asked, half-stated, not possessing enough of a reserve of self-worth to run the risk of being wrong.

DeKray's ribcage jerked up half a centimetre, paused for five long seconds, then deflated again. Never had less than a thumb span of movement caused such loud cheers. But before there could be any back-slapping, more work needed to be done.

"Okay," Lana said after the silence had deepened back to its usual nihilism. "We have at least one survivor. What's next?"

DeKray's sarcophagus darkened to an orange so deep that it almost matched the colour of Tuesday's urine. A helpful little message popped up: ESTIMATED TIME OF DEATH: TWELVE MINUTES.

"Something fast, I'm guessing," Trace said dismissively.

Jimmy carefully ran his index fingers over the bracket of ports the Slidge had drilled into both his temples. Examining DeKray's crispy head as best he could, feeling the ridges and counting the bumps, Jimmy came to a conclusion.

"I kind of..." he started, pushing the words out despite how much he dreaded them, "I kind of have an idea, I think?"

*

It only took moments to prove Jimmy's guess was correct: the brackets of sockets that he, Trace, Lana and Tuesday had installed just above their cheekbones all had the same tiny little prismatic Thoughtplane logos stamped into them, and were an almost perfect match for what Professor Karl DeKray, Neurovirologist, had implanted in his own scone. The "plan," if you could call it that, was more obvious than the grass being green, the sky being blue, and Indian food being a lot more pleasant going in than coming out.

Of course, leaping into an unknown virtual environment that may be totally and utterly corrupted wasn't the safest of prospects, especially seeing as though two-hundred-and-fifty-five geniuses had mysteriously died within it without leaving any clues as to what had snuffed them all. It was quickly agreed to put hopping blindly into VR on the backburner until other, safer options could be explored. As it was just over nine minutes until DeKray was due to flat line like all the other Professors, this was an appropriate moment to start meatball planning at its most desperate. The first half-decent idea was to find a way to communicate with DeKray's excised mind in some other way, but it proved to be impossible to communicate with anybody or anything within this virtual Construct from the Actual, and it took a minute and a half to figure out why.

"I know there are some unbelievable time dilation effects in play within the Construct, but what this screen is telling me is just ludicrous." Lana scoffed, calling up numerous displays from her Omni. She may have taken twenty precious seconds to safely ascertain that the security feedback in this room wouldn't fry her like a sausage, but she was staying alert just in case that situation changed. "Let's just say that communication between the Actual and the Construct is impossible. It'd be like trying to understand a conversation where each word stretched out for a thousand years, or a million words in under a second, depending on what side you're standing."

"So DeKray's brain is currently experiencing things way too quickly for us to understand them?" Jimmy asked with surprising accuracy.

"From a research perspective, it makes sense." Lana confirmed. "They needed a cure for The Trance ASAP, right? Why not cram each second out here with a month in there? Why not dial it up all the way?"

"I don't want to do it," Tuesday said sharply.

Lana raised an eyebrow.

"Do what?"

"I seen you lot comparing those ports in DeKray's melon to ours," Tuesday snapped. "I can see they're a good enough match. So I know you're about to suggest we kick a bunch of icky mummies out of their sarcophagi and plug ourselves in with their wet plugs. Well, I'm not doing it! I don't care if it's Mankind's only hope. Something killed all these scientists, and I don't want to meet whatever it was. Understand?"

Jimmy gave Tuesday a look of pity.

"Dude, we already discussed this not five minutes ago. Weren't you listening?"

Lana leaned in close to Tuesday, her face blank and cold with hatred.

"You already made one Universe extinct today," she growled, low and dangerous. "I think it's well overdue for you to prove to us that you're worth the air you foul, hmm?"

"Hey, Tuesday?" Trace said sweetly, causing him to turn. She instantly drilled her meaty fist over his entire face in one wallop, sending his brain bouncing off the inside of his skull like a spring-loaded toy. He splashed heavily into the mud. "Does that smell like knuckles to you?"

CHAPTER THIRTY EIGHT

While Tuesday slept, his snores blowing bubbles in the muck, everyone else got down to the unpleasant business of ejecting four skeletons from what should have been their place of eternal rest. Thankfully, the smell of graves was like a particularly dusty attic in a retirement village, as the stench of rot and foulness had long-since withered away.

Respectfully setting aside the bones and waving away the piles of grit, they loaded Tuesday into one of the pods like lowering a caged canary into a suspect coal mine. As somebody who was no stranger to Wakky World cortical-shunt amusement parks, Lana made sure all fifteen of the neural cables were inactive before inserting them into Tuesday's temple brackets. Screwing the lines into place, Lana clicked-and-dropped Tuesday's consciousness into standby mode, readying him to meet what remained of Professor Karl DeKray's mind in the Construct at the same instant as everyone else. Tuesday's head didn't explode, which technically counted as a success. As Tuesday had zero chance of suddenly developing Involition Syndrome, there was no need to freeze him.

"Lana," Jimmy said from his freezer, burning an instant they didn't have to spare. He paused, wasting another irreplaceable second, before blurting out a whole headful of thoughts. "With all these coincidences with the Thoughtplane brand and the same plugs and brackets we all have and how all the humans with The Trance are all piped up like we were..."

"Jimmy," Lana said softly, more than intuitive enough to know exactly+ what he was really asking, "if you're wondering if Tuesday's actions with the Generation Gun never happened and we've all been recaptured by the Slidge and jammed into another software loop, then yes, there's a chance that's happened. But regardless, you have to remember something."

Jimmy was all ears. "What's that?"

Lana leaned above the lip of her freezer to make eye contact.

"Thinking like that will make you insane. Look how happy Tuesday is not knowing what day it is. Maybe we could learn something from him?"

There was a moment of deathly silence, followed by hysterical laughter from three of the five occupied pods.

Unable to understand what was so funny, Skagen unfurled the Scroll computer to make sure everything was gravy. Lana's face darkened at how he was treating the delicate antique. She resisted the urge to tell him that scratching it so hard with his fingernails would leave rough spots.

"Okay," Skagen warned, "I'm going to give you lot precisely half an Actual second in there. This should give you days, if not weeks, of dilated time to do whatever it is you need to do before DeKray...well, you know. Like with any Immersive, you should be able to shape the Construct as you see fit, and you, Lana, will have full access to your Omni. Do keep in mind we still don't know who or what blasted the Weavers or killed the scientists, let alone how they did it or whether they can do the same thing again, so be prepared for hostiles. Assume anyone you see is insane and wants to kill you, but also be as friendly as possible. Any questions?"

"One," Trace growled. "Are you going to hit the button, or keep talking until DeKray flat lines?"

Skagen's face twisted a little, biting back some choice words. Instead, he gave

Trace a wink.

"See you lot in half a second."

*

There was no feeling of transition from Actual to Virtual. This Construct was a highly efficient, industrial-grade simulated environment designed to calculate the most impossible of equations, to map hypothetical patterns that stretched over millennia, to count up to infinity and beyond. If The Needle of Asclepius had existed a few generations back, Mankind might not have engineered itself into a living death with a defective neural vaccine.

Skagen's finger flicked down, replacing reality with a low-res pearly white expanse. There was nothing to see, hear, feel or smell. Aesthetically speaking it was utterly vile, an empty block only meant to serve as a temporary placeholder while a proper virtual environment was loaded in. A lack of stimuli could send the most balanced Human insane within days, and it could be permanently mentally damaging to spend just a few hours in such a void.

Nevertheless, here they were.

Understandably, Lana, Trace and Jimmy felt more comfortable looking at each other's colourful avatars than the emptiness. Despite standing in a Construct generated by the most powerful computer on the planet and powered by the most hard-core fusion reactor ever conceived, each of their avatars were composed of about eight hundred polygons or so, at the most. You could easily tell who was who from their silhouettes and the way they moved, but it was unsettling to see somebody you knew represented by less visual information than a plucky anthropomorphised bandicoot in a platformer game on a late 20th Century home console. In an unexpected and amusing twist, Tuesday was sprawled unconscious on the snow-white floor, and the shiner that took up his entire face was rendered with three shades of purple and two of grey.

But it turned out they weren't in an empty Construct. Their sight adjusted, and soon they could discern a complex network of midnight wire framing that divided this anti-abyss of pale cream into blocks and spheres and other basic three-dimensional shapes. From there, the shapes made up discernible objects, becoming bookshelves and square tables and high-backed chairs and throw rugs and dart boards and massage recliners. Although devoid of colour this was clearly a recreation room, perhaps the sort you got at trendy companies that treated their staff to free breakfasts, unlimited breaks and six-figure salaries. Seeing as though the Professors were literally the most important people on the planet and this trip was guaranteed to be one-way, providing a generous rec room for downtime was the least they could ask for.

Taking a few hesitant steps, marvelling at how good the anti-nausea feedback was compared to a Wakky World cortical shunt park, Lana took a close look at one of the shelves. The bookcase swept out like wings, but was as empty as an autumn vase. Running her finger along one of the mantels, colours sparked in tiny fireworks displays, only to vanish just as quickly. A second touch caused a book-sized block to appear in high-resolution, adorned by an old-fashioned mechanical lighter resting on a colourful nebula. It disappeared again without fanfare.

Lana stood up straight.

"These shelves used to contain Immersives," she said with surety. "Hundreds of thousands of them. But they've all been deleted."

She examined the cluster of square tables towards the centre of the rec area. Their chairs looked comfy.

"And I'd bet that's where they used to sit to mainline them."

"Single player or multiplayer?" Jimmy asked, surprised by his voice sounding unchanged.

Trace huffed. "Really? Does it matter?"

"No," Lana shook her head. "It doesn't."

The background silence was broken by a sharp tapping, the sound of a dog with long claws trying to sneak across a tiled kitchen. Turning, Jimmy found he was being enveloped by the legs of a gigantic black spider. Freezing in abject terror, all Jimmy could do was gape up and up and up at the arthropod's multi-elbowed limbs as they gently curled around his avatar, pulling him into an intimate embrace. From point blank range he could see the spider was a billion squiggles of tightly-bundled wire framing, and their cold touch sent ice down his virtual spine.

Jimmy summoned all his bravery to say what needed to be said.

"Meep."

"Jimmy, don't move," Trace growled, playing the role of Captain Obvious. "Lana, do we have weapons in here?"

Unfortunately, Lana's exasperated look couldn't be properly conveyed by a face with so few polygons, so she gave a knowing nod. Somehow picking up on what Lana was trying to convey, Trace casually circled around the ten-legged spider on its right while Lana went left, flanking the beast. Of course, there was no real way to predict whether the bug could hurt them or if they could hurt it back, but as Jimmy was about to be given an unwanted cuddle by something twenty times his size, this was the best possible time to find out.

Drawn into the deep, empty core where the long limbs met, clusters of black wireframe spheres began to appear a matter of centimetres from Jimmy's face. They randomly stretched and warped into ugly, bulging, inhuman faces before deflating back to their original shape and size. It was almost as though they were trying to...say something? Squinting at the odd bubbles, his virtual body shimmering and going low-res from terror, Jimmy's fear switched to confusion as a block of royal blue letters superimposed themselves over the so-called spider.

They said, "Professor Phergo Saleh, Director."

Sharply holding up a hand to still Lana and Trace, silently warning them to back off, somehow Jimmy found the courage to move closer to where the ten legs met. He examined the bubbling faces from centimetres away, trying to understand what their lips were silently mouthing.

"Are you one of the scientists?" Jimmy asked softly.

The cluster of limbs nodded in an uncoordinated bowing motion. There was some sort of audible chittering from its depths, quickly coalescing into something closer to language. Backing away from Jimmy, giving him some much-deserved personal space, the spider's limbs twisted against each other like thin copper filaments, forming and reforming until there was the vague sense of a bipedal creature. It was like a child had taken a sheet of chicken wire and attempted to twist it into an effigy of a person. Just as fingers and facial details began to form, however, the mess lost all cohesion again, collapsing into black threads on the white floor. It rattled in anger and frustration, but not with words.

"It's okay," Jimmy said soothingly, slowly kneeling and reaching out towards what used to be a Human mind. It stopped vibrating as violently, and calmed to a gentle purring. "You've been in here a long, long time, I know. It's okay if you can't make yourself look like you used to. It's okay."

The puddle extended a long, crooked black branch dotted with twigs. Growing longer and longer, the sapling twisted towards Jimmy's outstretched hand, and he instinctually reached out to make contact. Trace snapped an order, causing Jimmy to freeze just millimetres away from Saleh.

"Shouldn't play around with anything you can't describe in five words," she said harshly, snapping her teeth together as punctuation.

Jimmy gave her a "What the spug is wrong with you?" kind of look, before turning back to the wireframe plant.

"Don't worry about what you look like," Jimmy said softly. "We're here to help. I don't want to put any pressure on you, but is there any way we can talk?"

The lines vibrated, as though trying to flex a muscle that hadn't been used in a century, then gave a second, more violent rumble, probably from frustration. Its wire framing jolted, and the midnight pile formed into a huge, crude mouth. Twitching, making sounds like a malfunctioning speaker, Professor Phergo Saleh said something for the first time in millennia. It took a bit of imagination to translate it unto Unglish.

"All...dead?" he sort-of asked.

Jimmy glanced over at Lana. She shook her head. Jimmy looked back at the mouth, which had downturned the edges of its lips in annoyance.

"Almost everyone. Karl DeKray has a few Actual minutes until he flat lines. To be honest, we thought he was the only one still alive in here. Was your body on the upper levels, or something? We didn't see your fridge when we were looking around."

"Death didn't..." Saleh almost sounded pleased with his next word, "...take."

Jimmy nodded, despite not having any idea what that even meant. Chewing his lip, he got to the point.

"Like I said, we're here to help. Could you..."

The lines rumbled, as though offended. They slowly calmed down.

"Cannot...affect..." it took some time for the puddle to finish its line of thought. After some nonsense chittering and ugly noises, it finished its words. "See...DeKray."

The blackness faded, dripping away into nothing after holding together for far too long. Its movements wound down towards stasis. Jimmy leaned closer, as though Saleh was merely having trouble hearing him. He asked his next question a lot louder, just in case.

"How do we see Professor DeKray?" Jimmy asked. "Where is he?"

A crude wireframe hand emerged from the vanishing mass, and its index finger pointed towards the beige ceiling of the rec room. For some reason, Saleh flipped his hand around to give the roof The Finger before fading into nothing. Whether he was dead, asleep or just hiding in the substrate of the Construct wasn't clear.

"What did he...?" Jimmy began to ask, looking up.

His words vanished as the rec room's ceiling was torn away like a sticking plaster to reveal a giant, churning star sitting almost close enough to touch. Far larger than the Sun that had warmed Mankind's birthplace since Earth accreted from stellar debris, the red giant dominated the sky from edge to edge, and no matter how far you panned your head around there was only more of it. It resembled old, congealed blood, but if you squinted you could make out orange, yellow and even white threads edging its swirls, almost like the star equivalent of getting your highlights done at a hairdresser.

Impressive as it was to see a star from point-blank range without frying away into a brief sizzling noise and a bad smell, seeing something awesome was not today's objective. They had work to do.

"Any idea what we can do with a virtual star?" Trace growled.

Lana narrowed her eyes, panning across the bloody orb with little discomfort. She spotted a tiny white dot that was surprisingly easy to pick out from the rest of the churning chaos, and pointed at it. Her hand motion accidentally superimposed a tiny emerald grid over her target, tracking it for all to see. Pretending she had done this deliberately, Lana clicked her fingers to get everyone's attention.

"Look," she said simply. "Look real close at the green box."

Zooming in closer than their retinal screens in the Actual ever could, Jimmy and Trace startled at an unexpected sight: it was a person with two arms and two legs and a head and everything, floating a kilometre or so from the red. He appeared to be drawing a long, thin multi-coloured spiral from the star, something along the lines of a giant double-helix of DNA but formed from boiling gases, dragging it out and out and out until he suddenly stopped deep in the outer corona. Once the twisted rope of colour stopped extending, the guy started tracing along it carefully, as though looking for something.

Lana made a noise in her throat.

"I think we've found DeKray."

*

As distance and gravity didn't hold any real sway in the Construct, flying was as easy as thinking it. Besides the eighteen sexual experiences everybody secretly tried out in Virtual but politely avoided discussing back in the Actual, flight had always been the most popular simulated experience. Every half-decent Construct had flight coded in as one of its most basic features.

Rising from the rec room, crossing the mighty gulf towards Professor Karl DeKray in what felt like seconds, while the crimson eternity didn't seem to alter in any major way, the last of the trapped scientists grew and grew until he was close enough to wedgie. Unlike the ruins that had once been Professor Phergo Saleh's mind, DeKray looked normal. To be specific, he looked like Generic Scientist 4B from any first-person shooter video game that incorporated science fiction elements, but it was better than a stick figure spider. His avatar's quality was roughly on par with that of his visitors, though perhaps ever so slightly more detailed.

If DeKray noticed his visitors he gave no sign, seemingly content to mess about with the long, thin cylinder spiral he'd drawn out of the star. From point blank range, it turned out DeKray was manipulating multi-coloured spirals of complex code that were intertwined like strands of DNA. His fingers brushed the weaving at choice points, altering their waveforms into slightly different curves, shifting their colours along the entire visual spectrum and beyond. Still not paying his visitors any attention, he twisted the cylinder closed and casually allowed it to retract a thousand kilometres into the star.

Seeing an opening, Lana went to announce her group. She had carefully formulated exactly what she was going to say to guarantee this meeting would be as civil and productive as possible. Unfortunately, Tuesday picked this moment to wake up.

"Where the SPUG am I?!" he screeched. Thrashing about in mid-air, not having the faintest idea how or why he was suddenly floating in a low-res purgatory, Tuesday gathered his bearings quicker than usual. He gave a long, pained groan. "You arse-headed pox-faced tampons! You plugged me in when I specifically said not to!"

"Not now, Tuesday," Lana growled out of the side of her mouth. She was all smiles as she turned back to DeKray, who was examining a distant spot of roiling gas for something only he could make out. "Professor DeKray, my name is Lana Slade, and I..."

DeKray turned slowly and made eye contact with her. She had never been looked at like that before. It was like being regarded by an intelligence so ancient and terrible and cold that only a fool would seek it out. His words were clear, but contained an undercurrent of menace that could only be described as demonic.

"I know my cycle," he said simply, dismissively. "I am still eight weeks away from going insane again. In over a hundred-and-twenty-five-thousand years, this pattern has remained unchanged. You are unwelcome to disturb me until I am due to be psychotic. I'm going to ignore you now."

DeKray casually went back to what he was doing: scouring the star for something. Raising a finger, Lana's words caught in her throat as she realised something.

"Wait..." she said.

Glaring towards where DeKray had compressed the cylinder of colourful helixes, she focused on the red skin surrounding it. If she looked in just the right way, she could see the entire so-called star was actually made of glowing, tightly-packed circles. They ranged in size from pinheads to heavy transit vehicles.

"This isn't a star..." she said slowly. "This is The Equation, right?"

DeKray didn't respond, but that didn't stop Lana from barrelling on.

"This is the giant ball of math your team has been working on all this time, a hunk of calculations and pattern mapping and neurological mock-ups and genetic charting and DNA comparisons and ancestry cross-references and all sorts of other..."

DeKray didn't respond, but he make a noise in his throat that stopped Lana's spiel. Kicking off violently, DeKray swept away from his visitors at Mach Five, obviously still convinced they were a figment of his deranged imagination. Tired of being treated as fictional, Trace swooped in at Mach Six and picked up

DeKray by his collar. Shocked he was being touched by somebody, DeKray gripped Trace by her huge biceps and blinked in confusion.

"The hallucinations never touched me before," he managed, tilting his head back and forth like a bird that had just bounced off a window. He gave them all an agonised expression, pushing his rendering to the limit. "But you can't be real. You're just characters from Immersives I used to play, Immersives that The Director deleted eons ago." He got nose-to-nose with Trace and hissed his words. "Am I completely losing it? Is my brain finally breaking like Saleh's?"

Trace got eyeball-to-eyeball with him.

"Either you listen to what we have to say, or I'm going to find out exactly what damage I'm capable of doing to you in here. I've got weeks of Virtual until you die for real. Don't test me."

Glancing from avatar to avatar, DeKray relaxed for the first time in what must have been centuries.

"Okay," he said simply. He gently pried Trace's fingers from his collar. "Okay."

*

As DeKray's tortured mind had technically existed for longer than an Ice Age, he had the attention span of a two-year-old on coffee. Even after he'd agreed to sit down for ten minutes to talk, DeKray spent most of that time asking people to repeat themselves, as though his short-term memory could only commit to fifteen-second blocks. Just to make communication even more impossible, the Professor was a constantly shifting pattern of strange movements and noises, kind of like he was testing out the index section of an encyclopaedia about Tourette's syndrome at random to see which combination of tics he liked best.

Just when the "genius" seemed to be getting a grip on the situation, DeKray suddenly twisted about violently as though sensing some terrible threat. He stood arrow-straight and declared he had to get back to work. Despite it being a waste of time so far, Trace wasn't going to let him fly away from this pow-wow.

"Damn it, DeKray, it's quitting time," Trace snapped, waving at The Equation as its colours burned like nuclear fusion. "Don't you see? Your team is dead, and that nonsense over there isn't solving squat. I'm no mathematishun, but I'm pretty sure all that red means the calculations aren't working, right?"

This got DeKray's attention. Stopping cold, regarding Trace with a billion-year gaze he'd had lots of time to perfect, he finally managed to answer a question.

"Right," he said in a little, depressed voice. "It's all nonsense. And every day, I make it a little bit worse. It gets bigger, and it gets more wrong. But I need to keep at it."

"Please, just hear what we have to say," Jimmy said kindly. "If we can't work something out…"

DeKray's eyes snapped wide in terror.

"But what if The Director sees me slacking off? You have no idea what he's like, what he can do to me!"

Trace gave a chuckle.

"The Director? Have you seen him lately? He's corrupted into scrap code. He's not hurting anyone anytime soon." She gave a gross snort. "How exactly did he end up like that, yet you're still…" Trace regarded DeKray for a time and did her best to not be hurtful. "Well, you're clearly mental as a frog in a sock, but at least you're in the shape of a person."

DeKray swallowed heavily. "That's because The Director's dead. The other survivors were sick of the torture sessions and reload-deaths, and pooled their resources to find a way to kill him in the Actual like he'd been doing to the ones who didn't toe the line. And, well, they succeeded."

This got Jimmy's attention.

"Wait. You're saying The Director's body in the Actual is dead? How did his mind remain alive in here after meat-death? Isn't that impossible?"

DeKray gave a sad smile. "No idea. My personal theory is he found some way to stay hooked into the substrate of the Construct like a tick, burrowed in somewhere really deep, where he couldn't get dislodged."

"What did the others think?"

DeKray's face darkened.

"No idea. When Saleh died, he took all the conspirators with him. I was the only one not brave enough to try and overthrow him, so now I'm the only one who…"

He went rigid as a plank. Unblinking and silent, it was as though DeKray's brain had temporarily shut itself down as protection from the horror of existence. He slowly came back to the present with a polite, slightly dazed smile. "Sorry, where were we?"

Tuesday raised a finger. "Question. So Saleh killed everybody? He was able to kill bodies in the Actual from in here?" Tuesday didn't allow any time for an answer before issuing his follow-up question. "Another little query: could he kill us in the Actual?"

DeKray nodded. "If you're plugged into this Construct the same way as all the others, then yes, he probably could. Not sure if he's still got power over life and death in his current...well, in his current state...but..."

Tuesday kicked violently at the air.

"That sorts it. Unplug me. Unplug me now."

"We weren't entirely sure how The Director was killing people in the Actual, to be honest." DeKray went on, as though Tuesday didn't exist. "Turns out he hacked all the local Weavers, and use them to do all kinds of things...like pinching off oxygen tubes in specific coffin fridges, sending violent electric shocks through the cardio-regulator patches, reversing the faecal extraction pipes at ten times the safe force..." DeKray was silent for a time, but whether in meditation or from catatonia was uncertain. He suddenly looked back to Lana, clearly knowing who served as the brains in this outfit. "So what do you suggest, then? What breakthrough do you have that the greatest geniuses in the most powerful computer couldn't sort out in an eighth of a million years?"

Lana tapped at the spot between the thumb and index finger on her left hand.

"Let's hope this works," she said far too loudly for everyone's hope levels.

It took a moment, but a holographic screen the span of a family-sized pizza appeared above her wrist. It displayed the image of a small black cylinder, which unfolded into thousands of black right-angled triangles before returning to its normal form, displaying dozens of master template menus in distinct colours: white for medical, red for military-grade destruction, green for terraforming, purple for interstellar manipulation, light blue for genetic engineering, pink for developing and harnessing latent psychic abilities...

"It's a Universal Fabricator," Jimmy said proudly.

DeKray shrugged. "I'm familiar with the concept. Does it have a cure for Involition Syndrome?"

"No," Tuesday interrupted, always happy to be the bearer of bad news.

"Then what good is it?" DeKray demanded.

"Because we can use it to make people," Jimmy said. "We can use the Universal Fabricator to record an image of a living person, and reproduce them exactly as they were in that moment."

"So what happens if we record somebody who's been a zombie from The Trance for seventy years?" DeKray asked.

"We're happy to create as many zombies as you want," Tuesday snarked.

Somehow Tuesday didn't get a slap, but Trace gave him a warning glance. DeKray shook his head.

"I'm certain there aren't enough survivors to make that work. Unless your idea of a solution is to create a population so badly inbred that they'll be headless crab people within three generations, I'm afraid your little Universal Fabricator isn't of any use."

"Thought you'd say that," Lana noted. She flicked at her Omni, and five thousand mugshots poured out, swirling around in a miniature tornado until settling into a neat grid. She pointed at the individual squares, and they expanded to show every possible detail. "We managed to get our hands on five thousand detailed medical scans. None of them are directly related, they're all free from just about every medical condition or inherited disease in the book, and we can start pumping them out as soon as we can hook up the Universal Fabricator to..." Lana's words faltered. "Shit."

"What?" DeKray prompted, his hopes swanning towards dashed.

"Ah." Jimmy said, picking up the ball and running with it. "Yeah. So, the plan is to brew up these five thousand people once per Arcology Cluster, and to keep the Clusters separated for two centuries or so. Enforced quarantine, or something. After that, you'd need a reproduction schedule between the Clusters to make sure there's enough genetic div...div..."

"Diversity," Lana said helpfully.

DeKray raised his hand, stopping Jimmy's spiel cold.

"Uh, no, back to you, Miss. You think I didn't notice your mile-wide confession that there's some major problem with this plan, did you? You want to elaborate a little?"

Lana nodded seriously. Hiding anything at this point could lead to total failure. If DeKray wasn't sold on their idea, this would be where Mankind officially ended. The future of all sentient life in this reality was at stake.

"We need one hundred-and-fifty terawatts to operate the UF," Lana said in a small voice.

DeKray maintained a steady gaze. After eight long seconds, he nodded.

"Okay. That's doable."

Everyone took a few moments to absorb this answer. A few glances were exchanged, as though checking their virtual ears weren't malfunctioning. Lana went to repeat his words, but could only mouth a confused nonsense noise. Her second attempt was more lucid.

"Wait, you mean you have a power source strong enough to power the UF? Where?"

DeKray extended his arms, waved them like he was making a snow angel, and snapped them down against his waist.

"Why, all this, of course. The Needle of Asclepius is the biggest fusion reactor on the planet. Once I flush all of this..."

Jimmy somehow choked without any virtual saliva.

"You're going to just flush The Equation? Are you serious?"

DeKray shook his head softly.

"It's garbage, the entire thing. Always has been. And all I've done is corrupt it more and more. This project is a total failure. It's time to realise that, and move on." He clapped his hands in a way that made it clear everyone had overstayed their welcome and should go home this instant. "Now, by the time my Actual body dies, everything should be ready for the next stage. This is all going to take a lot of work on your part for a very long time, but as I'm sure you understand," DeKray nodded at them solemnly each in turn. "Sometimes sacrifices must be made."

Jimmy and Lana went to offer their thanks, but with the way DeKray barrelled on through their accolades it was clear he wasn't in the science game for the back-slapping.

"Look, with so little Actual time until my body flat lines, I need to get busy," DeKray stated. He locked eyes with The Equation in hatred, then back at Lana. "None of you need to stick around. I can take care of everything. To be honest, I will experience some notable satisfaction at hitting the Delete key really, really hard."

*

Lana's eyelids had only just closed in the Actual before opening again. Back in her body without any uncomfortable feelings of mind fragmentation or download psychosis, she didn't have enough time to get her bearings before a medical siren went off. Blinking, only half-taking in Skagen's panicked voice and the burning hum of cardio-stimulator equipment, she already knew what had happened before sitting up all the way.

"No!" Skagen screeched, pounding and kicking at DeKray's freezer, a combination that didn't help anyone, let alone the flat lined corpse.

Feeling woozy, Lana turned her head and the mossy, salty, moist complex zipped by, almost causing her to vomit. Leaning over the cusp of her freezer, she locked onto the coffin that contained Professor Karl DeKray, and watched without feeling as his stick figure body mercifully died. Skagen kept zapping the mummified remains over and over, and didn't stop until Lana unhooked her cables, splashed over and put her hand on his shoulder. She could sense the other three stirring from their half an actual second of time spent within the Construct, but for now she focused on Skagen with a kind smile.

"It's okay," she said simply.

Looking at Lana in total confusion, Skagen's words were interrupted by an unexpectedly beautiful choir of soft whirring. Above, the absently buzzing Weavers swooped down from the ceiling in an impressive formation, finally coming back to their senses after a long, long time of mental distress.

All the freezers switched off one by one, their red hazard lights and essential systems all halting on queue. A rising howl sounded from pipes and valves and cables and engines as the considerable mental might of The Needle of Asclepius switched to a new function.

Jimmy gave a squeak as the pocket on his neon-yellow MacDeath fry cook apron tore along its seam. Opening the flap wide, Jimmy's Universal Fabricator floated up into the middle of the room, instantly growing from the size of a cigarette to a span big enough to contain a basketball court. Within it, a Man and a Woman began to form, first from shadow, then from marrow, then from bone. Muscle threads traced over their skeletons, followed by clumps of skin sewn together by invisible forces.

"Everything is okay," Lana repeated softly, watching the beginnings of tomorrow. "It's going to be okay."

www.ingramcontent.com/pod-product-compliance
Lightning Source LLC
Chambersburg PA
CBHW050112120726
47904CB00004B/1318